Interfictions 2

an anthology of
interstitial writing

Edited by Delia Sherman
and Christopher Barzak

Introduction by
Henry Jenkins

Interstitial Arts Foundation
Boston, Massachusetts

Interstitial Arts Foundation
P.O. Box 35862
Boston, MA 02135
www.interstitialarts.org
info@interstitialarts.org

Distributed to the trade by Small Beer Press through Consortium.
Printed on recycled paper by Cushing-Malloy. Text set in ITC Esprit.
Library of Congress Cataloging-in-Publication Data available on request.

ISBN-13: 978-1-931520-61-4

First edition: 1 2 3 4 5 6 7 8 9 0

Contents

*To Terri and Charles and Midori and Kate and
Sarah and Warren and Ellen and Gavin and Kelly,
who were there at the very beginning.*

Introduction
On the Pleasures of Not *Belonging*

Henry Jenkins

"Please accept my resignation. I don't care to belong to any club that will have me as a member."

—Groucho Marx

Let's start with some basic premises:

1. I do not belong in this book.
2. The contributors also do not belong.
3. You, like Groucho Marx, wouldn't want to belong even if you could. Otherwise, you probably wouldn't have picked up this book in the first place.

Let me explain. The editors of most anthologies seek stories which "fit" within prescribed themes, genres, and topics; the editors of this book have gone the opposite direction—seeking stories that don't fit anywhere else, stories that are as different from each other as possible. And that's really cool if the interstitial is the kind of thing you are into.

At the heart of the interstitial arts movement (too formal), community (too exclusive), idea (too idealistic?), there is the simple search for stories that don't rest comfortably in the cubbyholes we traditionally use to organize our cultural experiences. As Ellen Kushner puts it, "We're living in an age of category, of ghettoization—the Balkanization of Art! We should do something." That "something" is, among the other projects of the Interstitial Arts Foundation, the book you now hold in your hands.

Asked to define interstitial arts, many writers fall back on spatial metaphors, talking about "the wilderness between genres" (Delia Sherman), "art that falls between the cracks" (Susan Simpson), or "a chink in a fence, a gap in the clouds, a DMZ between nations at war" (Heinz Insu Fenkl). Underlying these spatial metaphors is the fantasy of artists and writers crawling out from the boxes which so many (their publishers, agents, readers, marketers, the adolescent with the piercings who works at the local Borders) want to trap them inside. Such efforts to define art also deform the imagination, not simply of authors, but also of their readers.

All genre categories presume ideal readers, people who know the conventions and secret codes, people who read them in the "right way." Many of us—female fans of male action shows, adult fans of children's books, male fans of soap operas—read and enjoy things we aren't supposed to, and we read them for our own reasons, not those proposed by marketers. We don't like people snatching books from our hands and telling us we aren't supposed to be reading them.

One of the reasons I don't belong in this book is that I'm an academic, not a creative artist, and let's face it, historically, academics have been the teachers and enforcers of genre rules. The minute I tell you that I have spent the last twenty years in a literature department, you immediately flash on a chalkboard outline of Aristotle's *Poetics* or a red pen correcting your muddled essay on the four-act structure. Throughout the twentieth century, many of us academic types were engaged in a prolonged project of categorizing and classifying the creative process, transforming it to satisfy our needs to generate lecture notes, issue paper topics, and grade exam questions. After all, academics are trapped in our own imposed categories ("disciplines" rather than "genres") which often constrain what we can see, what we can say, and who we can say it to. Academics are "disciplined" through our education, our hiring process, our need to "publish or perish," and our tenure and promotion reviews. Most academics read or think little outside their field of study. As Will Rogers explained, "there's nothing so foolish as an educated man once you take him out of the field he was educated in."

I may gain a little sympathy from you, dear reader, if I note that for those twenty years, I was a cuckoo's egg—a media and popular culture scholar in a literature department—and that I am finally flying the coop, taking up an interdisciplinary position at a different institution, because I could never figure out the rules shaping my literature colleagues' behavior.

Many literature professors may hold "genre fiction" in contempt as "rule-driven" or "formula-based" yet they ruthlessly enforce their own genre conventions: look at how science fiction gets taught, keeping only those authors already in the canon (Mary Shelley, H.G. Wells, Margaret Atwood, Thomas Pynchon), adding a few more who look like what we call "literature" (William Gibson, Octavia Butler, Philip K. Dick), and then, running like hell as far as possible from any writer whose work still smells of "pulp fiction." Here, "literature" is simply another genre or cluster of genres (the academic midlife crisis, the coming-of-age story, the identity politics narrative), one defined every bit as narrowly as the category of films which might get considered for a Best Picture nomination. I never had much patience with the criteria by which my colleagues decided which works belonged in the classroom and which didn't.

What I love about the folks who have embraced interstitial arts is that some of them do comics, some publish romances, some compose music, some write fantasy or science fiction, but all of them are perfectly comfortable thinking about things other than their areas of specialization. In that sense, I do very much belong in this collection as a kindred spirit, a fellow traveler, both phrases that signal someone who does and does not fit into some larger movement. Maybe we can go to each other's un-birthday parties and not belong together.

To be sure, academics are not, as Buffy would put it, "the big bad." We may have gotten inside your head but with a little mental discipline, you can shove us right back out again. Most interstitial artists ritually burned their old course notebooks years ago. They started to write the stories they wanted to be able to read, only to be told by their publisher that their book would sell much more quickly if it could be positioned into this publishing category for this intended audience, and to achieve that you just need to cut back on *this,* expand on *that,* and add a little more of *this other thing.* I often picture James Stewart in *Vertigo* gradually redressing, restyling, and redesigning Kim Novak's entire identity, all the while creepily asserting that it really shouldn't make that much difference to her. That's the process those of us who sympathize with the concept of interstitial arts are trying to battle back into submission or at least push back long enough so that we can demonstrate that there are readers out there, a few of us, who want the stuff that doesn't really fit into fixed genres, though it may bear some faint family resemblance to several of them at once. Viva the mutts and the mongrels! Long live the horses of a different color!

So, you are now about to enter the Twilight Zone, where nothing your freshmen literature teacher taught you applies, where we eat with the wrong forks and wear white shoes after Labor Day. But it doesn't mean that academic genre theory has nothing to contribute to our efforts as readers and writers to step across the ice floes and navigate the shifting sands of the interstitial. For the next few pages, I will be proposing a more contemporary account of how genre works in an era when so many of us are mixing and matching our preferences and defying established categories. The work of genre is changing as we speak—in some ways becoming more constraining, in others more liberating—and genre theorists are rethinking old assumptions to reflect the flux in the way culture operates.

To start with Genre Theory 101, all creative expression involves an unstable balance between invention and convention. If a work is pure invention, it will be incomprehensible—like writing a novel without using any recognizable language. Don't worry: a work that is pure invention is only a theoretical possibility. None of us, in the end, is all *that* original; we borrow (often undigested) bits and pieces from the already written and the already read; we all construct new works through appropriation and transformation of existing materials. As Mikhail Bakhtin explains, we don't take our words out of the dictionary; we rip them from other people's mouths and they come to us covered with the saliva of where they've already been spoken before. Sharing stories is swapping spit.

However, if a work is pure convention, it will bore everyone. While most of us feel gratified when a work sometimes meets our expectations, and most of us feel somewhat frustrated when a work fails to deliver those particular pleasures we associate with a favored formula, none of us wants to read a book that is predictable down to the last detail. All artists fall naturally somewhere on the continuum, in some ways following the dictates of their genres, in other ways breaking with them. And most readers pick up a new book or video expecting to be surprised (by invention) *and* gratified (by convention).

As they seek to satisfy our desires for surprise and gratification, genre conventions are both constraints (like straitjackets) and enabling mechanisms (like life vests). They are constraints insofar as they foreclose certain creative possibilities, and they are enabling mechanisms insofar as they allow us to focus the reader's attention on novel elements. In the Russian formalist tradition that shaped my own early graduate education, we didn't speak of "rules"; we spoke of "norms," with the understanding that a work only achieved its fullest potential when it, in some way, "defamiliarized" our normal ways of seeing the world and ordering our experience. Or in another familiar paradigm, the auteur critics embraced those filmmakers who were "at war with their materials," that is, who followed the expectations of genre just enough to continue to be employed by the Hollywood studio system but also sought to impose their own distinctive personality by breaking as many of those rules as possible.

Now, let's consider how some of the writers featured on the Interstitial Arts Foundation website are confronting these competing pulls towards convention and invention as they think about their work. Some are seeking to break with the conventions of genre more dramatically than others; they each lay claim to different positions on the continuum between convention and invention.

Here, for example, is Barth Anderson:

> If the work comforts, satisfies, or generally meets the expectations that viewers might carry of a genre in question, then the work is genre. This might even apply to works attempting to redefine genre or works which introduce alien elements and disciplines into the genre mix . . . Interstitial art should be prickly, tricky, ornery.

> It should defy expectations, work against them, and in
> so doing, maintain a relationship to one or more genres,
> albeit contentiously. . . . Interstitial art is often upsetting.
> It rocks worldviews, political assumptions, sacred cows,
> as well as bookstore shelves.

Anderson values surprise and sees genre primarily as a constraint.

Susan Stinson, by contrast, sees the artist as moving between the pleasures of operating within genres and the freedom of escaping their borders:

> The gifts of being in a genre—reading the same essays
> and stories; seeking out the same mentors; publishing
> with the same magazines and presses; writing books that
> share shelf space; gathering at workshops, retreats, and
> conferences often enough to know each other—create a
> common language . . . I've felt both embraced and con-
> stricted by the conventions of those worlds. . . . The
> interstitial idea of thriving in cracks and crevices feels
> like [another] kind of home. Nurturing active, creative,
> receptive, demanding relationships and institutions that
> welcome genre-bending and respect a wide range of
> sources, traditions, and affinities sounds so good that it
> scares me. The expanded possibilities for joy are worth
> the risks.

Stinson acknowledges the gratifications of consuming genre entertainment and understands genre formulas as both enabling mechanisms and constraints.

Anderson speaks about the interstitial as "prickly, tricky, ornery," while Stinson sees it as welcoming, "nurturing," joyous, and "receptive." One stresses radical breaks from the genre system, while the other is negotiating a space for singular passions within the system.

Most current academic thinking dismisses the idea that genres are stable and essential categories, that we can determine what genre a work belongs to once and for all, and that doing so tells us all we need to know about the example in question. Instead, this new scholarship talks about what genres *do* rather than what genres *are* and describes the processes by which works get classified and reclassified over time.

When these categories are deployed as a system for regulating the production and distribution of culture, The publishing industry is misusing genre theory. As music critic Simon Frith notes,

> Genre maps change according to who they're for . . . A committed music fan will soon find, for example, that she's interested in sounds that fit into several categories at once and that different shops therefore shelve the same record under different labels. . . . It's as if a silent conversation is going on between the consumer, who knows roughly what she wants, and the shopkeeper, who is laboriously working out the pattern of shifting demands. What's certain is that I, like most other consumers, would feel quite lost to go to the store one day and find the labels gone—just a floor of CDs, arranged alphabetically.

So, for Frith, genre categories have some temporary use value in helping consumers find the music they want to hear. But those categories are also subject to recall and modification without notice and are often deployed in idiosyncratic ways, reflecting the personalities of the owners of different record shops or even the whims of the clerks who shelve particular titles. If you print the genres on the book jacket, you automatically limit their shelf life by restricting your ability to shuffle the pieces to reflect changing tastes and perceptions. The result will be as much bad business as bad art. Of course, on the consumption side, we all adopt very idiosyncratic systems for shelving our books anyway: that's the pleasure of reading other people's bookshelves as maps of their minds, displaying what things interest them and the perceived relationships between the parts.

You might think that this "shelving" metaphor for thinking about the cultural work of genres would break down quickly in a world where fewer and fewer books are purchased in brick-and-mortar bookshops and more and more of them are being bought online, where listings can be easily reconfigured, where the same book can be listed in an infinite number of categories. Paradoxically, though, genres have had a tighter hold on our imagination in recent years as the range of cultural choice has broadened and audiences have fragmented. Film historian Rick Altman tells us that far from imposing rigid boundaries between genres, the old studio system depended on the idea that the same film could appeal to multiple audience segments at a time when pretty much everyone in the country went to the movies once or twice a week. Hollywood films rarely fit into some narrowly composed category: the same film had to appeal to men as well as women, the young as well as the old, by signaling different entertainment elements ("Comedy. Romance. Action. Exotic Locales. Singing. Dancing....")

Over the course of the twentieth century, however, genre categories have become ever more specialized as media industries refine techniques for monitoring and targeting particular clusters of consumers. These more rigid and precise subgenres are the product of a more general tendency toward what anthropologist Grant McCracken calls "specification." Subcultures break down into smaller subcultures, niches become smaller niches in an eternal dance between our desire to differentiate ourselves *from* and affiliate ourselves *with* others who share our tastes. There are more different categories of books, records, and films than ever before; all that diversity produces an anxiety that is being met by more aggressive policing of boundaries. Using more sophisticated tools, media consumers are trying to find the "perfect choice," rather than taking for granted that a work designed for a general audience is going to contain some things we like and some things we don't.

And where the market doesn't impose such specifications, we add them ourselves. Catherine Tosenberger has argued that the best fan fiction is "unpublishable" in the sense that it operates across the genre categories, aesthetic norms, and ideological constraints that shape commercial publishing. Fans self-publish in order to step outside those filters. Yet, the fan community also imposes its own categories, which help readers find the "right story" through author's notes that tell us, for example, which "ships" (relationships between specified pairs of characters) are being explored, offer a rough sense of their sexual explicitness or emotional tone, warn us about vexing themes, and so forth. And if you read the letters of comment, there's enormous anger directed at any writer who asks a reader to read a story that doesn't deliver what was promised and, even worse, gives them something they didn't ask for.

All of this focus on using genres to classify and shelve works assumes that we know where one genre ends and another begins and that genre works stay where we put them. Genres may be optical illusions, which come and go like mirages, depending on the ways we look at the texts in question. In one formulation, genre classifcations offer reading hypothesis: we start a book with the assumption that it will follow a certain path; we read it *as* a mystery or as a romance or as a fantasy, and as we do so, we look for those elements that match our expectations: depending on our starting point, we may notice some things or ignore them, make certain predictions or avoid them, value or reject certain elements, form or dismiss certain interpretations. Start from a different hypothesis and you will have a different experience. Some critics are rereading familiar texts through alternative logics: so, for example, queer cultural critic Alex Doty has made the case for *The Wizard of Oz* as a power struggle between butch and femme lesbians, Jason Mittell has read the HBO series *The Wire* as a video game, and Linda Williams reads pornography in relation to Hollywood musicals. Might we see such essays as interstitial criticism?

For some readers, there is a certain pleasure in playing a game where all the parts match our templates (much as a sparrow feels more like a bird than an ostrich does). For other readers, there may be a pleasure in the unanticipated or the indeterminate. Let's hear it for the duck-billed platypus!

Tzvetan Todorov has talked about the "fantastic" as playing with this uncertainty about classification. For instance, most ghost stories create a special pleasure from our uncertainty about whether we are supposed to believe there really are ghosts or whether we are to come up with a natural, logical, real-world explanation for the events. The pleasure, he says, is in toggling between multiple interpretations, not knowing what kind of story we are reading: there *was* a ghost; the narrator was crazy; or in the Scooby Doo version, it was all a scheme by the guy who runs the old amusement park.

Even when we kinda knew where the ghost story was going, the process of hiding and unveiling can be as much darn fun as a good old-fashioned striptease. What if we were to imagine the interstitial as another kind of indeterminacy, one that flits between genres in the same way that the fantastic flickers between levels of reality? Maybe this is what Heinz Insu Fenkl is getting at when he writes:

> Interstitial works make the reader (or listener, or viewer) more perceptive and more attentive; in doing so, they make the reader's world larger, more interesting, more meaningful, and perhaps even more comprehensible. The reader, who has been seeing black-and-white, suddenly begins not only to see color, but to learn how to see other colors.

Just as there are systems of cultural production in which audiences express confusion if a work straddles genres, there are others in which artists thrive upon and audiences anticipate mixing and matching genre elements. Take for example the so-called masala films that come out of the Bollywood film industry in India and are popular across Asia, Africa, and increasingly the West. The same film might move between historical and contemporary settings, might mix comedy and melodrama, might follow an intense (and disturbing) action sequence with a musical number, might mix the most sudsy romance with social uplift and political reform, and might acknowledge both Hindu and Islamic traditions. The descriptor "masala" refers to a mixture of spices used in Indian cooking. Just as one would be disappointed if an Indian dish contained only one spice, the Bollywood spectator would be disappointed if a Hindi film contained only one genre.

We are seeing greater cultural churn as more and more works move across national borders, get picked up by new artists and audiences, get combined in new ways, paving the way for nouvelle culture in the same way that the global availability of spices and ingredients has led many of our best chefs to experiment with radical departures from and reinventions of traditional cuisines. The anthropologist Renato Rosaldo has contrasted a classic understanding of cultures as so many exhibits in an ethnographic museum with a more contemporary notion of cultures as garage sales, where people push, pull, and paw over other people's used stuff before taking it home, trying it on for size, and altering it to suit their needs. Many young American consumers are using the Web in search of Korean dramas, Japanese anime, Latin American *telenovelas*, or Bollywood films, anything that takes them outside the parochialism of their own culture. The result really does defy any classification: look at something like *Tears of the Black Tiger*, which starts as a classic Thai novel, throws in a little opera, adds a much more intense color palette, and tells the man's story as a western and the woman's story as a '50s-style melodrama to suggest that the two protagonists are living in different worlds.

Globalization is simply one of a number of forces which are breaking down the tyranny of genre classifications and paving the way for experimentation within popular storytelling. In his book *Everything Bad Is Good For You*, Steven Johnson makes the argument that the most popular forms of entertainment today are popular because they make demands on our attention and cognition. For example, a television show like *Lost*, one of the top ratings successes of the past decade, demonstrates a level of complexity that would have been unimaginable on American television a few decades ago—with its large-scale ensemble casts of characters, its flashes forward and backward in time, its complex sets of puzzles and enigmas, its moral ambiguities and shifting alliances, but also its uncertain and unpredictable relationship to existing television genres. If we knew what the operative genre model was, we might figure out what's really happening on the island, but without such a clear mapping, we remain pleasurably lost. Such dramas thrive in part because they support robust Internet communities where readers gather online to compare notes, debate interpretations, trace references, and otherwise have fun talking with each other. Its interstitial qualities are essential to *Lost's* success, even as they account for why other viewers got frustrated and gave up on the series, convinced that it was never going to add up to anything anyway.

Lost illustrates another tendency in contemporary popular culture towards what I call transmedia storytelling. *Lost* is not simply a story or even a television series; *Lost* is a world that can support many different characters and many different stories that unfold across multiple media platforms. As these stories move across media platforms, *Lost* also often moves across genres: not unlike early novels, which might be constituted through mock letters, journals, and diaries, these new stories may mock e-mail correspondence, interviews, documents, websites, news magazine stories, advertisements, computer games, puzzles, ciphers, and a range of other materials which help make its world feel more real to the reader. These transmedia works will add a whole new meaning to the concept of interstitial arts.

So, to borrow from Charles Dickens (who borrowed from everyone else in his own time), this is the best of times and the worst of times for the interstitial arts. In such a world, the interstitial thrives and it withers. It finds receptive audiences and harsh critics. It gratifies and grates. It inspires and confuses. Above all, it gives us something to talk about. It opens us up to a world where nothing is what it seems and where little belongs, at least in the narrow sense of the term. We're going *Out There*!

What happens next is in your hands. Read. Enjoy. Debate. Tell your friends. But also create. Write. Appropriate. Remix. Transform. Just leave your cookie cutters and jelly molds at home. We can figure out what shelf this belongs on later.

Ellen Kushner, "The Interstitial Arts Foundation: An Introduction," in *Nebula Awards Showcase 2005*, edited by Jack Dann (ROC/PenguinPutnam, March 2005), http://www.interstitialarts.org/why/theIAF_an_intro1.html

Delia Sherman, "An Introduction to Interstitial Arts: Life on the Border," http://www.interstitialarts.org/what/intro_toIA.html

Susan Stinson, "Cracks," http://www.interstitialarts.org/what/reflection Stinson.html

Mikhail Bakhtin, *The Dialogic Imagination* (University of Texas, 1982).

Heinz Insu Fenkl, "The Interstitial DMZ," http://www.interstitialarts.org/why/the_interstitial_dmz_1.html

Barth Anderson, "The Prickly, Tricky, Ornery Multiverse of Interstitial Art," http://www.interstitialarts.org/what/reflectionAnderson.html

Simon Frith, *Performing Rites: On the Value of Popular Music* (Harvard University Press, 1998)

Rick Altman, *Film/Genre* (British Film Institute, 1999)

Grant McCracken, *Plenitude 2.0: Culture by Commotion* (Periph: Fluide, 1998)

Catherine Tossenberger, "Potterotics: Harry Potter Fan Fiction on the Internet," Dissertation, University of Florida, 2007

Alex Doty, *Flaming Classics: Queering the Film Canon* (Routledge, 2000)

Jason Mittell, "All in the Game: The Wire, Serial Storytelling and Procedural Logic," in Noah Wardrip-Fruin and Pat Harrigan, *Third Person: Authoring and Exploring Vast Narratives* (MIT Press, 2009)

Linda Williams, *Hard Core: Power, Pleasure, and the "Frenzy of the Visible"* (University of California Press, 1999)

Tzvetan Todorov, *The Fantastic: A Structural Approach to a Literary Genre* (Cornell University Press, 1975)

Renato Rosaldo, *Culture and Truth: The Reworking of Social Analysis* (Beacon Press, 1993)

Charles Vess, "Interstitial Visual Arts: An Impossible Marriage of Materials," http://www.interstitialarts.org/what/marriage_of_materials.html

Steven Johnson, *Everything Bad Is Good for You* (Riverhead, 2006)

Kristin Thompson, *Breaking the Glass Armor: Neoformalist Film Analysis* (Princeton University Press, 1988)

John Caughie, *Theories of Authorship: A Reader* (Routledge, 1981)

Peter J. Rabinowitz, "The Turn of the Glass Key: Popular Fiction as Reading Strategy," *Critical Inquiry*, March 1985

The War Between Heaven and Hell Wallpaper

Jeffrey Ford

Just before I dozed off to sleep last night, I had a vision. I saw, with my eyes closed, a room that was wallpapered with the most amazing scenery of a battle between angels and demons. It was brilliantly colorful and so amazingly detailed. I can still see the deep red of the evil horde, their barbed tails and bat wings—classic Madison Avenue horned demons, but playing for keeps, slaying angels with their tridents. The angels wore billowing white robes and, of course, had feathered wings in contrast to the slick rodent ones of the enemy. Halos, gleaming swords, harps to call the troops to charge, they poured out of the clouds, riding beams of light toward Earth where the demons crawled out of cracks in the ground, smoking volcano craters, and holes in giant trees. The middle part of the wall, from just above knee-height to the top of the rib cage, was taken up by the actual battle. The upper part held scenes in heaven as the troops made ready to descend and the dead and wounded were brought in. The lower part of the wall was the stalactite-riddled caverns of burning hell, showing the incredible numbers of Satan's minions. If you've ever seen the *Where's Waldo* books—it looked like one of those, or at least every inch was as crowded with as many characters, painted in the style and color of Mathias Grünewald. One thing to keep in mind—I knew this was a war *between* Heaven and Hell, not the war *in* Heaven in which Lucifer and his posse were evicted.

The sight of this wallpaper jazzed me back to consciousness, and I said to Lynn, who was dozing off, herself, "I just saw War Between Heaven and Hell wallpaper." She was silent for a while, but I knew from her breathing she wasn't asleep. "What do you think of that?" I said. She laughed. "I have to get up early tomorrow," she said. A few moments later I was describing it to her. When I was done, I said to her, "What do you think that means?" "You've got a screw loose," she said. "It was so colorful and intricate," I told her. "Great," she said, and a few seconds later, she was lightly snoring.

I lay awake for a while and contemplated the War Between Heaven and Hell wallpaper. In my imagination a woman got this wallpaper installed in a room in her house. Eventually she noticed that the scenes changed each day while she was at work. On the days when she had a bad day at the office, Satan's troops had gained the advantage, and the days when things went well for her, Heaven took the lead. Months went by and Heaven really started to kick ass, pushing the demons back into Hell and then invading the smoky underworld in order to finish them off. The last battalion of winged demons had pulled back into the frozen parts at the center of Hell where they'd amassed their infernal artillery and battle beasts, falling into a siege amid the ice mountains. The angels surrounded the last bole of Hell and used long bows and spears.

For the woman to take all of this in each night, she had to get down on the floor and move a desk out of the way to see the spot where the final battle was taking place. Just as it looked like the demons were going to be obliterated, she started to feel badly for them. She felt an uneasiness with the lack of balance represented by the wallpaper's scenario. Since the wallpaper scenes had something to do with what happened to her through the day, she decided to try to turn the tide of the battle by performing acts of evil, things that would reflect badly upon her and ensure she would have a bad day. She put her plan into practice, and the demons began to rally. A call came through on her cell phone, and Satan engaged her as an agent in the War Between Heaven and Hell. That's when I fell asleep.

I woke up this morning from a dream of a kind of monastery in a snowy wood. I think a monastery is a place where monks live, but this place had Catholic priests living in it. Lynn and I came to it after slogging through swamps and through a snow-covered forest. We were totally lost. The place was built from the most marvelous-smelling rosewood, and it seemed to have been carved from enormous blocks of it rather than put together with nails and screws. The trees came right up to the sides of the walls as if the monastery had been there for a very long time and they had grown up next to where it was built. There were a number of larger buildings linked to each other by screened hallways. Some of these buildings were more than one story and were decorated with gargoyles in the shapes of demons and angels.

We were met by a priest out in the yard behind the open gates at sundown. We were weary and hungry. He told us to hurry if we wanted to eat. We followed him through the winding, dark hallways of the place. The shadows were kept at bay only by lit candles. We were led to a small kitchen and given a piece of stale bread and a bowl of onion soup. The priest introduced himself as Father Heems. He was a very downtrodden-looking fellow, his face filled with worry lines and his hands shaking slightly. He told us the place was haunted by the Holy Ghost, and that the spirit was angry. Just the night before we arrived it had strangled the caretaker, whose body he pointed out to us lying next to the stove wrapped in black plastic and tied at the feet and head. "You've got to keep moving. You can't sleep till dawn. If you doze off, the Ghost will strangle you through your dreams. A breeze will pass over you, and you will feel it tightening its fingers around your throat."

We got up from the table and started walking. "That's it," cried Heems, "keep moving." Three other priests, two very old ones and a slow heavy one, and Lynn and I, along with Heems, moved through the corridors of the place—up stairs, down stairs, through catacombs, along balconies. When we passed through the dungeon, there was a cell with straw on the floor with about a dozen young children milling about behind the bars. The heavy priest told us that the children were safe from the Ghost at night behind the bars. I asked, "Why don't we go in there too?" And Heems yelled, "Pipe down and keep moving." Every time I'd begin to feel tired and slow down, I'd hear the wind blow outside and feel a breeze creeping down the hallway.

Somewhere in the middle of the night, Father Heems called out to one of the other old priests, as we made our way along, "Where is Father Shaw?" This almost made me stop in my tracks, because Father Shaw was the head priest at the church I went to as a kid. He was stern to the verge of cruelty and looked like an emaciated

3

Samuel Beckett. We all hated him. Even the parents hated him. When we kids went to the church for any kind of instruction, like before First Communion or for confirmation training, he'd appear and spew rants about how we were a bunch of little sinners and he wished we could feel Christ's pain from the crucifixion. Any time I ever went to confession and that little door in the dark confessional would slam back and I'd see his profile through the grating, I'd nearly crap my pants. The prayers he'd give you to say for even some minor infraction of disobedience would be an onerous weight.

Soon after the mention of Father Shaw, daylight came and we could finally stop walking. In some kind of weird chain of events and reasoning, Heems made me the new caretaker for the time Lynn and I would stay there, which if I had my preference was not going to be very long. First, though, we had to figure out where we were. Once the other priests left us alone for a few minutes, Lynn asked me, "What's with the kids in the dungeon?" "That's not cool," I said. But then Heems was back with a canvas bag for me with a shoulder strap on it and a long stick with a nail poking out the end. I got the idea that I was meant to police the grounds. So I started around the outside of the building, poking candy wrappers (there were a lot of candy wrappers for some reason). When I made my way around half the building, I came to a little alcove, and lying in the middle of it on the snow was Father Shaw—dead. He was leaking from somewhere onto the snow, and the snow had turned the color of Mountain Dew. His flesh was rotted and yellow. The second I saw him I started breathing through my mouth as to avoid smelling him. I thought to myself, "Do I have to clean this shit up all by myself?" Time skipped here, and I was tying a string around the plastic that covered his legs. I woke up.

While eating breakfast, I realized why Father Shaw had appeared in this dream. I'd mentioned him to Lynn not two days earlier. We were at a wedding in South Jersey, staying in a place called the Seaview in Absecon. It's a really old hotel and golf resort. That's where the wedding reception was being held. Lynn had stayed there once for a conference she was participating in, and she told me that the hallways of the place reminded her of the hotel in *The Shining*.

After the reception was over, we went and got our room, hung out for a while, and then headed downstairs to the bar to have a drink. On the way, we passed a room like a study, with wooden paneling and stuffed chairs and glassed bookcases with a plaque over the door on the outside that read "Shaw." I immediately thought of Father Shaw and told Lynn about him. The memory of his face prompted me to recall that my father was in the hospital to have a cyst removed once when we were kids, and when he returned from his stay, I'd overheard him say to my mother that Shaw had been in there at the same time, dying of cancer. "All of his great solace in God went right out the window," my father said. "Shaw wailed just as loud as the rest of the sinners." At the moment he said this, he was eating a cracker with a sardine on it. He gulped down the cracker in one bite, licked his forefinger, his thumb, and then smiled, giving the advantage to either Heaven or Hell. I'm still not sure which.

"The War Between Heaven and Hell Wallpaper" is a completely true story. I saw the wallpaper in my mind as I dozed off, I woke up and told Lynn, I tried to confabulate a story for it, I fell asleep and had a real dream, and then the next day I remembered something that had happened to me that might have initiated the chain of events. I have a feeling these kinds of incident/experience/thought trains happen to us frequently, but usually we are too distracted by life to notice the connections. The wallpaper vision was probably only a portal into this chain of events and dreams, which stretches way back to when I was a kid encountering the church and will more than likely move forward as my life progresses. It could be that our lives are woven from these long thematic threads and only at certain magical times like in the twilight between consciousness and sleep they are momentarily revealed to us. I don't really know enough about the concept of Interstitial to say how this story qualifies. What I do know is that I could feel when I was writing this piece that it was different in some fundamental way from other stories I'd written. The whole idea of it seemed kooky as hell, but it felt good to follow it, so I did.

Jeffrey Ford

The Beautiful Feast

M. Rickert

October evening, 1969. Golden leaves spiral down. Johnny tries to catch one. His fingers touch the whisper of leaf but close on air. It doesn't matter. He spins across the yard, dodging gold bullets. He's hit! He's hit! He falls to the ground, rolling in leaf, grass, sticks, and dirt. In the distance, a dog barks. The boy lies still, arms spread, legs at odd angles. Dead. He is dead when the car pulls up in front of his house. Heart beating wild from all his spinning, he is dead, trying to still his breath when the doors slam shut and shoes click up the sidewalk, dead when a man's voice says, "Mrs. Harlyle?" dead when his mother screams, a siren-sound that falls to the ground like leaves. The boy is dead when he opens his eyes, looks at the sky, darkly now. Dead as he lies there, waiting for God, angel, or ghost. Dead as one leaf spiral-lands on his cheek. He sits up slowly. Stands to brush the leaves, sticks, dirt, grass from his clothes before he takes serious steps across the lawn and up the cracked sidewalk, like one returned from a terrible mission. He has seen terrible things. He reaches for the doorknob, opens the door, walks into the room where his mother sits weeping on the couch between the two soldiers. Gone are the golden leaves, gone the innocent dream. She looks at him, and for a moment he is worried that she is gone, too, lost somewhere inside herself, but she pulls him close, smashes his face against her collarbone. She is holding him too tight, he can hardly breathe, though he will not struggle for breath. He will give her everything. Gone is the selfish little boy. "Oh, Johnny," she rocks him, "pray for your father." She releases him just enough that he can nod, before she presses him close again.

Later, he will lie in his room, on his twin bed, listening to the neighbors, his aunts, uncles, cousins, people from the church. He will lie there in his clothes, right on top of the covers, and he will smell the food they bring but forget to offer him. He will stare at the simple walls of his childhood, the window with the drawn blind. He will try to pray for his father but he will find it, too, gone, this belief in God, fallen from him as if he were the tree and God the leaves, fallen in the yard where he has left his childhood, where he was shot down, where he died and no one noticed, no one at all. That boy is a ghost. He rolls on his side. Stares at the wall until sleep comes for him on her silent feet and enfolds him in her dark wings, takes him to that magical place of forgetting. Too soon, morning arrives and he is returned to his little room where, at last, he weeps.

The Time Between

They call Johnny "that poor boy." Teachers whisper his story to each other, and he develops an ability to hear it even at some distance. He likes to swing, he likes to run, but gone is the desire to play war, though sometimes, over the years, when the leaves spiral down around him, he hears gunfire.

Johnny kicks cherry blossoms while his mother finds his father's name on the wall. "Here is your father," she says.
     My father is not a stone, he thinks.

They are in a Chinese restaurant with "a man from Washington," as Johnny's mother puts it. When the man leaves to use the bathroom, Johnny's mother applies red lipstick and neatens it with her fingernail. She leans across the table to whisper to Johnny, "He's going to help us find your father." Johnny holds his breath against the terrible scent of his mother's perfume, the plastic smell of her lips, the pork and alcohol. When she leans back, looking pleased as a cat with an overturned fishbowl, Johnny says, "Mom, he's dead." She slaps him so hard his cheeks burn red for years.

On her deathbed, Johnny's mother hands him the incriminating evidence. "What do you want me to do with this?" he says.
     "You've always been too timid," she replies. It's the last thing she says to him before she dies.

2005

Johnny is a man on a mission. Every Monday he sends another letter. About once a month he gets a reply. "I am sorry about the loss of your father. He has given everything a man could give to his country. Please accept my condolences." It is a form letter. Johnny knows this, because on occasion he rents a mailbox under a different name, and the letters he receives there are exactly the same as the ones sent to his house. Sometimes he changes the details, but no matter what he says, he always gets the same reply. It irritates him. One Monday the variation of his letter alludes to that irritation, and a week later, two men with badges come to his office.

He has only one chair, but they are not interested in sitting so Johnny retains it for himself. They ask a lot of irrelevant questions. Does Johnny own a gun? Does he expect to travel any time soon? What political groups does he belong to? Johnny answers shortly. Yes. No. None. What does any of this have to do with the issue?

The men look at him as if he has said something inscrutable. "What issue would that be?"

Johnny reaches for the file drawer. At last he has their interest. He pulls out the photograph and hands it into the long fingers of the chief interrogator. The man hardly looks at it before he passes it on to his partner, who laughs. "It's grass!"

Johnny waits for the other one to explain, but when he doesn't, Johnny peers over the man's knuckles at the photograph. "Look closer; see how the grass forms numbers?"

The man nods, slowly.

"That's my father's secret code. For if he was captured. He was shot down in 1969. That picture was taken in 1982. He's still alive. Well, at least he was then, and I have seen nothing since to make me believe he's dead."

They look at him with new appreciation. Their expressions remind Johnny of all those years ago, the faces of the soldiers when he walked across the room to his mother.

Johnny objects when the man tucks the photograph into his pocket, but they tell him that they'll make sure the right people see it.

Johnny shakes their hands. Only later does he realize he should have gotten their names.

He waits.

Eventually Johnny takes the American flag down from his front porch and doesn't put it up again. No one is going to do what he should have done years ago.

Vietnam

Time has fallen into a turbine, wildly spun into strange green days and purple nights. Johnny is a friendly giant. He greets the villagers, using the phrase from his tourist book, but sadly retains nothing more of the language. What is spoken by these small people remains mysterious until the day Phi Nuc Than enters the noodle shop, and comes to stand by Johnny's table. "I have been told you need a guide."

At the sound of such clear English, Johnny feels as though woken from a long coma. He concentrates, blinks, frowns, smiles, nods, shakes the small man's hand, insists he sit, orders more noodles. Only then does Johnny explain how he has come in search of his father.

"They say there is one American, but we would be foolish to try to find him. He doesn't want to go home."

"Not wanna come home? Are you saying he's crazy?" And when Phi Nuc Than looks at Johnny with a frown, he repeats "crazy," rolls his eyes, sticks out his tongue, shakes his head, doing his best pantomime of the word, all of which is unnecessary. Phi Nuc Than's English is excellent.

"Not crazy, a Lotus Eater."

"A Lotus Eater?"

"It is probably just a legend."

"Why wouldn't he wanna come home?"

Phi Nuc Than is concentrating on his noodles and does not look up as he shrugs.

Johnny sits back. It never occurred to him that his father might not want to be found. "Wait," he says, though Phi Nuc Than has made no move to go. "He left his secret code in the grass, the way

9

he was taught. I had a photograph of it, snuck to my mother by a friend of hers."

"When was that?"

"It was a long time ago, but why should I believe he's dead? The only proof I have is that he's still out there, waiting. I'm going to bring him home. Will you help?"

Phi Nuc Than is hard to convince. He has a wife. Kids. He doesn't like the jungle. At each objection, Johnny raises the price he's willing to pay. Eventually, Phi Nuc Than agrees. Johnny pays him handsomely but promises double upon their safe return.

They meet the next morning, leaving the village together; Johnny dressed like a soldier, carrying a backpack of supplies, and Phi Nuc Than dressed in the simple clothes of a peasant farmer. "I wasn't sure you'd actually come," Johnny says (and, in fact, Phi Nuc Than had been more than an hour late, which Johnny decides not to mention).

Phi Nuc Than nods. "My father, too, is missing. I know your heart."

This is the nicest thing anyone has said to Johnny in a long time. He rests his hand on Phi Nuc Than's shoulder and when the small man looks up, Johnny calls him "friend." Phi Nuc Than doesn't seem to know how to respond to this, but later that day, when Johnny loses Phi Nuc Than, then finds him again, the small man smiles broadly and says, "There you are, my friend."

Over the following days, Johnny is surprised to discover that his companion is a terrible guide. He walks too far ahead and frequently loses Johnny. It is a miracle every time Johnny finds him. Both men are bitten by insects, but Johnny is clearly the one who suffers the worst, and when he comments on it, his friend shrugs and says, "This is my country," as if that explains the insects' preference. Neither man is skilled at making the small fires necessary for heating the food, and neither is very good at rationing. Both can see that they are exhausting their supplies much too quickly. As for searching for the American, who may or may not be Johnny's father, who may or may not truly exist, both men seem equally at a loss as how to go about it, pretending (Johnny is fairly certain Phi Nuc Than is pretending) to read clues in the strange markings on trees, or the various leavings of scat. Johnny and Phi Nuc Than begin fighting. At first they are mild spats, "You walk too fast," "Well, you walk too slow," "Your breath stinks like a goat," "Well, your breath smells like farts," but then they become pointed: "This is a stupid idea," "Maybe it wouldn't be so stupid if I didn't have such a stupid guide."

The night comes when they make camp with broad leaves and bamboo, sharing the almost empty backpack as a harsh pillow, and Phi Nuc Than tells his story.

"We did the same thing with the French, years before the American war. We called them pearls. My country was willing to keep their end of the bargain. Pay us for the pearl, we bring him to you. We need the money, you understand? America measures time like a child, but we are very patient. We waited. All we wanted was the money that your president promised, but the Americans refused to pay. What can I say? Our officials did not believe Americans would leave their own soldiers behind. Our officials thought they were bargaining.

"The soldiers guarding the prisoners grew tired of their duty, but if any of them left his post, he was punished with death. Either stay with the pearls or die. No choice.

"My father was one of the jewelers. Yes. That's right. How do you think I know so much? My father used to sneak home to see us. The last time he did, he told us about the Lotus Eater. We never saw my father again, though my mother says she sees him standing on the hill, but my mother is old and who knows if she sees what is true or what is desired?

"The Lotus Eater, my father said, was shot out of the sky into the lake, and when the people pulled him onto the land, he already had lotus blossoms in his mouth. His body was broken, and they tried to break his spirit. Some said his spirit was never broken because his mind was. Others said his spirit hadn't been broken because he walked through death's door and came back. Not ghost. Not alive. Someone who exists in both places.

"My father was given the special duty of guarding him. He told us how the American ate nothing but lotus and emitted a sweet perfume. No one knew where the lotus came from. Put him in a cave, put him in a box, tie him down, still he was found with lotus. One of the guards told my father that he had observed the prisoner pacing the small yard, lotus blooming beneath his feet. When this same guard suffered a terrible snake bite, he approached the Lotus Eater, who touched his finger to the wound and healed it. Yet another time, the group came upon a dying water buffalo; the Lotus Eater touched it, and wept over it, but it died anyway. The guard said that proved his theory that the Lotus Eater existed in both worlds, a creature of heaven, with all its miracles, and a creature of the earth, with its terrible limitations.

"This guard insisted that the Lotus Eater was Buddha and began to include him in their circle at the end of the day. One evening, he gently tapped the Lotus Eater on his arm, the way friends do. The Lotus Eater shook, trembled, and with a roar turned into a tiger and ate the man. After this, my father became a fugitive. He snuck home one more time and promised he would come back, but as I've said, we never saw him again. Except my mother.

"They say the Lotus Eater roams the jungle. Some say he's holy. Some say he is a demon. Some say he's not real at all, just the dream of men like my father who lost their minds to the war. War is a terrible monster. You and I are the sons of this monster, but we do not have to be its victims. Let's sleep and in the morning return to the village. My wife will make us a good meal. She said it was foolish of me to take this trip, and she was right. Sometimes I do unreasonable things because I want to find my father, but let's leave our fathers to the world of dreams. Let us return to the land of the living. That is where we belong. No good can come of trying to find them. Even if we find them, they no longer belong to us, my friend. We have made a terrible mistake. What is it that you Americans say? Life is too little? Life is too little for us to spend our days like this."

Johnny didn't come all this way for a bedtime story, or a lecture, but to be respectful, he lies in silence when Phi Nuc Than is finished.

Later that night, a tiger comes to the edge of their camp.

Johnny's heart beats wildly. Beside him, he hears his friend wake with a start. Both men hold their breath as the beast slinks past. Johnny whispers, "Was that him?" Phi Nuc Than answers with a shush. Eventually, Johnny falls asleep. When he wakes up, his friend is gone.

When?

He wanders the jungle in the rain, the mud, the heat. Is this how it's been? All these years, so many days and nights, hours and minutes filled with hunger and loss? Why not eat the Lotus and forget everything and everyone? How long? How long can a man survive on the memory of love when all around him the jungle threatens? How long before the autumn leaves fall around him and he lies dead in the grass, breathing the sweet scent of dirt, end of summer, end of everything? How long before he asks, what is my measure? If not time, or skin, or place, what? How long before he pulls the Lotus to his mouth, the soft, velvety texture against his tongue, the terrible taste of forgetting, the succor it brings. Not sated, exactly, but satisfied, he lies beside the water. When the old man comes to stand there, dressed in Lotus blossoms and teeth strung like jewels, they watch each other before the elder begins scavenging for what the younger has not taken, a scarce feast of Lotus, but this is a dream, of course, this is all the dream of a boy shot dead on the grass by the falling golden leaves, or a dream that comes later than that, the dream of a boy who listens to relatives mourning his missing father, a boy who falls asleep hungry, and alone in his bedroom, or later still.

When the waiting tiger pounces, Johnny opens his eyes. He sees a flash! Oh! He thought it was a beast, but it is fire. All is red, all is pain, all is falling leaves, golden, like rain. This is not happening. He reaches for the doorknob, opens the door, walks into the room where his father waits at the table, beckoning. Johnny takes serious steps across the room, like one returned from a terrible mission. He has seen terrible things. He sits at the table across from his father. The steaming plates set before them emit the sweet scent of Lotus blossoms, and for a moment, this singular moment in all the years, months, hours, and days of his life, Johnny remembers this feeling and he thinks his friend was right, what had he said, the words are gone, here is his childhood home, here is the promise of his life. Johnny is spinning, spinning, wildly spinning even as he forgets everything, he remembers how beautiful, how tender, how delicate the taste of breath, and when the feast is over, he stalks away, languid almost, to drink from the lake. Startled at first by the reflection there, he drinks.

I went through a period in my life of reading Robert Pirsig's *Zen and the Art of Motorcycle Maintenance* every so many years. Each time it was a different book. A road story. A father/son tale. An exploration of quality. But there came a time when, possibly because of the rootless nature of my life then, I came dangerously close to understanding the Zen in the book. There is a reason why the Zen tradition is a teacher/student one, but I was alone when I had this experience, which was basically the sense of falling off the world. This is not as fun as it may sound. It can actually be quite frightening to recognize that life is not bound the way we bind it. The question is, if it isn't reality, what are we living? Luckily, I was able to reel myself in from the precipice, and once recovered from the shock, have been trying to define that sensation of transcendence ever since. How to describe the limitation of words while using words to describe it? How to translate the freedom of transcendence while remaining safe in the shared world? Likely, it can't be done, but most of my work seeks to do it. Who knows why? Doomed to fail, I just keep trying and have discovered that failure, in itself, carries an element of transcendence. "The Beautiful Feast" is a continuation of my search for the transcendental. It is also an exploration of failure. This is true for both Johnny and me. Some people might think this is a sad account. Only those of us who roam the jungle of fail know the secret beauty there, which, to be clear, doesn't mean that it is an easy journey. Failure is a hungry tiger, it hurts every time. And yet ...

M. Rickert

Remembrance Is
Something Like a House

Will Ludwigsen

Every day for three decades, the abandoned house strains against its galling anchors, hoping to pull free. It has waited thirty years for its pipes and pilings to finally decay so it can leave for Florida to find the Macek family.

Nobody in its Milford neighborhood will likely miss the house or even notice its absence; it has hidden for decades behind overgrown bushes, weeds, and legends. When they talk about the house at all, the neighbors whisper about the child killer who lived there long ago with his family: a wife and five children who never knew their father kept his rotting playmate in the crawl space until the police came.

The house, however, knows the truth and wants to confess it, even if it has to crawl eight hundred miles.

The house isn't stupid, of course. It knows that leaving in the morning when that middle-aged lady strolls across its overgrown lot would attract attention. So, too, would leaving at any other daylight hour, even though by then most of the neighbors have gone to work. A beginning is the most noticeable time of a secret journey.

The house is patient. It's waited three decades and it could probably wait another three, though it isn't sure if people live that long, especially *its* people. They seemed upset and harried when they left everything behind but what fit in their arms, and that can't be a healthy way to live. The Maceks could well be dead, but the house doesn't think so. It doesn't feel so, either.

At dusk the house decides to leave. Shadows from the rotting trees conceal its departure, though it isn't auspicious: the house shudders its frame and groans forward two inches. Afterward, exhausted, it sighs through its yawning windows and leaking attic with a wood-filtered moan.

Then it tries another two inches, and another two after that. They get easier, once the house gets some practice and learns just how to tighten the posts and shuffle forward.

In the coming weeks, the walking lady doesn't notice the house is moving. She just changes her path to compensate, not even realizing she's doing it, until one day she stops coming around at all. Maybe she goes back to work or finds a brighter place to walk. Maybe she just gets a bad feeling about the lonely house in the woods, some chill that it was almost alive. The house gets that a lot.

With no witnesses, the house picks up speed and moves ten feet an hour on level ground during the daytime and even faster at night. The breeze passing through its dormers and eaves exhilarates the house, and sometimes it doesn't care if anybody sees its shadow crossing the rising moon.

The house keeps to the woods and meadows between properties, because it wouldn't do to be found and restored. You can't go all the way to Florida with a family of four living in you, the house likes to say to itself. The house has lots of wisdom to impart but nobody to whom it can impart it, like a newer house or even a shed.

For instance, it would like to tell someone that traveling in the wilderness is risky. Sometimes the weather is bad and you slip down a hillside in the mud. Sometimes your shingles get scraped away by low-hanging brambles. More than once, raccoons tumble down the chimney or through a window to nose through food the Maceks left behind. The house tries to shimmy in a scary way, thumping the old black-and-white framed photos on the wall, but the raccoons don't seem to care. They pull away a fuzzy rotten chicken bone or a green roll while the house glowers.

When it rains, water seeps through the grey insulation and bulges in big lumps in the ceiling. Sometimes one will burst, splattering plaster and moldy water across the carpet. The house winces when this happens and tries to stick closer to the trees for shelter.

~

The house waits beside Highway 61, wondering how it will ever get across. A car passes every few minutes, just enough to make a foot-by-foot march across the pavement risky.

The house squats by the side of the road, watching for the darkness to come. When it finally does, the house crosses the first two lanes of the road as best it can, rattling its windows and cracking its siding to all but gallop to the median. There it rests, hoping to look inconspicuous—like someone just built a house in the middle of the road, or like the state is preserving a historic building by running the highway around it.

After the house has caught its second wind, it begins to cross the other lanes. Just when the dotted white line exactly bisects it, light fills all its easterly windows.

The house panics, though it isn't easy to tell: only an architect could see the corners go out of plumb and the walls buckle like that, though he or she wouldn't believe it.

Behind the windshield, the truck driver doesn't seem to believe it either. He blinks, screams, and veers the truck into the other lane. The steering wheel shudders in his hands as the trailer skids.

The house, not ready for sixty thousand pounds of truck to crash through its timbers, shuffles as best it can to the other side. There it watches the wheels catch, lock, and then thump back onto the highway as the driver gains control again. The trailer totters left and then right, but the only likely casualty is the driver's heart rate. Probably the house's too, if it had one.

The house hates fences, especially the barbed wire ones. It has broken through many a wooden rail fence with relative ease, but the barbed wire ones drag behind the house for hundreds of yards. The house then has to gingerly slither across the wire to leave it behind, losing sometimes minutes or hours.

Probably fifty or sixty people have broken into the house since it left the foundation. The house grumbles at the lost time, but sometimes visitors are nice, especially when they leave. Some of the kids break bottles and light bulbs, and the house doesn't appreciate that. Sometimes they take things, a couple of portraits or an old fork or some other souvenir of that "creepy shack in the woods." The house wishes it could stop them, but it already has one big job to finish.

Bums rarely stay the whole night. They'll nap a few hours on a bed and root around for some liquor, but then something calls them back outside—maybe a train whistle or an unfinished mission or an unpaid debt. Whatever it is, the last thing those guys seem to want is a house. Which is good, because the last thing the house wants is a bum.

Nine couples have made out on the old moldy couch, green water squishing between their fingers from the cushions as they press together. The house remembers when Mr. and Mrs. Macek did that once when the couch was clean. They both were drunk on gin-and-tonics, and she started it by unclasping the right shoulder of his overalls. The kissing kids aren't as smooth—they just shove each other on the couch, grope awhile, and then go straight to the thrusting.

Rivers and creeks are a mixed blessing. They're difficult to cross, but the current can take days or even weeks off the journey if the house navigates them right. It still floats more or less, though water washes in through the front door to the back, leaving behind silt and weeds and even flopping fish.

The house has never seen a waterfall, but it imagines one would be bad news.

In North Carolina, the house has interesting visitors: two boys and a girl, early teenagers, sweaty and sunburned from a summer vacation spent running all over the wooded mountains.

The house can tell they're adventurous, like the Macek children were before Mrs. Macek took them away. Still, they're respectful—climbing in through the kitchen window, yes, but only one already shot out by a drunken hunter.

They walk around, peeking into the stove at Mrs. Macek's forgotten roast and flipping through the stack of brittle newspapers by the green chair. They talk about the big mystery, what had happened to the people inside.

"They left so much behind," says the girl. They call her Amanda, the house discovers.

"Look at this," says the bigger boy, Michael. "There's still food on the table."

Not much after so long, of course, just scattered pebbles of dried corn and black circles where rolls used to be. Muddy animal tracks speckle the table.

"It's like the *Marie Celeste*," says the smaller boy with the big eyes, Jeremy. "Lost at sea, adrift for months."

You don't know the half of it, rues the house to itself.

"You think they got killed?" asks Michael, the one who keeps looking at the girl when she bends over the tables and shelves. The house doesn't appreciate him at all.

Neither does Amanda, it seems. She catches him staring and says, "Stop it." Then she turns to the smaller boy. "There's no sign of it. No blood or anything, at least."

"Maybe they were poisoned and they crawled outside, choking on arsenic to die in the yard or something," says the smaller boy. The house likes his insight: yes, the Maceks had been poisoned and crawled out all right. Just not by arsenic.

"Good theory," says Michael, punching him on the arm.

Amanda spreads out the newspapers on the table, the ones Mrs. Macek saved after Mr. Macek's arrest. After half a century, those lurid headlines crackle on the yellowed paper as the kids gingerly turn the pages with pinched fingers. Amanda reads them aloud, probably because Michael can't read. He looks the type.

"*Local Girl Missing for Three Days*," reads Amanda. The house remembers that, all right. Policemen walking the streets, swinging their lights from one side to the other, calling out her name. Women gathering in clots on each corner, whispering with their hands held to their mouths. Cub Scouts crawling in the bushes. Teenagers in trucks rumbling by late at night, chuckling over their dark jokes.

The house, of course, could do nothing to help.

Jeremy reads the next: "*Body Found in Crawl Space by Detectives.*" That actually wasn't true. A police bloodhound named Jenny dragged Kathy Henderson's bludgeoned body out from under the house while the detectives gaped. The dog pulled and pulled, and the house wished someone would just help, would just break through the rest of the rotten lattice to get her out. But they all just stared, and of course the house could do nothing.

Mrs. Macek fainted on the porch. Mr. Macek had a lot of questions for the police, but they didn't speak Polish. Not that they were listening anyway.

"*Foreign Handyman Arrested,*" says Michael. He would pick that one, wouldn't he, the article with the picture of Mr. Macek being dragged from the house in his grey overalls, squinting in the flash bulbs, wincing as cops twisted his arm more sharply than they had to? There were lots of boys like him back then, too. They just happened to be wearing uniforms.

The house remembers the casseroles brought for Mrs. Macek and her children right after the arrest, the offerings of neighbors who didn't believe her husband could do such a horrible thing.

"*Immigrant Pleads Not Guilty to Child Murder,*" crows the next headline in Michael's voice. "Dude looks crazy." He sidles closer to Amanda, but she sidles just as far away. "The kind of guy who'd kill a girl and stuff her under the house."

"*Crazed Handyman Offers Garbled Defense at Trial,*" whispers Jeremy.

The house remembers, too, how the casseroles came fewer and fewer, stopping altogether when the autopsy photos were shown. The Macek daughters came home from the park crying, and the Macek boys came home from the baseball diamond angry.

Amanda doesn't have to read the last one: *Guilty.* It's from August 9th, 1938, and nobody bothered to cut it from the newspaper like the others. The kids can read advertisements for $50 refrigerators if they want to, but they're all just staring at Mr. Macek's horrified expression instead.

August 9th, 1938—the day Mrs. Macek, mortified by her husband's guilt and their neighbors' reaction, ordered the children to take whatever they could carry and stuff it into the car. The day they left everything behind, not just dishes and pictures but questions, too. The day the doors clattered, the lights dimmed, and the house was left to itself.

"Cool!" says Michael. "It's a Kill House!"

The house hates to be called that.

"I wonder where he did it." He looks around, grinning. "I bet there's a ring of blood still in the tub."

He leaves to go check and Amanda follows.

Jeremy squints at the newspapers and says to nobody, "Wait. These newspapers are from Ohio."

He follows his friends, silent now as though afraid to wake up the house, and steps gently down the hallway, looking into each of the bedrooms. Blank patches on the yellow wallpaper show the ghosts of pictures fallen from the walls.

The first bedroom looks like three boys shared it, two in bunk beds and one in his own. Their dresser drawers are still open with pants and sweaters spilling out of them, and metal toy soldiers lie wounded on the floor. Jeremy picks one up but then puts it back.

The second bedroom seems to have been for the girls of the family, two of them if the beds are any sign. They'd left everything behind like their brothers had: a few drawings from school hang crookedly above one bed, and a bundle of letters tied in a pink ribbon rest on a nightstand beside the other. The letter on top has the print of someone's lips. Amanda holds it up and sniffs it.

In the master bedroom, the blankets are thrown back from one bed but the other is still made. An old clock has wound down, dying three minutes past eleven. An oval dresser mirror leans away from the wall, its left half broken away. Rusted hairpins lie beneath. A closet door swings from one hinge. Metal hangers dangle between coats and dresses with ragged sleeves.

Michael leans over a nightstand to pick up a wallet. It's the one Mr. Macek had taken from his overalls when the police came. He flips it open. It has long ago been emptied of cash, but he grins and slips it in his pocket anyway.

"What are you doing?" asks Jeremy.

"I'm just taking a little something away, that's all. A real-life murderer's wallet."

"You can't just take that."

"It's not like he'll need it. Guy's long been executed."

The walls of the house creak as though resisting a heavy wind.

Through the windows, however, the leaves hang motionless.

"Put it back." Jeremy points, his finger shaking.

"It's like robbing a grave," says Amanda from the doorway. "It isn't right."

Michael laughs and steps backward. He jumps up onto a bed and spreads open his arms. "You gonna take it from me?"

The house wishes the ceiling hadn't already collapsed above him some half a decade ago.

"Come get it, Amanda," Michael says, swaying his hips.

Jeremy and Amanda trade glances and frown. Then they both step forward.

The bed creaks beneath Michael's weight as he bounces on his heels. The tired wooden frame finally gives way and he falls backward to the floor, crunching on broken glass. He groans though he isn't cut. The house had hoped otherwise but then it realizes that it doesn't want to carry a corpse to Florida.

Jeremy pulls the wallet from Michael's hand and sets it back into the dustless square on the nightstand while Michael staggers to his feet.

"I could be dead," he whines. "Stupid kill house."

Neither of his friends say anything. Quiet and maybe embarrassed, they return to the kitchen and climb back out through the window.

Michael stomps the faucet before slithering through.

The hardest thing about crawling across the country is keeping plumb. Even if you're a good 1921 Craftsman-style bungalow, your beams and crosspieces will be torqued to their limits over all that terrain in all that weather.

Tornadoes hit in Georgia, some forty years after the house leaves Ohio. By now, the house is gray and its siding curls at the ends like a dead man's fingernails. The wind, green with stolen earth, blasts through the broken windows and tears the curtains away. Moss on the roof peels from the corner like a scab before tumbling into the vortex.

The hail rattles against the roof. The rain shoots sideways through the door. The newspapers dissolve. The couch bloats.

With nowhere for the wind to grab hold, the tornadoes move on to more satisfying victims. They wobble away, leaving the house bewildered in the middle of a field.

The house gathers its wits and crawls away through the broken branches, onward to Florida.

There aren't houses like this house near Fernandina Beach, and you'd think it would be embarrassed. It isn't. The clean adobe houses in the retirement community are full of Formica and fiberglass, slathered pink and teal with concrete seashells hanging by their doors. They've never had a baby born inside. They've never seen a really good teenage argument or a night of gin spilled in the master bedroom. Their pastel walls flicker with reruns.

The house sticks to the woods on the edge of the development, circling from the north and sensing the last of the Macek family, the commander of the toy soldiers, Julian Macek.

Of course he likes to walk still, young Julian. He always liked it back in Ohio, even in the middle of the night. He'd sneak out of his window and patrol his town like an amateur watchman. Of course he still does that today, eight hundred miles and seventy years away.

Now he carries a broom handle walking stick. He's driven a finishing nail headfirst into the end, just the thing for spearing a paper cup or an attacking animal's eyeball. He shakes it much like his father did at the kids who rush past his house on their bicycles and skateboards, not quite sure if he's missing something important and American.

The house watches Julian on his daily patrol. He follows the walkways through the golf course though he does not play. He squints at the other old men in their plaid hats and white shoes, sometimes raising the broom handle at them in either salute or warning. They chuckle and wave back.

The house realizes that it has never thought of how to call attention to itself. On windy days, you can hear the groan of rotting joists and the whistle of split shingles, but the air is stagnant during the Florida summer and the high drone of locusts would conceal

23

them anyway. It can't whistle or snap its fingers, and houses can only whisper to their occupants.

After a week of waiting fifty yards off the seventh hole for Julian Macek to get a funny feeling on the back of his neck, the house decides to risk everything and just edges its corner onto the fairway.

Julian Macek sees it first one rainy morning. His broom handle clunks upon the concrete but stops about thirty feet from the house. He stoops, peering past the pine trees and curving palms at the leaning wreck, more snail than house.

Julian looks over his shoulder to the left and then to the right. He steps across the grass and touches the corner. A charge crackles along the old cloth-sheathed wiring.

Come inside, the house wants to say.

Julian limps around the house, examining every side: the missing back steps, the jagged windows, the wavy porch planks. The house waits and hopes for any sign of recognition.

Julian staggers back, holding his hand over his mouth. He bends gasping toward the ground while the house worries.

I traveled a long way, the house wants to say. Come inside.

Julian's face is white, but he steps onto the porch and tries the door. The last few months of humidity and vibration have finally rusted away the tumblers in the lock. The knob falls into Julian's hand and the door swings open.

Come inside.

Julian, holding his broom handle like a spear, walks into a living room he last saw over his mother's shoulder. He grimaces at the kitchen table. Cans and candy wrappers crunch under his feet as he shuffles from one room to the next.

In the master bedroom, he picks up his father's wallet in his shaking hand. He opens it, sees the Ohio license, and then drops it to the floor.

He runs now through the house, crashing into one wall and then the next, clutching his narrow ring of white hair. He drops his broom handle in the hallway. He slips on the mold-slick carpet and crawls the rest of the way from the house.

Wait. Wait.

Julian Macek, the son of a convicted and executed child murderer, scrambles for his life from his childhood home.

That's not the way it was supposed to go at all, thinks the house. Confession turns out to be harder than it expected.

The house has a speech prepared, though it has no way to deliver it. "We're brothers, you and I," it would like very much to say. "Maybe we both crawled to get here, but we're both still standing. We wouldn't have made it this far carrying the things we know if your father hadn't done a good job. He was for building things, not destroying them."

But eloquence doesn't come easy to a house when all its words are only architecture. There's only so much to say by standing still, by still standing.

Just as the house resolves to finish the journey and crawl the quarter mile to Julian's backyard, a flashlight beam bobs over the fairway, coming closer. Julian, a bottle in one hand and the light in the other, cracks his knees against the porch and curses. He totters back and walks up to the door.

"I've spent my whole goddamned life running from you, and now here you are," he says, narrowing his eyes to focus through the dusty glass.

You didn't have to, the house wants to say. That's what I've come to tell you.

Julian can't hear it, of course. He stomps into the house, crunching across a fish skeleton from somewhere in Kentucky. He glares down at it confused. Then he stops at the doorway of the room he shared with his brothers, dead twenty years ago. He bends to the floor and picks up one of his old soldiers. Clutching it in his fist, he continues to his parents' bedroom.

There he sways, staring at their beds.

"I watched everything I did, just in case," whispers Julian. "I stayed away from children, even my own, just in case. I stayed away from girls. I married late, too late. I yelled and fumed to let out whatever he might have given me. All I wanted was to forget him, but here you are to remind me."

It was me, the house wants to say.

"Is this like the mystery stories? The scene of the crime comes back to visit the criminal?" Julian stamps his foot and pipes clank against the beams.

The house tenses, hoping he'll hear, hoping he'll do it again if he doesn't.

"They already got him," shouts Julian. "Are you happy?"

No, thinks the house. I killed her.

Julian shatters the bottle against the wall and vodka soaks into the yellowed wallpaper. He watches it, considering. Then he stoops and flicks open a lighter. Flames crawl up the wall.

Julian's father built the house almost entirely from wood that came on a truck as a kit from Sears. Niklas Macek, a skilled carpenter, carefully fitted each piece to the other and nailed them square enough to travel eight hundred miles farther than any architect had ever imagined.

Fire scurries from joist to joist and beam to beam while the insulation smolders. Paint bubbles on the walls in streaks. Plaster crumbles and furniture flares. The house holds together.

Julian stares at the empty squares where the family portraits once hung. Mama died soon after the move. Anja and Maria left as soon as they could, marrying the first cretins they met, hoping to start better families than their own. Theodore ran away to the war, and Peter was spacey and silent the rest of his life. They're all dead now.

The house can't get away, even if it wanted to, not with fire to spread like typhoid anywhere it goes. It can't just die, either, not yet, not with Julian still mistaken.

The house inhales. Hot air flows up to the attic and cool air sucks in through the broken windows. It has no lungs or voice box, but the fire itself will have to do. Maybe a ten penny nail shrieks from two boards prying apart or expanding gases split an ancient rusted pipe; all the house knows is that it manages a single scream— one very much like Kathy Henderson's all those decades ago.

The difference is that someone hears it this time. Julian spins to his left and to his right, looking for the source. Was there someone still in the house? His worry clears his mind enough so he can race from room to room to find her.

Of course it is a *her*.

Unable to find anyone, Julian lopes outside and searches around the foundations. He bends to check the crawlspace, and glowing embers barely show the pipe, black and rusty and blood-stained. Can he see?

She crawled under after a cat, the house wants to explain. One of the calicos from Mrs. Pettyjohn's yard. She crawled under and cracked her head. She bled all over, and I couldn't stop it. I'm sorry. It happened so fast, too fast for a house.

Julian crawls backward to escape the crashing beams and soaring sparks, and the house wonders if he understands. Blood and mud and rust look a lot alike, after all. It's a long shot, much like coming all the way to Florida in the first place. Julian does look amazed, surprised, his eyes wide. He doesn't look as slumped and heavy, at least.

Relieved, it settles exhausted into the fire and sleeps.

"Remembrance Is Something Like a House" started as a crime tale with a supernatural element, a house crawling across the country to confront a murderer. I had a tough time finding the correct voice and point of view in the first few attempts, but everything changed when I said, "To hell with it. I wonder what would happen if I told it from the perspective of the house?" It was a strange, risky, and counterintuitive choice—one I couldn't have made earlier in my career when I was still scared to break rules.

If "Remembrance" is anything to go by, interstitial fiction is fiction that, regardless of the tropes and traditions involved, taps into universal emotions with a certain verve, awe, voice, enthusiasm, risk, and abandon—a tossing aside of normalcy in the brave pursuit of some aesthetic or thematic end. Interstitial stories tend not to care what genre they belong to, what traditions they confront or invent, what audience they find. Their writers have simply written with every tool they've got: robots, ghosts, creeping houses, whatever. They've held nothing back, even risking embarrassment or failure.

"Remembrance" is good only because I took a big, scary chance that it would be bad. Perhaps that is what makes interstitial fiction so powerful.

Will Ludwigsen

The Long and Short of Long-Term Memory

Cecil Castellucci

It had been forty-six years since Dunbar had visited the moon. He stood in his bathrobe at the scenic window taking in the view. The black sky, the craters, the landscape were exactly as he remembered.

He cursed.

Dunbar was a research scientist at McGill University. He thought it was funny that he was studying the biology of memory in Quebec, a province whose motto was "I remember." He saw it everywhere on the license plates. "Je me souviens."

I remember.

Dunbar remembered many things from his past. He remembered his first telephone number. The number of steps from his front door to the playground two blocks over. The exact color of his shirt when he graduated from sixth grade. The words to the poem "Kubla Khan." The way the first car he owned had to be finessed when he shifted from first to third.

Je me souviens.

Was the province worried that it would forget? What would it forget? Dunbar could find no clear answer.

He had come here to study memory so that he could learn how to forget.

"One interesting aspect of animal and human behavior is the ability to modify behavior by learning."

"There are two kinds of memory. There is declarative and procedural."

"The number of neurons in the brain is 10 to the power 10. Each neuron in the brain receives, on average, 2,000 to 20,000 synapses, or connections, from other neurons."

"Every human brain has the same general blueprint for organization, but the experiences that you have make every single brain unique."

Each semester, Dunbar told his students all of these things in his Intro to Neuroscience lecture. It was always the same lecture, because even if more and more was discovered about the mechanics of memory, the basics didn't change.

Each semester, the students were the same. They sat, sleepy eyed, scratching the words that he said into their notebooks or laptops, hoping that something that he said would be on the exam.

He wanted to tell them that there was no way to be sure that we remembered anything correctly; something would be lost, something would be discarded.

But in the end something would also be retained. Even if it was something that you wanted to be forgotten.

Slide 1: The Neuron

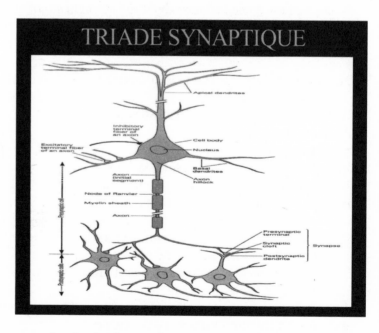

"The neurons in the brain produce action potentials. In other words, they secrete neurotransmitters to communicate with each other at the synapses. The chain of neurons creates various neural pathways. Some neural connections are stronger than others and they can be modulated, or changed, following learning or during behavioral modifications."

DUNBAR: How do you choose what you remember?
DUNBAR: Which pathway in my brain is the one that holds that memory?
DUNBAR: Scientifically, how do I answer this question?

Often, he asked himself these questions. All he knew was that the brain retained information if it was interesting and exciting. If it wasn't, then it would ignore it.

DUNBAR: But how do you *choose?*

No matter how much he knew about the mechanisms of memory, he could not pick and choose what he remembered. He could not forget what he wanted to forget. And Dunbar very much wanted to forget.

DUNBAR: How do you choose to forget?

1. First Memory

It was not a cage, he thought. *It was a crib.*
He was supposed to feel safe there; the mattress was soft. But the young Dunbar knew one thing. He wanted to get out. He pulled himself up by his tiny hands, using the bars to steady him. He used his small muscles to bring himself to the top of the bar. He teetered on the edge and then flung himself over and fell to the floor.
Once there, he felt pain. And so he began to scream.
His mother came into the room and picked him up.

His mother sat in her room. She was eighty-eight years old and she remembered nothing. Not even who he was.
"Who are you?" she asked.

"Dunbar," he said.

"That's a terrible name," she said. "You can bring me a (sandwich) (Coke) (sweater) (magazine)."

So he did.

He would sit there and have the same exact conversation with her twenty-two times before he would feel that he had done his duty as a loving son and finally leave the hospital.

He envied his mother. She could not remember all the pain that life had caused her. Not his angst-filled teenage years when he had tormented her with worry. Not the loss of her husband of forty-eight years, without whom she never imagined she could live.

Conveniently, all was forgotten, and she was happier than she'd ever been in her life.

Her brain had saved her from the pain of her past.

He thought that she was *lucky*.

If he could suppress that one thing in his mind, the thing that his mind found so interesting and he found to be pure torture, then perhaps he could finally be happy, too.

Long-term memory. When the synaptic pathways are fluid and used, memory is easily accessible.

There were 241 students in the Intro to Neuroscience class, and one of them was a girl with long braids piled up on top of her head. He noticed her because she looked like Heidi, from the storybook. It bothered him when she came up to him after class and told him that her name was Heidi and that she had some questions, not because he did not want to answer the questions of an eager young mind, but because his bladder was full from the terrible coffee from the break room that he'd drunk all through the class, and now he had to urinate.

"I have a few questions," Heidi said.

"Let's walk and talk," Dunbar said. He was snapping the laptop bag closed and rushing to get out of there. Heidi followed him through the halls.

～

HEIDI: How do you choose what you remember?

DUNBAR: You cannot.

HEIDI: But how do you choose what is important or exciting, or to be discarded?

DUNBAR: You don't. Or, you can try to practice, to give certain ideas a better chance at consolidating in your memory, like when you study.

HEIDI: But you still might forget the thing you want to remember.

DUNBAR: Yes. It is possible.

HEIDI: But how do you make sure that you will?

DUNBAR: Is there something specific that you want to remember? Because the good news is that then you probably would find it interesting, and your pathways will take care of it on their own.

HEIDI: I want to remember Every Single Thing.

2. Second Memory

He had been making fried chicken in the deep fryer. Placing the pieces in, one by one. He was making dinner for his molecular biology study group. They were due at 6 PM and it was 5:50 by the digital clock on the stove. He was rushing to finish preparing the meal. He had come home late. The subway had been evacuated because of a strange smell, and he had had to take the bus, which was much slower.

There was something comforting about the methodical action of dipping the chicken into the oil, and as he got into the groove of it, his mind began to wander as though he were dreaming.

His mind swirled with a jumble of images cobbled together from the movements of his day. How he tied his shoe in the hall next to the water fountain. The lost glove he found outside the classroom. The piece of rhubarb pie he ate at lunch. The yellow of the ball he served in the tennis match against his thesis adviser.

Dunbar was dipping the next piece of chicken into the boiling oil when the doorbell jolted him out of his reverie. His study group had arrived.

But Dunbar screamed. He had stuck his whole hand into the fryer.

His study group kindly called 911.

Slide 2: Simple Reflex Experiment

Le réflexe de retrait du siphon et de la branchie et ses
modifications dues à l'apprentissage.

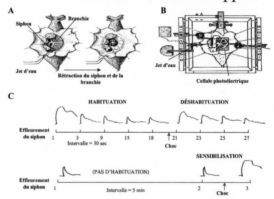

12

The simple reflex in the snail *Aplysia* is a good example of the sorts of things that happen in our own brains when we learn things.

In the experiment, the withdrawal reflex of the snail is evoked, and the first response is big. Then, with repetition, the amplitude of the withdrawal reflex diminishes. If you record the activity of the motor neurons of the reflex, there is less excitation arriving to the neurons. As the reflex goes down, the excitation goes down, as well.

With rest, the reflex can recover.

By adding more stimulations over days, the same withdrawal reflex can be diminished and remain diminished for several days or weeks. This is a simple form of learning. If we now look at the motor neurons involved in the reflex, we come to realize that not only are their connections diminished, but their structure is changed. For example, they now have fewer transmitting synaptic buttons than before, leading to less effectiveness in their messages.

If by using another experimental protocol, such as giving a shock to the tail of the snail, the reflex is facilitated, the same motor neurons will now be more excited; and if the change is long lasting, we can observe that the synaptic buttons will be more numerous.

Thus the brain is continuously removing or adding connections according to the learning that has happened.

Dunbar's experiments using this simple reflex and other model systems led him to find some molecules that could enhance synaptic transmission and therefore improve memory.

A drug was being developed to enhance memory.

The developer, a private company called Memory, Inc., had head-hunted Dunbar after reading his recent paper, "Molecular Strategies for Diminishing Consolidation of Memory looking at CAM kinase II."

Memory, Inc., had hired Dunbar for his expertise. His research in the mechanisms of memory was something to behold. With their funding, he believed that he could finally accomplish what he had set about as his life's work.

Memory *suppression.*

"You can build your own team," they said.

He thought of Heidi.

Heidi was his most difficult student. She wanted to remember, and he had wanted to forget. They were at odds with each other, but it seemed logical that if one of them could succeed in the lab, it would benefit the other.

They became collaborators.

HEIDI: How do I make sure that I can remember everything?
DUNBAR: How can I forget one specific thing?

In front of them, they had the model systems of *Aplysia* and the hippocampal structure of the vertebrate brain. They looked at how these systems learned and forgot.

∽

Dunbar knew if he could figure out the right chemical cocktail to prevent the neurotransmitters from consolidating, he could successfully eliminate an experience from turning into a long-term memory. He did have some success, but the trouble was this: if he successfully eliminated consolidation, how could he be sure which pathways in the brain were associated with a specific memory? He might wipe out other important aspects of a person's personality.

In theory, the chemical cocktail and the molecular strategy worked. But how could you look at a brain and say what specific structure held what specific traumatic memory?

He did not mention the flaw to his superiors. He just presented the fact that it seemed possible, in theory. They were sold on the idea that memory suppression would lead to memory enhancement. They reasoned that if you could figure out how to turn it off, you could figure out how to turn it on. They continued to fund his lab.

And while Dunbar failed, Heidi had some small success.

One type of intelligence is measured by the ability to recall details. And Heidi had found a way to make everyone remember the details.

She had three different memory enhancers in Phase IV of the trials.

But every time Heidi had a success, she reminded Dunbar of the thing he was trying to forget, and he did not like that.

He began to resent her.

Worse, he did not like that she had taken the drug she created herself.

That she'd use perfume to cover up the fact she didn't bathe when she was running an experiment.

That she looked gaunt and worn down.

That she was essential to his science and that he could not function without her.

That she deserved equal partnership in their papers.

Heidi became an emotional wreck. It was not a pretty sight.

Heidi could not forget anything, no matter how big or small.

Betrayal. Jealousy. Love. Happiness. Regret. Hope. Frustration. Euphoria. Empathy. Disappointment. Disgust. Interest. Pity.

These feelings and more were her constant companions.

Heidi hadn't considered the fact that remembering everything meant that she would remember every single emotion associated with every memory, as well.

Heidi began to despair. But the pharmaceutical companies were very excited. The board members, all elderly, all facing their own degrading memories, were waiting for the drug to be approved.

But before that could happen, the bioethics community had a meeting about the goings on at Memory, Inc.

"Memory suppression has many good uses," Dunbar said in front of the bioethics committee. "Think of the soldier who is at war and sees unspeakable things. When they come back, they have posttraumatic syndrome or PTSD. If we could effectively suppress the memory that is causing the trauma, the individual could regain a more normal life."

The bioethics committee had their own opinions.

"The trouble with memory suppression or memory enhancement is the fact that the misuse of such knowledge can have devastating effects on the individual. If a person were to have certain memories suppressed, never to be retrieved, that would be akin to brainwashing. This leaves the door open for mass behavioral modification."

The drug was not approved.

Memory, Inc., folded up shop but appealed the ruling. Eventually, they would have their memory enhancement drug.

After his failure at Memory, Inc., Dunbar went back to teaching at McGill.

He was amazed by the passage of time. By how a place could have so many memories pressed over it. A simple walk down a certain street could bring to mind moments in his life at twenty-two, thirty-six, forty-five, or sixty walking down that same street. The time he found that nice table in the trash. The time he picked up a bottle to recycle. The time he got a parking ticket. The time he slipped on the ice.

And on top of those memories, Dunbar knew with certainty that every single time he walked down St. Laurent street, the memory that he wanted to forget got stronger. Even if he walked one street over, sometimes the wind would still blow the smell of the smoked meat from Shwartz's, and like anyone would tell you, smell is one of the biggest triggers of memories that there is.

Two steps.

Four steps.

Six steps.

And then the smell would be left behind him, but the memory was always there.

Why would smoked meat remind him of the moon?

It was a mystery.

Dunbar had turned sixty-eight earlier that year.

He was here to get an award. The lifetime achievement award for the IAAS (the International Association for the Advancement of Science).

Why they held the party on the moon was anybody's guess. Perhaps the association felt that the moon was more international.

3. Third Memory

It was the middle of February. The days had been bitter cold and relentlessly gray for weeks. The night before had dumped another ten inches of snow.

But that day, it was sunny.

Dunbar watched his students as they sat at their stations in the lab dissecting *Aplysia*s and running their experiments. He noticed that they never looked out the window at Mount Royal, which was shining bright with the pure untouched snow. It was the kind of day that Dunbar had loved as a child.

Dunbar made a decision.

"OK, everyone, lunchtime. Put your coats on," he said. "We're going out."

He marched his entire lab to the mountain, buying some toboggans on the way.

Dunbar went sliding down the toboggan run successfully five times before the snow got so packed down that it exposed a root from a tree. The root made his red plastic sled crack in half, which sent Dunbar flying into the air and smashing straight into a tree.

His students laid him on the other toboggan and slid him down the mountain so that the ambulance could take him away.

He had broken his leg in three places.

Sometimes during his lecture, he reminded his students that time had passed. That day-to-day lives were lived differently.

"Imagine," he said. "How much life was changed when these things were introduced."

The push-button phone.

The remote control.

Cellular technology.

The portable personal computer.

The Internet.

Nanotechnology.

Retinal ID chips.

Gene therapy.

Civilian space travel.

Dunbar believed in the collective memories of generations who had useless skills in their old age.

In his youth, for an undergrad experiment, he had brought in groups of people at different ages and left them with old technology and new technology.

Mostly, the old people could figure out the new technology, but the young people could not figure out how to use old technology.

It was not a part of their collective memory.

When he said this, the students did not look up from their desks. They just kept taking notes. He had meant to say these things to excite the students. To give them some pause. To make a big change in the synaptic pathways in their brains. To jog something loose.

Nothing.

They didn't even read scientific papers that were published over ten years ago. They thought old science was useless.

Dunbar turned back to his Powerpoint presentation and clicked to the next slide.

Slide 3: The Hippocampus

LOCALISATION ET STRUCTURE DE L'HIPPOCAMPE

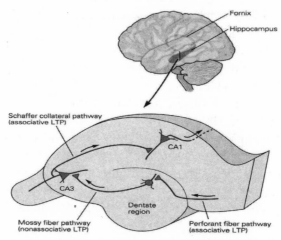

Figure 63-7 The three major afferent pathways in the hippocampus. (Arrows denote the direction of impulse flow.) 10

Patient HM

The hippocampus is the place in the brain where some types of memory begin to be formed and consolidated. Consolidation is the switching from short-term memory to long-term memory which happens when synaptic connections between neurons are made more permanent. In some diseases of the memory, the important step of passing from short-term to long-term is impaired. There is an inability to form any new long-term change of synaptic connections.

Dunbar told his students about the case of the famous patient HM.

His hippocampus had been removed to cure the recurrence of large seizures. The seizures stopped, but the brain operation resulted in a total collapse of the ability to store new information. Patient HM experienced every day, every moment as a completely new one. Patient HM could remember things that occurred in long-term memory, his childhood, how to read, how to make conversation, how to drive, but HM could not store any new information in the brain. The endless loop of meeting people for the first time happened every single day, even with the doctors who had cared for him for decades.

Dunbar wondered if it would be better to be senile in order to forget. He wondered if it would be better to be like his mother. Or patient HM? Or Heidi?

Heidi had remembered Dunbar's lecture on patient HM and did something terrible to herself. She reasoned that if she damaged her hippocampal structure she could block the storing of new information and stop accumulating new details of her life. She flew down to a hospital and had her hippocampus severed.

Dunbar went every Wednesday to lunch with her at the hospital.

DUNBAR: Heidi. How are you today?
HEIDI: Dunbar! It's so nice to see you.

DUNBAR: Heidi. How are you today?
HEIDI: Dunbar! It's so nice to see you.

DUNBAR: Heidi. How are you today?
HEIDI: Dunbar! It's so nice to see you.

After a few years, he stopped.
Heidi did not notice.

He had been a young man the first time he had come to the moon, and here he was again.

"Are you ready, sir?" asked the young man who had been assigned as his handler.

"One minute," Dunbar said.

He needed to look out the window for a little bit longer. He was now dressed, except for his shoes. He could not bear to put them on. They were a little too tight, because of the difference in gravity.

He was being rewarded for all of the work he had done on memory techniques. And here he was, standing in the one place he wanted to forget.

4. Fourth Memory

Dunbar and Gertie had come to the moon for a romantic weekend. It was expensive and decadent, but they felt that they were more the type of couple that would go to the moon than to a tropical island. So when the prices came down low enough for civilian space travel to be affordable, they jumped at the chance to go.

"We are going to the moon!" they said.

They kissed the whole space flight up. They marveled at the architecture of the space station. They enjoyed the free shampoos in the bathroom of the hotel.

"Newlyweds?" the bellhop had asked.

Gertie blushed. Dunbar had wanted to ask her, but he was slow and shy.

Once in the room, they made love with the window shade open so that they could see the earth rise. There were three hurricanes on the Atlantic.

They were in each other's arms when the conversation went from lover talk to something else. Something dark. Something ugly.

A suspicion.

"You were checking up on me?"

"I had to know."

"How much I loved you?"

"It was because I loved you so much. I loved you with all of my heart."

"Why didn't you leave it alone?"

"I'm not comfortable with your jealousy."

"You're not happy unless there is an argument."

"You kept it from me."

"That was my right. I am my own person."

"By doing that, you betrayed us."

"But I had to know. You left me no choice."

"You broke the trust."

"It was only that one time. I wouldn't ever again."

"I don't know if I could ever love you the same way now."

"You are a coward."

"You are disgusting."

"You are weak."

"I hate you."

"I can't stand that look in your eyes. Hard."

"I will never forgive you."

"I wish I had never met you!"

Dunbar got out of bed and put his pants on. He got out of bed and cursed her out.

He got out of bed and left the room. He got out of bed and slammed the door.

There was no relation between the door slamming and the crack that had been building for months in the window of their room, but after the fact, it seemed like it because just as Dunbar slammed the door, the window gave up on itself and began to splinter.

By the time Dunbar was stomping down the clear tube to the bar in the hotel, the crack had gotten larger.

By the time Dunbar had gotten his drink and sat by the scenic window, fuming, swearing that he would make her sorry, the window had shattered. All of the contents of the room, including a naked, crying Gertie, had been sucked out into space.

By the time the emergency bells went off and the guests were escorted to safety, Dunbar realized that he would never be able to take his terrible curse back.

Dunbar left the moon screaming.

This time there was no one to comfort him.

Dunbar had his lesson plan in front of him. He had made copies available to his students at both the university bookstore and online. But he knew for sure they were not listening.

How many times had he taught this lecture? How many times had he said these words? Showed these slides?

He could imagine how strong the information was in his brain. The memory of talking about the mechanisms of memory was a permanent memory trace. It was like riding a bike. He could say the lecture in his sleep. He could pick it up from any section of the slide show. The students may have changed, the styles of their hair changed, the technology that they preferred changed.

But the lesson plan was always the same.

"I'm ready," he said to the young men. The one at his door and the one he used to be that lived in his head.

Dunbar walked down the scenic hallway to the room where the ceremony was taking place. There were other scientists there, as well. All older, like him. They all wore tuxedos or ball gowns. They all wore their academy pins. And when the evening was over, they would all be wearing medals around their necks.

Dunbar sat at his table, making chitchat with the other table mates. He was polite and interested. He ordered another Scotch and didn't eat much lamb. He listened to the other winners' speeches and clapped when appropriate.

That was the benefit of long-term memory, knowing how to fake behavior in social settings.

He drank his Scotch and realized that the scene outside the window was the same as it had been the last time that he had been here, when the alarms had gone off. His bow tie seemed tight; he felt as though his body were swelling. He loosened his tie, wanting to get some more air.

They called his name and his handler helped him to the stage, not because he was so old, but because he was a little drunk.

The lights were bright as he stood on the podium, now wearing the medal, a bit heavier than he'd expected, around his neck. He looked out at the audience. They had finished clapping, and now they were all trying to be quiet with their dinnerware. Dessert had just been served.

He could smell toast.

"I can't tell you what an honor it is to be here," Dunbar began.

"I am a man of memory, and I have a strong memory of the moon. Here, on the moon, lies the very reason why I went into neuroscience, to study memory. To study the mechanisms of it. To see how we remember and how we forget."

His tongue suddenly seemed thick. Very thick. He felt as though he was slurring, and he had only begun his speech. He had never needed to use index cards before, he didn't even have them. But he realized that he could not remember the next thing that he was going to say.

He blinked. His vision a bit blurry. Was he crying?

He blinked.

He took a deep breath.

Toast.

He smelled burnt toast.

And realized that he did not know where he was.

A warm rush in his face. He knew what was happening.

"Thank God," he said as he fell to the ground. "It's finally over."

My first job was at fifteen, working as a gal Friday to the Nobel Prize-winning neurobiologist Dr. Eric Kandel, with whom my dad worked. I had a slightly punk attitude, artistic temperament, and free spirit but was stuck photocopying data and feeding the aplysias. Science, memory, and DNA were always topics of conversation at the dinner table growing up. Last year, recovering from a psychological trauma, I moved back in with my parents in Montreal. One day my father, now vice dean at the University of Montreal, was giving a lecture to the undergraduate Intro to Neuroscience class. Since I had never seen him lecture, I went. Listening to him talk about the mechanisms of memory while clicking through the slides highlighting experiments explaining how the brain learns and forgets and stores long- and short-term memory, I was riveted. I was particularly fascinated with patient HM, whose hippocampus had been severed, with the dramatic result of his having an endless loop of old memories but never remembering anything new. I began to think about the mechanisms of memory in light of my own situation. Could a specific traumatic memory be removed? What would the moral and philosophical implications of that be? I wanted to forget, but

I knew people, like my friend's parents, who suffered from Alzheimer's or dementia, who were desperate to remember. On our way back to the car, I remarked that the license plates in Quebec sported the provincial motto: *Je me souviens*: I remember. I wanted to write a story from the point of view of someone who has access to all the secrets of how memory works. By mixing fiction, philosophy, and portions of the Intro to Neuroscience lecture my father gave that day, I hoped to get to the heart of the very human desire to forget emotional trauma.

Interestingly, Dr. Kandel is now actually working on a pill that would enhance memory, and the day after I submitted this story to *Interfictions 2*, patient HM died.

Cecil Castellucci

The Score

Alaya Dawn Johnson

> Don't matter what we sing
> Every window we open, they jam another door
> They gladhand, pander, lie for the king
> It's our song, but their score
> > —Jake Pray, "What We Sing"
> > (first documented performance:
> > February 15, 2003 at the pre-invasion
> > anti–Iraq War marches in New York City)

Gmail – Inbox – jimmy.sullivan@gmail.com – chat

me: violet, i'm so sorry. if you need someone to come over . . .
Sent at 3:16 PM on Sunday

Violet: he never liked you, you know
Sent at 4:43 PM on Sunday

Violet's new status message—
Two bleeding hearts drank ginger beer / and mocked and stung their gingered fears / to know the future, and still die here. Rahimahullah, Jake.

NEW YORK CITY MEDICAL EXAMINER

NAME: Jacob Nasser	AUTOPSY-NO: 43-6679
SEX: Male	DATE OF AUTOPSY: 3/21/2007
RACE: White (Arab)	TIME OF AUTOPSY: 3:36 p.m.
DOB: 2/1/81	DATE OF REPORT: 4/1/2007
DATE OF DEATH: 3/17/07–3/18/07	

FINAL PATHOLOGICAL DIAGNOSES

I. 25 MICRON TEAR IN CORONARY ARTERY, POSSIBLE INDICATION OF SPONTANEOUS CORONARY ARTERY DISSECTION

II. MINIMAL DRUG INTOXICATION
   A. Probable non-contributory drugs present:
      1. Acetaminophen (2 mg/L)
      2. Cannabis (30.0 ng/mL)

OPINION

Jacob Nasser was a 26-year-old male of Arab descent who died of undetermined causes. The presence of a 25-micron tear in his coronary artery might indicate SCAD (Spontaneous Coronary Artery Dissection), however it was deemed too small to lead to a definitive finding. The presence of cannabis was small and non-contributing.

The manner of death is determined to be: COULD NOT BE DETERMINED.

M. Andy Pilitokis
M.D., LL.B, M.Sc.
Chief Medical Examiner

Andrea Varens, MD
Associate Medical Examiner

Jake Pray (Jacob Nasser) prelim autopsy notes **[Recovered]**
Last saved with AutoRecover
4:33 AM Thursday, March 22, 2007

Andrea Varens
3/21/07

The subject was first discovered dead in his holding cell the morning of March 18 in the "Tombs" Manhattan Detention Center. The subject was discovered with a rope in his hand, and so police at first surmised it had contributed in some manner to his death, but there are no consistent contusions on the neck or, indeed, anywhere else on the body.

A preliminary physical examination reveals what looks to be a normal, healthy twenty-six-year-old man with no signs of ill-health or infirmity (beyond the obvious).

Drug interactions? Probably SCAD, poor fucker.

I saw him. I went to the hallway to get a coke from the machine and I saw him. Leaning against the wall looking out the window. Oh, fuck. Fuck fuck fuck. I've been staring at his sorry face for the last two days, I oughta know. Maybe he has a long-lost twin brother?

Mom was right, I should have gone into

The New York Post
Anti-War Songster "Scored" Dope, Autopsy Says
April 2, 2007

Bad news for the anti-Bush peaceniks who've turned Jake Pray into a martyr: turns out he was stoned on dope (the equivalent of "one joint of strong chronic," according to a well-placed source) when police took him into custody. And he died of a "spontaneous" heart attack. Not police abuse.

Of course, you didn't hear any of that damning data at the packed memorial service in the ultra-liberal Riverside Church this Sunday. In fact, Pray's memorial service sounded more like an anti-war rally.

Violet Omura, a Columbia grad student who spoke at the memorial, had nothing but contempt for the city's Medical Examiner. "It's ridiculous," she said. "It's like if you shot me in the head and the autopsy said I had died due to 'spontaneous brain leakage.'"

Pray's fellow protesters were convinced police abuse

was responsible. "[The police] really picked on him at the rally," said Billy Davis, a close friend who had been present at the protest. "Guess they saw his skin and hair, you know, and drew their conclusions," Davis said, referring to Pray's Palestinian heritage. "They called him a terrorist. Said ragheads like him were responsible for bringing down the Twin Towers." Davis also accused the officers of using Tasers on the unruly protestors. Conspiracy theories abounded at the memorial of how the nonlethal crowd-control devices could have contributed to his death.

In a statement issued today, the Police Commissioner denied all accusations of wrongdoing by the officers on the scene and restated the findings of yesterday's autopsy report. "Should any new evidence surface regarding this case, rest assured that we will pursue it with all due diligence."

Rock & Rap Confidential
"What We Still Sing"
Issue 4, Volume 78; May 2007

Jake Pray may never have had a hit song, but to the latest crop of anti-war protestors, "What We Sing" has the same iconic resonance that "Bring the Boys Home" or "Masters of War" had for their parents. And over three hundred youngbloods turned out for the memorial of this iconoclastic musician, held this past March in Riverside Church.

Jake Pray was born as Jacob Nasser to Palestinian immigrants; the family settled in suburban New Jersey when he was just three years old. His father, a professor of Linguistics and Cultural Anthropology at a university in the Gaza strip, was forced to emigrate after he received death threats for his political positions.

Not surprisingly, Pray became a lightning rod for activists across the world when his life ended in Manhattan's "Tombs" detention facility. He was arrested after an incident with police during the anti-war protests this March. The autopsy report declared its findings inconclusive. The police commissioner, in a written statement, called Pray's death a "tragic incident." The arresting officer had taunted the twenty-six-year-old man with racial slurs like "raghead." He had shot 50,000 excruciating volts of electricity into his body and then detained him in unspeakable conditions for endless hours. A *tragic incident*? The mind would boggle, if this weren't so painfully predictable.

The larger meaning of Jake's life was best captured by Violet Omura, a twenty-five-year-old graduate student in the Physics department at Columbia.

Perhaps the experiences of his parents in the occupied territories influenced his decision to turn to political activism and the thankless efforts of those who argue from right, not expedience. But I think, perhaps, that he mostly just wanted to tell, he just wanted to sing, he just wanted others to know they had a voice. Our parents were optimists. They gave us "Imagine," and "Blowin' in the Wind." We're not pessimists. God knows Jake wasn't a pessimist. But he wasn't so sure that singing could change anything. Some people complain that "What We Sing" is bleak. I disagree. It's furious, it's strident, and it's real. Jake wanted to change the world, but he couldn't hide from the fact that it might never change.

Billboard Pop 100
Top Ten
Issue Date: 2007-5-19

#1: Beyonce & Shakira: Beautiful Liar
#2: Gwen Stefani featuring Akon: The Sweet Escape
#3: Fergie featuring Ludacris: Glamorous
#4: Avril Lavigne: Girlfriend
#5: Diddy featuring Keyshia Cole: Last Night
#6: Tim McGraw: Last Dollar
#7: Mims: This Is Why I'm Hot
#8: Jake Pray: What We Sing

#9: Gym Class Heroes: Cupid's Chokehold
#10: Fall Out Boy: This Ain't a Scene, It's an Arms Race

MSNBC TRANSCRIPT
" > TUCKER" with Tucker Carlson
Original Air Date: 5/20/07

TUCKER CARLSON: Jake Pray has been in the news a lot lately. After all, the blame-America-firster's mysterious death in police custody, his illicit marijuana use, and his surprise hit song, "What We Sing," have made him the perfect martyr for self-defeating liberal elitists.

But now, one of Pray's own radicals has come out against him. In a damning exposé published in the online fringe-left newsletter *Counterpunch*, James Sullivan has laid bare the despicable anti-Semitic and vitriolic anti-American hate that underlies the rabid far Left.

Welcome to the show, Mr. Sullivan.

JAMES SULLIVAN: Thank you very much for having me.

TC: We know you were detained with Jake Pray at the Chelsea Piers before he was taken to the Manhattan Detention Facility. How well did you know him?

JS: Well, when you're as heavily involved in the peace movement as I was, you kind of get to know everyone. Jake was, you know, dedicated. A bit too dedicated. He was a musician, but you could tell it wasn't really about the music for him. It was about the fame. People loved him. I did, too, for a while.

TC: But eventually you realized—

JS: Yeah, you know, he was just full of—sorry, yeah, full of it. A bit of a megalomaniac.

TC: I understand that you're also a musician? Did he ever support you, or...

JS: Never. Jake really resented the presence of another musician in the, well, what he would have called the "inner circle."

TC: Now, I'm going to read a passage from your *Counterpunch* article. It's pretty damning, detailing what happened the afternoon you were both detained by the police. You write: "Pray was furious after the arrest. On the ride down to the pier he just sat in the police truck shaking and clenching his fists. His girlfriend, Violet Omura, tried to calm him down, but he just lashed out at her, called her an 'ignorant bitch' and a few other expressions I'll choose not to print here. He was always like that, in fact, willing—and sometimes eager—to take out his own personal frustrations and failings on others. Billy Davis and Violet and his other cronies are trying to claim that the police officers called him a 'raghead' that day. If they did, I never heard it." And then, further on, you write: "Around the police, Pray was like a rabid dog. At Pier 57 it was like something had popped. He wasn't quiet anymore. We all heard him: Violet and Billy and the rest who are trying to pretend that it didn't happen."

You go on to list some of the epithets Pray hurled at our men in blue, some of which are not, um, fit for television. Could you share some of the milder ones?

JS: [*Laughter*] Yeah. They're—sure. "Filthy murdering bigots," that was one. He said they were all "closet fags," and accused them of, ah—"practicing on Abner Louima." He just wouldn't stop. Finally, one of the officers tried to get him to calm down. He had dark curly hair, a big nose—you know, obviously Jewish, and Jake nearly tackled him. Said "his kind" was supporting genocide and maybe "they deserved what they got."

TC: "Deserved what they got." What do you think he meant by that?

JS: I think it's obvious. He was saying the Jewish people deserved the Holocaust.

TC: Wow. Now, I hear you're starting to distance yourself from all this and the so-called peace movement.

JS: Yeah. Actually, I'm [*Laughter*] yeah, I'm halfway through *Atlas Shrugged*.

TC: [*Laughter*] How do you like it so far?

JS: Really good. It's giving me a new perspective.

JakePrayTruth.org
Action Statement

Jake Pray, the radical anti-war protestor and singer, died as a result of police abuse on the night of March 17, 2007. This fact, supported by activists present during his arrest and reports from within the holding facility itself, has been systematically covered up by the New York City Police Department and coroner's office. This is just a part of an overall, covert strategy to undermine the vocal anti-war movement with acts of state-sponsored terror. Jake Pray, whose anti-war songs had energized a new generation of protestors, was first on their list because of his growing influence. COINTELPRO had thousands and thousands of pages about John Lennon in their files, because he posed a similar threat. In this age of increasing government control and ongoing illegal wars (one million dead and counting!), Jake Pray's powerful voice and even more powerful message posed an unacceptable threat.

But guess what? So do we. And we resolve to uncover the TRUTH about Jake Pray's murder and bring his message to the world.

—Billy Davis
Founder, JakePrayTruth.org
December 15, 2007

[UPDATE 1/3/08: For our official statement on the allegations made by James Sullivan, please visit our FAQ.]

Just Another (Libertarian) Weblog: Ron Paul 2008!
Rockin' for the Fatherland
Posted January 4, 2008 5:45 pm by BigFish

Well, Billy Davis over at JakePrayTruth has finally responded to the accusations James Sullivan made such a big splash with a few months ago.

Short version: 'Ole Jimmy is an opportunistic lying asshole.

Still, we have to thank him. "Practicing on Abner Louima" is an expression now enshrined in my soul. Hey, Jake, wherever you are, I never look at a toilet plunger without thinking of you. (Unfortunately none of the inexplicably frequent ghost-sightings of Pray these last few months have involved home plumbing equipment. Though I hear he was spotted outside the Pink PussyCat last Thursday).

In other news, the redoubtable Jimmy Sullivan has made himself a webpage! Check out the "latest music" section. And here I had thought right-wing volks-rock had gone out of fashion in the Third Reich.

Oh. Never mind.

Sieg Heil!

To: Professor Violet Omura < vomura12@nyu.edu >
New York University
Department of Applied Physics

From: Zacharias Tibbs < zachknowsthelord@cheese.org >
15 East Rock Way
Topeka, Kansas

March 16, 2015

Dear PROFESSOR Omura:

I hope you are prepared & have sat down to read this letter for I have here enclosed the most ASTONISHING and SECRET mathematical formula whereby all events heretofore UNEXPLAINED by the greatest scientists of the world are rendered clear by a simple proof. If you do not believe this, don't trust me, but read on for yourself!

I see from reading your very fascinating articles and biography that you once had the privilege of knowing the great Jake Pray, whose every album I own. Would you believe me if I said that this GREAT MATHEMATICAL PROOF would even make clear the mystery of the rumors of his ghostly resurrection and spectral warnings of future wars & conflicts? Have I intrigued you? Yes, of course, for you have a keen intellect and open heart and would surely not want to deny your colleagues the benefit of the knowledge I have so HUMBLY stumbled upon.

Merely scroll down to see the world's greatest secret revealed. . . .

$$p(R) = (As * (t(d)/Gw)) * B/V$$

Thus, the probability of any INDIVIDUAL, upon their DEATH & DEPARTURE from this world, becoming a REVENANT is revealed...

Where As = Astrological Sign, with the following values assigned:

Aries = .2

Taurus = .5
Gemini = 1
Cancer = 5
Leo = 1
Virgo = 3
Libra = .7
Scorpio = -1
Sagittarius = 2
Capricorn = 0
Aquarius = 1
Pisces = 2

As determined through intensive STUDY of GOD'S HOLY WORD & observations & deductions of a PERSONAL nature.

t(d) = the time spent in the process of dying

Gw = the number of GOOD WORKS performed in their lives, with the average being 500 for a CHRISTIAN and less than 100 for ALL OTHERS (& in particular those of the apostate MORMON faith)

B = that which belongs to BEELZEBUB, otherwise known as SATAN or the DEVIL. The values are assigned thusly:

If the subject is a Mormon, B = 1000, for all MORMONS shall surely walk the EARTH for ETERNITY
For ATHEISTS, B = 500
For CHRISTIANS of pure and godly EVANGELICAL faith, B = 0.1
For ALL OTHERS, B = 1

V = the number of verses in our HOLY BIBLE the departed knew & memorized in life

But perhaps you, in your SECULAR University and GODLESS education, do not understand the true significance of explaining the REVENANTS among us. For do not mistake me, the revenants are responsible for all manner of WEIRD & UNEXPLAINED events. Not merely ghosts (like that of your (sadly GODLESS) REVENANT & FRIEND Jake Pray), but also such sundry as possession by DEMONS, ALIEN ABDUCTIONS, and sightings of UFO'S!

Even the INEXPLICABLE behavior of SUBATOMIC particles through the EXTRA DIMENSIONS is caused by these revenants & of course not to mention the riddle of GRAVITY.

I am sure you can see the potential of this astonishing EQUATION and I will be happy to travel to the GODLESS city of New York to discuss it with you further. Though you are only an Assistant Professor, I feel you are the perfect VESSEL of this KNOWLEDGE.

Yours in RESPECT & ANTICIPATION,

Zacharias Tibbs

From: Violet Omura [vomura12@nyu.physics.edu]
To: zachknowsthelord@cheese.org
Date: March 18, 2015, 4:13 am, EST

Dear Zacharias:

you can bet that I have no aspirations to be the perfect VESSEL for your KNOWLEDGE, or even the person who has to open your crackpotty emails (what, you didn't think I got the first three?)

but I'm drunk and bored and this is definitely the worst day of my year, so I'll bite. taking it as a given that you wouldn't know a quantum theory of gravity from a hemorrhoid, why don't all these horrible sinners and atheists and (!) mormons just go to, you know, hell? seems easier than having billions of revenants wandering the earth like thetans or something. you're not a scientologist, are you?

I don't know what you might have read or whatever about jake and me but you honestly can't believe that a godless intellectual like yours truly believes the woowoo crackpots who say he still shows up at their rallies?

god i wish he did.

(I mean 'god' in a purely rhetorical, godless way, of course).

violet, future revenant

From: zachknowsthelord@cheese.org
To: vomura12@nyu.physics.edu
Date: March 18, 2015, 6:21 pm, CMT

PROFESSOR Omura:

Disregarding your DRUNKEN (and, indeed, Godless) aspersions on my theory & character, you have indeed hit upon the crux of the matter.

For through other EQUATIONS & RESEARCH, I have hit upon the fundamental truth: these revenants do not go to HELL, for we are ALREADY LIVING THERE.

Yes, I say. The present EARTH merged with BEELZEBUB'S kingdom on the night of MARCH 20, 2003.

I trust you recognize the date? Yes, for your friend Jake Pray was present at every RALLY and PEACE MARCH in protest of this war, which I of course included in his calculation for GOOD WORKS.

Contemplate our SINFUL world and tell me that you do not agree. We have been DENIZENS of hell for the last twelve years!

And as a side note, I am of course entirely OPPOSED to all false gods, including the ABSURD teachings of

SCIENTOLOGISTS. I must thank you for reminding me of them, for both they AND Mormons should receive a Beelzebub score of 1000...

When would you like to meet?

Zacharias Tibbs

Warp & Weft: An Inclusive Community for Alternative Paradigms and Progressive Politics
Virtual Town Meeting (Excerpt)
Transcript and Audio archived on the community bulletin board
Original event April 1, 2017

[**Rose_Granny**] Thank you all for inviting me here today. I'm Rose, and as my husband used to say, I don't look much like my avatar. [*Laughter*] I've never really believed in ghosts. Oh, I've heard stories and some were eerie enough to make me shiver, but I've lived a long time and I had never seen anything to make me believe that any part of us could survive after death.

When my husband died last year, after a long and painful fight with liver cancer, I was devastated. I decided that it was my duty to make Harold's life count as much as it could, by taking his ideals and courage and using that to further work he would have approved of. So I became, at age 75, a political activist. I attended rallies. I spoke up at virtual town meetings like this one for our local congress members. I made signs, I wrote letters, I organized petitions . . . and I discovered Jake Pray. I'd heard "What We Sing" on the radio years ago, of course, but at the time I hadn't paid any attention to the man or the story behind the song. When I learned of how he died, I was shocked. How could such a young man, with such promise of the future, die so suddenly? He had no serious drugs in his body. There were no signs of violence, self-inflicted or otherwise.

He was found dead on the floor of his holding cell, with a bit of rope in his hand.

And then I saw him. Perhaps it will not surprise most of you to learn that I mean this literally. I saw Jake Pray, sitting beside me in the dark early-morning during a sit-in protest in front of the White House. A rope was wrapped around his left hand. He looked very young—the exact image of the twenty-five-year-old I'd seen in all the pictures. Still, I tried to rationalize it as an uncanny coincidence, a kid who happened to look just like him.

"Aren't you cold?" I asked, when I saw his short-sleeved T-shirt. He smiled and shook his head. The cold obviously didn't bother him. That's when I knew he was a ghost: it was at least twenty degrees that morning.

All these questions bubbled inside of me, but I was so nervous I didn't know if I could get them out. "Do you think we'll be able to stop this escalation with China?" I finally asked.

He looked very sad. Just then, a friend tapped me on my shoulder. I glanced away for just a second, but when I turned back, he was gone.

Would it surprise you to learn that I attended that sit-in on March 15? And, yes, India sent the first cruise missiles into Nanjing two days later.

Warp & Weft Message Boards
Topic: Jake Pray was MURDERED and gov't is COVERING it up!
Username: FightAllPwr4
Date: April 2, 2017 – 3:34 EST

Rose_Granny is a government dupe. She says "there were no signs of violence," but how can we trust the coroner's report when it was commissioned by the same government that first marked Pray for assassination?! That's like trusting the tobacco industry to give an accurate autopsy to the Marlboro man! Billy Davis, who was THERE, said the arresting officer called him a "fucking raghead" and "commie" and that he was a "mass murderer" who "flew the planes into the Twin Towers." This jerk couldn't wait to get his hands on Jake. Just consider a few things:

Why is the coroner report dated APRIL 1?! A subtle hint, maybe, that all is not what it seems? APRIL 1, 2007, was a SUNDAY. Who publishes a coroner report on a SUNDAY? This is a fucking ten-year-old April Fools' joke, people!

He had a "spontaneous cardiac artery dissection" but he only had a 25-micron tear? How was that enough to kill him? Do you know how big 25 microns is? Half the width of a STRAND OF HAIR!

Where did this famous rope come from? Violet Omura, a respected physicist, was his lover at the time. She visited him a few hours before he was discovered dead. She says he seemed distressed by the racist cop's treatment but showed no signs of chest pain or anything that could lead to his "spontaneous" death! Significantly, *she saw no rope anywhere in the cell!* Where did it come from? The forgotten remains of a top-secret government "alternative interrogation" technique, imported from our gulags in Guantanamo, Stare Kjekuty, and Iraq?

Jake Pray was tortured to death by our own government. Maybe the reason he's haunting us, Rose_Granny, is because he wants the truth to come out!

JakePrayTruth.org

Warp & Weft Message Boards
Topic: Re: Jake Pray was MURDERED and gov't is COVERING it up!
Username: SweetGreenOnions
Date: April 2, 2017 – 3:45 EST

omura did it. evidence from "not a factor," the last song he ever wrote:

The invisible hand blasts the cradle
Spreading peace by throwing bombs
We feast beneath the master's table
Sating growls with salvaged crumbs
Save the world? It's just a song

she told jake to provoke a fight with those officers. the
NSA i > paid < /i > her to be the yoko ono of the antiwar
left.

Excerpt from *Real Ghosts: The Warp & Weft Guide to Spec-
ters and Revenants of the 21st Century* by Dede Star Flower
(New York: HarperPenguin, 2018)

The accuracy of his revenant predictions is quite remarkable. Two days after the New York Medical Examiner
saw Pray's ghost in her office building, the Iranians kid-
napped fifteen UK soldiers. In 2009, a cocktail waitress
sighted Pray in an alley, and that very night the United
States dropped the first round of tactical nuclear weapons
on Iran. In 2011, Amina Okrafour was marking the an-
niversary of John Lennon's death in Central Park when
she saw Pray's ghost. The next day the Chinese government shipped one thousand support troops to the Iranian
front. The list goes on: thirteen activists see Pray at an
antiglobalization rally in Sweden; the next day India tests
a nuclear bomb and the cease-fire ends in Kashmir. When
San Francisco representative Linda Xiaobo reported seeing
Pray during a ceremony in the Mojave desert, we all knew
that the talks to bring India into NATO were a certainty.
Sure enough, a few days later, the United States honored
its obligations under the treaty and declared itself officially
at war with China and Pakistan.

As a revenant, Jake cannot stop these horrors from occurring, but he can stand witness to them. He can accuse
us, like Hamlet's father, of not doing enough.

Written Communication from Zacharias Tibbs, Topeka, Kansas
To: Violet Omura, NYU, Department of Applied Physics
Date: November 18, 2020 – 10:44 pm, EST

[**Sender:** Verified]

Professor Omura:

Perhaps you have wondered why I have not yet responded to your Communication which you sent to me this past April. In fact it is because I have UNDERTAKEN to follow your kind & SAGE ADVICE and read those very ERUDITE & SCHOLARLY works by the great Einstein, Feynman, & Chatterjee. I found the latter's work on M-THEORY and the QUANTUM GRAVITY SYNTHESIS most Fascinating, though I must confess that I found a great deal of it Difficult, and indeed, sometimes quite IMPOSSIBLE to understand. GOD, it is clear, has GIFTED her with a great mind. As did HE to YOU.

It's strange, I thought upon my completion of these works, how very CLEAR my errors in the past are to me now. Though I maintain my belief in REVENANTS & the HOLY SPIRIT, it is clear that my EQUATIONS & THEORIES, which I had thought could explain the WORLD, were not worth a Greasy Rag. I see the DEPTH of THOUGHT of those PHYSICISTS exploring the universe, and I feel a small INCHWORM in comparison. I must thank you for your most UNUSUAL & FAITHFUL correspondence over the years. Without it I fear I would never have understood my Gross Errors.

I have also Considered your Strange words to me regarding your SAD & PAINFUL feelings of guilt & regret over some mysterious Life Event. I say to you that your grief GRIEVES ME, for I know that you, too, could find solace in the LORD, if only you would open your heart to

HIM. You say you Cannot, because "a scientist does not work from faith, but evidence." This is a Worthy Philosophy, but I say that because I KNOW GOD EXISTS, the EVIDENCE for him will someday be FOUND. Cannot you SEE His HAND in Chatterjee's Equations?

Can you not SEE that the reason your friend Jake still WALKS AMONG US is because he is a Revenant on Earth?

I await your Response with great Eagerness & Anticipation.

Zach Tibbs

Excerpt from "Changing the Score: My Life with Jake Pray"
Vanity Fair, May 2025
by Violet Omura

Before I say anything else, before I tell my story, or what little I'm privileged to know of Jake's, let me make this perfectly clear:

I loved Jake Pray. For a certain period of time he, and the anti-war movement, were my entire life. When he died, that life fell apart so completely that for the first and only time I considered suicide. In some ways, on some nights, that pain has never left me. I could never have harmed Jake. Those who suggest otherwise reveal a lack of understanding about our relationship so profound I can only pity them. To those whose critical faculties have not been addled by baseless conspiracy-mongering, I offer my story.

I first saw him at the West End, in December 2003. I was a senior at Columbia, a physics major so obsessed with quantum mechanical particle interactions and Feynman diagrams that I had only dimly registered our country's illegal invasion of a sovereign state. (Such ignorance was possible, then; over a certain income level, foreign wars didn't touch your daily life.) I gleaned my news from articles my sister sent me, or my suitemates' overheard conversations. I felt the appropriate outrage and promptly forgot about it. What, after all, does outrage look like at the Planck scale?

Later, while drunk, I would amend that rhetorical question: what does it *sound* like? The bar was packed that night. Some were the typical Friday-night crowd of loud freshmen and bored frat brothers, but others had heard Jake at the big rally in February and were excited to see him again. He didn't even perform "What We Sing," the song that was already turning into an anthem. It didn't matter. Jake had a voice that stuck you to your chair and forced you to listen. Almost gentle, with an ironic bite. "Like fresh ginger," a simile-inclined local reviewer once called it (and Jake and I laughed until we had to stop to breathe; we ate in Chinatown that night, and he bought me ginger beer). His falsetto was eerie; his bass rough. Sometimes his vibrato wavered so wildly you thought he might lose the note, but he never did. His lyrics were passionate and only sometimes political. He had thick, wavy brown hair; a high forehead; wide eyes with camel's lashes; and a chin that dimpled when he smiled. He was young, talented, and beautiful. I was twenty-two, and I felt as though I'd just crawled from Plato's cave.

I introduced myself after the set. He bought me a drink. We talked, I don't remember about what. For all I know I babbled about brane theory and quantum gravity all night. I had never been very good at talking to people. But he didn't seem to mind me. He told me a little about himself. He had graduated from NYU that year as a film major, but he didn't want to make movies. And the usual: he was appalled by the Iraq War, President Bush, our foreign policies. He quoted Chomsky, which was familiar, and Said, which surprised me. He said he had met Edward Said as a child, when his parents had first moved to the States from Palestine. I asked him if he was Muslim; he said he was a "closet atheist." He asked me if I was religious; I said I was a physicist.

He took me back to my dorm that night; my philosophy of alcohol consumption at the time did not include moderation. He kissed me as he pressed the call button for the elevator, as though I might not notice if he were doing something else.

"Do I get your number?" he asked.

What odd syntax, I thought, many years later. Like it was a game show and my number was the all-expense-paid trip to the Bahamas.

My good friend Billy Davis, who died last year, spent his life advocating for a full inquiry into Jake's death. I find it ironic that even now, in the midst of our global war with China and Iran, the relatively insignificant Iraq War has so much cultural relevance. Perhaps because it is the first moment when our generation, collectively, began to realize that something had gone terribly wrong in our political and social system. Jake's death symbolized too much of that moment for us to ever let it go.

They took us to Pier 57, that detention-center-turned-toxic-waste-dump where they liked to herd activists during overcrowded demonstrations. Jake was furious that day, on a manic high. He was no stranger to racism—was any Arab living in New York City after 9-11?—but the arresting officer that day reveled in a particularly nasty brand of invective. "Raghead" was the least of it (and if Jimmy Sullivan can even tell the difference between his mouth and his lower orifice, I've yet to see the evidence). After they arrested us, Jake could hardly sit still. The floor was covered in an unidentifiable sludge that slid beneath our shoes and smelled like decomposing tires. We were all chilly and desperate to get out. Jake went to ask the officers when they would release us. I never heard what they said to him, and I never got to ask. Jake started yelling and shouting. His hands trembled as he gesticulated, like a junkie coming off a high, though I knew that he hadn't had more than half a joint. I remember being terrified, afraid that they would shoot him. When they set off the taser, he dropped to the floor like a marionette loosed of its strings. He groaned, but he couldn't even seem to speak. The police officers laughed, I remember.

What did he yell? "Pigs," certainly. But Jake hated few things more than he hated the ongoing Palestinian/Israeli conflict, and he would have *never* used the despicable anti-Semitic tripe certain opportunistic faux-rock musicians attribute to him. We had been unlawfully detained and verbally abused. Did Jake's behavior represent a failure to turn the other cheek? Of course. But he never meant to be a martyr.

I went to the Tombs late that night, after they released us from the Pier and arrested him. His lawyer said the police insisted on detaining him for questioning and were charging him with "disorderly conduct." Jake was happy to see me. The police had confiscated his guitar, and one of the officers conducting the interrogation was a real (to put it more genteelly than Jake) ignorant racist. I asked Jake if he was okay. He said he was, but he couldn't wait to get out of there. There was no rope in the cell that I can recall.

He was acting a little more restless than normal. Tapping his fingers against the bars and rocking back on his heels like a drinker with the DTs. It didn't seem remarkable at the time, and it might be that I am merely creating false positives, searching for a clue where none exists.

He held my hand before I left and kissed my palm. He liked romantic gestures.

"There's something happening here," he sang softly. Buffalo Springfield.

I kissed him. "I'll get Neil Young and the gang down here tomorrow."

"I'll see you, Angel."

It was the last thing he ever said to me.
But he had never called me "Angel" before.

Written Communication from Violet Omura, NYU, Department of Applied Physics
To: Zacharias Tibbs; Topeka, Kansas
Date: December 25, 2025 – 1:05 am, EST

[Sender: Verified]

I woke up twenty minutes ago and couldn't fall asleep. Chatterjee has posted a new paper on the public archives. Did you see it?
It's been a while. Hope you're doing okay.
Merry (godless) Christmas, Zach.

Written Communication from Zacharias Tibbs, Topeka, Kansas
To: Violet Omura, General Communications Inbox, Columbia University Physics Department
Date: March 18, 2027 – 6:01 pm, EST

[Hi! This message has been approved by your filters, but contains some questionable material. Would you like to proceed?]

[Okay! Message below.]

Professor Omura:

Though I know you have not heard from me these past two years, I hope you do remember our long correspondence and will still read my messages despite your new Tenured Position at the venerable Columbia University.
I have not Written due to increased Problems with my Health and also, perhaps more importantly, a crisis with my Faith. You might think that facing Death & the Great

Beyond, as I am (a persistent Cancer, which no medicine can treat) would drive one in to the Bosom of their Lord, but I find myself instead Contemplating the letters you have sent me over the twelve years of our correspondence.

You have presented to me a mind steeped in rationality, who does not even let deep grief over personal loss sway her to the side of a comfort that she does not feel has a basis in reason. Is Faith a Good Thing? I ask myself. As a child, I loved mathematics. At the library, I read books about Pythagoras and Newton and Einstein. But in the end I preferred Money to Knowledge, as any Ignorant eighteen-year-old might. I passed over my chance at College. My Father got me a good job as an auto mechanic in his Cousin's shop. Last year, I retired. I had worked there for Sixty-Five Years. I had kept my Faith and raised children. I had read the Bible and tried to use Math to Prove the Beauty of it.

I have wondered why I still Wrote to you, Professor, when you so Clearly held my Views in Disdain. I think now that I Respected the Knowledge you held. The Mathematics that I had loved in Childhood are your Life's Work. I thought if I could Convince you of the Truth of my Faith then it would not be Faith any longer but Reason.

And now, I think I have failed. I face death without the solace of Christ and I think it is not as Hard as I imagined in my youth, but hard enough.

With My Thanks and Respect,

Zacharias Tibbs

Written Communication from Violet Omura; Brooklyn, New York
To: Zacharias Tibbs, Topeka, Kansas
Date: March 19, 2027 – 3:20 am, EST

Zach,

Call me Violet. Would you like to meet for lunch sometime soon? I know of a great fondue place on Flatbush Avenue (that's in Brooklyn, where I live).

Violet

Audio-Visual Transcript of U.S. Internal Investigations files Originally archived on the diffuse-network, proprietary Global-Net, intercepted and transcribed by Chinese Intelligence
Subject: Omura, Violet; U.S. Scientific Authority and Academic;
Status: Dissident
Date: September 12, 2027 – 2:22 am, EST

The subject's apartment is dark. She walks to the window overlooking the street. She removes her shoes and stockings (a run in the back: 4.2 cm). The subject's hair is styled in an elaborate bun. She removes several bobby pins and tosses them to the floor. The subject empties a small, gold purse onto her coffee table.

Contents:
One (1) funeral program. The cover reads: *Zacharias Tibbs: He was Right with Our Lord*
One (1) small rolled marijuana cigarette.

The subject lights the cigarette with a match. Upon completing half the joint, she extinguishes it on the windowsill.

OMURA: [*Soft laughter*]
OMURA: [*Inaudible*]

The subject turns from the window. She abruptly ceases almost all movement. Her breathing resumes after 2.4 seconds. It is at this point that the subject begins to behave very erratically. Her eyes are fixed at a point in the room, as though she is interacting with a person, though motion sensors and audio bots indicate she is alone. The subject has no known history of mental illness. [NOTE: However, our own psychiatrist has stated that her behavior here strongly indicates a psychotic break possibly triggered by the marijuana usage. Hearing voices is common in such incidences.]

OMURA: What . . . Jesus Christ. Jesus Fucking Christ, what's going on?

The subject pauses. Her body relaxes and her head movements are consistent with someone listening to someone else in conversation.

OMURA: Jake? Holy fuck, what was in that pot?

The subject takes two steps forward. [NOTE: The consulting psychiatrist has determined that the person to whom she believes she is addressing herself is standing between the coffee table and her couch.]

OMURA: What do ghosts look like at the Planck scale . . .

20-second pause.

OMURA: Zack did this?

3-second pause. She shakes her head.

OMURA: Maybe. Yes. In a strange way. He could have changed the world. But he fixed other people's cars.

The subject begins to cry. Her hands have a pronounced tremble.

OMURA: Jake, oh fuck. Fucking God, why are you . . . why now? I never believed, not once, and fuck do you know how much I wanted to? I could kill you! Christ, Jake, 30 nanograms of *pot* and not a fucking drop of lithium!

12-second pause. A siren is heard in the background.

OMURA: I knew that. You think it makes me feel better? I should have known! The DTs, I said. Like you were manic. I saw it all then. I've known it all for years. 30 nanograms of pot, 2 milligrams of Tylenol. 0 nanograms of your fucking life.

The subject steps closer.

OMURA: Then why did you? Oh, you came back from the grave for me? God, my maudlin subconscious.

11-second pause.

OMURA: Like Hamlet's father? Did the ghost love?

2-second pause.

OMURA: Like me. Jake . . . if you're real and not my own degenerating brain . . . I'm sorry I asked you taunt—no, listen, I should have known what you were going through. I shouldn't have put you in that position. Not with those trigger-happy assholes. Engineer a conflict? Get it on the news? What a fucking cunt I was.

The subject is silent for nearly one minute and thirty seconds (1:30). Halfway through this period, she closes her eyes and shudders. [NOTE: From the heat patterns in her body, it appears as though she is having a sexual reaction.]

OMURA: The last thing you said to me, what did it mean? Why did you call me Angel?

The subject opens her eyes and looks around. Apparently, the room now appears empty to her. She staggers backward and sits on the couch. After a minute (1:00) she begins to cry with audible sobs.

OMURA: I don't know either.

Associated Press
War Desk: For Immediate Release

September 14, 2027 (SEOUL): Accounts of Chinese war-
ships equipped with long-range nuclear warheads heading
into the Hawaiian archipelago have been confirmed, and
evacuations of major targets on the United States West
Coast will begin within the hour.

"The Score" was born out of an extended period of reading political
and scientific blogs. These venues incubate conspiracy theories like mi-
crobes, most often through their comment threads. September 11 tru-
thers, global warming denialists, germ theory denialists, you name it,
comment sections are a fascinating record of the ways people are able
to delude themselves into believing the palpably untrue. As my idea for
the story grew, it encompassed music and cult followings and the social
effects of post–World War II U.S. foreign policy. This I projected onto a
future that is not so much dystopian as barely functional. The end result became interstitial, I think, because I needed to use the techniques
of so many different modes and genres of writing to convey these disparate pieces of the puzzle. I read *CounterPunch* and *Rock & Rap Confidential* and odd left-libertarian weblogs. I've seen people with writing
styles more exuberant than Zach's in my piece, peddling theories even
less coherent. It's in the spaces between the pieces of this puzzle that
the reader finds a story.

Alaya Dawn Johnson

The Two of Me

Ray Vukcevich

I was not quite ten when Renata grew up out of my right shoulder like a second head. She was just a blemish at first, a smudge that looked a little like the state of Florida. Then she was a squashed spider mole, then she was a monster, a mewling, squirming mass of purple flesh that smelled like raw chicken, and then she was just Renata, my little sister, saying let me have the arms, Davy, I need the arms, my nose itches, please please please, give me the arms, so I can scratch my nose!

I'll scratch your nose, I told her, hold still, okay, here we go, honk honk, ha ha!

You're so mean, Davy! She was about to go off like a fire alarm in my ear. I hunkered down for it, but she changed her mind and switched strategies so smoothly you had to think she was planning this from the beginning—tears and puppy dog eyes, not that they were so easy to see that close up, but I knew what she could do with those eyes. I'd seen her use her big brown eyes on other people—oh, you poor thing! Let me get you a glass of juice, would you like a cookie? Don't cry. Let me see that big girl smile, I know you can do it. Yes, you can. Here, here's your cookie. Davy, hold the cookie for your sister.

Jeeze Louise.

They're my arms, I said. Get your own arms.

I'm trying! she yells. You know I'm trying, Davy!

I do know that. I can see she has shoulders now. She didn't have shoulders before. It's like she's rising up out of me. Some day she'll be all out of me but her feet. I'll be down here, and she'll be up there, and I'll be her big brother bunny slippers, and then one day, plop, she'll pull one foot out, and plop, she'll pull the other foot out. Then she'll run off into the woods throwing flowers to the left and to the right and back over her shoulders.

When I get my arms, I'm going to strangle you, Davy, she says, spooky voice, I'm coming to get you, I'm creeping up on you, here I come now, boo! Giggling. She knows that I'm the one who could do some serious strangling, since I have the arms, but she also knows I never would. I take a deep breath and let go of the control of my right arm. She can feel me do it. Her smile is so big and bright. You just get the one, I tell her. Oh, thank you, Davy! She closes my right hand into a tight fist then opens it up and spreads the fingers. She lifts the hand to her face and scratches her nose and sighs and sighs and sighs. It seems to me she is getting an indecent amount of pleasure out of a simple nose scratching, but then I see that she is looking at me out of the corner of her eye, almost smiling, she's up to something, and before I can grab control of my arm again, she gives my nose a retaliatory honk.

So there! So there! So there!

She had her own arms by the time we got to high school. Things were getting a lot more crowded with us. I had to look up to see her face. But wait, there's more—as her shoulders emerged from me, not only arms were revealed but also a couple of hideous growths on her back. Wings, someone said, and someone else said yes, that must be what they are. Everyone was so sorry for her, like she didn't have enough to worry about being so tightly attached to me who could be known for not always being so nice. Poor Renata! All the time having to be superduperglued to a smelly boy. And now wings.

Once, before she got her arms all the way out, I put a paper bag over her head when I wanted a little privacy. She put up such a fuss people came running to see what the matter was, and when they saw her, saw us, the two of us, Renata with the bag over her head, and me being, well, me, she making a Middle Eastern ululation of despair that she had picked up from watching public television, and me all what? What? She's fine. She didn't look fine when I snatched off the bag to show everyone how fine she was, she looked terrified and lost, but I knew her well enough to know that a lot of it was for dramatic effect. She played our keepers, our fosternistas, like stringed instruments, a big bass for Charlie, who was really the nicer of the two, and a squeaky squawky fiddle for Debbie, who was like a rat terrier. Renata was wailing and Charlie was looking at me so disappointed and Debbie was yapping and I was the rat. I wished Debbie would just bite me or something and get it over with, but she didn't.

Shortly after that, Renata got her arms, and we settled the privacy issue. I opened the bag and put it on the table in front of her and ignored it. It only took a couple of minutes for her to pick up the bag herself and put it over her own head. You pervert, she muttered, and that was that, no fuss, some muss.

In most other ways, she was a lot harder to live with once she got her arms all the way out of me. Not to mention the growths on her back, which by then were clearly wings. There were no feathers. We both wondered if she'd ever get feathers, but there were never any feathers. Her wings reminded me of unborn things. You could see the blood pulsing in them if you looked closely, and given my position, I was always able to look closely. They were a strange pale greenish yellow color with just a little of the pink the rest of her had become, and I should mention by this time we were both in our early teens, and girls grow up quicker than boys, so there was some hullabaloo made over the fitting of feminine tops and attaching them in the back between the ribs and the "wings," and I was not to look, and I pretty much didn't, yes, yes, we fought all the time, but we were so close, it was easy imagining how she felt, or maybe it was just that she was so good at showing how she felt. You never had to wonder. It was all deliberate. She used the display of her feelings as a subtle tool. She knew you could see just how she felt, so when she wanted something, she opened up wide, and it was really really hard to say no, since you knew exactly how she felt. Like alone together in the dark at the end of the day, do you think we'll always be like this, Davy? I don't think so, I told her. Think about it. Every year you grow more and more out of me. It makes sense that some day you'll just be out and can walk away on your own two feet. Do you really think so, Davy? I really do.

And I really did, but I didn't mention that I sometimes imagined her flying away. One time I dreamed her wings were out and big and had all of these black and white feathers, she looked magnificent, and when she beat her wings, the wind blew my hair back like I'd stuck my head out the car window going 60 mph, but her feet were still attached to me, so when she finally lifted off, I came along, too, like a fish in the talons of an eagle.

When her wings finally did fully emerge, they were nothing like eagle wings. In fact, they were very ugly. They were the kind of ugly that people go all white in the face over. Oh, they're not so bad, I told her. I hate them! I want to tear them off my back! Wasn't it bad enough I had to be born attached to you! Wasn't it bad enough I had to have any wings at all! Why does God hate me? Who? Oh, never mind, I'm going to jump off a building! You'll just fly to the ground. You'll be all oh goodbye cruel world, and you'll jump, and then just like you can't kill yourself by holding your breath, your wings will start flapping, and you'll start flying, and that will be that. You'd pull me down, she said. You'd be heavy enough so we'd both go splatter on the sidewalk. Would you really take me with you, Renata?

No, not really.

By the time we graduated, and we did graduate, you wouldn't think we could, but we did, she was almost out, which made the logistics of getting around pretty difficult. Imagine walking around with a 105 lbs seventeen-year-old girl with stubby wings standing on your shoulder. Charlie rigged some scaffolding with wheels, squeaky hard-to-control shopping-cart wheels, and lots of aluminum bars. You might call us a two-story student—me plodding along on the ground level holding onto the bars with both hands and pushing the whole contraption down the high school hallways, and Renata up there like a queen of the parade shouting down greetings to her friends, making jokes, smiling smiling smiling, or pouting if someone had hurt her feelings, Bobby talking to Karen and not even seeing Renata as she rolled on by, slow down, Davy, slow down! Her biggest problem in those days, aside from having to crouch down whenever we went through doorways, was keeping those wings covered, not because she thought people didn't know about them, but because they were still so ugly.

Once she dragged (or more correctly directed) me around to thrift shops looking for feathers. Peacock feathers, feathers in your cap, old arrows, a couple of feather pillows, and when she had enough, she spread out her supplies on our bedroom floor, it

looked like a bombing in a bird store, and took her glue, not su-
perglue we should thank the heartless deity who had kicked this
whole mess off in the first place, but white glue like kids use in
kindergarten, and she glued the feathers to her wings. She really
couldn't reach them right and was making a mess of it. I didn't
say a word, but she could see the judgment in my eyes, so she
got me to do it, so she would have someone to blame when it all
turned out badly. And it did turn out badly. She looked awful—
she had been bamboozling the town folks with some kind of dance
hall and gambling scheme, and they had had it up to here. They'd
gotten mad as hell and weren't going to take it anymore, so they
tarred and feathered her and rode her out of town on a rail. What
does it even mean to be ridden out of town on a rail? If she were
to be ridden out of town, she would be riding me anyway. Charlie
and Debbie gave us grief about the feathers, but the worst part
was the way they looked at us like could there be anything more
pathetic than you two?

I have to hand it to them, Debbie and Charlie, they did come
to our graduation. They were out there with all the parents and
siblings as Renata and I rolled together up the ramp and onto the
stage. Renata had to be especially careful holding her arms out like
a tightrope walker to keep our balance, and I had to push especially hard to get us up the ramp. It was touch and go there for a moment. It would have been just perfect if we had fallen over, people
running around shouting and trying to get us up, looking at us like
that, but we didn't fall. We made it to the podium, and Mr. Hodges
reached up and gave Renata her diploma. Then he reached down
and gave me mine. I pushed our scaffolding off the stage. Lots of
people clapped for us. We're like dancing bears, Renata whispered,
but she didn't sound bitter.

We came apart that summer before college. It happened just as
I always imagined it would. Renata was sitting on the bed, and I
was sitting on the floor. I had been able to see the tops of her feet
for days, and now I could see most of the sides of her feet. And her
toes. Just as soon as her toenails had dried and hardened up, she'd
painted them bright red. The fumes from the polish made me dizzy.
Oh, don't be such a big baby, Davy. Don't you just love this color?

I could take it or leave it.

And then it was like she was only resting her feet on my shoulder, me on the floor, her sitting on the bed, the late afternoon summer sunlight making the room too hot, but not so hot it was worth it to get back into the scaffolding and go outside.

And then I could feel her moving her feet back and forth on my shoulder, a little to the left, a little to the right, and I knew she was loose, but I didn't want to admit it just yet. I could tell she knew, too. This was our big moment. There should be a band. The sky should open up and a Big Face should scowl down at us and say, okay, that should teach you two a lesson! A parade, noisemakers, corks popping. Davy and Renata, two people, separate at long last.

She lifted her left foot off my right shoulder and put it back down on my other shoulder. I leaned back against the bed. Then I leaned over and pressed my face against her right leg, the one that might still be attached. No, I knew it wasn't. I rested my cheek against the warm skin of her leg. She put both hands on my head and moved them around gently like my head was a hairy crystal ball and she was reading our future.

Would she fly away now like some kind of angel? Well, maybe if all the world's a barnyard, and plucked chickens have angels. She'll be running around flapping those awful wings and going nowhere fast. Then she'll put on a big coat and take a cab, or she'll get on a horse and ride away, wings scooping at the air but not even lifting her butt up out of the saddle, or maybe she'll buy a motorcycle.

And I'll go around town pushing my squeaky scaffolding, and people will all the time be saying, hey, Davy! Where's that beautiful sister of yours? And I won't know what to say. What in the world will I say?

"The Two of Me" comes from a challenge to write a story based on a drawing by Rhiannon Rose, a young writer/artist in my workshop. Isn't that a cool name? Wouldn't we have to make her up if she didn't already exist? Isn't it strange the way you never know where a story will pop up next? I like to look at things and write stories about what they bring to mind. In the case of looking at someone else's artwork, it is a kind of collaboration in that the object is talking back with its own point of view and agenda even if what you are hearing isn't what it is saying. The result is something between where you start and what the object wants. I am a chicken or an egg or maybe both at the same time. This is the way I've been writing for years. I'm not sure I could do it any other way, but it's nice to finally have a theory! I'm almost always after a story that is simply itself. Yes, stories talk to stories, and I always listen, but I doubt if I'm qualified to file a report on their conversations. Sometimes a voice in my head scolds, "You can't do that!" And the rest of us smile. Those are some of the best times. If a story really is just itself, it will probably be hard to categorize and might fall through the cracks. That's not always a pretty sight.

Ray Vukcevich

The Assimilated Cuban's Guide to Quantum Santeria

Carlos Hernandez

I was heading toward Parking Lot Four on the east side of campus, mentally reviewing the interview I'd just had with NPR's *All Things Considered* about my new book, when I almost kicked a pigeon. I'm a physics professor at CalTech specializing in quantum entanglement and unspeakable information, and my new book is called *The X Axis of Time*. The idea is this: what if time, a dimension we normally think of as a one-way line, has *width* as well as length? What if it is traversable in two dimensions? Well, my book contends, it would explain a lot about our universe: like, for instance, entanglement. Uncertainty. How the universe can be expanding faster than the speed of light. It is, you know. Nothing can exceed the speed of light—except the whole damn universe. A 2-D model of time offers at least one explanation as to how.

The book is the kind of speculative, sweeping thought experiment that all the cool physicists are writing these days. I am probably wrong about almost everything. But I hope I'm wrong in the ways that will someday lead us to science. That's exactly what I said to my kid-gloves NPR interviewer, and she seemed, in her throaty, liberal-media way, duly impressed.

And then I almost kicked a pigeon. Though I was too distracted to see it at the time, in hindsight I can describe exactly what happened: the pigeon stood in place as I approached, as inert as an abandoned football, watching me approach with one curious eye. Only at the last moment did its little birdbrain realize that I was about to kick it, and, once kicked, there would be no turning back on this *XY* point on time's Cartesian grid, and the pain and consequences of the kick would forever be a part of its history. It therefore decided to get out of the way, with a commotion of wings that startled me back to our shared dream of the world.

There on the sidewalk, surrounded by the cool of an autumn night in Pasadena, I got down on one knee and said to the pigeon, who was now eyeing me gravely, "Sorry, little fella. Didn't see you there."

All was forgiven. It immediately came ambling up to me, eager for a handout. I laughed. And when I find something funny, I often switch to Spanish. "¡Ay, pero niño!" I chastised. "¡No debas ser tan confiado! ¿No sabes que cuando yo era un niño, maté a puñaladas una paloma...."

I fell quiet. To the pigeon, who stared at me with one curious eye, it must have looked as if I had suddenly shut down, like an unplugged robot. And in body I had. But my mind, like a ghostly projector that had started itself, began playing the reel of the time I killed a pigeon in the kitchen sink of my boyhood home.

I had to. The heart of a pigeon was the last ingredient I needed for the Santeria ritual I was performing so that Papi could find love again.

Mami died the summer before third grade. Doctors were removing a benign tumor from her uterus when . . . well, we weren't allowed to know exactly what had happened. One of the conditions of the settlement was that all documents relating to the case remain sealed. The official cause of death on her death certificate is "cardiac arrest," but her heart was doing just fine prior to surgery. They must've done something to her.

Once the settlement came through, Papi didn't work full-time anymore. He had been teaching senior math at Samuel Adams High School in Handcock, Connecticut, since before I was born, and substitute teaches there to this day. At Samuel Adams they call him "The Professor," partly because he has a PhD, but mostly because he *is* a Professor, capital P. You know the type: the kind of man who has to bite down on a pipe (or, in his case, a puro) to remind himself that he has a body as well as a mind, whose eyes are always looking past you and into a reality that is somehow less substantial and more consequential than the one you exist in. It's one thing when these professor types are tall, bearded, tie-choked, corduroy-jacket-wearing sages who are as white as the faces on

Mount Rushmore. Then they're easy to spot. But on the outside, Papi is as Cuban as they come: five-foot-five, fat as a top and just as agile, with a nose like a head of cauliflower and Wolfman hair growing off his ears—and always, always wearing a pastel guayabera, even in the ice-age middle of a Connecticut winter. He looks like a guajiro who just needs to pick up his machete to be ready for a full day of cutting cane. But then, just as people start feeling superior to him, he starts talking mathematics—in virtuoso English that will send responsible listeners scrabbling for their dictionaries. It takes just one meeting. After that they call him "Professor."

We were the only Cubans in town. Therefore, the Connecticut Yankees of Handcock thought all Cubans were like Papi. So did I. Using a kind of commutative-property logic, I reasoned that, since Papi was Cuban, all Cubans were Papi: intellectual, distracted, blunt, cheerful, apolitical, and immune to neurosis of any kind. Kind of like Mr. Spock, but with a better sense of humor. And a *lot* more body hair.

I got to hear from other kids how much better Cubans were than other Latinos, who sent their kids to American schools even though they were illegal. They were poor because they were lazy, and the only reason they couldn't speak English was because they didn't try hard enough. You speak English, Salvador, why can't they? Stick those stupid spics in Special Ed with the other retards.

I agreed with them completely. You see, while they were insulting those other Latinos, they were complimenting me.

I forgot at those moments that, as hard as she tried, even after years of study at the Vo Tech, Mami still struggled with English, and that whenever we went shopping without Papi she always sent me to talk to Customer Service. But at night I would remember. When I spoke to Mami then—surrounded by a darkness so complete I wasn't sure I still had a body—and asked her why she left Papi and me alone, and when she was coming back, I spoke to her in halting, failing Spanish.

When I was eight, it was dinosaurs. When I was nine, it was magic. And when I was ten, I got into Santeria.

Not even a month after starting third grade, I got in a fight with a kid at school because he said Mami didn't die, she'd been deported, because eventually that's what happens to all spics. I was Latino small, so the kid, Timmy Andersen, thought I was an easy mark. Big mistake. I rushed him, but instead of taking a swing, I yanked down his pants. And his underwear, perhaps understanding the justness of my cause, slid down like they'd been buttered. I will never forget the sight of his tiny white penis: it looked like one of those miniature rosettes adorning the edge of a wedding cake. Little Timmy screamed and tried to pull his pants up, while I, almost leisurely, pushed him to the ground, grabbed his hair in two fists, and bashed his head into the playground loam. It's the third happiest moment of my childhood.

Because little Timmy was more embarrassed than hurt—his forehead was red and plenty dirty, but no lump emerged—the principal took it easy on me. He just sent me home for the day with a note for Papi to sign. Because it was too early to take the bus, Mrs. Dravlin, one of the assistant principals, drove me home. She and I were buds; I had known her since I was in kindergarten and had always been one of her favorites. She wasn't as pretty as Mami or as chubby as Mami or as vivacious as Mami, and she didn't know any more Spanish than you need to get licensed as a teacher in Connecticut. But she smiled as big as Mami, a huge, scary, dental-exam smile, as if she wanted you to be able to count her teeth.

I loved her teeth.

She wasn't smiling then, though; she had to watch traffic as she drove, but she kept sneaking fretful, motherly looks at me and saying things like, "Salvador, you're too smart to get in fights," and "I want you to apologize to Tim tomorrow," and "Maybe you should have your dad call me."

I wasn't at all sorry about pounding stupid Timmy's head into the ground, but Papi had taught me to respect teachers, even when they're wrong. So I agreed with everything she said, and, once she had parked in my driveway, I said to her, "I'm sorry I was bad, Mrs. Dravlin."

Something in the way I said it? She cried exactly three tears. The first two tumbled out of her eyes like the boulders of a surprise avalanche. I was a little scared; I'd never seen an assistant principal cry before. As she erased the tears from her cheeks with the back of her hand, a third skittered down her face without her knowing and hung pendulously from her chin. It refused to let go of her face as she spoke. "Listen to me, Salvador. You are not bad. You're a very, very, very good boy." Then she leaned over to the passenger side and hugged me. The tear on her chin sank through my T-shirt. Long after it must have evaporated, I felt its warmth and wetness on my shoulder.

I waved goodbye to Mrs. Dravlin, who was waiting to make sure I could get in the house, and "snuck" past Papi. After the settlement came, he was always home. He sat in the living room with his chin in his hand, studying a Rithomachy board on the coffee table; I could've brought a dead cat into the house and he wouldn't have noticed me. To prove it, when I was nine I actually did bring a dead cat into the house, but I'll tell you about that later. For now, I went to my room.

On the bed lay an illustrated encyclopedia of dinosaurs. It was the biggest book I'd ever seen, even bigger than Mami's Bible. The inscription inside read, in Papi's plain and serious script, "The best way to honor Mami is to better ourselves."

At the end of that school year I became the youngest winner ever of the school's science fair for my project "How the Dinosaurs Really Died," where I explained, based on the exciting new research of this wicked-smart Latino named Walter Alvarez, that the dinosaurs had actually been killed by a huge chondritic asteroid with the cool name of Chicxulub that had blasted the Yucatan Peninsula about sixty-five million years ago. The judges must've known Papi wrote it, gathered the research, made the graphs—this was stuff even the science teachers hadn't heard about yet. But, in my defense, I *memorized* every last bit of it. I won because it's cute to hear an eight-year-old say phrases like "unusually high concentrations of iridium" and "nemesis parabolic impactors."

To celebrate, Dad bought us tickets to go see locally famous prestidigitator Gary Starr make a giraffe disappear. But Papi was unimpressed by Gary Starr; he told me after the show, "That guy couldn't even fool his own giraffe." But after seeing with my own eyes a full-grown camelopard disappear off the stage and reappear in the theater's parking lot, where it was waiting for us, next to a Gary Starr flunky selling Gary Starr T-shirts and Gary Starr pre-packaged magic tricks, I was hooked. Papi wouldn't buy me any Gary Starr tchotchkes, of course, but he would gladly take me to the library. I checked out the fattest magic books they had.

By the time I was nine, I had become a not-too-shabby magician and could even fool adults right in front of their faces. You know the trick where you cut the rope into pieces, only to pull on both ends and—tada!—it's back together again? I did that one for show-and-tell and pissed off my fourth-grade teacher, Mr. Liss, when he couldn't figure out how I did it. And, of course, I wouldn't tell him. Magician's code.

But my best trick of all was a bit I did with the help of Roadkill the Magic Dead Cat. Roadkill wasn't a stuffed animal. Roadkill was a dead black cat, stuffed and mounted and made—why?—into a piggybank. The taxidermist had done a good, if clichéd, job with her: she had a permanent arch in her back, an eternal horripilation of the hair along her spine, and a look in her glass eyes that said, "I am three-quarters demon." I got her for ten bucks from Mr. Strauss at the magic shop I frequented after school because he was getting remarried and his wife hated it, had threatened to call off the wedding if he didn't get rid of it. I think he made up that story just to get a sale, but who cares. A dead-cat bank for ten bucks?

Here's how the trick went down, as per the performance I gave to Mr. Liss's class. I went to the front of the room and put Roadkill on Mr. Liss's desk. Everyone said, "Ooh!" One girl, Jenny Chalder, said, "That's gross."

I said, "Ladies and gentlemen, allow me to introduce you to Roadkill the Magic Dead Cat!" I pulled out a phone book and handed it to Mr. Liss. Then I turned back to the class. "My dad's a math teacher, and he's always saying that math lets you do magic, but I didn't believe him until I got Roadkill. Roadkill's going to predict what name we pick out of a phone book, using math."

Jenny Chalder said, "Cats can't do math."

I pulled a slip of paper and a new, sharpened pencil out of my bag. "First, we have to give Roadkill stuff so she can write her answer down." I stuck the piece of paper in Roadkill's mouth, then used the eraser end of the pencil like a ramrod to jam it down her throat.

Jenny Chalder said "Don't hurt her!"

And I said, "You think that hurts, watch this!" Then I took the pencil and strugglingly pushed it all the way in Roadkill's mouth. Kids squealed and laughed, in that order.

"Okay," I said, "Roadkill has paper and pencil. She's ready to predict which name we pick out of the phonebook. So now we have to pick the name. Mr. Liss, call on someone."

"Why?" asked Mr. Liss. His brain was working overtime, trying with all its might to figure out the trick.

"So everyone will know I'm not cheating. Everyone knows you would never help me."

"You got that right." He scanned the room, then villainously smiled. "Okay. Jenny Chalder."

Everyone oohed. Perfect choice.

"Okay. Jenny, say a three-digit number."

She scrunched her face at me. "What's a three-whatever number?"

"Pick a number between 100 and 999, Jenny," Mr. Liss explained.

She scrunched her face again and said, "I don't know. 1-2-3."

I said, "Okay, one-hundred and twenty-three. Mr. Liss, can you go to the board to do some math for us?"

Still suspicious, he asked, "Why don't you have a student do it?"

"Because kids are always messing up math, and the trick won't work if the math is wrong."

He went to the board. I said, "Okay, please write 123 on the board." He did. "Okay, now reverse it and write down that number." He wrote 321. "Okay, subtract 123 from 321." That gave us 198. "Okay, reverse that number." He did; 891. "Okay, what's 198 plus 891?" He did the math: 1089.

"Okay," I said. "That means we go to page 108 in the phone

book and go down to the ninth name. Can you find that, Mr. Liss? Don't tell us what it is. Just find it."

Mr. Liss went to the phone book, opened it to page 108, and dragged his finger until he got to the ninth name. "Got it," he said.

I picked up Roadkill and said, "Okay. Roadkill's going to give us the answer now." I put Roadkill over my shoulder like I was burping a baby and patted her on the back. "Okay, she's got it!" I said, and brought her over to Jenny Chalder's desk. "Okay, Jenny, reach in to Roadkill's mouth and pull out the answer she wrote down."

She flared her nostrils. "I ain't putting my finger in no dead cat's mouth."

Instantly the class exploded in yells and boos. Two cannonballs of paper bounced off Jenny's head. Our resident bully, Willie Toomer, got up from his desk and made like he was going to whale on her right there, but Mr. Liss made him sit down again.

Jenny was so intimidated she said "This thing better not bite me" and stuck her finger in Roadkill's mouth and hooked out a slip of paper. "Okay. Read what the paper says to the class, Jenny," I said.

Jenny was having trouble with the last name; she practiced a few times to herself, mouthing the syllables like a dying fish gasping for air. Finally she said: "Rosa Ber-to-li-ni."

"That's impossible!" said Mr. Liss, charging for Jenny Chalder's desk. When he got there, he said, "Let me see that," and snatched the piece of paper out of her hands. He read it over several times, flipped it over, rubbed it between his fingers, even smelled it.

The whole class waited for his judgment. One kid fell out of his desk, he was leaning forward so far. Finally, quietly, he said, "It's not even your handwriting, Salvador." And then he smiled. "The cat got it right, children! The name in the phonebook is Rosa Bertolini!"

Children shot out of their desks and formed two circles: one around Mr. Liss and the phonebook, where he happily showed them Rosa Bertolini's name, and another around me and Roadkill. They asked me over and over if she was really a magic cat. Over and over I said, "Yes."

That moment remains my second best childhood memory. I

walked from the bus stop with Roadkill under my arm, thinking that maybe I would be a magician when I grew up. But, as I walked up the driveway to my house, I could feel that something wasn't right. My chest suddenly felt like I had swallowed a beehive. As I got closer, I thought I saw the house . . . waver. Like a mirage. And then, like any good mirage, it became solid again, reasserted its reality.

There were voices coming from the house. One was Papi's. He was shouting. Papi never raised his voice about anything anymore. And there was someone else in the house shouting at him. In Spanish. A woman.

I walked in. There was Papi, in the living room. "It's just a stuffed cat . . ." he was saying.

But Mami interrupted him. *"¡No te atrevas hablarme en inglés!"* she screamed.

Then they both saw me. They went quiet, just like they always used to when I caught them fighting.

I looked from Mami, to Papi, to Mami, to Papi. He shot me a look that said, *She's in one of her moods. Don't say anything to make her angry.*

Mami came over to me, knelt so she was at eye level, hugged and kissed me. *"Ay, mi hijito,"* she said. *"¿Cómo te fue la escuela?"*

Her eyes were less green than I remembered. They were more of a hazel that went green the closer the irises got to the pupils. "Good," I said. "I did magic today."

She laughed. "Do no' tal' to jour Mami *en inglés,*" she said. "Tal' to her *en español. ¿Hiciste magia hoy?"*

"Sí."

"¿Y te fue bien?"

"Sí."

"Qué bueno," she said, and impressed another kiss on my forehead. *"Pero tenemos que hablar seriamente de algo."*

I didn't quite follow. My Spanish was rusty. Papi said, "She wants to talk to you."

Mami shot him a look that said *I know how to talk to my own son.* Papi put his hands up, took a step back. Mami looked at me again, sweetly. *"¿Sal, por qué estás andando con ese gato negro?"*

I understood "cat" and "black" and deduced she meant

Roadkill. "It's for..." I started, but then, catching the look on her face, tried Spanish: *"Es... por... magia."*

She patted my head. *"'Para.' Es para la magia,"* she corrected. *"¿Pero por qué tienes que usar un gato negro? ¿No sabes que ése es símbolo del Diablo?"*

I couldn't follow her. I couldn't understand my mother. I said in English, "I don't know." And I added, sotto voce, "I can't understand you."

She looked at Papi. This time she wasn't angry; she looked worried. *"¿Qué le pasa?"*

"Nada más que necesita un poco de práctica con el español, mi vida," said Papi.

"¿Práctica?" said Mami. She looked more confused than I did. *"¿Mi hijo necesita práctica en español? Yo le hablé esta mañana, y le dije que dejara ese maldito gato aqu" en la casa, y él me dijo, 'Sí Mami' como un niño bueno, y me entendió perfectamente."*

She was getting pissed again. She stood up to face Papi, looking glorious and powerful and unmistakably alive. *"Pero me desobedeció, por qué tú le diste permiso a traer ese gato endiablado para hacer magia negra. ¿Y ahora tú me vas a decir en cara que él no me puede entender?"*

Papi stumbled out the beginnings of a response, but she cut him off: *"¡No quiero la magia negra en esta casa!"*

She charged for the door to the house, then turned one more time to Papi. *"Voy a dar una vuelta por el barrio. ¡Cuando yo regreso, si ese gato no está en la basura, se va a formar el titingó!"* Then she looked at me. Her face was both soft and stern; she pointed at me and said, tenderly, *"El titingó."* Then she walked out of the door.

The beehive in my chest stopped buzzing. I turned back to Papi. "Papi?" I asked.

He knelt so we were eye to eye and put a hand on my shoulder. "I don't know, Sal," he said. Then he looked past me, at the door, and started carpet-bombing the carpet with his tears. "We'll just have to wait and see."

We stood for a long time, hands on each other's shoulders, watching the door. But she never came home.

~

90

"Salvador, is your father okay?" asked Mrs. Dravlin. I mean, Ms. Anbow. She had gotten divorced last year, much to the delight of the fifth-grade boys who were just coming into their first erections.

Papi wasn't okay. The day Mami came home for a few hours cut a permanent, diner-sized pie slice out of his will to live. It was bad enough that Mami's return was illogical, impossible, and, for all that, irrefutable. It was that they had fought. They had spent that last precious coda of their marriage fighting over a stupid dead cat. *My* stupid dead cat.

But I wasn't going to tell Ms. Anbow any of that. I just said to her, "He's okay."

She looked at me askance. "I called to tell him that we're awarding you the Science Student of the Year Award. Again. Most parents would've been thrilled. Do you know what your father said to me?"

"No."

"He said, 'Science is just the lie of the moment. Like religion. Or astrology. Or alchemy. Right now it's science.'"

I just waited for her to continue. "Your dad has a reputation for being one of the smartest teachers in Connecticut, Sal. But this . . . well, I don't know him very well, but that didn't . . . that's not the sort of thing I would expect him to say." She gripped her nose, shook her head. "I'm sorry. I'm not making any sense."

I just kicked my legs and looked at her.

She came around her desk and to the chair I was sitting in, kneeling down to look at me eye to eye. Her blouse bagged; she had on a practical tan bra. "Sal, I want you to let me know if you need anything. Sometimes it takes years to work through the grief of losing someone you love, like a mom, or a wife. Hey," she said kindly, pushing my chin up with a single finger so I would look at her eyes. "You're doing great. Your dad, too. But everyone needs a little help sometimes. I want you to let me know if there's any-thing you want to talk about. I know I am your principal, but I am also a trained psychologist. I can help you, if you want me to. I just want to help. Okay?"

When I went home that day, I said to Papi, "Ms. Anbow is worried about you."

He sat on the floor, in front of his shrine to Elegua. He had set it up in the living room a few weeks after Mami had come back—had gone—and hadn't much moved from it since. It was decorated with a red-and-black runner and candles and rumshots and hard, brilliant candies and old fruit collapsing in on itself and a big coconut with shells for eyes and mouth. And Mami's wedding picture, dead center.

Papi sat in a half-lotus in front of it, dressed all in white, except for a necklace of red and black beads. He had shaved his head, his beard. He looked thinner and younger. But older, too, because though he had lost weight, he still had all the skin that had bagged his fat for so many years. Now it hung off his skeleton like the wrinkly hide of a shar-pei. Without turning to me, he said, "Let her worry."

I walked up behind him. There was a new addition to the shrine, next to the coconut: a painting of a young boy. Bright colors, almost psychedelic. The boy looked like he came from a couple hundred years ago. He had on a cloak and a hat with a feather in it, and he carried an empty basket and a staff with a gourd hanging off the tip. Putti flew around his head and smiled down on him.

"Who's that?" I asked.

"That's Elegua."

I pointed at the coconut. "I thought that was Elegua."

"That's Elegua, too. See, when the Africans were enslaved and taken from their home countries and brought to the Caribbean to work the fields, they weren't allowed to practice Yoruba, their own religion. But they were allowed to be Christians; they could have all the Christian icons they wanted. So they practiced Yoruba by using Christian saints. All of their gods got assigned one: Chango got Santa Barbara, Oshun got Our Lady of Charity, and Elegua got that little fella: El Santo Niño de Atocha."

"So Elegua is a little boy?"

"Kind of. He is an old man with a little boy's face. That's because he is eternally young and playful. But wise, too; he is the pathfinder god, the guide to travelers. He helps you find your way when you are lost and takes care of you along the journey."

"Really? He can do that?"

Papi looked away from the shrine, at me. Some of the old irony came back into his face and made him seem more himself. "I don't know," he said finally. "I don't know anything. Before I met your mother, back when we were in Cuba, I was a Santero. A cabeza of Elegua. But I gave it up for her. She was a Catholic and thought Santeria was all black magic. It really scared her. She equated it with witchcraft, and the Bible says witchcraft will get you a one-way ticket to hell, and then she would spend all eternity without me." He laughed. "That woman. She was so sure she was going to heaven! Well, long story short, she cried and cried until I finally gave up my religion and became a Catholic."

"We used to be Catholic," I said. I had forgotten.

He stood and went to the shrine and picked up a shot of rum and dumped it down his throat. He looked at the coconut and said, "Don't worry, I'll get you a refill."

Then he turned back to me. "When your mami died, I thought God was dead, too. But then your mami came back. We both saw her. She kissed us both that day, you on the forehead and me on the lips." He got on his knees in front of me, locked our eyes. "And that ruined everything. Because it's impossible. Your mami is dead. But there she was, in our living room, kissing and fighting with us like she had never gone. It's like there's a parallel universe out there where she and you and I are still a family, with small argu-ments and small problems . . ." he was crying now ". . . and all the unspoken love. And only God brings people back from the dead. Only God can do magic."

"I do magic," I said quietly.

Papi didn't hear. He took a second shotglass from the altar, but this time he poured a trickle of rum on the coconut. "Okay?" he said to the squinting Elegua. *"¡Pare jodiendo entonces!"* He drank the rest, and breathed through his teeth for a second, and then, still looking at the coconut, said, "I don't know what to believe anymore. So I'm going back to the start. This is where I started, as a child of Elegua. So this is where I'll begin again."

He laughed without joy. "I've forgotten almost everything I used to know about Santeria. I can't find the things I need to perform the few rituals I remember. Connecticut isn't exactly a

Santeria mecca, you know. Where the hell do you get aguardiente in Handcock? But Santeria was born of adaptation. I will do the best I can with the materials at hand. If Elegua wants to hear me, he will hear me."

We stood quietly and together studied the altar for a while. And then, pointing at El Santo Niño de Atocha, I said, "He kind of looks like me."

Papi looked at the picture, then at me. "I guess he does, a little. Hey, you're going to be ten soon. You want me to get you an outfit like his for your birthday?"

"No!" I yelled, and laughed; Papi laughed, too, which made me feel better. That's when I knew I was on the right track. That I needed to learn everything I could about Santeria.

Papi was right; Connecticut in the '80s was no Santeria mecca. My library didn't have a single book on Santeria. They did, however, have lots of books on psychology. I found a book on grief written for the parents of grieving kids called *Child of Mourning*. It featured chapter titles like "The Maze of Grief: The Child's Journey through Suffering"; "Voicing Pain: Giving Your Child the Words He Needs to Grieve"; and, my favorite, "Telling Time: How to Align Your Adult Internal Clock with Your Child's." You see, adults think of time as linear, a one-way street with a consistent speed limit. But not children. They think time can go forwards, backwards, sideways, and loop like a Hot Wheels racecar track. You need to understand how children see time to help them understand that the dead stay dead forever.

Unless the dead show up one day to tell you to get rid of your stuffed black cat.

One chapter towards the end of the book I did find useful. It was called "Love Again: How to Bring a New Member into the Family without Destroying your Child's Trust." Apparently, it's very natural to fall in love again after your husband or wife has been dead for a long time. It's nothing to be ashamed of. Your departed loved one would want you to be happy, would want your child to grow up in a household with both a mommy and a daddy. But your child—young, ignorant animal that it is—may not understand that it's okay for you to love again, may feel that you are betraying the memory of the deceased parent. So here are several steps you can take to prepare your child to welcome a new member into the family.

But I didn't need to read the steps; I got the message. Papi needed to fall in love again. It was natural. It was good. It would help him find his way.

Now, who would make a good wife for Papi? A good mom to me?

Ms. Anbow handed me a thin book with a heavy green cover; on the inside flap was stamped "Property of the University of Connecticut Library System." Printed in gold lettering on the spine was *The Ebos of Santeria*. It was a typewritten manuscript that had been the master's thesis of a student named Ines Guanagao. Recently, in a fit of nostalgia, I tried interlibrary-loaning it, but it seems to have gone missing in this timeline. I'm jealous of the Many Worlds that still have a copy. I would've loved to have Proustianly perused it again as an adult.

"It's the only thing I've been able to find so far," Ms. Anbow said back then. "The librarian from my alma mater said she'd keep looking for more, but she said, 'Don't hold your breath.'"

"Thank you," I said. "Did you read it?"

"I flipped through it." She studied me for a moment, then asked, "Santeria is a religion?"

"Yes. It's my dad's religion."

"Okay." She seemed unconvinced. "It's just that this book looks like . . . well, like a spellbook." She smiled. "You're not going to cast any bad spells on me, are you?"

I smiled back—Papi would've known I was lying—and said, "Magic isn't real, Mrs. Dravlin."

"Ms. Anbow, Sweetheart. I'm divorced, remember?"

"Oh yeah," I said, tucking the book in my bag. "I keep forgetting."

An Ebo to Remove Evil Spirits from your House. An Ebo to Bind Good Luck to You. An Ebo to Sharpen Your Mind. An Ebo to

Bring Ruin Upon Your Enemy. An Ebo to Discover Hidden Money. An Ebo to Ward Against the Evil Eye. An Ebo to Win a Case in Court. An Ebo to Make a Man Infertile. Getting closer. An Ebo to Destroy a Marriage. An Ebo to Stop a Husband from Cheating. An Ebo . . . there it was. An Ebo to Attract a Lover.

Whoever Ines Guanagao was, she wrote one hell of a thesis. As a master's student, her job wasn't to write an exhaustive book on Santeria, but it was her introduction to the thesis that gave me a functional understanding of my father's religion. Oh, so that's why Papi wore a necklace—sorry, an *ileke*—of black and red beads: those were the colors of Elegua, whose name can also be spelled Elegguá or Elegba. Oh, that's why he called himself a *cabeza* of Elegua—when the spirit "mounted" him, he became the "talking head" of the god. Aha! So that's why Mami's picture was dead center in the altar: she was Papi's main eggun, the pantheon of protector ancestors who basically hang out all day waiting for you to call and ask for help.

Papi was trying to commune with Mami, but he wasn't doing it right: at least not according to Guanagao. He shouldn't have a single altar for both Elegua and his *eggun*. Your *eggun* should have a dedicated *bóveda*, with a white runner, and nine glasses of cool water, and flowers, preferably white, and, sitting on the floor in front of the *bóveda*, a shot glass with a little clear rum and a cigar in it, and next to it a cup of black coffee, in case you poured too much rum and they get drunk and need to sober up fast.

Mami never drank when she was alive. Had she started after death? Nothing left to lose?

There were lots of ebos for making people fall in love with you. Most of them were disgusting—even to a ten-year-old boy. Every single one in Guanagao's thesis required some mix of pubic hair or urine or poop or blood or head hair or nail clippings or some other body part from the person you wanted, and sometimes you had to throw in your own pubic hair or urine or etc. as well. And since I wouldn't be performing the ebo for myself, but on behalf of Papi, that meant I'd have to gather gross stuff from *two* people: him and Ms. Anbow. Wasn't gonna happen. Plus, most of the ebos required other weird stuff I wasn't going to be able to find. Papi

96

had complained about not being able to find aguardiente, but that was nothing. Where was I supposed to get sea turtle eggs, preferably powdered, or whale oil, or smoked *jutia*, or *amasa guapo*, whatever the heck that was?

There wasn't a single love ebo in the thesis I could—or would—follow all the way through. But there were ingredients of different love ebos that I didn't mind, like cinnamon sticks and wine and hard candies and incense and borax. So why couldn't I combine those to make my own ebo? Papi said that Santeria was born of adaptation; if the orishas wanted to help me, they would. I just had to prove I was sincere. Serious. Willing to sacrifice for the sake of my desire.

Sacrifice. According to Ines Guanagao, the orishas needed food. Blood. The sacrifice of animals is vital to the rituals of Santeria. As life leaves the sacrificed animal, it radiates outward, bathing the participants in the mystery of life, carrying them out of the bounds of normal reality and into the realm of the spirit. Minds grow sharper, senses keener. Souls awaken from their quotidian slumber and stand ready to receive the wisdom of the gods.

Guanagao's rhetoric, fantastic and sincere, utterly convinced me. My soul definitely needed to awaken from its quotidian slumber and hear the wisdom of the gods. I needed a sacrifice.

In several of the love ebos, one consistent sacrifice was the heart of a "*paloma*." Guanagao left the word "*paloma*" untranslated, so I looked it up in our Spanish/English dictionary. I found two main definitions: (1) a dove; (2) a pigeon. At first I thought the ebos probably called for dove hearts. Doves are beautiful and beloved and are symbols of peace and hope. And "dove" rhymes with "love": game, set, and match, right? But then I read in the thesis that Olodumare, the father/creator of all the orishas, didn't like animal sacrifices of any kind, and he was symbolized by a dove. You can't possibly be allowed to symbolically sacrifice the creator of the universe, right? So the paloma hearts in the ebos *must* be referring to pigeons.[1] That made me feel better: there were

---

1   I have since discovered that doves are used all the time in Santeria rituals. So much for logic.

always a few doves in cages in the magic store, so I had formed a bit of an attachment to them. I didn't think I could kill one, even in the name of love.

But nobody liked pigeons.

Nobody, that is, except for Handcock's resident crazy lady, whom we affectionately called Miss Pigeon. And even she only liked to eat them.

Miss Pigeon was the most efficient can collector in town. Her shopping cart bulged with can-stuffed garbage bags so full, they made that homely cart look like a steampunk flying machine. She had further customized the cart, housing it with what looked like a pantry cupboard that had been ripped out of some country-kitsch kitchen. In it—all the kids in town had been dared at one time or another to sneak a peek—she kept a small electric deep-fryer; some staples, like corn oil and Veg-All and potted meat; extra yellow kitchen gloves (she always wore a pair, which made her look kind of like a superhero); a huge jug of Clorox; a lunchbox, square and gray; and a Cabbage Patch doll so mangled someone should've called Children's Services to put it in foster care. For her lunch she always went to the park that surrounded City Hall, where she would douse a park bench with Clorox, take a seat, and, still wearing her kitchen gloves, daintily pick at what looked like deep-fried chicken, but what any local would tell you was deep-fried pigeon.

Everybody in Handcock, CT, had received an involuntary education on how to catch, prepare, and eat a pigeon. Most members of polite society would pretend to avert their eyes, but even the most squeamish among us would pause to watch her nab one. She was a master. Her favorite hunting ground was the park, where stood the remains of a wall where, it is said, generals Washington and Rochambeau debated the merits of attacking the English in New York. Pigeons had since "whitewashed" that wall with their droppings. Miss Pigeon'd sidle up to the wall, where the birds stood packed together like targets at a shooting gallery. They'd hop and flap and caper in pigeony fashion as she approached, delighted to see her. She would lean against the wall, wait for just a second or two, and, in one elegant motion, swipe at the wall with her

Grendel-like arm, dragging whatever she caught into a sack she kept just for that purpose. Sometimes she'd catch two; most of the time she got one; every once in a while she missed. Whatever the result, afterwards she threw some bits of bread at the pigeons. They exploded into an ecstatic battle for those crusts. Then she slung the rice sack over her shoulder and headed back to her cart.

Nobody talked to her, interacted with her, or, by the way, tried to stop her. We just watched from a distance and tittered and judged. So imagine her surprise when one day, a ten-year-old boy who didn't quite look all-the-way American came up to her and asked, "What's your name?"

She stopped dead. She looked at him as if through a fog. She squinted, cogitated. And then she said, "Maggie."

"Thank you," said the little boy. Miss Pigeon immediately turned back to her cart and started pushing. The little boy ran home. He was happy. Excited. He now had the last ingredient he needed for his ebo. One that would compel Miss Pigeon to help him. One he made up himself, though it was based on many others he had read. "An Ebo to Make Someone Help You," he would call it. He wondered if it would end up in a book someday.

An Ebo to Make Someone Help You
One iron nail
One coconut
Black, red, and yellow ribbon
Rum (aguardiente is preferred, but if you live in
    Connecticut, rum will do)

Wash the coconut with a sponge dipped in rum, asking Elegua to assist you. Heat a nail over a flame (a gas stovetop works perfectly). Drive it into the coconut, then yank it out. Pour some rum into the small hole (but not so much that your Papi will notice you stole his rum). Tie black, red, and yellow ribbons to the nail. Push it back into the same hole in the coconut you made before. As you do, repeat seven times the name of the person you want to help you. Sleep with the coconut in your arms that night. The person will be willing to help you the following day.

Miss Pigeon—Maggie—didn't recognize me the following day. I caught up with her as she approached the pigeon wall, yelling "Miss Maggie, Miss Maggie!" She slowly turned around and stared at me, squinting and straining her memory to figure out how this little boy had come to know her name. "Hello?" she said cautiously.

"Hello, Miss Maggie. I'm the little boy from yesterday."

"I don't remember anything," she said.

"That's okay."

She laughed. "Says you."

I held out an empty hundred-pound rice sack. (Papi always had some lying around.) "I was hoping you would do me a favor."

She stared at the rice sack and said nothing.

"I was hoping you would catch a pigeon for me."

Instantly she said, "Okay."

"Thank you. It means a lot."

"Okay."

We stood there looking at each other. Stood. There. Looking.

I said, "So, should we go now?"

"Okay," said Miss Pigeon, and took the rice sack out of my hand. She trundled over to the wall, took her customary place. The pigeons danced for her. She threw her patented left hook and swept one into my bag; the pigeon pecked ineffectually at her yellow kitchen glove as it went in. For a few seconds it looked like grenades were going off in the rice sack, but soon the pigeon stopped rioting. Miss Pigeon took a crust of bread out of a pocket and threw it to the other pigeons on the wall, who fell upon it in a catastrophe of wings. Then she trundled back over to me, the sack held before in modest triumph.

"Here you go," she said, handing me the sack. After a second, she added, "You gonna eat it?"

The pigeon came to life again in the bag, but I held on firmly. "Yes. Santeros always eat their sacrifices, unless they're using it to remove a curse or an evil spirit from themselves. Then they can't eat them. But most of the time they do."

She understood nothing of what I had said, I could plainly see. Still, she said, "If you're going to eat it, make sure you deep-fry it."

"Why?"

"Because pigeons are filthy. Full of lice and disease. You got to kill the germs, okay?"

"Okay," I said. After a moment's thought, I asked, "Miss Maggie, if pigeons are so gross, why do you eat them?"

"'Cause they're free, okay? That's a whole wall of free food over there. And they taste good, once you kill the germs." Then she gave me a look that I think was meant to be motherly and said, "You're a boy. You're young. You want me to kill the pigeon for you, okay?"

"No thank you, ma'am," I said. "I have to perform the sacrifice myself, or Elegua won't help me."

Though again she didn't understand me, she said, "You're a good boy, okay? Remember to kill the germs." Without another word she turned and headed back to the wall to catch herself tomorrow's lunch. The pigeons cavorted with joy.

On some of the points along the X axis of time, at least a few of the Salvadors, marching beside me on my right and left like my reflection in a pair of opposed mirrors, must have felt a little trepidation about killing the pigeon I had in the bag. But not this Salvador. I was excited. My test ebo had worked perfectly: Miss Pigeon agreed to help me so quickly that she must have been enchanted. And that meant, even though I had no idea what I was doing, even though I had never been initiated into Santeria, the gods were on my side. They wanted to help me, had accepted the ebo I had made up on my own. Maybe Mami, my main eggun, had helped convince them. And that led to one evitable conclusion: if the gods and my mom were willing to help me, that meant they thought I was on the right track.

Papi was almost always home: except that day, he was running an SAT-prep seminar at Samuel Adams after school. This was my one chance to kill, eviscerate, cook, eat, and dispose of the pigeon without Papi ever knowing. I had even bookmarked a recipe for deep-frying a pigeon in *The Joy of Cooking*. (Actually, it was a recipe for squab, but close enough: I wasn't eating it to delight my palette.) Papi had the 1962 edition, which begins with an epigram from Goethe's *Faust* that reads: "That which thy fathers have bequeathed to thee, earn it anew if thou wouldst possess it." Yet another clear sign from the gods.

All the way home, the pigeon insisted on reminding me it was alive. It batted its wings and tossed itself around the bag and, during periods of rest, cooed plaintively. I didn't feel bad for it, exactly. But all the way home I wondered if its primitive bird brain had figured out it was going to die. That would be just like Elegua, trickster that he was—to whisper into the pigeon's ear the fate that was about to befall it, inspire fear in it, make my job that much harder.

I opened the front door, shed my bookbag in the entranceway, and trotted, the rice sack still struggling for its freedom, to the kitchen. I switched the sack to my left hand and got to work: emptied the sink of the breakfast cereal bowls; brought out the cutting board; took out Papi's Cutco French Chef knife; decided it was too small and went to the garage and got his machete; slowly, one-handedly, washed the machete in the sink; got a bowl for the blood and the entrails and the heart; another, bigger one for the feathers. Okay. Everything was ready.

Now then. How to get the bird out of the sack. Hadn't thought of that.

Suddenly I was terrified that it would fly out of the bag and perch somewhere where I wouldn't be able to get it. Papi would come home and hear the pigeon cooing and then look up and see the pigeon and it was obviously my fault that it was there and how would I explain it?

I gripped the sack in both hands. With all my strength I heaved it in the air and brought it crashing to the floor. The pigeon cried, flapped, fought for its life. I heaved it again. Again. Four, five, six times. It stopped fighting after the third, crying after the fifth. I had to be sure. Seven. Eight. Nine.

Ten.

I bent over, huffing. I hadn't noticed I'd started crying. I wanted to wipe the tears off my face, but I was afraid to release my two-handed chokehold on the neck of the sack. So I just let them fall. They beaded on the rice sack before scurrying off.

I looked at the kitchen clock—it was one of those weirdo Kit-Kat clocks with the moving eyes and tail—and watched it for two full minutes. All the while I listened. No sound came from the sack. No movement.

Slowly, cautiously, I grabbed the lips of the sack and opened its mouth a little, ready to squeeze it shut if the bird tried to escape, and peered in.

The pigeon blinked. It was alive. But it lay crumpled at the bottom of the sack. Awkwardly angled: living Cubism. I'd broken the one wing I could see and a lot of bones I couldn't. Blood pooled behind its blinking eye.

"I'm sorry," I said. I opened the sack as wide as it could go. "I'm sorry," I said, and cautiously reached into the bag. The bird seemed to watch me, but I thought with all the blood filling its eye it was probably blind. "I'm sorry," I said, and gently grasped the pigeon in both my hands. It should not have felt that soft, that cartilaginous. It did not resist. I lifted it up; the head swung loosely on its shoulder. It opened its beak in surrender, but then, slowly, willfully, closed it. "I'm sorry," I said, and carried it to the sink.

I placed it in the sink on its side as gently as I could. There was no risk of its flying away now. I put the bowl for the blood and innards in the sink next to it, brought the feather bowl a little closer to my work area. Guess I wouldn't need the cutting board after all. Or the machete.

I took a breath. *It's okay,* I thought. *Just stay calm and work fast.*

I clutched the knife in my right hand, held the pigeon steady in my left. Should I cut off its head first, put it out of its misery? I was afraid I would do it wrong, that I would cut indecisively and have to hack at the neck, torturing the bird even more. I was desperate to kill it mercifully, quickly. With my left hand I lifted its useless wing. With my right I guided the knifepoint to where I thought its heart was. "I'm sorry," I said. "I honor your sacrifice. Thank you." Then as hard as I could I pushed the knife all the way through the bird. My brain burst into a swarm of bees. The knifepoint gouged the sink's porcelain.

The front door opened. Papi. Home early. The pigeon lay dead in the sink, transfixed by the knife still in my hand. I looked around wildly, sought any means of escape, but it was as if my fingers were glued to the knife. I couldn't let go.

Wait. No. I could let go. I just didn't want to. I wanted to be punished for what I had done. I took a breath and faced the kitchen's swinging doors.

Mami shouldered her way into the kitchen, struggling with three paper bags overflowing with groceries. She couldn't see me over the bags. "Sal, I'm home!" she yelled, loud enough for me to hear her in any room of the house. In English.

"Hi Mami?" I asked.

"Oh! Jou're in here?" She laughed. *"¡Bueno, no te queda parado cómo un bobo!* Come hel' jour Mami with these bags." But she was already putting them down on the kitchen table. "¡Tonigh' we're goin' to have a feas'! I goin' to ma'e jour favorite. *¡Boliche!* I was at the estore, and I saw . . . *¿Qué te pasa?*"

She stopped dead, stared at me, her eyes following my arm, to the hand, to the knife grip. I stared back. Then I started to cry.

"¿Qué te pasa?" she repeated, terrified, running over. She looked in the sink.

Covered her mouth. Screamed into her hands.

"¿Qué hiciste, Sal?" She yelled. She started crying, too. *"Bendito sea Dios. ¿Qué hiciste?"*

I started to respond through my bawling, but Mami slapped me. I instantly tasted blood, stopped crying. She slapped me again. *"¡Dime que diablera hiciste aquí!"*

Oh, yeah. I'd forgotten Mami was a hitter. She took off a sneaker and proceeded to give me the walloping of my life.

It was the happiest moment of my childhood.

When Mami disappeared again, slipped off the tightrope of my *Y* time and tumbled into another, I knew I had to look for conclusive evidence to prove to Papi she had returned. And of course I found none: time retroactively righted itself the moment she vanished.

The only thing it left were the marks she left on me. Shoe welts on my back and legs. The cut she slapped into my lip.

Nevertheless, when Papi got home, I told him everything: I showed him *The Ebos of Santeria* and described my encounter with Miss Pigeon and showed him the pigeon I sacrificed, still in the sink, and pointed to my lip. "Mami did this," I said.

"Did you get in a fight at school?" he asked.

"No. I told you what happened."

He picked up *The Ebos of Santeria*. "This book told you to kill a pigeon?"

"No. Not exactly. I made up my own ebo. But I used it as a guide."

"Where'd you get it?"

"Ms. Anbow."

"Your assistant principal?"

"Yes."

Papi called information and got her number and even paid the extra twenty-five cents to put him through immediately. "Ms. Anbow? This is Augustín Vidón, Salvador Vidón's father. I'm sorry to bother you at home, but we need to talk. Now. In person. Would you mind if we went to your house?" He looked at the sink. "I'd invite you here, but my house is a little messy right now."

I don't know exactly how long I spent kneeling on that Cal Tech sidewalk speaking cooingly to the pigeon I'd almost punted. I didn't stop until my cell interrupted my reverie. Caller ID showed the number. Home.

I flipped it open and said "Hi, Mom and/or Dad."

"It's both of us," said Mrs. Dravlin. I mean Ms. Anbow. I mean Mom.

"We heard you on the radio," said Papi, his voice younger than it had been for the span of years when he'd been unmarried.

"How'd I sound?" I asked. Fishing for compliments like a ten-year-old.

As always, Mom obliged. "Like a genius," she said.

And, as always, Papi said, "Well, . . ." He made that word four syllables long.

"Oh, don't start, Auggie. He sounded brilliant, and you know it."

"Of course he did. But that NPR reporter: what an idiot! Couldn't they find someone who at least knew the first thing about quantum physics?"

"No, they couldn't, because nobody knows the first thing about quantum physics. Except maybe Elegua." Suddenly inspired, Mom added, "Hey, Sal, you know what would make this moment perfect?"

"What?"

"Your mami."

"Don't say that," I knee-jerked. "You're my mother."

"Oh, don't be so sentimental. I know that. I'm just saying it'd be nice if Alma were here to see this. Don't you think, Auggie?"

Papi went quiet; we listened to him think. Then he said, "Well, sure. If only that were possible."

"You know what," Mom said, startlingly chipper. "I forgot I need to pick up some things for dinner tonight. I need to run out to the store." And then, her voice devoid of connotation, the way only psychologists master, she said, "You boys be good."

"Love you, Mom," I said. I heard her smile before she hung up.

Papi and I waited until she shut the front door behind her. Then Papi said, "Now all we need is a pigeon."

"No worries, Papi." I held out my hand, and the pigeon I'd almost kicked trundled toward it happily, as if it were as pleased by this serendipity as I was. "I've got one right here."

Ashé O.

Borges's "The Garden of Forking Paths" gives us one possible way to create an infinite book. It's not unlike—forgive me, Borges—a Choose Your Own Adventure, though in Borges's story the book loops around like a Rolodex and is therefore infinite. But it's a small infinity: a unidirectional line that circles around to bite its own tail.

While I was thinking about Borges and time, I was also thinking of my *abuela*, who was senile and dying. She was a Santera. She used to plant curses (ebos) in my mother's garden. She didn't like Mami.

One I remember was an egg left to rot beside a rose bush. I think it was meant to dry up Mami's womb. Anyway, Mami would find these ebos and grow terrified. She would tell Papi, and one time Papi got so angry that he beheaded the statues of all Abuela's gods. Papi would fight any god, any time, any place. Abuela bought new gods, and the cycle began anew.

In my house, Santeria was tantamount to black magic. It was the opposite of Catholicism and, therefore, the opposite of the Good.

I went to college. I learned that Santeria wasn't black magic, but a religion, an act of defiance created by Caribbean slaves so that they could hide their faith in plain sight from their captors. I learned it was a vital part of Cuban culture. I learned it was a difficult thing to learn: practices varied a great deal, and little was written down.

And now Abuela was senile and dying. I could never know what she knew about Santeria.

This is how histories fall out of time. This is how we forget.

But sometimes histories don't fall away completely. Sometimes they get stuck in the interstices. There they lie, waiting to be excavated. You won't find much in your digs—a femur, a shard of pottery, a strip of paper inscribed with ideograms from an undeciphered language. But from these bits, a vision of the past emerges—wavering like a mirage in the desert, but a vision just the same. And, for one delicious second, the tyranny of time is broken.

Carlos Hernandez

Shoes

Lavie Tidhar

He remembers going to Sanara when he was young, standing barefoot in the water off that great bleached-white stretch of dazzling sand, and fishing. Now they used bamboo for a rod, and the line and hook were cargo, had come on the ships from the waetman's distant countries. Back then he had used a bow and arrow, to shoot at the fish as they pooled beneath the cool shadow of the great black stones. He guesses it doesn't matter. The fish are still there, and the naura too, the sweet white meat enclosed within an armorial shell, that one needs only dive for.

When he was a child (but how long ago was that? he no longer knows), he went to Sanara almost every day. It was, is, his family's land: his land. Back then the only things that washed on the beach were driftwood and coconuts. He remembers it years later, when his son, David, who was now a policeman in Santo, was merely a boy, and the Americans had come and there was a war. There were five Americans living up on the hill above Mosina. There was a great tree up there, and they had built a house at its top and put a bed there, and each of them spent six hours at a time sitting antap with binoculars, looking out for the Japanese. His boy, David (was he a policeman now?), helped carry food for the Americans. He was there when the man in the tree discovered a sea monster, its body rising from the deeps between Vanua Lava and Gaua, and the sun caught its metal hide and betrayed it.

The man had scrambled down the tree as fast as he could, and when he came down his hands were raw and took a week to heal. He spoke to his captain, and the captain used the great machine blong toktok and half an hour later airplanes came, with a great buzzing excitement like a cloud of flies, until they had located the monster, which the Americans said was a submarine. Neither he nor David had seen a submarine before; it seemed as impossible as an airplane.

The airplanes circled high above, but one by one they darted low, and as they did they seemed to defecate on the monster, but they were planes, not flies, and the things they had released were bombs.

On and on they went, one after the other, and the water in the distance rose high and made clouds of tiny drops, and rainbows arced between them, until there were no more bombs.

He was in Sanara when the debris of the dead monster began to wash ashore the next day. Broken crates, and bottles with a strange curved script on them, so different from the Europeans, and shoes. He remembers the shoes best. There had been no bodies, and he thought then that it was better that way, that the soldiers inside that metal hulk were better off left in the sea as they had lived. He had only seen the soldiers once, and that was before, at Surevuvu, though he had not realized it then.

So there were no soldiers. But shoes there were, and as the years went on, as his son grew and became a man and had children of his own, their country was changed, and the waetman brought with him new things beside religion, and chief among them was footwear, shoes, and ol slipa, what the waetman called flip-flops, and now every time he went to Sanara more shoes were washed ashore, enough to fit an entire village, and when the pikininis came with him they ran along the shore and tried them on and walked in them for a while and then discarded them again.

But now that he is old, he knows the danger of shoes and does not wear them himself. For he is old, and there is no arguing the point, but he had been young once, more years ago than most people believe.

"Angkel," his niece says, and the old man turns and regards her with a puzzled expression, and yet smiling, "kam insead long haos. Wind ia I kolkol."

But the old man waves her away with a vague gesture, for he is not cold, and the wind is pleasant. That language, too, which when he was young was called beche-la-mar, after the sea slug that the traders lusted after, and was now called Bislama, it, too, was a mark of change, and now all the children spoke it, and it was no longer a pidgin but a creole—that is, a language one spoke from birth: a mother tongue. When he was young, they each spoke the language of their own village or island, and there was no common tongue, so that sometimes you did not understand the man from the village just down the beach, on the other side. But Bislama came with the Europeans, like shoes or fishing lines, and the old man could speak it well; for they had come even before his time.

"Angkel?" His nephew comes and sits down with him, and the old man smiles. His nephew is a good boy; he still remembers him as little more than a baby; they had taken him to Sanara once, and he had climbed a great black rock and could not come down again and had cried. He has become a good man who knows kastom, and the old stories and the dance. He knows, and that's important, the old man feels, that he is not the owner of this land, but its caretaker. The Europeans never understood that, when they spoke of traditional landowners. You did not own the land as much as it owned you. "Shall I make a fire?"

The old man makes the same vague motion with his hand. He looks out, but his eyes are not good and he can no longer see the volcano, and it is getting dark. Beyond the volcano is Surevuvu, the hill of the dead, and the old man knows that soon he will have to go there, as is right; and besides, he has been there before: he knows its secrets.

"I would like to go back to Sanara," he says dreamily. "You and I should go. Is the old bush path still there?"

"It is only beyond the hill," his nephew says. "We will go soon."

But of course he will never go beyond the hill again, for his body is too old to travel even that short distance. His grandchildren and their children are the ones to follow that ancient trail through the bush now, and fish beneath the great black stones, and dive for naura, and sleep in the shade of the elder trees . . . He had a good wife, and she loved him, and he cared for her, too, and they had many children. But sometimes at night he still thinks of Metér, and the ship, and the far distant country of the waetman, and he misses her.

"We will go soon," his nephew says again, no doubt thinking to humor the old man, and the old man smiles and stares out to the sea. His nephew is a good man. He works for the province (had they won independence then? were the British and the French really gone?), and pilots a boat, and knows the pathways of the sea amid the islands. For him, waetman and blakman are natural facets of humanity; he does not remember a time before the waetman came.

But the old man remembers this place before it was a town, and before it was a plantation, before the coconut trees were planted and buluk were brought on the ships and bred and ate the grass between the trees, and there were horses. He had been a child when the *Southern Cross* came, the way it had come in his father's time, and the men on the shore looked and saw white men and thought they were ghosts.

But they were missionaries. When they came ashore, his father told him, he had been afraid. They were vui, ghosts, come from the land of the ancestors in the giant hulk of a spirit ship, and they had lost their native tongues; their speech was fathomless.

Yet they did not prove dangerous; not then, at any rate, the old man thought. The white men had wealth, had cargo, and they exchanged many things for food and hospitality, but they were particularly interested in the young. There was a school, they said. A fabulous school on an island far away, where the teachings of their powerful god could be shared. His father had been unsure what a god was. He knew of Qat, the trickster, who had come from Vanua Lava—from their own land, in fact—and Qat could perform many miracles, could shrink and sail in a shell of coconut and hide his brothers in the beams of a nakamal, and he fought Qasavara many times, and made the tree grow until it stretched from Gaua to Vanua Lava, and his stones were everywhere. The waetman's god had no tambou stones, but it only needed one look at their ship and their clothes and their guns to know that he was powerful indeed.

And so his father had gone with them. Sometimes he had told him stories of it, of the school on Norfolk Island, where they dressed like the white men did, and learned to read the waetman's books, and learned of Jesus. They were fed well.

There were people there from other islands, other nations, and many from the islands of King Solomon, and his father learned with them, and sometimes he exchanged his own knowledge with them, too, although the missionaries didn't know this and would have been angry had they known. There was magic in the Solomons that was new to his father, of which the most prominent was the knowledge of sea ghosts. Indeed, Bishop Patteson was eventually killed by sea ghosts, off the island of Nukapu, where the islanders had mistaken his mission for the man stealers, and their chiefs raised the sea to protect them. Patteson was the first martyr.

When his father returned, he was a Christian, and he brought up his son to be the same, and why not? Their god was a powerful one, and had cargo. But he also taught him the old ways, the way to speak to vui and to prevent nakaimas and to spot, amidst the dogs walking down a road of an evening, which one was real and which a man in different shape. And when his mother died, his father had taken him to Surevuvu, when he was young, and together they danced the rusrus dengé in the dark with the other men and raised her, and he got to speak to her one last time and tell her that he loved her.

The missionaries settled at last on Mota, which they had called Hat Island, and which you could see from the shore of Vanua Lava every day even when clouds formed like a screen. And they took on the language of Mota, and taught in it, and their ship, the *Southern Cross*, made frequent visits to the islands of the Banks, as the white men called them, and they still took young boys to their distant school, and returned educated and dressed in the waetman's fashion. And their god was all-powerful, beating even Qat.

So when his own time came—the old man, who was then not old at all—he, too, had wanted to go and learn of the power of their magician-god. And when he saw the *Southern Cross* approaching the bay, coming across the point which they now called Port Patteson, he was excited, and waited for the bishop (it was Wilson now, after Patteson's death and Codrington's short service) to come on shore, and vowed to join him.

But the bishop didn't come on shore. The ship remained in the distance, and the boy could see, faintly on the deck, the figure of a man in the robes of the bishop, making gestures with his hands as if blessing the island. A small boat came from the ship, with two men in robes sitting inside it, and they said the bishop was ill and had to remain on board, but that he would love to see his friends again, and anyone who wanted to come to the school at Norfolk Island should come on the boat with them.

And he had gone. His father had bidden him goodbye, and gave him a stone, and as he did a shark surfaced in the water ahead and then disappeared, and his father said, "Remember Surevuvu when you need it."

Then he had gotten in the boat with the two white men, he and several of his friends, young men and a couple of the women, too, and they went to the *Southern Cross* and boarded it, and the ship departed, sailing away from Vanua Lava.

But it was not the *Southern Cross*.

He remembers the captain's laugh as the ship sailed away from Vanua Lava and headed south, and into open ocean. Ross, the others called him, and when he laughed his whole body shook, like a man sitting around the fire enjoying a good joke just told.

"The missionary gambit!" he bellowed, "The missionary gambit works every time!" and he addressed them in fragmented Mota and in beche-la-mar, the pijin English they hardly understood then but learned to speak so fluently once they got to the plantations of Queensland and worked the sugarcane. "Yufala I go wok kwiktaem, kanakas," he said, once laughter had drained out of him like mud. He called them kanakas. "Yu laki tumas, from yu go wok long Kwinsland, hemi wan kantry blong waetman ia."

Queensland. He remembers Queensland the way it was, the heat of the sun, naked torsos gleaming black in the fields, and the overseers shouting, and there were men and women from every island, and no one spoke the other's tongue. They communicated in pijin, and they worked, and they slept, and sometimes they loved, but love in a foreign land is hard and can be taken away from you.

But that first night on the ship, helpless, he had merely sat with the others, and there was no escape; the sea was their jailer then, and the white men had guns. And yet as he watched the islands receding in the distance and saw the arm of the Milky Way reaching from one end of the sky to the other, dense with untold stars, a wild joy rose in him, unbidden and unexplained, a feeling that stole on him like a rush of wind, for there was a strange freedom in his exile, and the world grew large, expanding like a growing tree.

There was a girl with them, Metér, a name which had once meant a leader of women, what the white men called chief. She was from Mosina, the village on the other side from his home, and the two of them could talk. He had comforted her that night, a solid, strong girl, her hair tawny and her bare arms black, and they talked quietly in the dark, and made plans, and thought they'd see the world, and the place the waetman came from, and dreamed of returning to their homes laden with knowledge and cargo. Ross made them sign a contract, and said it was for three years, and after that they could return to their homes. He had heard of people like Ross, of course, for the man thieves had come before, and one heard of them in every island, but he had not thought it would be him to be so caught. Like fish, he thought, and found comfort in the comparison. Caught like fish. At least that was something he knew about, and he also knew sometimes fish struggled, and sometimes they broke away from their hunters. Sometimes.

The journey was long and hard, though he could not compare it to any others. They had stopped at other islands, and anchored a distance from the shore, and Ross dressed in the robes of a bishop and paraded on the deck, and his men rowed to shore and told the people there that Bishop Wilson wanted them to come on board and greet him, and then there would be a hasty retreat and the ship would be crowded further.

Two weeks into the voyage one of the sailors wanted Metér, and he woke up to her screaming as she was dragged out of the hold, and he tried to rise against them and was butted with a gun and kicked until she was removed.

He was angry that night, and he clutched the stone his father had given him, and he called on the shark spirit, the 'ataro as it is called in San Cristoval, and it came to him, and with it came the sea ghosts, and they rose out of the depths of the sea. At that there was a commotion on deck and the running of many feet and the firing of muskets, and he and the others, too, came onto the deck, and he saw Metér again, for the sailors had to abandon her when the sea ghosts came.

The sea ghosts rose out of the sea and their bodies were fishes, shaped into the form of a man, and their weapons were swordfish and they fired stone-fish onto the deck, and one of the sailors fell badly ill and his leg was amputated when they got to Queensland; he had gangrene. The sailors shot into the waves but they could not hurt the vui, and the sharks circled the ship and the water churned foamy-white and hot, like an oncoming fever.

But Metér was safe then, and he came to her, and held her hand in the dark, and let drop the stone; and his shark departed, and the sea ghosts sank back into the sea. The captain swore and shouted and cursed the rocks and the sharks as though he could not see the ghosts at all, and his men were frightened, and the prisoners were allowed back into the hold and were not disturbed. And he had spent that night with Metér, who lay against him in the darkness of the hold and was herself as hot as the ocean and as deep, and he had felt like a man who had gone too long and too far into the sea in a canoe and could no longer find his way back.

"Angkel? Yu save gerap?" It is his niece, shaking him awake, and the old man stirs, and for a moment feels himself a bird, light-boned, filled with air, as insubstantial as a vui. "Yes," he says, "I was only resting a moment." His niece nods, and there is something in her eyes, like a sadness, but luckily it is gone too quickly. "Bae mi karem kakai long yu," she says, and she goes, and returns with food, a plate of rice and a boiled yam and two white-fish boiled in coconut milk, and he eats.

In Queensland there was plenty of rice, and there was the meat of buluk, red and heavy, which he had tasted a few times, and always there were the sugar canes, and they had seemed a great delicacy to him then, and more than that he remembers Metér's love for them, the way she would peel the bark off the cane and

LAVIE TIDHAR

drink the juice inside and spit out the remains, and she laughed as she did it. Once there was a dance, and she wore a European dress and he a European suit of clothes, and they danced the Europeans' way. He had a polished cane of dark, rich wood, and he twirled it and wore a hat tilted at an angle, and she laughed; she was barefoot in the dress and tall, and her hair was a rich yellow like the sun, and they danced a long time under the electric lights. The overseers worked them hard, but there were other white people, like missionaries, or if not olsem exactly then semak lelebet, who came to look at them and to make sure they were not abused, or not too much, at any rate, and to teach them about their god Jesus, who could save their immortal souls, if only they repented from their heathen ways and accepted him.

It seemed easy enough to do, and many took it on with enthusiasm. You could get many things that way, like shoes, and many people wanted guns, too, which they could take back to their islands and fight their neighbors with, who would be bound to try and steal their lands if they did not return. Many of the Europeans were glad to sell them, and the overseers were happy to give them in payment when the workers left. When he was only a boy, his father had taken him to the land of the great waterfall in the west of Vanua Lava, where they had family, too, and there they took a canoe and came to a small landing and hiked a short distance through the bush and came to a cave, dry and secluded and sloping down into the rock, and there he saw many skulls, which had once belonged to their enemies.

"Do they still have them?" he says, not realizing he is speaking aloud, and his nephew looks startled for a moment and says, "Have what?"

"The skulls in the cave. Did I take you there once?"

"I took some tourists there last week," his nephew says, "for the festival. They have a festival there now, once a year. There are many kastom dances, and string bands. I bin gat plante plante kava—" and he grins, for his nephew is a pikinini blong kava, one who likes to drink until he is drunk. Many nights he returns from the nakamal, weaving a makeshift snake dance as he walks, and when he arrives he lies down on a mat outside, where he sleeps.

116

But the old man doesn't say this and asks only, "Did you go to the cave?"

But his nephew is not interested in old skulls, and he shrugs and says, "The tourists went. But there are few skulls left. Men have been throwing them into the sea, and making plaeplae we-tem. Now the chief keeps them somewhere else and only puts them back when the tourists come."

The old man sighs, but a part of him is happy. For they have no guns now, beyond the few muskets used for shooting flying fox, and there is no war in the islands, and the people are peaceful, though there are so few of them now, so fewer than there had been before. The waetman's sickness had killed many, too many, more than guns could ever kill.

When the sickness came to the camp, it came swiftly and with-out mercy, and the waetman blong Jesus stopped coming, too, for they were afraid despite their god. At first it was nothing, a mere irritation, and then one and then another man fell sick and couldn't work, and they were afraid. Many died, and their bodies were burned, but he was well and did not know why. He lived with Metér then, as husband and wife, and their nights were happy, and she was become thick with child, which the overseers didn't like.

When she became ill, he was angry, though it shamed him to feel it. He was angry at her for being weak, and for succumbing to the sickness, though he knew that was wrong. He sought a klever, a man of kastom medicine, and together they searched hard for the leaves that might help her body struggle, and he danced for her, with the other men, and he even prayed, to the god of the waet-man, but the sickness had taken so many, and was too strong, and Metér stopped working and lay in their hut and didn't eat. He sat with her, and told her of their island, of Vanua Lava, and said that when she was better they would go back and build a house at San-ara, and eat fish and lobster every day, and have many children, and he thought it made her happy. Her face eased when he spoke, but perhaps it was just on hearing his voice.

She died one afternoon and he wasn't there, for the men were few now and had to work harder even than before, and so she died alone and was burned with the rest.

That night he tried to follow her, remembering his father's words, and he drank kava with the men in the nasara until it sent him to a drugged sleep, and then he flew away from the plantation in the shape of an owl, flew away from Queensland and the waetman's bigfala aelan and across the sea and over Tanna, Efata, Malekulah, and Gaua, until he reached Vanua Lava at last and saw in the distance one hill shining with a pure white light and knew it was Surevuvu, the meeting field.

When he landed there, he changed back into a man, and the hill was full of people. He wandered amongst them, and some welcomed him as a friend and some shied away from him, and some seemed not to know he was there.

He called her name.

He wandered through the hill of the dead and sang out her name, calling Metér, Metér, but he could not find her. He saw the moon rising and falling over the sea and once, in the distance, strange men oli no blong ples ia, with slanted haunted eyes and unknown uniforms, who seemed lost and silent here.

He felt the pull of the sun and knew the day would soon come and that he must return, but yet he persisted, calling out her name, walking Surevuvu as if he himself was a vui, and at last he found her.

She was standing alone on a ridge and looked east, toward Mosina and the small island, Lenoh, that lies off it, close to where Sanara lies. Her hair was as tawny as he remembered it, her eyes as dark, but there was no laughter in her anymore, not then, and they didn't speak.

She tried to hold his hand, but her hand passed through his, as insubstantial as ocean foam, and as the sun rose he changed back into an owl and raced away and took only that memory of her with him.

He had lived a good life. When he returned to the island he married a good woman, wan woman Mota, from the hat-shaped island across from Vanua Lava, and they had children and had been happy. But sometimes he remembers that night when the air was full of sound and she was dancing in her dress, and her bare feet moved across the packed-earth ground as if stamping them into solidity, and on those nights he thinks of Sanara, and of standing on the rocks catching fish when he was young. He had wanted to take her there with him, but he never did.

Living in Vanuatu means having to accept two worlds existing at once: the everyday and the fantastic. In the sea where you fish there are also shark-familiars, and in the forest where you might go gather wild yams also live the uturgurgur, the little people of the bush. Rocks are really legendary beings and objects, frozen into the landscape: the great snake of Sola is now a hill where the Anglican diocese stands, and the black rocks off the coast are Qat's canoe. Men talk matter-of-factly of sorcerous battles carried on in dreams, of people changing into the shapes of animals, of curses being laid and warded. The spirits of the ancestors still gather at the great volcano of Gaua island and on Surevuvu, the hill of the dead on Vanua Lava. Everything in this story is true. Which is to say, it is woven from the stories that still shape life, daily, on those remote Pacific islands where clouds obscure volcanoes and children shoot at fish with bows and arrows, where tabu sticks can still be found in the sand and men measure worth by their rank in the suqwe, the secret societies of the islands. Life and *storian*—the art of telling stories—can't be separated in Vanuatu. Nor should they.

To research this story I climbed volcanoes, traveled in boats through stormy seas, talked to people in hushed, smoky *nakamals*, and once stood on the beach in Sanara, where shoes still float onto the sand. This is a story. This really happened. Or at least, it might have . . .

Lavie Tidhar

Interviews After the Revolution

Brian Francis Slattery

Charles Patrice Hodges, entrepreneur: The swifts gave me the idea, there in the narrow streets of the old city at the top of the hill, overlooking the bay. It was the way the birds rocketed around the houses and through the alleys, through the ruins of the church at the summit. I stood there in the dirt streets as the sun was going down, and I put out my arms, and I swear the swifts all swarmed around me. Like I was at the center of a whirlwind.

Anastasia Godunov, project manager, SMQ Investments International: We lost track of him for three days, and thought the worst. Stood around the doorway of the hotel near the shore, waiting for a ransom note. Two million, maybe? But then he just appeared, a million little scratches on his skin. Rats? I said. No, he said. Birds. And he wanted to invest in San Marco. What do you have in mind, I said. I was thinking a textile mill, shipbuilding maybe. [*Laughs.*] A party, he said. But San Marco already has a nightclub, I said [*the Good Foot—ed.*], this rickety place built right into the seawall that they'd hollowed out the first floor of, had apartments above it. It was packed every night but flooded once a month. Charles laughed. No, no, he said, a *big* party. The glammest the world's ever seen. I said to him, you realize this country's in the middle of a civil war? He shrugged. Wars end, he said.

Hodges: The party circuit needed a new destination, and I saw a massive business opportunity in San Marco. The city was so beautiful, so undiscovered. The price of real estate was unbelievable. All it needed was the facility—a spectacular building, a destination within a destination. A hotel, a club, a resort, an everything, put together in one place. So I bought land, see? All along the top of the hill overlooking the city and the ocean. These old places, most of them didn't even have glass in the windows, but people lived in them all the same. Sleeping in chipping plaster, covered in dust. Terrible conditions.

Godunov: They were refugees, I think. From the war.

Hodges: When the war ended, I gave them all jobs tearing the buildings down, until there was just the old church at the top and those twisting streets. It looked like a map of the city up there for a while. And I waited, and the sun started to go down, and the swifts were there again, funneling into the church steeple. I broke ground for the palace the next month.

Q: Ms. Godunov, did you get any other investments in development projects that year?

Godunov: No. Too risky, everyone said. [*Pause.*] I have to impress upon you just what kind of a place San Marco was. And still is. It had two heydays—two more than most places get—the first one four hundred years ago, the second maybe seventy-five years ago. Everything that was built was built then, and in between, there was no money to keep them up. So the buildings are covered in moss, dripping wet, and vines crawl all over and crack walls, sidewalks, streets. The San Marcans like to say that the jungle outside the city has been trying to eat them for five centuries, but it can't finish its dinner because the San Marcans are too bitter.

Hodges: In the spring, the whole town bursts into bloom, a hundred species of flowers, and swarms with birds and insects. It's marvelous.

Godunov: But the poverty. I can't tell you. San Marco is and always was a working port, so it wasn't as bad off as other places. But the murder rate there was the highest in the country, even in peacetime. Drug runners and other smugglers. Prostitution. Extortion rings of various kinds. They used to say that San Marco was the other capital, for the other government, the people in the black market. And then during the fighting—

Hodges: The town never got hit when I was there.

Godunov: There was a local joke about that, too: they said it was because nobody wanted the place. And they didn't. Until you built your palace. Everything in San Marco changed after that.

Q: For better or for worse?

Godunov: [*Pause.*] It's more complicated than that.

* * *

Pato Rochereau Paraguana: My brother, Pedro, was born on the floor of our apartment. That was when we lived above the Good Foot. It was three-thirty on a Saturday morning when my mother pushed him out. Downstairs in the club, my father used to say, there was a band playing with twenty drummers, two basses, two guitars. Big horn section, lots of singers. It was some party down there. My mother said that my brother didn't cry once. He just hit the floor, put his ear against it, and started taking it all in right then. The band, the cheers from the crowd, the stomping feet against the club's floor. He never cried. But never slept either. Just listened and listened.

Q: So you knew he'd be a musician early?

Paraguana: From birth.

Q: How did you become a fisherman?

Paraguana: A bet. Nothing else to do. School and I, we never shook hands. I was on my first boat by the time I was sixteen. Pedro was in his first band when he was six.

Q: What did he play?

Paraguana: Whatever they asked him to.

Oroyo Batide, bass player, the Silver Diablos: He could play bass, drums, guitar, guitarrón, requinto, mbira, banjo, violin. Some trombone. And he could sing. You've heard the bootlegs. So you know. I had only been playing a year when I met him. He was seventeen already. He heard me playing in a *vale callampa* band—a very bad one—and asked me to play with him instead. I knew who he was. We all did. Why do you want me to play with you? I said. I don't understand what you do. And he took both of my hands in his and said, these do.

Buto Longo, drummer, the Silver Diablos: We practiced together above the Good Foot for a few weeks. That was all. Then we played the Good Foot. They invited us back, and we played there, oh, many times. Soon we had gigs all over the place, in the towns all around here, in the capital. That was when the war was still on, before the peace accords. There were firefights in the jungle, militias going up and down the highway, ambushing each other, and here were us three musicians in a little green truck with all our gear in the back, trying to make a living. The things we saw on the road. [*Shakes head.*] I could tell you some stories. We came across roadblocks all the time. Sometimes they took all the money we'd just made. Sometimes they threatened to take our instruments, but somehow Pedro always talked them out of it. We were just kids, though sometimes the fighters were younger than we were. They'd put the barrels of their guns right in our faces. You could see the rifling on the inside. [*Pause.*] We should have all been dead a long time ago.

Q: When did you first hear the name of Charles Patrice Hodges?

Batide: Who? [*Laughs.*]

Paraguana: Right after the peace accords. A month or two after, maybe. They brought in big yellow wrecking machines and just razed the top of the hill. I thought the war was over, I remember thinking. Why are they destroying the city now? Then they started bringing in all this . . . metal and plastic, by the truckload, by the shipload. So many ships. Some days, we had to stay out to sea. One day, a third of our catch rotted in the hold. But when our captain complained, they [*Hodges Enterprises—ed.*] paid us for it anyway. The captain came back, shaking his head and laughing. We ought to catch rot more often, he said.

Hodges: The metal and plaster was what E.G. Saro [*architect of Apus Apus—ed.*] had called for. They really built the building in Malaysia, I think, then took it down again and brought it over piece by piece and fit it all together in San Marco. Those soaring wings—I had told Saro about the swifts, you see—came off the boat already in flight. Apus Apus was up in a week. It was marvelous.

Longo: But then for the first nine months, it was dark.

Celine Newton, general manager, Apus Apus: There were, how to put this, numerous unforeseen obstacles to creating a destination like Apus Apus in a place like San Marco. For starters, there was no beach to speak of, and I told Mr. Hodges that he'd best make one before the first party if he hoped to have another one there after that. Within days it was also clear that we would need our own power supply. Food was a nightmare, at first. The people at Development International were concerned, they said, that we weren't creating sufficient sustainable employment for the San Marcan community. I told them if they wanted us to create something sustainable, they could start by having someone grow some fresh basil. I know how uncharitable that sounds. But I don't get paid to be charitable, and, frankly, I don't think people like being treated charitably. Which is why I disagreed so much with the way that Mister Hodges dealt with people there. They didn't want handouts. They wanted jobs.

Masashi Shimura, relief worker, Global Crisis Response: I don't think the Apus Apus folks ever understood how dangerous the situation really was. It was common knowledge that the only reason the rebels signed the peace accords was because they ran out of bullets. There were rumors that the army had bombs planted all over San Marco, and if it ever looked like the rebels were going to take the place, they'd just blow the whole city up. Nobody ever found any bombs after the accords, but a lot of people here still think that's because the army just hid them really well, and now they're all still here, ready to go off. If Miss Newton had ever gone to a party at the Good Foot, she would have understood a little better, I think. In that place, people say they dance like they're going to die tomorrow. Because the next day, a couple of them always do.

Longo: [*Laughs.*] You know, all of these people—the government people, the aid and relief workers—they mean well, they really do. I know that. But whenever they want to talk about how dangerous it was, they always put a story in our mouths. San Marcans say this. San Marcans say that. I'm not saying they're liars. Maybe someone told them those things once. But I never say any of those things, and I don't know anyone who does. I also don't think San Marco has ever been as dangerous as they say. You just have to know who to stay away from. Who not to look at. But it's not hard to learn those things. [*Pause.*] I think they see what they want to see. They make up the story they want to tell. But who doesn't?

Q: What was the first party at Apus Apus like?

Batide: Like an invasion. They had lights on the outside walls; searchlights sweeping the sky, back and forth; and this throbbing dance music going boom, boom, boom. [*Accents with fist.*] The speakers they must have run the sound through, I never got a good look at them, but they must have been something. Then a flock of helicopters flew over the city, a fleet of ships landed in the harbor, and the people on them were driven up in jeeps with fresh coats of red and white paint. More jeeps came down the highway from the capital, same new paint job. They were all in by midnight, and then Apus Apus really lit up. My mother watched the whole thing from the roof of our house. Is the war on again? she said. I said no, it's just a big party. And she gave me this look, and I could tell she was wondering what the difference was.

Longo: Nobody thought it would be like that. The size of it, and how long it lasted.

Batide: Looked like fun.

Hodges: Yes, the first party was a massive success, a full week of the best music I could buy, the best food, the best accommodations, for a few thousand people. A small village. It got a little out of hand, you know, the way it's supposed to. More people started coming on the third day, after word got around that the party was good.

Q: Where did the people come from?

Hodges: Everywhere. Tokyo. Shanghai. Singapore. Bratislava. Johannesburg. Buenos Aires. São Paulo. They couldn't have all stayed at Apus Apus, I don't think. Though I don't know where they stayed if they didn't.

Batide: We saw them sleeping on the street in the morning, or in the black sand on the shore, looking like they fell out of the sky with their bright clothes and dirt on their knees. Or they'd wander around town, so altered they didn't know they'd left the party. I remember one of them stopped me and asked where the beds were. I pointed back up the hill, and he said—really, my English isn't good, but I'm pretty sure he said thank you, Purple Walrus. And made a motion in the air like he was shaking a tusk.

Alfonse Guerrera Machado, former mayor of San Marco: Of course there were robberies the first year. People taking advantage. I tried to warn the manager that would happen, but either she didn't believe me or she lost control of the situation, or maybe let it get out of control. But then the second year, there was much less crime. And the third and fourth years, almost none at all.

Paraguana: Well, the crime went down because Apus Apus started paying people more not to mug the partiers than they'd ever get by mugging them.

Q: How did they know who'd been doing the mugging?

Paraguana: They had their own security force, lots of cameras. Which was how they caught us later. Anyway, some of the seediest people in San Marco started showing up in the banks with checks from Apus Apus. I don't know whether to cash it or frame it, one of them said, but of course he cashed it. You could always tell who'd tapped the Hodges fortune. New cars, fancy clothes. An expensive wedding. Other things, too. Lots more smuggling boats coming into the harbor a couple of weeks before the parties. Someone else bought up some jungle not far out of the city, cleared it, and started growing . . . basil, I think. All I know is that all that money wasn't making the fish come any closer. But the paying people not to rob—that was what gave my brother his big idea, though he would never have guessed how big it would turn out to be. He might still not even know.

Q: You don't think he knows what happened here?

Paraguana: My personal opinion? No. If anyone even reported it, wherever he is, I doubt he read about it.

Q: You sound envious.

Paraguana: [*Pause.*] Sometimes I feel like I'm walking backward all the time, always looking at what happened years ago. To this country. To our parents. My brother never fell for that. He just worked with what was right in front of him, what he could put his hands on. And I think that's how he got out, while the rest of us are still here.

～

Batide: All Pedro wanted was a gig. He was hoping for a set a day, but he would have settled for less. On the dance floor if they wanted, or in one of the bars or lounges. By the pool. Anywhere at all. I told him it was a bad idea. They're not interested in our music, I said. If they were, they would have hired us by now. Because Pedro really was the best at what he did. I saw other guitarists put away their instruments when they saw him walk through the door. Three or four younger musicians, teenagers, followed him around town, staring at his hands. Too afraid to talk to him. He was a hero to them, or a ghost. Something unreal.

Newton: I know that Pedro Paraguana came to visit me, but in all honesty, I can't remember talking to him. I've had to look at the security tapes to see what happened. He looked to me like the men who worked at the pier, except skinnier and quieter, and he had a beat-up old guitar case with a broken handle, held shut by a piece of rope, that he was carrying under one arm. He had a stammer. What do you play? I said. San Marcan music, he said. And I said, yes, like what they play at the Good Foot. That's right, he said. I play there all the time. I'm not sure we're the right place for you, I said, but if you have a recording, I would love to hear it. He said he didn't have a recording, and he started to get out his guitar. I must have said something disparaging then, or maybe the look on my face was enough, because then he got very quiet, and he tied the rope around the case again and patted it, saying it's okay, it's okay. As though it was his child.

Batide: After the peace accords, things got so bad. A lot of the people with money left the country, and *pffft,* there went the parties we used to play in the capital. The weddings, the holidays. Just like that. We sold the truck to buy strings and fix a crack in the back of Pedro's guitar.

Q: Did you still play?

Batide: Oh, all the time. There just wasn't any money in it anymore. But I don't think Pedro could have stopped playing if he wanted to, and we didn't want to stop playing with him. There was something in his music, something you couldn't destroy. And the worse things got, the happier the music became. [*Pause.*] I miss him so much.

Longo: But money is money, and Pedro is no fool. He knew how much Apus Apus could give away just to keep people pacified, and he figured that the people who came to the parties probably had a lot more than that. But it wasn't just the money. I believe to this day that if Apus Apus had given Pedro Paraguana that gig, none of what happened would have happened. What else could have been the signal?

Shimura: There's no question that what Pedro Paraguana and the Silver Diablos did started everything. And on the other hand, you could argue that if that's all it took, then anything at all could have triggered it. Anyone who was there at the time could see it. A quarter of the ships coming into San Marco were carrying guns, and they weren't for the army. There were rumors—more than rumors—that the rebels were training again, in the jungle where the government helicopters couldn't see. Every other night at the Good Foot something seemed to go down, a lot of money moving around, people shaking hands. Now and again, someone getting shot in the back of the head. People said they were rooting out traitors early, not that the police ever found any evidence. Oh, they investigated, but it always ended in nothing. Or a detective would get shot, and that was it.

Q: What about the army?

Shimura: [*Pause.*] Let me tell you something. I worked in the clinic in San Marco near the water, and I was involved in knife fights and shootouts. I saw a man almost beaten to death with a hammer. But I never felt more unsafe than I did when the army showed up.

Q: So given the choice between the rebels and the army—

Shimura: Look, I just worked in the clinic there. I'll be back there again in a couple of months. I treated the sick and the hurt; I didn't ask what their politics were. It wasn't in my job description. But to be unaware of what the different sides meant for my safety and the safety of most of the people in San Marco, who just wanted to get through it—to not know it or act on it would have been naive, bordering on stupid. You don't get involved, but you don't stay out, either. And you never give a straight answer if you want to get home.

Q: Did you know the rebels were moving guns through San Marco in the Apus Apus days?

Machado: [*Pause.*] Turn that recorder off, and I'll tell you some stories. [*Laughs.*] I'm not an idiot, and I know that politics don't follow the laws of physics. But sometimes they do. You have a balloon full of hydrogen and a match. What do you think is going to happen?

Batide: Pedro first told me about his idea after a gig at the Good Foot. I thought he was joking, but he wasn't laughing. We haven't really had a decent gig in six months, he said. Six months isn't so bad, I said, though Pedro could tell I was listening, that I needed the money. Then he said, if we do this, we can make enough for the next six years. All we have to do is disappear for a while, meet somewhere else, far away, and we can play what we want to.

Longo: I thought it was a great idea. The only trick was what to do afterward. You had to take the money and then disappear from San Marco, never see the piers and the boats, or the Good Foot, again. Not so hard a trick, you say. But we're all San Marco boys. Which is why Batide and I ended up in jail, then back here worth nothing, and we haven't seen Pedro Paraguana in ten years.

Paraguana: My brother was so quiet about it, I didn't know what he was planning. I didn't see him bring in the uniforms or the guns. He must have done it in his guitar case. But then, two days

read in the papers, never on what the plac
saying that the papers made anything up
the crime way out of proportion, and it al
people commented on it, because many of
elsewhere, and isn't it just as true there? If
paper in any city, you would never go. If yo
never leave the house. But the same peopl
own papers with skepticism were complete
read the news from San Marco. It just did

Hodges: But everything was beautiful whe
really was. The people, the clothes, the m
birds, as always, under the lights in that
like I've never felt anywhere else. I have p
can remember the colors of it, the motion.
remember the way the food tasted, or the
sounded. In my head, it's something rarifie
fect. I was heartbroken at what happened t

Newton: What was considered to be the bes
was on the stage, halfway through their
phone started in on its panic ring—which h
til then. But before I could even answer it, t
and there were four men with rubber mask
machine guns in among the musicians. Thr
just strutting around the stage. The fourth
singer's back and was whispering in his ear.
fessional even under such circumstances—s

Jeremy Goddard, singer: I said, the armed
says that he and his compatriots are represe
Revolutionary Front of San Marco and now
annexed to their territory. As we speak, reb
city and will defend it to the death. It is th
you leave your valuables on the ground in fr
from the country as quickly as possible, lest y
of the new regime. [*Laughs.*] Or something li

before, he took me out to the Good Foot and said the drinks were on him, which he'd never done in his life. Then he told me that he loved me, and he'd always respected what I did—being a fisherman, he meant. He said he was almost a little afraid of it, because I did something that fed people, and what did he do? Make noise. You can't feed people on noise, he said. Then he told me about his plan. Did I want in. I said yes without thinking. We had to help each other home afterward, and all I can remember is me lying in bed, and him in the next room playing guitar and singing to himself, and the window open and the sounds in the harbor coming in, the waves against the shore. I haven't slept like that since.

Godunov: It's not news how controversial Apus Apus was from the beginning, even before the news got out about how the city had helped Mr. Hodges buy the land. I know the San Marcans always said that Hodges could have done more. But they never talked about what Hodges did do. The commerce—legitimate commerce—he brought to the port, freight and passengers. Additional income for local farmers.

Q: But Apus Apus never hired anyone from San Marco to work inside the facility, where the money was.

Godunov: We and the development people talked to Mr. Hodges about that many times. But you have to understand, also. He needed people with significant experience in the high-end hospitality industry, no, don't interrupt, because I know what you're going to say: couldn't he have trained San Marcans to do the work? The answer is obvious: yes. But to me, Apus Apus never quite realized its enormous potential. It ran, what, five years? And not full-time. That's just enough time for a venture like that to figure out where the bathroom is. I think if Apus Apus had lasted ten years, fifteen, twenty, you would have seen local training and employment, community projects, infrastructure improvements, maybe some social services. But people can't wait that long. Not that I blame

them, but that's where the tragedy lies.
great, and the remedy takes so long.

Newton: I remember that last party being t
ing at the books, I know it wasn't. Ther
fewer people at it than there'd been at the
band. Which meant fewer support staff.
tered. All the way down the line. Perhaps i
in my mind because it was the hardest to pu
appearing. Trucks from the capital bringin
things—linens, liquor—kept being held up
more than before. A few of the trucks vani
right there, but it wasn't any better. I unde
the rebels, making a last sweep before the
time, it was just a logistical nightmare. In
ing our own planes, our own helicopters,
expensive items we needed. [*Pause.*] You kr
that this one was going to be a real loss. It's
said, in that quasi-mystical way of his. He
the party. Honestly, I don't know how he ev
ful. They always call him a visionary busir
of the visionary, but not much of the busi
you can imagine that we were very worried
guests to and from the facility without then
put this, pieces of their persons. If I had to c
have demanded big raises, for me and my st
in San Marco, of course, the strength of our
ing what it was. But for us to go back home
before the whole thing started, about a do:
Have you been reading the paper? they said.
they're saying about San Marco? They descr:
phone. Sounds like every other piece I've rea
wanted to say, but I'd already lost them as cli
would have said might have tarnished the bra

I do have to say that I always thought Sar
was never quite deserved. It was all based or
because I know you're a journalist, but it was a

Newton: One of them fired his rifle into the ceiling, then leveled it at the crowd. Well. I've never seen so much money and jewelry hit the floor at once. Not just that. Shoes, watches, sunglasses. And the sound it all made, this long rustling slide. Like chains falling onto the floor.

Goddard: Then the other three went running through the crowd, collecting it all in big plastic bags. I remember one of them took a pair of shoes, tied them around his arm. The one with the gun on me stood right where he was. And when nobody was looking—nobody believes me when I tell them this, but he leaned in and said, in very hesitant English, I love your singing.

Q: What did you say?

Goddard: Thanks. [*Laughs.*]

Newton: They were gone in ten minutes, and after that, Apus Apus was in complete chaos, there's a war starting, there's a war starting. [*Pause.*] It was kind of genius, I think, the way they played the crowd. Played to their fears and insecurities about where they were. The people who came to that last party, I think, were ready to believe that the whole country was ready to blow. They were primed. All those four did was spark them off. But I was skeptical even then. It didn't look right. The guns were real, the clothes, even the masks. But if there really was a war on, why were there only four of them? I knew from the beginning it was all a hoax, and for what? six or seven hours? that's what it was. Then, all of a sudden, it wasn't.

Rodrigo Vincente, minister of commerce, former unit leader in the Southern Liberation Front: Preparations to continue fighting in earnest had been underway for quite some time. When the storming of Apus Apus occurred, we had standing units across the country, arms and stockpiles, and there had been discussions among the leaders of the units as to when the best time to attack would be. We had agreed it would be in the next few months, and that we should all attack together, but there were no details worked out—well, not that I knew. You have to understand that communication among the units was quite poor. It had to be sporadic to avoid detection, and there were serious technical problems with the equipment we were using. It was always breaking down, and the messages that did get through were often garbled. Orders were unclear. It felt as though we were pieces in a game, being moved around, and we could not understand the rules or see who was doing the moving. [*Pause.*] We were in the jungle about sixty kilometers from San Marco, in command of two hundred men, and we had heard nothing for four days. So we sat there under the trees, sweating in the rain, arguing over whether it was quiet because there were no orders, or because ours or someone else's radio was broken. Then the news came that revolutionaries had attacked Apus Apus, and we figured that there must have been orders to move. So we radioed to . . . I don't know, at least seven other units that we were moving, too. Other units must have done the same thing, but it's hard to be sure. What is clear is that the revolution began that night. But we learned how it had really started only later.

Q: Did you know what happened?

Batide: No, no. Once we were out of Apus Apus, we just got down to the docks as fast as we could and got on a boat out of the country.

Q: Who was on the boat?

Longo: Batide, myself, and the two Paraguana brothers.

Batide: And what turned out to be enough cash and high-end merchandise to live off of for a long time. We all could have started very comfortable lives, and at the time, I think we all thought we could do it. When we got to Mumbai, we all just shook hands and made plans to reunite in the same place in a year, after our trail was cold. But we couldn't do it. Three of us were back here within the year.

Longo: Where was I going to go? I was back in four months, and Pedro's brother was already here, working the docks, though he was calling in sick a lot. That was a flimsy cover. At least I hadn't had a job when I left, so nobody thought it was weird that I was sitting around doing nothing, though they did wonder where I'd gone. Then Batide showed up a couple of weeks later. Just came up and knocked on the door. I knew you'd be back already, he said. Then we sat and waited for Pedro. And here we are. Still waiting.

Q: When did you realize what had happened while you were gone?

Batide: The day I got back, when I asked why there were so many holes in the buildings. The people in the Good Foot looked at me like I was a moron. Where have you been? There was a revolution, man. For two months. No way, I said. Who started it? [*Pause.*] When they told me, I went home and threw up.

Vincente: Would the revolution have occurred if there had been no takeover of Apus Apus? Probably. But would the revolution had gone as it did? With such energy and enthusiasm? I'm not so sure. There was something iconic about what they did, storming the playground of the lords of global commerce, that said what we wanted to say. Blurry lines came into focus, and the image was so indelible that even after we found out that the people in San Marco hadn't been revolutionaries at all—just three poor musicians and a fisherman—it lost none of its clarity. It's possible that the symbol they created is one of the key reasons that the revolution was successful.

It is ironic that, had they been true revolutionaries, they would have been granted amnesty, but because they were thieves, they ended up with five years in prison apiece and their assets taken away.

Q: Couldn't you have given them amnesty, as well?

Vincente: Well. As you might imagine, both Hodges and his clients were unhappy about what they'd done. And Apus Apus had them on security camera, did some investigating afterward, noted their disappearances and reappearances. Then looked into their finances. It was enough to bring them to trial. You must realize, between the four of them, they really did abscond with assets worth a great deal of money. But I realize you're asking the larger question here. [*Pause.*] Before you are in power, nothing gets you in faster than denouncing the lords of commerce. But once you are in power, you understand, all at once, that it is all far more complicated even than you thought it would be when you thought it would be complicated. You realize that you must deal with them. You must compromise. It doesn't have to invalidate the things you said to get into power, though—just as the symbolic value of what the four of them did is not diminished by knowing why they did it.

Q: Even though Pedro Paraguana wasn't ideologically motivated.

Vincente: On the contrary. It may be exactly what makes the symbol so powerful.

Batide: We have a standing gig at the Good Foot now, me and Longo. The house rhythm section. We back up singers, guitar players, horn players. But really, we're still playing with Pedro, still bouncing off the way he put down a beat. No matter who's really in front of us, all we see at the microphone, all we hear through the speakers, is him.

Paraguana: The town government says they're going to put up a statue of my brother on the shore, facing the city, a guitar in one hand, a gun in the other. Something stupid like that. I understand why they want to do it. He's a convenient hero. But if he were here now, he'd never have a gun. Just the guitar. And sometimes I wonder, if he were to knock on the mayor's door today, would the mayor give him a place to play?

Q: Where do you think Pedro is now?

Longo: I have no idea. He must have gone back to Mumbai a year after we got there, expecting to find us, but we were already in prison by then. [*Pause.*] I keep expecting to hear him on the radio, or on an album from another country, a big star with a different name, singing in a different language, doing a different style of music, maybe playing a different instrument. But I would recognize him instantly, I'm sure of it. He couldn't hide from me or from Batide. Or from his brother. [*Laughs.*] We would never give his secret away, even though that means we'll never play with him again.

Another part of me, though, thinks that wherever he is, he's living as he did here, when he was a kid. He probably plays in a local club somewhere with another band, and the people who hear him wonder why he isn't famous. They probably tell him he should go for it, start playing out in the big clubs in the big cities. And I imagine him smiling and nodding, and then going home and playing just for himself. I like to think that he plays the San Marcan music like we played it then. But I know that's just my nostalgia. Pedro Paraguana always seemed like a balloon to me, ready to float off into the sky. All he needed to do was cut the string. And he did.

Hodges: When the revolutionaries came into power, they offered to buy Apus Apus back from me. I'd heard there'd been some fighting there, that the place had been set on fire. There were questions as to how much it was all worth. So I went to see for myself. [*Pause.*] From the shore, the place looked tired, but not so different. As we got up closer, though, we started to see. Half the windows broken. Bullet holes in the plastic. Lots of things stripped off, light fixtures, wiring, carpeting, ceiling tiles, appliances in the kitchen. Somewhere in San Marco, a family of ten is making goat stew on one of the most expensive stoves in the world. There were already squatters there, many of them. Children playing handball in the dirt and glass in the courtyard. A cluster of tents and shacks around the swimming pool, which had been filled in with dirt, and they were growing vegetables in it. A total loss, we all agreed. I collected from insurance, then sold it to the government, and wrote off the losses. All in all, I believe I still came out ahead.

It was getting dark as we were leaving, and one of my lawyers looked out over the city and asked me why I'd built Apus Apus in the first place. He couldn't see what I saw in the place. But I looked up, and there they were, that swarm of swifts, pinwheeling overhead, funneling into the tower at the top of the complex. I don't even remember what I said to him. I just couldn't stop looking at them. They flew with such speed and grace. Almost violent. I think that every week, I still dream about them.

I'm one of those people who thinks that nothing is stranger than the truth. I like writing fiction, but when I do, I'm always a little annoyed by its formal constraints, and more than a little envious of those nonfiction writers who have found a story that blows the mind in a way fiction never quite can. Fiction, after all, must have a beginning, middle, and end, whereas nonfiction has no such limitations; to be compelling, fictional stories must be on some level plausible, whereas some of the best nonfiction stories are so good precisely because they are so implausible. It's irritating.

"Interviews after the Revolution" is the first story that I wrote to completion, threw away completely, and then wrote all over again from start to finish. I really liked the plot, which I would never have been able to work out except by writing a draft of it, but I had told it all wrong. Too many of the plot's elements were too implausible for fiction—but not, I realized, too implausible for nonfiction. Would the plot work better if I told it instead as an oral history? Having finished the story a second time, I still don't know; but I do know that using a nonfictional form opened up the story and the characters in a way that most written fictional forms don't allow, and allowed me, at last, to keep my own mouth shut.

Brian Francis Slattery

Count Poniatowski
and the Beautiful Chicken

Elizabeth Ziemska

My father wanted to write his memoirs, but he didn't have enough confidence in his English to pull it off on his own. He had come to this country in 1974; after thirty-five years he still had trouble with his pronouns and verb tenses. Nevertheless, he did not want to produce such a document in Polish. America is where my father met his second wife (finally, a soul mate), where my half-brother and sister were born. Feeling the need to record his life on paper quickly, he decided that I would become his amanuensis. The choice was obvious, as my father had agreed to subsidize my college education even though I insisted on studying comparative literature over the more practical engineering. He is the sort of man who likes to see a return on his investment.

We met over three consecutive weekends in July at a modest resort in the Catskills, my father dictating in Polish while I translated into English.

Before I tell you the story he told me about his encounter with Count Stanislas August Poniatowski, the last king of Poland, I need to explain a thing or two about my father. For the past three decades he had been working for the same engineering firm in Manhattan, until it was sold to a large multinational corporation. Not long after the merger, my father was deemed redundant. He found himself suddenly at home, alone (his wife worked, the kids were already out of the nest), with nothing to fill the next seven years before he reached retirement age, at which time he could allow himself to behave like a retiree.

My father repainted the apartment a calming shade of blue: the color of the sky the day he met his second wife while taking a stroll after Mass one September afternoon. A complete stranger to popular culture, he decided to educate himself by going to the movies every weekday afternoon, when the tickets were half price.

He read three newspapers each day, cover to cover. For a man who had been earning his living since he was sixteen, none of these activities could make him feel like a productive human being. He felt spellbound, worthless, miserable. Unbeknownst to his family, or even to himself, he began to search for a Great Deed.

One thing my father did enjoy was taking his lunch al fresco, a pleasure he hadn't had time for since childhood, when he and his brothers would take chunks of bread and cheese into the forest behind their grandfather's country house and pretend that they were woodland creatures. So it was that on a crisp, russet-hued fall day my father crossed Cabrini Boulevard heading toward Ft. Tryon Park, brown bag in hand, his head full of childhood memories, and was run down by a gunmetal gray Hummer H3.

The driver, a young German with a blond crew cut, could not have been more apologetic. He simply hadn't seen my father in his brown wool suit, camouflaged so perfectly among the dying autumn leaves of the tree-lined street. The unfortunate driver was articulate in his mortification over the accident, promising to pay for all medical expenses; all my father could hear was his German accent. And all he could think about, as he was strapped into a gurney and hoisted into the ambulance, was the day the Panzers rolled into Warsaw.

In the hospital where he stayed for two weeks while his bones knit, my father's already somber mood descended into melancholy retrospection. Why had he survived the accident? Was it a coincidence that the driver was German? Was it some sort of sign? Although he had worked hard his entire life, was his real work about to begin? He made a mental inventory of his accomplishments. Immigrating to a new country: check. Successfully raising not one, but two, families: check (though if he were entirely honest with himself, one more successfully than the other). Building a career in his profession (as opposed to driving a cab, or running a candy store, as many other immigrants must do to survive): check. Were these enough to constitute a successful life? Surely there were other things he could have done, could still do, now that he had been spared, once again. Every night before he fell asleep, he tried to work on a list of future accomplishments, but he could never get beyond item number one. The youngest of five brothers, my father was just three years old when Germany invaded Poland on September 1, 1939, but he remembered with great clarity the day his family hid in the basement of their apartment building. Polish fighters had managed to keep the Germans out of Warsaw for eleven days of a siege before they ran out of supplies. Panzers broke through fortifications and rolled down the streets while German soldiers swarmed the city, going door to door, looking for Polish soldiers hiding among the civilian population.

My father's oldest brother was at the age when little boys fall in love with war. In the family's rush to get downstairs, no one noticed that he had brought his favorite hat into the basement, the one that superficially resembled the square *czapka* with the scarlet band of the *Zandarmeria*, the Polish Military Police. When the gunshots, the screams, and the smoke had cleared, the Germans discovered that their fugitive Polish soldier was just a ten-year-old boy.

Out of the hospital and recuperating in his tranquil blue apartment, my father took his pain pills and reviewed what he knew about the sequence of events from the German invasion of September 1, 1939, to the partition of Poland, just one month later, by Germany and the Soviet Union. He confirmed that nothing could have been done in those thirty-odd days to prevent his brother's death. Really and truly the only way to undo that past event was to prevent World War II, the first and only item on his To Do list.

My father is an engineer, not a historian. He spent six months at the Tennessee Valley Authority Reactor Facility, reworking the electrical grid to harvest the nuclear energy more efficiently. He can track the path of an electrical current through conductors and resistors. He understands the laws of cause and effect. He was convinced that there was a specific moment, a *prima mobile* in the timeline of Polish history that was responsible for the sequence of events that occurred in the basement of his childhood apartment building. He started reading history books. It was not long before he found what he was looking for.

～

Between 1764 and 1795, Stanislas August Poniatowski was King of the Most Serene Republic of the Two Peoples, also known as the Commonwealth of Poland and Lithuania. The official motto of his kingdom: *Si Deus Nobiscum quis contra nos?* (If God is with us, then who is against us?). Sadly, God could not protect Poland from its aggressive neighbors, Prussia, Austria, and Russia. As it turns out, King Poniatowski was little more than a puppet, having been forced onto the throne, against the wishes of the Polish nobility, by his former lover, Catherine the Great of Russia, who then virtually controlled the country. The one and only independent (one might say, rebellious) act of his reign was the brilliant speech he made upon the adoption of the new Polish Constitution of May 3, 1791, a constitution written and ratified without the approval of King Poniatowski's puppeteers. What happened next was the *prima mobile,* and my father was sincerely convinced that if he could make Poniatowski retrace his steps of the night of May 3, 1791, he could change the course of Polish history, and thereby change the history of Europe, and thereby bring his brother back from the dead. How to make a king take counsel from a humble engineer?

I had no idea what was going on inside my father's head when finally I convinced him to spend a few days with me and my husband in sunny Los Angeles. I remembered from growing up in New York how bad it got by February, when the charming snowdrifts left over from the Christmas holidays turned into sooty hills and valleys dotted with frozen dog shit, extremely treacherous terrain for a fifty-nine-year-old man on crutches.

As soon as I saw my father at the airport, I could tell that something was troubling him besides the weather and his leg.

It was the lack of purpose that got him down, I rationalized, a temporary depression brought on by the early retirement. Had I known that he was revising mental blueprints for a fantastical contraption he had once made me, I would have marveled at the coincidence of taking him to see the Überorgan at the Getty.

When I was ten years old, and my parents still had one good year left on their marriage, my father built me a beautiful little windmill.

It was science fair time again at my school; this year I was determined to win first place. With the help of World Book Encyclopedia (birthday present), I created a self-sustaining environment by filling a Ball jar with water, snails, and aquatic plants. The plants were supposed to feed the snails, and the poop from the snails was supposed to feed the plants. It was simple and elegant, but it only got me an honorable mention. I vowed to do better the following year, so I came to my father and asked for his professional advice. In just a couple of hours, after dinner and before the evening news, he had transformed the contents of our junk drawer into a windmill. I marveled at its miniature perfection, two feet high on our kitchen table, cute little blades spinning when I connected the red wire to the green wire. No amount of patient explanation could make me understand how the thing actually worked.

Needless to say, my submission to the science fair was disqualified for cheating (those were the days when it was forbidden for kids to turn in work that was actually done by their parents). I was humiliated. My father felt even worse for setting me up to fail, albeit with the best intentions. It had never occurred to him that I wasn't able to comprehend the mechanism of the windmill even though I sat at his elbow during its construction. My father could never understand why everyone didn't see the physical world as clearly as he did, why simple things like mathematics and science provoked confusion, distrust, and sometimes even hostility.

For instance, how would I have reacted if I'd figured out that what my father had made me was not just a clever toy, but a time machine? Had I known that my father had given me the means to fast-forward to a time beyond the havoc of my parents' divorce, would I have used it? Had I known that I could skip past the 1980s and '90s and settle gently into the place where I am now, at peace with myself, would I have done it? Would I look ahead, given the opportunity to use the windmill today? Probably not. Nature shows us only the tail of the lion.

The Überorgan could have been the intestinal tract of an enormous creature made from cardboard tubing, tinfoil, dry cleaner bags, and electrical tape, except it played music. My jet-lagged father stood inside the light-filled atrium of the Getty Center listening to the hooting strains of Bach coming out of toilet paper rolls and promptly reminded me that he had worked on the Tennessee Valley Authority Nuclear Power Plant. He wasn't interested in children's toys cobbled together from bits of junk.

I was deeply disappointed that my father failed to make the connection between the Überorgan and the windmill he made me. Perhaps he didn't remember the windmill. Why should he? How could he be expected to remember an insignificant event in the childhood of his first child, the one he only lived with for ten years, the one who came before the two new children, whose elementary school years were fresher in his mind?

But I was wrong to underestimate the power of the Überorgan. It jogged his memory the same way it did mine (though it was only several months later, when I sat down to transcribe his words, once again at my father's elbow, that I finally, fully, understood the mechanism of the windmill). That night, after a light dinner, my father emptied the contents of my junk drawer into a shopping bag and locked himself into the spare bedroom.

Having already mapped out his *prima mobile* around the afternoon and evening of May 3, 1791, my father was still left with the "wet" problem ("wet" referring to the humid, mycelial world of human interactions, as opposed to the "dry," hygienic world of science) of manipulating a monarch. By employing the principles of electrodynamics in combination with a reverse cause/effect vector and the information he had gleaned from his history books regarding the life cycle of the average head of state, my father concluded that favorable results would follow if he approached King Poniatowski not at the height of his reign, the previously mentioned May 3, 1791, but at its absolute nadir.

By 1798, Catherine the Great was dead and Count Poniatowski was no longer king of the Commonwealth of Poland and Lithuania. In fact, there was no commonwealth: it had been torn to pieces by Prussia, Austria, and Russia. Despised by his countrymen and practically a prisoner in his own house, Count Poniatowski was forced to swallow his pride and accept an invitation from the new emperor of Russia, Paul I, the crazy son of Catherine the Great and her only official husband, Peter III. The new tsar had invited his mother's former lover to live out the rest of his days in St. Petersburg, with a modest pension provided by the Russian crown. Being a connoisseur of irony, Paul I even offered Poniatowski the Marble Palace in which to live, the exact same mansion his mother had built for her other lover, Gregory Orlov, who had replaced Poniatowski in her heart and bedchamber (and whose brother had killed the father of Emperor Paul I).

With all this history carefully plotted in the form of a circuit diagram, my father taped this "map" to the wall of my spare bedroom and dumped the contents of my junk drawer onto the quilt I had purchased earlier in the week in anticipation of his visit. He sorted through greasy gaskets, bent paperclips, lint-covered gum balls, rusted nails, used twist-ties, packets of soy sauce, keys to forgotten doors, a mouse trap, Hershey's Kisses, matchbooks without matches, a tape measure, a box of regular strength Ex-Lax, and a water pistol, keeping an inventory of everything. By midnight, he had finished reconstructing the windmill time machine.

Time is an arrow. Time is a sphere without exits. Time is the reef upon which all our frail mystic ships are wrecked. Time is the fire in which we burn. Time is the longest distance between two points. *Tempus fugit.* Many fancy things have been said about time, but one thing everyone can agree on is that time, like space, is three-dimensional. It follows that just as one is able to move freely through a three-dimensional space, one should be able to move freely through three-dimensional time. The easiest way to move freely through time is via the fourth dimension. But what is the fourth dimension?

You know when a wheel spins so fast that at a certain point it looks as if the center of the wheel is spinning in the opposite direction from the rim? Well, it does. The centrifugal forces created by a spinning wheel begin to generate, following Ampères Law, a weak electrical current. This is not unlike what happens in the solenoid in your car, in which a three-dimensional coil wrapped around a metallic core produces a magnetic field when a current is passed through it. Thus the center of the windmill produces a weak magnetic field which begins to drag on the fabric of space-time until there's a snag and a pucker and an accumulation of extra fabric. This extra fabric is the fourth dimension.

And if you reach with nimble fingers into the center of a reverse-spinning wheel and pluck at a bit of that fourth dimension, you'll find that it yields to your touch, and that it is extremely fine, and practically invisible. And if you pull and pull on the fourth dimension, you'll pull out enough for a handful, and when you examine it you will find that it's quite flexible. And if you keep pulling, you'll eventually pull out enough to cover your entire body, like a pair of footsie pajamas, plus hood. And if you step into this garment made from the fourth dimension, you can go *anywhere*, because an additional property of the fabric of the fourth dimension is it *pelastricity* (penetration and elasticity). You can go anywhere; all you need is a map. Time is on the side of the outcast.

In 1798, St. Petersburg experienced an exceedingly mild February. The Neva was slushy, not frozen. On Millionnaya Street, just one block in from the Gulf of Finland, where the Marble Palace stood out from the candy-colored townhouses like a displaced family crypt, the arctic wind did not peel the skin from my father's forehead, as it should have done at this time of year. Though the Marble Palace was far superior to the Getty Center with regard to its form and the quality of its building materials, there was no doorman to greet my father as he climbed its wide front steps. The gardener had neglected to wrap the boxwoods in burlap, and they had died in the first frost of the season. A brass lion's head door knocker, completely black with tarnish, produced a sound like rocks falling down a mineshaft. My father could barely contain his nervous excitement at these signs of neglect.

The door swung open on creaking hinges, and my father beheld Count Poniatowski. He was older, of course, than the robust image preserved by the court painters, but he was still as tall and handsome as in his prime. Wisps of fine silver hair framed his high forehead. He was dressed in carpet slippers and a blue velvet sable-trimmed robe. A beautiful white chicken was perched on his left shoulder; she, too, had fine silver plumage on her aristocratic head. My father bowed deeply and introduced himself. Poniatowski offered his thin old man's hand to be kissed.

That a countryman from another century had come to visit him in his exile did not disturb the former king of Poland. He had met many exotic people during his active years, both during his youth, while attached to the diplomatic corps in St. Petersburg, and in his own court. Now, left with no retinue except the old nursemaid who had taken care of the infant he had fathered on Catherine the Great (alas, mother and daughter were both dead now), Poniatowski was glad to have someone new to talk to.

The count closed the heavy wooden door and invited my father to follow him into a pale gray marble sitting room. It was bare except for a small Bukhara rug, a shabby divan, silver candelabra, and two Karelian birch armchairs. An imposing black marble fireplace, tall enough for Poniatowski to stand in, consumed smoldering remains of the furniture that must once have decorated this room. Smoke backed out of the fireplace and crept up the marble walls; it had been years since the chimney was swept. Despite the embers, a subterranean chill hung in the air.

Poniatowski offered my father one of the armchairs and took the divan for himself. They sat in silence for a few minutes, my father stealing glances at the chicken, Poniatowski examining his neatly manicured fingernails. The chicken eyed my father in between bouts of grooming its topknot of decorative feathers. It really was the prettiest chicken my father had ever seen.

Before too long, a very old woman shuffled into the room carrying a silver tray with two cut crystal glasses. She offered one glass to my father and the other to the count. Then she settled down into the other armchair, placed the silver tray under the chair, pulled an embroidery frame out of the pocket of her apron, and began to work.

Count Poniatowski raised his glass. "*Sto lata.*" (One hundred years.)

"*Sto lata.*" My father clinked glasses and downed his vodka.

Having grown up in communist Poland, my father never felt comfortable among aristocrats. For instance, a completely trivial problem gnawed away at the resolve with which he had arrived at the Marble Palace: what to do with the vodka glass? Eventually he gathered his wits, placed the glass on the rug under his armchair, and came right to the point:

"Count Poniatowski, I have studied your reign and the long and sad history of our country in great detail. I realize that I am a man of no consequence, nevertheless I believe that God has chosen me to come to you with a plan that will help you reclaim Poland." Satisfied with the way his speech came out, my father wasted no time in producing from his briefcase a thick document, complete with diagrams and bibliography.

Poniatowski accepted the document with a sigh and let its bulk settle onto his lap. The beautiful chicken shifted her perch and clucked. The nurse made no sound at all.

"It's really quite simple," my father continued. "All you have to do is go back seven years, to May 3, 1791, to the day you made your triumphant speech in front of the Assembly of Noblemen."

"That seems like a lifetime ago," Poniatowksi replied sadly. "I can't even remember what I said last week, let alone the supposedly triumphant speech I made seven years ago."

My father gets very impatient with people who refuse to understand the thing he's trying to explain to them. But he mastered his irritation and continued.

"You made a speech to the assembly upon signing into law the new constitution. And for six glorious months, before the new government was overturned by a royal decree sent from Russia, you were able to unite the fiercely independent Polish nobility for the first time in the nation's history."

"Yes, I do remember those bickering idiots, the 'Polish nobility.' What a nuisance it was to be their king," Poniatowski sniffed, stroking the elegant feathers of his hen.

"If I may be so bold, Your Majesty," said my father, the vodka loosening his tongue, "it was the first time in your twenty-seven-year reign that you had power independent of the Russian crown. Now, all you have to do is go back with me to the precise hour of your speech (he had made an additional pelastric suit for Poniatowski), right after you received the standing ovation from the members of the Assembly, and, instead of going home to tend to your art collection, you will come with me to see your nephew, Prince Adam Czartoryski. You will lay your crown at the feet of Prince Adam—a born leader and warrior, if you'll continue to forgive my boldness—who will then lead the Polish army to victory in 1792, and, like Garibaldi in Italy (but how could you know of Garibaldi, forgive me once again), would have united the Polish states. A unified Poland would have been able to rebuff the imperialistic designs of Empress Catherine and her devious ally, Frederick the Great of Prussia. A united, independent Poland would have grown and prospered at the same rate as every other country in Europe, so that by the time the German Panzers came rolling across the border in 1939 (for the Germans will come back, they always come back), instead of the sad spectacle of the Polish cavalry (horses fighting against tanks!), Hitler would have encountered a modern, fully equipped Polish army bound in steel! And while Poland held the Germans in check on the eastern front, the French would have had time to mount their offensive (900 division, 1,500 tanks, 1,400 planes) and attack Germany's western flank, thereby stopping their military machine in its tracks and ending World War II before it even began."

My father concluded his speech with a short bow and wiped his brow on his sleeve, panting softly. He retrieved the glass from under his chair and tipped the last drop of vodka into his parched throat.

Poniatowski smiled and nodded. He was a good listener, but, of course, most of what my father said to him made no sense at all. Except for one thing. "I accepted the throne of Poland only because I thought that Catherine would marry me if I, too, were a monarch. All of Europe thought the same."

"You were her puppet!" My father could not control himself any longer. "All of Europe knew that. But everything changed after your speech. That was the moment you showed your true self, your brilliance, Your Majesty. You could have done great things for your country had you simply done as I have just described."

"Kings are the slaves of history," Poniatowski murmured sadly and reached up to stroke his chicken. She dipped her white plumed head under his caresses and shook out her tail. A single milk-white feather flew up, caught a draft, and landed on my father's knee. He picked it up and tucked it into the breast pocket of his sport coat.

Poniatowski wiped a tear that had escaped from his rheumy old man's eyes and rearranged the folds of his velvet robe. "You are wrong about me. I never had power other than the power Catherine gave me. I was not born to do great things. An excellent education enabled me to conceal my mental and physical defects. I have sufficient wit to take part in any conversation but not enough to converse long and in detail on any subject. I have a natural penchant for the arts. My indolence, however, prevents me from going as far as I should like to go, either in the arts or in the sciences. I work overmuch, or not at all. I can see the faults of any plan but am very much in need of good counsel in order to carry out any plans of my own. In short, I would have made Catherine a good husband. Why do you think she stopped loving me?"

The vodka buzz had worn off, and suddenly my father felt sober, cold, and tired. Though not an intuitive person, he now saw Poniatowski more clearly and realized that there had been a flaw in his approach. The former king of Poland was ruled not by his mind, but by his broken heart.

"I understand," my father said evenly, as if trying to calm a child who has broken a favorite toy. "I, too, was once married to a Russian woman. Though she wasn't a tsarina, she carried herself as one. I remember the day I came home from work to find the apartment completely empty. She had taken everything—my furniture, my daughter, even the cooking pots."

My father looked up to find Poniatowski nodding sympathetically. "Catherine also took our daughter away from me. A child for a throne. I never saw her again." A second tear slid down Poniatowski's withered cheek. "She did not live past her second birthday. Is your daughter alive?"

"She's alive, thank God," my father put his hands together and glanced heavenward. "I should have gone after them, but something stopped me. I should have at least tried to take my daughter, but times were different then. Divorce courts almost always granted custody to the mother. I also believe that the child, especially a daughter, should stay with the mother, but I still regret not doing more. It wasn't until she became an adult that my daughter and I renewed our relationship. In short, I understand how difficult Russian women can be."

"But Catherine was German," Poniatowski protested.

"Only until she came to Russia, and then she was more Russian than the Russians," said my father.

"What does that mean?" Poniatowksi leaned forward and rested his elbows on his knees, finally interested in what my father was saying.

"Nobody knows. The Russians can't even decide what it means to be Russian. In any case, I'm sure Catherine loved you. Women only torture the men they love."

Poniatowski clapped his hands. "Bravo!" The beautiful chicken flapped her wings and settled back down on his shoulder. "You understand everything. I promise to read your proposal, but not until tomorrow morning, after we've both had a good night's sleep. In the meantime, you shall have supper with me."

Not having any relatives in eighteenth century St. Petersburg to stay with, my father gladly accepted the count's hospitality. For dinner they would have a simple omelet. Poniatowski told my father how he had learned to cook in Paris, during his first trip abroad. Now that he was older and had a sensitive stomach, it gave him great pleasure to eat at home rather than in one of those expensive St. Petersburg restaurants, which he could no longer afford anyway. My father, who hated to waste money, was glad that he and Poniatowski were able to agree on something besides the curious nature of Russian women.

In the basement kitchen of the Marble Palace, my father sat on a high wooden stool and watched Poniatowski cook. The beautiful chicken walked around the rough wooden table pecking at breadcrumbs.

"Why do you examine each egg over a candle flame before breaking it?" My father was hoping that the question about the eggs would lead to an explanation about the chicken. In lieu of an explanation, my father got a story.

"I used to sneak into the aviary of the Summer Garden in the morning. It was Catherine's favorite place to have her intimate dinner parties," Poniatowski began. "I spent many a pleasant evening there in my youth, back when I used to be invited to her parties. The aviary has fallen into disrepair since Paul became tsar. Now I visit the place for an hour or two each day, to keep the birds company. I pick up an egg every now and then, not wanting them to go to waste."

What harm was there in stealing eggs from a dead lover, especially when one is poor and hungry, my father wanted to ask. But he kept silent.

"The Summer Garden reminds me of when Catherine was young and I was the love she had not found in her marriage," Poniatowski continued. "She was beautiful back then, and absolutely fearless. She would sneak into my rooms dressed as a cadet, in breeches and boots with shiny silver spurs, wrapped in a fur-lined cloak. In her later years, she grew fat and pitifully prone to flattery. Her last lover before she died was an insipid boy of twenty-six. Can you imagine? I was once such a boy."

My father nodded. He, too, had once been such a boy.

"I still laugh when I recall the antics—I never really liked sex. Did you know that she was my first lover? I found it degrading the way she used to ride me around the bed like a pony, though I will never forget the feeling of her powerful, slender thighs clenched around my back. I tried to talk to Catherine about my love for her, that it was so pure as to be almost platonic, but she just laughed in my face. She liked to sing during our lovemaking, compose little operettas, dress me up like a doll. All idiocy. I can just imagine what it would have been like for her last Favorite, what the New One thought when a graying mountain of a woman climbed on top and grasped him with her old-womanish hams . . . but that's all in the past now."

My father, who hated to interrupt someone in the middle of a story even more than he hated to listen to people talk about intimate matter), cleared his throat and said, "You were going to tell me about the eggs."

"I understand," Poniatowski smiled. "You want to know about my chicken."

153

My father began to protest, because he felt it was important to continue in the charade that the chicken simply wasn't there, or that it wasn't odd to meet a former monarch living with a pet chicken, but the count waved him off with another laugh.

"One morning I returned from the Imperial Aviary with a pocket full of fresh eggs. When I tried to crack the first one, it cheeped back at me! It was fertile, and, moreover, the chick inside had been just minutes from hatching when I so rudely invaded its shell. So I took the egg, which was largely intact, though cracked, and placed it inside a fur-lined glove. Eventually, pieces of the shell flew out of the glove, and I was able to sustain the newborn chick on mashed flies and droppers full of water. One day a perfect little yellow chick emerged, and now look at her," Poniatowski grabbed the chicken and kissed her fine feathered neck. "Isn't she beautiful? She's a gift, after all my suffering."

Let me repeat: my father is a scientist. He deals with the physical world, governed by the predictable laws of cause and effect. He has no mental construct for the metaphorical (or metaphysical) significance of a chicken born from a lover's garden. Or so I thought. Nevertheless, he made no comment about the chicken-and-egg story, simply agreeing with his host that she was indeed a handsome bird.

Poniatowksi and my father finished their meal in companionable silence and wished each other pleasant dreams ("*Spokojny sen*"). It really was an unusually warm night in February. There should have been piles of snow along the embankment, but the sleepless citizens of St. Petersburg were strolling about amid daffodils tricked into premature bloom.

Later that night, there was a terrible storm, one of the hundreds of storms that regularly flooded the city until Brezhnev dammed the Neva River in the 1970s. Sometime after midnight the air changed from a caress to a claw. The waiting winter cold rolled in, making the Neva thrash in her canals like a sick man upon a pillow. The howling wind and rain and wicked waves stalked thieflike through the empty streets, creeping under doors and through partially opened windows, breaking up the bridges and sweeping out the foundations like coffins from sodden graveyards.

My father, exhausted from his journey through the centuries, slept through it all, until the wraith like figure of Count Poniatowski in a nightshirt bent over his bed and inadvertently dripped candle wax on his forehead. "You must help me!" He cried. "It was so warm, I left the window open, and now she is gone. I've searched the entire house. She is out there in this storm. Please help me."

Outside, the wind tore at their hair and clothing. Frigid water gushed out of the canals and numbed their feet. People driven from their ground-floor beds ran through the streets, scrambling over each other to get to higher ground. But Poniatowski did not seem to feel the sting of the sleet on his face. His eyes were fixed on a single spot on the embankment, where a beautiful willow swayed in the midst of a broken pile of pleasure boats. There, perched on a bobbing limb, was a luminous white speck, a ghostly flutter of wing. And then a wave came down upon the tree, and the speck was gone.

"Catherine!" Poniatowski wrenched himself from my father's grip and ran for the tree. My father ran after him, clutching at the hem of his cloak.

In the morning the world had turned to glass. Crystallized leaves fell from the trees onto the newly frozen ground with the plinking sound of a celestial harpsichord. Bodies trapped under the ice and snow would remain there until spring, immobilized like pike in a frozen pond. Survivors of the night stayed indoors with the curtains drawn.

Poniatowski lay inside his Marble Palace like a corpse in a mausoleum. My father had carried him home during the night. He and the nameless, wordless nurse had put the count back into his bed. Having weathered several winters in wartime Poland, my father knew that you could survive this kind of cold only if you kept your head. He broke up the Karelian birch armchairs for firewood and gathered together the count's fur-lined cloaks—the red one, the black one, and the silver one with the chinchilla lining— wrapped himself and the nurse and the count, spooning together to conserve body heat. Toward dawn of the following day, death came softly on kitten paws and left behind an elegant corpse.

The weather had grown mild once again. My father handed the cloaks to the nurse and bid her good-bye with a short bow. In no time at all he was back in my spare bedroom. When he came down to breakfast the day after he arrived, he looked a little more like his old self. Six months later, he asked me to help him with his memoirs.

It was nine o'clock on a perfect July evening of our last session in the Catskills, and the sun was just beginning to set behind Slide Mountain. Dragonflies were dancing the mazurka with a flock of swallows as my father and I sipped vodka-spiked lemonade, gently rocking in our aluminum lawn chairs. We hadn't eaten since lunch, and I was starving, but there was still one question I wanted to ask. The fading light obscured my father's features, so now seemed like a good time.

"Why didn't you go back?"

My father put his drink down under his chair and shifted in his seat to stretch his bad leg.

"You could have gone back," I continued, "to an earlier time, when Poniatowski was a bit more lucid. Before he found his chicken, for instance. Maybe he would have listened to you then."

"Well, it's obvious, isn't it?" said my father.

I shrugged. Nothing in this story was obvious.

"Cause and effect," my father continued. "What have I always taught you? Follow the sequence of events to their logical conclusion."

I shrugged again, not sure if he could see the gesture now that it was full dark.

"If there was no war, the part of Poland in which I was born would not have become a Russian satellite state. I would not have gone to university in Russia, would not have met your crazy mother, and you would not have been born."

"Oh," I said, though this is what I had expected my father to say, exactly what a man of science *would* say in lieu of an apology. It was enough for me. To forestall the sentimental tears that threatened to mess up our beautiful moment, I tried to grasp the concept of my nonbeing. What I imagined was a vast marble room without furniture, weak northern light, a chill in the air.

My father pulled something out of the pocket of his short-sleeved shirt. It was a feather, extremely white in the dark, moonless night. He leaned forward and handed it to me. "You are my beautiful chicken," he said, "a gift after all my suffering."

I ran the feather across my cheek and smiled in the dark. Time heals all wounds.

❖

Dinosaur Eggs

I am grateful to the editors for giving me "interstitial fiction" to use in response to the question, "What sort of writing do you do?" Now I'm compelled to offer up another term in exchange: "concretion."

According to Wikipedia, a concretion is what you get when mineral cement fills the porosity (the spaces between grains) in a mass of sedimentary rock. This mineral cement is younger and denser than the rock in which it forms. When the sedimentary rock erodes, the concretion, usually spherical or ovoid ("time is a sphere without exits"), pops out of its mold. Although "concretion" comes from the Latin word "con," together, and "cresco," to grow, the more common name for these geological objects is "dinosaur eggs."

What does this have to do with writing interstitial fiction? I believe that interstitial fiction is created in exactly the same way as concretions: mineral cement (narrative) fills the porosity (imagination) in a mass of sedimentary rock (dreams, family history, objects and people you covet, allergies) to create an ovoid object (the story) that pops out once the sedimentary matrix erodes.

So here is how the concretion entitled "Count Poniatowski and the Beautiful Chicken" was formed: a pastel portrait of a white Polish Frizzle chicken purchased at a garden shop; the Tim Hawkinson Überorgan exhibit at the Getty Center, which I went to see with my husband (finally, a soul mate); the fifth-grade science fair; the humiliation of being disqualified for passing off my father's windmill as my own; Count Stanislaw Poniatowski, whom I encountered in a dishy biography of Catherine the Great (research for my novel-in-progress). What he wrote about himself touched me: "An excellent education enabled me to conceal my mental and physical defects." I hear you, buddy. All the rest— my father, the Catskills, time travel—is mineral cement.

Elizabeth Ziemska

Black Dog: A Biography

Peter M. Ball

The first time the Black Dog showed up, I was five. We were living in Miriwinni, and it lurked behind the low, chain link fence that marked out our backyard, hunkered down in the long grass filling the space between the fence line and the train tracks. Noone else could see it, not even my parents. It was good at hiding when other people looked.

I don't remember much about our house back then. My parents were teachers, so we moved a lot. I was five, and that means I'm working with hazy images here: I remember the house was on stilts, thick hardwood pylons that would keep the snakes out and keep us dry if the river flooded. I remember off-white weatherboards and a corrugated iron roof. We lived across the road from an endless expanse of north Queensland cane fields. They burned blood red and spat ash into the air during the harvest months. The town was just a school, a pub, and a corner store that sold fizzy drinks and cordial. Maybe a couple of dozen people lived around the train station, the rest spread out in the houses that nestled in the heart of the cane fields. My friends were mostly farm kids, seen only on weekends.

Miriwinni was the kind of place where adults were filled with conventional worries: a bad harvest, the bills coming due, snake bites while cutting the cane, a cyclone sweeping in over the coast. No one worried about the Black Dog except me. At first my parents would check the long grass when I spoke of him, just to make sure nothing was hiding there, but it didn't take long for their concern to falter. I was a child prone to imaginary friends and childish fictions. There was no reason to believe my stories. "It doesn't exist," they told each other. "He'll grow out of it."

One day, when my mother was taking me seriously, she convinced me that I should be making friends with the Black Dog. I was six, and I was terrified, and I refused to play outside. "It's time to conquer your fear," she said, handing me a fistful of sausages. They were slimy to hold, the meat squelching through my fingers. My mother held my other hand and dragged me down the back stairs. "Give them to the dog," she said. "Just throw it over the fence and let it know you want to be friends."

The Black Dog didn't want to be friends. It was already sniffing out my scent as I trundled down the back steps. I saw the wolfish head rise out of the grass, fixing me with its crimson gaze.

"Nice doggie," I said. I held up the sausages so it would know I was willing to try. The Black Dog just smiled and pressed its body against the chain-link fence. The silky midnight of its muzzle pressed through the links, the moist tip sniffing as I got closer. Mum was looking in the other direction, her eyes on the dark clouds that squatted on the horizon. Clouds were worrying things during storm season.

"Little boy," the Black Dog whispered, his voice just low enough that mum couldn't hear. "Yum."

I dropped the sausages and squirmed out of my mother's hands, taking the stairs two at a time as she yelled out my name and demanded I come back. I refused to leave the house, watching her search for the dropped sausages through the wire of the screen door.

Later that night she told my father what had happened, whispering the story in hushed tones after I went to bed, when they thought I could not hear. She couldn't work out how the sausages had disappeared.

When I was seven, my parents were transferred, so we moved south to the Gold Coast. I was happy to move. We settled into the suburbs, and the only thing behind the fence in our backyard was another backyard and the neighbor's pool. We envied that pool during the sweltering summer months, but most of the time I was just happy to have something good to watch on television. Having multiple channels seemed like a smorgasbord after Miriwinni's patchy reception.

I liked our new house. I had friends who lived in the same

neighborhood; they could come around and play after school. There were enough people around to play Frisbee or cricket in the backyard, as long as no one threw too hard or hit the ball high enough that it would go over the fence.

We had a big fence. An old, wooden thing with gray slats and pointed tips that was so tall even my mother couldn't peer over the top. My mother was the tallest person in my family, at least three inches taller than my father. It was her job to look over the tall fences; his job to repair the tall fences if anything went wrong.

My new bedroom was small, but so was I back then. It came with pictures of Donald Duck drawn into the walls and a built-in reading lamp that meant I could read in bed. I liked reading; my bookshelves were filled with fairy tales and the works of Enid Blyton. Reading was like having imaginary friends who did things on their own. It meant I didn't have to sleep.

I will tell you something true about the Black Dog. It can breathe fire. It could roast you in seconds, scouring you down to bare bones and ash. You can run away, but it will always come and find you. The Black Dog is persistent. It can smell your dreams in the warm night air as soon as you fall asleep, no matter how far you run. If the Black Dog wants to find you, there is nothing you can do to stop it.

When I was nine, the Black Dog found me again. I hadn't seen it for two years. First it slunk into my dreams and breathed its fiery breath. My skin crisped and flaked, the muscles and tendons melting away. I became a skeleton, blackened and crumbling, ready to be munched and crunched in the Black Dog's great jaws. I woke up screaming. My mother was sitting by the bed, wearing her pajamas.

"Shh," she said, cool hand on my forehead. "It's just a nightmare. It can't hurt you."

She told me the same thing, night after night, her face growing tight and disappointed. The Black Dog kept coming. I learned not to scream in my sleep.

~

low

People came to the Gold Coast because it had beaches and sun. The Black Dog hated the sun; I don't think it was too fond of sand. That meant it came to the Gold Coast because it was following me. It took up residence behind the fence again, hidden in the shadows of our neighbor's garden. I liked the high fence; it stopped the Black Dog from seeing me play in the backyard. If I was feeling brave, I could climb up and snatch a quick peek, trying to spot it among the delicate fingers of the neighbor's low ferns.

I didn't feel brave all that often. If we lost a Frisbee over the fence, I'd make one of my friends go and get it. Sometimes they wouldn't come back, and my parents would get concerned calls from their parents. Sometimes, late at night, I would hear the Black Dog swimming. It would splash about in the neighbor's pool, growling and baying at the moon. It didn't like sand, but I think it was starting to like the water.

When I say the words *Black Dog* I am not speaking in metaphor. I don't use it as slang or to hide another meaning. There are legends that say you'll die if you see a Black Dog, unless you take the time to tell someone about it before the next dawn. I never said anything about the Black Dog to anyone, not at first, but I kept on living anyway.

Legends tend to refer to black dogs as capitalized: Black Dog, something singular and dangerous rather than something generic. The Black Dog is not just any black dog; you aren't going to die just because your neighbors have a sooty Labrador in their back yard. The name Black Dog is specific; you'll know it if you see it.

I lived on the Gold Cost for eight years. The Black Dog lived there with me. Sometimes it would disappear for months; I don't know why. There was never any obvious reason for its absence. It still crept into my dreams, lingering on the edges two or three times a week, breathing its fire-breath and gnashing its jaws and reducing me to a screaming pile of black bones.

I didn't miss the Black Dog when it went away, but I didn't sleep well, either. I would lie awake, reading in the dim glow of my night light, delaying the moment when I had to close my eyes.

Sometimes, if I asked it nicely, the Black Dog would even give me the night off. I guess it had other places to go, other people's dreams to lurk in. Even Black Dogs can be busy.

I'll be honest: not all of this is true. I'm lying in places. I've left out the dull bits and built on old memories. It happens, in biography; some things are changed for the sake of convenience.

An example: We moved to Miriwinni when I was three, not five. We moved to the Gold Coast when I was six. I completely skipped the three years we lived elsewhere, hanging out in a country town with too many pubs and even more churches. We lived in more than one house on the Gold Coast; we moved across the suburbs like wandering stars for the first seven years I lived there. And the Black Dog never gave me a break, not even when I asked for it. It sat there, night after night, a malignant blot on the landscape of my dreams. The Black Dog was a bastard; he had no consideration for narrative momentum or character arcs.

The Black Dog ate my first girlfriend. Her name was Suzanna, and we were both sixteen. We'd met when I was eight, and she taught me how to throw a Frisbee. We were friends, originally, but there isn't much space for friendship when you're sixteen. Things evolve whether you want them to or not.

I was a much better friend than I was a boyfriend, even before my kissing her got Suzanna eaten. I was a sloppy kisser back then, and I was so nervous about being her boyfriend that I never had much fun when we were together.

She got eaten while we were hanging out on the balcony at her place. We were drinking instant coffee, trying to get used to the taste so we could go to cafés and drink lattes without seeming like children. We would boil the kettle, make a cup and then try to keep a straight face while we drank it down. Coffee isn't particularly bitter if you add six teaspoons of sugar, but the sharp kick of the sugar rush was as bad as the Nescafé bitterness.

We were on our third cup when Suzanna noticed me watching the fence line. I was a connoisseur of fences by then; I'd been studying them for years, rating them by how well they could keep the Black Dog at bay. I liked the towering fence at Suzanna's because it was made of orange bricks. By now I was afraid the Black Dog would work out that it could simply burn down the wooden fence we had at home.

"What?" Suzanna said. "Why are you looking at the fence?"

"Nothing," I said. The balcony gave us a good angle; I could just make out the Black Dog's hackles rising over the bricks as it hid on the other side. It was a big dog now, bigger than I remembered it.

"No," Suzanna said. "You always do it. It's weird."

"Maybe I'm just Paranoid," I said. Suzanna was into metal and had a love affair with Sabbath and Led Zep. I'd learned to weave the names of her favorite songs into conversations; a private joke. Suzanna picked at her black shirt, frown disappearing behind her ragged fringe as she looked down.

"Don't make jokes," she said. "I thought you loved me." I thought I loved her too; she looked so hurt that I told her the truth.

"There's this dog that follows me," I said. "A big, black one. It hides behind fences and wants to burn me with its breath."

Suzanna didn't say anything. Then she said: "My neighbors don't have a dog."

"It's invisible," I said. "I'm the only person who can see it. It's been hanging around since I was six. It creeps into my dreams and breathes fire."

"That's stupid," Suzanna said. "There's no such thing as invisible dogs that breathe fire."

"Well, I can see one," I said.

Suzanna laughed. I liked it when she laughed; it made her breasts jiggle. At sixteen I was acutely aware that breasts were very important things, and I liked the way Suzanna's moved. She smiled at me, her teeth showing.

"I get it," she said, even though she didn't. "You're having me on."

"Sure," I said. "If you like."

Then she leaned over and kissed me, her tongue worming its way past my gums and into my mouth. I closed my eyes. It was the first time she'd ever kissed me with tongue. She tasted like too much sugar and Nescafé, sweet and bitter all at once. I could feel her lips working against mine, trying to stay locked in the vacuum of the moment. She stopped and leaned back in her chair. I was still leaning forward, my eyes closed, trying not to drool in the aftermath.

"There," she said. Then I opened my eyes and the Black Dog was behind her, a massive blot of black fur and open mouth. It breathed in and out with harsh regularity, washing Suzanna in a blast of sulphurous breath. I hadn't been this close to the Black Dog in real life, only in my dreams. I gritted my teeth and waited for the fire to come. Suzanna didn't seem to notice. Not even when the black gums and gleaming white teeth snapped her up and swallowed her whole. She didn't even get a chance to scream.

"So," I said. "I guess it's my turn."

The Black Dog lowered its head and stared into me with its bright, crimson eyes. I closed my eyes and waited, wondering if being eaten would hurt as much as being burned alive in my dreams. I waited for a long time. I could feel my ankles starting to itch under my emerald school socks.

"Hurry up," I said. "Let's get this over with."

Nothing happened. I opened my eyes and the Black Dog had disappeared.

This is a list of things that have, at one point in my life, frightened me: Daleks; big snakes; Celine Dion; public speaking; that scene in *Indiana Jones* where they open the ark of the covenant and ghosts come out; nuclear bombs; really small snakes, the kind that can creep in through your window and wiggle up your nose and sting you in your brain. None of these things frightened me more than the Black Dog.

No one bothered asking questions after Suzanna disappeared. Her parents didn't call. Her friends didn't miss her. I wasn't even questioned by the police. That gave me chills for weeks after it happened.

I stopped listening to Led Zeppelin after Suzanna. It didn't seem fair to listen to them without her. I did keep her Black Sabbath

CDs, though; I listened to *Paranoid* every night, just before I went to sleep.

I got another girlfriend when I was seventeen. She was nice, but she thought I was weird, and I thought she was safe. She didn't care about my obsession with fence lines. The Black Dog waited eight months before it ate her.

When I was nineteen, I moved out of home. I was a uni student, kind of, so I moved in with a bunch of people who actually went to the classes I was ignoring. We had a unit on the waterfront in Southport, across the river from a theme park and the spit of land that separated Southport from the ocean. In the afternoons the water would turn a golden orange, like a slice of ripe mango wedged between a pair of sandy shores.

Our unit was on the fourth floor. The road behind us was a highway, lots of road noise and moving cars. The unit block didn't have any fences; it barely managed to lay claim to a yard. Our windows looked over the main road; it cost an extra twenty dollars a week to look over the water.

I figured there was nowhere for the Black Dog to hide. I'd be safe, physically, even if it could still sneak into my dreams.

The first night after we moved in, we stayed up late, drinking and waiting for the traffic noise to die down on the street below. I went to bed at midnight and looked out the window. The Black Dog was hiding behind the metal bus shelter on the opposite side of the road. It crouched over, trying to make itself small, but the black snout and shaggy tail protruded from either side of the metal bus shelter. I leaned my forehead against the glass and stared at it.

"Yo, Black Dog," I said. "I can see you."

The shaggy head rose up and glared at me. The red eyes were narrow and glowing.

Southport wasn't a good place to live when I was nineteen. It was an old suburb in a tourist town, one of those places that had had its day sixty or seventy years before. It was full of patched-up holiday units and summer shacks that were no longer rented to holiday makers.

165

The hospital on the edge of the suburb had shut down its rehab facilities and psychiatric wing a year before I moved there; we kept a blackboard in our flat that tallied how often we had a run-in with one of the random crazies or the junkies eager to offload their methadone for some quick cash. Every week the person with the fewest close encounters was responsible for buying the Friday night beers. Victoria won more often than not; she was beautiful enough to be worth approaching, even if you were crazy or strung out.

I lost a lot, but that was okay. I liked buying beer for Victoria.

This is what the Black Dog looks like: it's big, and it's black, and it looks like a dog. The Black Dog is never big the same way; the Black Dog has always been content to remain six inches taller than I am, growing as I grew. It took years before it was taller than my mother.

The Black Dog is black the way the night sky is black, a different shade every evening depending on the position of the moon and the stars. And it only looks like a dog because it seems unfair to call it a wolf; it holds onto its doggishness despite its sleek frame and lupine jaws.

This is what Victoria looked like: she wore black dresses and had hair dyed redder than henna, and her eyes were impossibly green as long as she remembered to wear her contacts. Her boots frequently came over her knees, black leather and shiny, the heels sharpened to a dangerous point.

I was twenty before Victoria and I got together. I had a thing for long courtships by then; the Black Dog had eaten another two or three girlfriends since it had snapped up Suzanna.

Victoria studied philosophy and stripped to pay the rent. She was beautiful and consciously sexy and sounded smarter than me when she talked. She smelled of clove cigarettes and patchouli oil; she tasted like aniseed and ashtrays. She liked to talk about the world's greatest minds and, when she'd been drinking, she'd focus on the extensive catalogue of ways they'd killed themselves.

Sometimes Victoria would take me shopping when she went looking for underwear she could take to work. I'd spend an hour standing in a store, shuffling from foot to foot, trying to pretend I was reading *On the Road* while Victoria disappeared into change rooms. My job was to offer a guy's opinion. I didn't get to see her wearing the outfits; I just got to see them on the hanger and make comments based on the amount of lace and frills. I spent hours imagining what they'd look like with Victoria inside them. I tried not to think about the stripping.

Victoria had a streak of self-destruction. I liked that; self-destruction seems inevitable when you're twenty. I had a feeling that the Black Dog approved of that.

This is how Victoria and I started going out: We were sitting in the kitchen just at sunset, the window looking out on the crush of the Tuesday night rush hour. Victoria smoked cigarettes, and I drank instant coffee, and the sun turned her hair the color of a cigarette ember. "What's that?" Victoria said. She pointed with her cigarette.

"It's a bus," I said.

"Not the bus," she said. "Behind the shelter. The black thing."

I looked. Occasionally you'd see crazy folks peeing behind the bus shelter. This time there was nothing there but the Black Dog.

"Must be the shadows," I said.

Victoria frowned. She had a great frown; her pale skin wrinkled like concerned silk. "You're telling me you don't see a wolf?" she said. "A big, fucking wolf?"

I blinked. "Sure," I said. "But you're not supposed to. The Black Dog's my thing."

"What the hell?" Victoria said. "How is a big fucking wolf in the middle of the suburbs supposed to be your thing?"

I changed the subject and Victoria changed it back, so I told her: Miriwinni, the Gold Coast, Suzanna being eaten and years of bad dreams. I hadn't told anyone the whole story before. It felt weird. Victoria gave me a strange look when I was finished.

"Shit," she said. "You're fucked up."

"I guess," I said. "But you can see it too."

"Too much acid," Victoria said. Then she added: "You know, I always thought you were a little too straight to be interesting."

I shrugged. I'd gotten used to the Black Dog being around. Then Victoria leaned over and kissed me. I was a better kisser by then, even when caught by surprise. It wasn't bad, as first kisses go. It should have led us toward better things.

In the end, we didn't have sex. We just made out and slept together, side by side in her bed, still wearing our clothes. Eventually Victoria got up and went to work. "Keep the bed warm," she said. "I'll be home in the morning, if you're willing to stay up."

It was strange, watching her get ready, head for the door after the taxi driver started leaning on his horn downstairs. She didn't get to wear her favorite dresses to work, but they insisted she wear the shoes.

I lay back and tried to imagine her naked. Soon there would be other guys watching her and then going home and doing the same thing. I wondered whether that should freak me out more than it did. Victoria's ceiling was covered with glow-in-the-dark stars, tiny constellations of luminescent shapes. Her bookshelves were filled with Sartre, Camus, and Plath. If I'd known better, I would have realised that none of these were a good sign.

The Black Dog sniggered outside. I tried to ignore it and go to sleep.

I was still awake at 2 AM. The Black Dog was still sniggering. It sounded snide, like it knew things I didn't. The Black Dog didn't normally laugh that much. Most of the time it was pretty quiet; a little bit creepy, but easy to ignore if you'd had enough practice. I checked the clock twenty minutes later. The Black Dog had sniggered for nearly four hours. I lay in bed and thought about how sick I was of hearing the sound.

I got up around 3 AM and went down to the bus shelter. I took half a pack of Victoria's cigarettes, a Zippo, and the fire extinguisher from the stairwell of the unit block. The Black Dog was still laughing; it didn't notice me crossing the road. I sat in the bus shelter and waited. I could hear the Black Dog's lungs working on the other side of the aluminium sheeting, the heavy thump of its flanks as

it breathed in and out. I rapped a knuckle against the aluminium.
"Yo, Black Dog," I said. "What's up?"

The Black Dog's laughter cut off, replaced by the soft pad of its paws. It circled round the bus shelter, black smoke trailing from its mouth, the cold bead of its nose sniffing its way towards me. The Black Dog's head lowered, drawing level with my own. I pulled the pin on the fire extinguisher and pointed it toward the Black Dog's mouth. Gave it a quick spray to make sure it worked, spitting white foam at the Black Dog's face.

The Black Dog eyed me carefully. Then it sat down, great haunches squeezed onto the narrow strip of curb, its long tail dangling into the gutter. "Hey, man," it said.

"Let's not get crazy."

"You're the one with a crazy laugh, Sparky. I was just trying to get some sleep."

The Black Dog growled, but it kept its voice soft. It barely even raised its lip to show me its teeth. I stabbed a cigarette into the corner of my mouth and started rummaging through my pockets for the lighter. Finally I just looked up at the Black Dog and pointed. "You want to help?"

The Black Dog exhaled and burning ember bloomed at the cigarette's tip.

"Thanks," I said. The Black Dog inhaled a strong whiff of cigarette smoke and then pulled a face.

"They smell bad," the Black Dog said. It sneezed twice, then settled back onto the ground, its red eyes narrowed as it watched me. I smoked the cigarette and stared back.

"So, Black Dog," I said. "Why aren't you off eating Vicky tonight?"

A big, red tongue lolled out of the Black Dog's mouth. "She's not my type," it said. "Not yet; I'm not big on fast food; the prepackaged stuff is never as filling as home cooked, you know?"

I nodded like I did, but I didn't. I hadn't eaten home cooking for months. "You," I said, "are one fucked-up dog."

The Black Dog snorted; I could taste the ashes on its breath. "Look who's talking," it said. "You should get going, kid. Your girl will be back soon."

It stood up, shaking itself off as if it'd been covered in water. Flecks of hot spittle dripped out of its mouth, creating black pits in the concrete sidewalk.

"It's been nice chatting, kid," it said. "We should have done it earlier." Then the Black Dog slunk back behind the bus shelter, settling its bulk against the side with a solid thump. A few seconds later it was snoring.

Victoria came home around six AM. She smelled of cold sweat, cigarette smoke, and the hunger of other men. I pretended I was asleep as she crawled into her bed.

I went and bought a portable fire extinguisher the day after I talked to the Black Dog. The extinguisher was small and compact, lightweight enough to fit in the bottom of my backpack. The guy who sold it to me said that they were designed to fit in the glove box of a car.

Victoria would spend her free evenings by the window in her bedroom, watching the looming shape of the Black Dog where it lingered behind the bus stop. She would write notes, smoke cigarettes, and sigh.

"What does it do?" she said. "It just sits there, day after day."

"It watches," I said. "It waits, and it plans its attack."

I was dreaming of the Black Dog every night. Victoria was added as a new feature. The Black Dog would eat her before it breathed on me, reducing me down to a familiar pile of bones and ash. I found the regularity of this exchange comforting; it reminded me that the Black Dog was still there, still doing the things it used to do, even if it wouldn't eat my girlfriend this time.

I wasn't a particularly good boyfriend yet, even with some practice under my belt. I was a better kisser, sure, and I wasn't as nervous as I'd been with Suzanna. I knew how to have fun by then. Sometimes we'd have so much fun that Victoria would laugh. Victoria wasn't big on laughing; laughter was a sign of weakness and stupidity. She'd perfected the art of the deadpan expression specifically so she could avoid actively laughing when she delivered jokes. Her laugh was nervous and hesitant, like a frightened rabbit sitting at the threshold of the warren.

I made Victoria laugh, but it was a rare event. Most of the time we got by on awkward passion and the knowledge that the Black Dog was watching us. I clung to Victoria despite the black pit that had settled into my stomach. Victoria hung with me because the Black Dog was there, and that was enough to make me interesting.

In the end, the Black Dog didn't eat Victoria. I think she was disappointed. She took the decision out of the Black Dog's hands while I was down at the pub. One of our flatmates found her in the bathtub and called the ambulance. They pulled her out and put her on a drip and stitched up the bits that needed stitching. They took her away, and Victoria spent three weeks in the hospital. We'd been going out for six months. We still hadn't gotten around to having sex.

Victoria became a lesbian after she left the hospital. We broke up not long after that. I just couldn't compete with the allure of women, not even with the Black Dog's help. I got kicked out of our Southport apartment because Victoria's new girlfriend didn't like having me there. My flat-mates took a vote to see which of us would stay; they wanted Victoria gone after the suicide attempt, but her name was on the lease and mine wasn't. They figured a little more melodrama was a small price to pay in exchange for not messing around with the RTA and finding the cash to cover her share of the bond.

I moved back into my parents' house. I was taller than both of them by now. The Black Dog moved back with me. It seemed happy to have a fence to hide behind again, even if I was tall enough to peer over the top when I stood on tippy-toes.

My stuff didn't seem to fit into my parents' place anymore. I found the picture of Donald Duck that filled the wall of my bedroom annoying now. I still liked the reading light, though; it made the room feel like home.

One night, a couple of weeks after I'd come home, I ducked out back for a cigarette. My parents were inside. I could hear one of them washing up, the other taking a shower in their en-suite bathroom.

I knocked on the back fence and held my cigarette up for a light. The Black Dog wheezed, produced a tiny ember of flame.

"Hey, Black Dog," I said.

"Hey, kid," the Black Dog said. He sounded happy.

I smoked. The Black Dog's heavy breathing rumbled on the other side of the fence. It sounded like it was waiting for something. I said: "Listen, stay out of neighbor's pool, huh? They've been complaining about the fur in the filter."

The Black Dog gave a low growl, a sound that was almost friendly. When I looked up, it was peering over the fence, its forepaws resting against the wood.

"I'm moving," I said. "This place feels too small now. I'm thinking of heading toward Brisbane, seeing what I can find there." The Black Dog didn't say anything. It just heaved big breaths, huffing and puffing, snuffling air through its smoke-filled nose. I finished my cigarette, stubbed it against the weathered fence.

"Hey, Black Dog," I said. "Could you eat her for me? Vicky?"

"No," the Black Dog said.

"What about me?" I said. "Is it my turn yet?"

"No," the Black Dog said.

"But it's coming, right?" I said. "How fat do I have to be before I'm considered a tasty treat?"

The Black Dog shook his head. I reached up and scratched its ebon muzzle.

"So, Brisbane," I said. "You coming? I'll have room in the truck."

"I'll think about it," the Black Dog said. "You planning on getting a place with a fence line?"

And again, yes, there are lies here for the sake of convenience. It's a flaw of biography, the assumption of an ending and a satisfying conclusion. The end point is always false, an attempt at poignancy that real life rarely provides. This is not how it ends, not really, but it's the way it ends here.

I moved to Brisbane when I was twenty-one, not long after my birthday. I found a unit block that didn't have a fence line.

The Black Dog didn't travel in the truck, but it made it here anyway. It spends its days lurking in the car park of my unit block, hiding behind the dumpster that holds our communal garbage. The Black Dog complains about the smell a lot. I keep telling it to find somewhere better to hide. There are cars down there, another bus stop if it gets really desperate. It never moves; it just whines and snarls every time I drop off my garbage.

Sometimes I'll invite it into the apartment, offer it a few hours away from the garbage stench and the exposure. Sometimes the Black Dog accepts my offer, and we spend the evening reading the work of the great Russian novelists. The Black Dog likes Dostoyevsky; it has a penchant for *Notes from the Underground*. I like *Anna Karenina*, but I read the Black Dog's favorites to keep the peace. It can still breathe fire when it wants to, and all the books are flammable.

Some days it seems like we're stuck with one another, just me and the Black Dog forever. Sometimes it just feels like we're waiting, but I'm not sure what for. I haven't had a girlfriend in a while now, but I'm not sure I'm ready to start again. The Black Dog tells me it doesn't mind so much. On the cool nights you can hear its stomach rumbling, a soft gurgle on the breeze.

Though I wrote "Black Dog: A Biography" as fiction, it pillages from my own life with a kind of reckless abandon. I've always thought there's something intriguing about the relationship between biography and fiction—biography may have the luster of truth about it, but I've never been able to accept it as such. Biography makes the private aspects of life public by excluding superfluous moments and reframing others to highlight their importance. It seeks to create cohesive narrative and meaning amid the chaos of personal history and recollection.

Everything in "Black Dog" started from something I think of as personal. Not necessarily a single experience or event, but things I valued and felt had shaped me as both a writer and a person—a long-remembered nightmare, a particular friendship from my teenage years, a few images from my childhood that weren't quite memories of specific events. For me it's as much biography as it is fiction, treading the line between the two as best it can.

Peter M. Ball

Berry Moon
Laments of a Muse

Camilla Bruce

There's a red, ripe moon, like a berry, in the sky. "Blood moon," they call it, "berry moon," I say. Juicy and full, that fat piece of fruit, makes me want to swallow it whole. A pearl of heaven's own blood in my mouth, and then . . . The sky surrounding my glossy morsel is brimming with purple champagne, foaming with stars. I wait for them to fall down and cover me in shimmering dust. Will it crackle and hiss when it touches my skin? Will it burn? Taste perhaps like ice and water, vanilla and nuts, when I lick it off my hands? It is my duty, you know, to eat it all up. "Greedy," you may say, but then, you still love me . . .

We grew up together, you and I, shaped by the same mold. We twisted and changed for a bit, learned our names and purpose. In the beginning we were equals; we had not learned our roles. We fed from what we saw, we grew, we shaped. We changed together, wove our worlds, created the universe all over again, with rocks and seashells, scissors and glue, thick crayons and cookie dough, glitter paint and colored paper. We made butterflies to hang from the ceiling, star-shaped gingerbread and faerie flowers. Those were times of wonder, dear sister. We were twins then, sharing a life. But then things changed again, and you became aware. You stiffened in a fixed shape, froze in your mask, and I was caught, beneath your skin, under the surface was I, glued to your form like a second skin . . . I was yours, and you were—awake.

I feed. I eat the sun on your skin, the pear-shaped lightbulb in the satin lamp above your bed, the pink and silver balloons that the girl in the park held so tightly . . . her dirty fingernails and brown braids. I feed, I eat it up, lick the traces of your memory and store it: The glossy red color of your new shoes, the scent of your boss's new perfume. We find a bubblegum wrap on the street; silver foil crushed into a froglike shape, tastes like mint and water lilies. The warm, glorious scent of your coffee at lunch; cinnamon and sugar. And you; blood and salt seasoning your skin. Artificial perfume; roses and orchids and musk. I feed, and when your silver-colored nails hit the keyboard at night, I spew it all out again: The balloons have become a state of mind, the silver foil frog leaps as mint-flavored kisses from the hero's lips onto the heroine's; her brown braids fall down her back, and he can smell the rose scent on her neck when he holds her tight. The hero's hands are dirty; he has been doing some serious work in the swamp, saving the heroine from grave danger—perhaps involving gators. He is bleeding from a shallow wound on his taut stomach, so she takes him home— and then, when they are all cleaned up, there are pears to be had, blushing with red, like *she* does when his gaze wanders, lingers . . . His eyes are cinnamon brown and his semen tastes like sugar on her tongue. Clickety-click, your nails type it down until I am drained and empty.—Not that I complain, it is always a pleasure when your reach inside and touch me like that, when the two of us meld together and become one. When we create, when you type it all out with your clickety-clicks, the release is exquisite, mingled with pain—when you penetrate my being with your mind, electric blue flashes and red hot pulses. Like fireworks. Exploding suns.

"I don't know where my stories come from," you say and sip your wine. Spill a little red drop of alcohol on your left stocking while you shift in your seat to cross your legs. Pure black silk, those stockings; you can't stomach anything else. You think it suits your artistic persona. "I don't know how I get my ideas," you continue as you light a cigarette and blow out the smoke, bluish-white tendrils that float like serpents, Chinese dragons, up toward the bright white lights in the ceiling. I laugh then, for I know, and am slightly annoyed that you don't. That you have forgotten me so entirely, your second skin . . . And you say: "It's almost magical how they appear out of thin air." You laugh, your friends surrounding the table laugh, over wine bottles and candles, a vase with one single rose. And I feed: the hostess's earrings, black onyx stones—black moons crying tears of silver. The texture of the tablecloth: fine, ironed linen. The rose has the color of peach bleeding pink, like a virginal wound, an ear shell of a maiden. The vase is crystal, reflecting the candle flames; liquid amber dance in the water, gems of fire . . . The man to your left, which your mind tells me is Bill, has a lavender-colored shirt on. It makes his eyes look a hazy blue, like bluebells, maybe, or the shadows under a willow tree at night after a rainy summer's day. "There is no secret," you say and smile at Bill. He smiles back at you and lifts his glass in a toast. Ruby red the wine in there, red heaven, red ocean. The bright electric light-bulb in the ceiling is mirrored in his wine, floating on the surface, like a blood-drenched sun. He drinks it all up. Like me.

And then there is Bill. Bill with the bluebell eyes and hair the color of ripe wheat, curly and soft to the touch. And you are in love, you think, and do not touch me anymore. I curse, I weep, and then I become silent. And while you love, I feed; I eat his soul like a can-died apple, consume his flesh and lick his bones while he sleeps so soundly beside you. And then it is over, and I add his carcass to your heap of dead lovers. You curse, and you cry, and then you fall silent. "I didn't love him anyway," you say on the phone and add another layer of nail polish to your claws. And of course you didn't, for you are mine, as chained by our pact as I am. No lover will ever know you as I do, from the inside out. Marrow, bones, and tissue. I am in every part of you, in every cell—even when you deny me.

And then you sit by your keyboard, before the shimmering screen, and you call for me, want to touch me—but I will surely not let you. You scream at me, and curse me, and drink far too much red wine. But why would I yield to a mistress who has treat-ed me so badly? Who has taken advantage of me and discarded me as soon as she found something else to play with . . . But then you are sweet and broken... and you miss me so badly I can feel it in every nerve, in every fiber of your being. And if hearts could cry, yours would cry a fat, black drop of sheer despair. And I open myself to you again and let you touch me.

You are always gentle at first when we reunite, then bolder, as you realize I am really there and won't disappear again anytime soon. Then you kiss me and love me like before. I could never stand your misery for long . . .

And we take Bill, like we have taken them all, and we transform him. We give him a mask and send him out on the stage so you can punish him as you see fit. He'll be a tragic hero or a villain—maybe the guy who dies. And you can shoot him or stab him . . . all that blonde hair covered in gore. I revel in it, you feel released, you close the chapter that was Bill and move on—and I feed you. Your nails go clickety-click as you see the world through my eyes . . . Perfectly entwined, you and I . . . And now you can write about the ripe berry moon, the sparkling stars, foaming champagne upon your brow, breasts, and thighs.

"Berry Moon" is an attempt to give the always working, never resting creative part of the writer's mind a voice and a personality of its own. It's a peculiar thing, often even to the writer, how his or her brain can take everyday occurrences, gobble them up, and transform them into shiny castles—how everything is inspiration, nothing is plain . . . As a writer (or artist, for that matter), a part of you is always detached from the real world, busy looking for food for the creative "magic." This, in my opinion, makes the writer somewhat interstitial by nature—walking in between the worlds.

This constant internal dialogue is, in many ways, far more intimate (and important) than a relationship with another human being can ever be, which makes the writer more or less self-sufficient when it comes to intimacy: no one can know you like you know yourself, even if you don't always quite understand exactly what it is that triggers and feeds your imagination. And nothing can satisfy you as completely as your creative work; to fill those pages and tell that story, to experience the sweetness of a creative "high" . . .

The relationship with the "muse," or creative self, is like a lifelong marriage: you fight, you love, you feed each other. Sometimes you want the stream of creative impulses to cease, other times you wish for it to flow—but then, of course, it won't . . . "Berry Moon" was written at a time when I had some doubts about this relationship between me and my "other self." We worked it out, though—we always do, as walking away isn't really an option. We both live here, after all.

Camilla Bruce

Morton Goes to the Hospital

Amelia Beamer

Most of Morton's weight landed on his left forearm. After he'd caught his breath, he flexed the fingers to check that nothing was broken. His hip hurt where it had hit the sidewalk, and his ribs. Still, he would not be put off his weekly lunch out. Since Marie had passed, it was the only time he ate anything other than what he'd heated from a can. More than that, he was a creature of routine. He was expected at Happy Family.

The street was empty, save his parked car, and a few others. He was relieved that no one was around to have witnessed his fall, and then he was bemused that no one was around to help him stand. What the hell had he tripped on, anyway?

Probably just your feet, Marie said.

He acknowledged the possibility with a nod. Morton had rules about speaking to Marie in public. It wasn't that he was crazy; he'd heard her voice in his head since before the cancer took her. Always coming up with some smart or insightful comment.

With some effort, Morton stood and dusted himself off with his good hand. His cane was nowhere to be found.

In the gutter, Marie said. *You know, you should really go to the hospital.*

Sure enough, it had landed in a puddle that was slick with something that might be soap. Who knew what was in this water?

Marie didn't offer an opinion. Morton liked that from time to time. Anyone who's been married can understand.

He had to bend over, bracing against a parked car, to retrieve the cane. Already there was some blood coming through his sleeve. He bled so easily these days, from the Coumadin. Sometimes he had nosebleeds that lasted for hours.

He walked the painful half block to Happy Family. Their normal table was still empty. Good, he wasn't late, not that Alice would notice. Morton used the time to check his wounds in the bathroom. His forearm was scratched up pretty badly. He'd ruin his shirt, at this rate. There were several welts on his side, and he took shallow breaths to minimize the pain when he breathed. He'd be OK for a while, he decided.

Morton used the toilet, which he often did these days, washed his hands, and went to wait. He read the menu as if he hadn't already memorized it, as if he ever ordered anything other than Orange Chicken, and wished—as he did every week—that he'd brought the newspaper. He watched the door instead.

Twenty minutes later, Alice came through, pushing a walker and shepherded by the young Hispanic driver. The kid had once told Morton that he locked the van every time he got out, so that the old folks didn't wander off. Morton was both grateful and a little resentful. The way it worked at Alice's home, you had to be on a list to check out a resident, as if the old folks were library books. It was a liability thing, for insurance. And Alice's daughter didn't like Morton; that was a liability thing, too. Alice had to ask for a ride just to get out and see Morton. She had a standing order.

Morton waved with his good hand. Alice saw him, he knew by the look of puzzlement that passed over her face. The look that said she knew him from somewhere. He stood despite the pain and kissed her dry cheek as she approached. Her helper sat her down, then left.

"Well, here we are," Alice said.

"It's Morton," Morton said. "Your old friend. Getting older every day. Alice, how are you?"

"Fine, thanks, and you?" She picked up the menu with her delicate hands and read it as if she'd never read a menu before. "They spelled *dinner* wrong," she said. "It's missing an *n*. And there's periods after some of the items and not after others." Her eyes were watery through thick glasses. Alice kept a packed suitcase in her room, for when she was to go home.

"You're proofing the menu again, dear," Morton said. He reached out to hold Alice's hand. She pulled away.

I do feel sorry for the poor dear, Marie said. *I don't know why you keep doing this to her, dragging her out.*

If she doesn't remember, what difference does it make? Morton thought. Maybe it was selfish of him, but she seemed to enjoy the food and the outing. Look, there she was, flirting with a baby in a nearby booth. The baby dropped a fistful of rice on the floor and smiled. It had tiny teeth poking up from its bottom gum.

I should tell you now, if you haven't figured it out already: Morton and Alice had a thing, back in the day. It lasted three years, from Christmas to Christmas exactly.

And I should tell you that it nearly destroyed him, Marie adds. Morton's dead wife wants to show you something, and though you wouldn't expect a disembodied form to have photographs, she does.

See?

She wants me to tell you about them. I have to be polite, plus I'm curious. Who'd take photos of a love affair they were trying to keep secret? So I look.

Our families were friends, Marie explains. The photos are Kodachrome, like the Paul Simon song, although I personally think everything looks better in black and white. They're curling around the edges, as if from repeated handling, although of course they're not actually real. The first shot is of a younger Morton in a Santa suit, with a thick tuggable beard. He's too skinny, and the red velvet is thin, also, but other than that he looks good.

This was taken before, Marie says. *He got stuck in Alice's chimbly. They had to call the fire department.*

Maybe this is what Marie had meant with *it nearly destroyed him.*

If a spot of dust could give you a look like your mother discovering you'd tracked mud all over her kitchen, Marie does this. I'm not used to having my mind read. You and I had better watch out. I'm doing this for your benefit, you know.

The next photo is a blur of a child running. What's most impressive is the green grass, the blue sky. There's a blanket under a tree in the corner of the photo, almost as an afterthought. A woman lies on the blanket, or at least I think it's a woman.

Morton is a fool to think I wouldn't find out, Marie says, but there is kindness in the ghost's voice. Poor woman. After all, she's dead, and that has to be hard on her.

That's not the story we're here for, Marie, dear, I tell her. We're here because something is about to happen.

Neither he nor Alice can eat much these days, so Morton ordered Orange Chicken and white rice. They'd share. On second thought, he added an order of Crab Rangoon for a starter. He was starting to feel woozy. Already he had bled through his sleeve, and the white cloth napkin he was using for a compress was showing spots. He'd have to tip extra. The food came, and they ate, and he paid, and that was that.

"Would you like to go for a drive?" Morton asked. He wasn't supposed to take her from the restaurant, but Alice liked to look at the big houses in the suburbs. As her memory receded, she had forgotten that she'd moved to California. She thought she was still in Chicago and would comment on the drive back about how the neighborhood had changed over the years. The brick was gone, for example. You don't see a lot of brick in earthquake country.

Alice assented, and Morton brought the car back half a block. He hurried despite the pain, conscious of their time limit.

Once they were on the freeway, Morton said, "You may remove your stuff."

"Thank God," Alice said. She took off her glasses, kicked off her sensible shoes, and stretched. They used to go through the litany from the Roald Dahl book (gloves, wigs, shoes), but it took too long, and Alice wasn't actually a witch. She just got better when she was going west. And worse when she was going east.

"I missed you," Morton said. Usually he would ruffle her hair, but he had to keep both hands on the wheel.

"Jesus, hon, you're bleeding," Alice said. "What happened?"

"No bother, just a fall. Stupid, my fault," Morton said. They had maybe fifteen minutes before he'd have to turn around or risk being late. After that was the eight-and-a-half-mile Bay Bridge, and then about ten miles of San Francisco before the ocean. "Alice, honey, do you remember what we did the last time we had a drive?"

She undid her seat belt and slid closer to him. "Just drove, and looked out at everything." Though she was lucid, Alice didn't seem to remember from week to week.

Morton took a breath. There was something he had to say, and he didn't care if Marie heard. Maybe she deserved to hear it.

"Alice, why'd we never do it, back in the day?" he asked.

"We probably should have," Alice said. "It would have been good. Just multiply the mistletoe." She sat in the middle seat of his old Buick, leaning her head against his shoulder. She should have been wearing a seatbelt.

Morton wanted to kiss her. He wanted to say something loving and charming and smart, something memorable. It tore at him. He wanted Alice to do something, say something, write her thoughts in a notebook while she still could. Whatever she should have been doing with this borrowed time, she wasn't doing it.

"I thought about you, though," he said. "I had conversations in my head with you every day. I still do."

"As did I. That's almost as good, right?"

It wasn't. All of us knew it, Marie and me and you, too, and not one of us said anything.

"I think it must be a polarization thing," Morton said to break the silence. "Because it's only when we're going west that you come back. Maybe there's something to do with the magnetic fields, the North Pole. If we could just figure out how it works—"

Alice interrupted. "When you only feel like yourself once a week for a few minutes, like waking up out of a dream, you—OK, well. I want it, of course I do. I miss being myself. When I'm coherent enough to notice." She put a warm hand on Morton's thigh. "The rest of the time, I don't care. I sit in the sunny spot, and it's enough."

"I can't believe that," he managed to say. Her hand on his thigh commanded his attention.

She teased his penis erect, through his khakis. He gasped, as much surprised at her action as his reaction. He hadn't had a willie since he started taking the blood thinners.

"Morton," Alice said. "I wasn't going to tell you this, but every time you take me out, I have to go back through it again. Losing everything."

Morton's hands tightened on the wheel. He was ashamed. Selfish, that's what he was, taking advantage of her. Marie was right, and she wasn't even going to *say* so.

Alice undid his zipper, and the feeling of her fingers on him, so dearly wanted for so long, made him forget what he had been thinking.

They were nearly to the bridge. Morton would have to turn around. If he didn't have Alice back to the restaurant in time, if the driver saw him pull up with Alice, he'd get in trouble; Alice's daughter would find out, and Alice wouldn't be able to meet him anymore.

He kept driving. Of course he kept driving.

OK, pause, Marie says. I figure dead people know everything, but it's clear she's as surprised as me. Maybe she thinks narrators know everything.

You're going to make them drive off the bridge, she says, upset. *Or they'll get in an accident, or they'll drive into the ocean.*

I'm not the one driving, I say. *Plus, you told me they'd had a thing.*

They did. That's obvious.

So you knew they never, ah, I say.

Marie's ghost seems to pulse. *You know how it feels, when you're having sex with your husband and you know he's thinking about someone else? He never said anything, but I could tell.*

Still mad? I hazard.

"Shut up, you two," Morton said under his breath.

"What, hon?" Alice, with her Western-going magic and her hand in Morton's trousers, didn't seem to hear us at all.

No, Marie says. *I love him.*

"Oh, sweetheart. Just wishing I could pull over. *Oh*," Morton said. It was suicidal, what they were doing. He was going forty-five in the left lane, still on the bridge. He was trying to remember how to get to UCSF, the medical hospital where he'd taken Marie so many times. If the doctors could see Alice, the change in her behavior, they could investigate. Maybe fix her. He didn't know what else to do.

You're going to betray her like that? Marie and I both want to know.

"What am I supposed to do?" Morton said. With regret, he gently grasped Alice's hand, trying to move it away from his penis. She moved faster.

"Just come, my love," Alice said. The skin of her palm was so smooth.

You try stopping the girl you're in love with from touching you. He groaned, realizing what she was doing, and his hand tightened on hers.

His weakened left hand wasn't enough to hold the wheel. The car eased itself into the embankment. They were hit from the back, and the car twirled and twisted. The airbags deployed, breaking Morton's nose, but it was the windshield that stopped Alice.

I can't believe you let that happen, you jerk, Marie says. *You know as well as I do that you're gone, just the same as them, once this story is over.*

Marie is right. Also, this is embarrassing for them as well as tragic. I'd wanted to end the story in the restaurant. After the meal, and after Alice's driver had picked her up, Morton would have stood with some effort, found his cane hanging on the back of the chair, and walked toward his car, with every intention of going to the hospital. How about that?

Ain't going to work, Marie says. *We may as well get comfortable.*

We sit on the curb inasmuch as two spectral beings can, waiting for the ambulance to arrive. Morton and Alice are both passed out; I can't feel anything from them. Which is probably good, because if they were dead already, they'd be with us. And we'd have some talking to do, for sure.

Somehow this is all my fault. It's terrible. But I did it for you.

The thing you don't know about dreams is the thing Marie teaches me as we follow the ambulance. When you fly in dreams, it's just like being dead. Being dead is just like flying. The trick is to keep going. Stay away from other people. They're just so *interesting*, it's hard to leave them be.

That was my problem, thinking their story is mine, but it's not. It's like quantum mechanics. If we hadn't been watching, I want to think that Morton and Alice would have had their boring normal lunch, and gone about their boring normal lives without really talking or touching, and finally died quiet, peaceful deaths. Comforting, but dull. Maybe we had to have the ghost of the wife, and the hand job, and the car accident, just to hold our interest.

On the other side of the bridge, Marie heads south with the ambulance and the freeway. I keep going west, towards the ocean and the sun.

And you. You stop here.

There is a trail along a creek bed near where I live. Exercise, and walking, in particular, is often useful for writing, so I took a hike one late Saturday afternoon and came up with this story. At one point, early on, my brain felt full, and I nearly turned back home to write it down before it all fell out; but I realized that I'd only found my characters and hadn't figured out what they would do. So I kept walking. By the time I'd completed the trail, I had all of the elements, so I went home and wrote the story. That's one version of its origins.

The other involves a long paper I wrote with Gary K. Wolfe, "21st Century Stories," in the British scholarly journal *Foundation* 103, for which we analyzed a number of stories associated with interstitiality, by authors such as M. Rickert, Jeffrey Ford, and Kelly Link. My fiction often ends up occupying interstitial territory—I get regular rejection letters from genre editors, saying that the speculative element isn't central enough, and have stories bounced from literary markets because genre work isn't serious enough—so it was neat to see how other writers used a combination of fantastic, postmodern, and what we in the genre call "mainstream" techniques. I kept this alchemical mix in mind while writing, and the story that resulted is a combination of my discovery of the characters and events, and a conscious dialogue with other writers. Though interstitial art is often defined as work that crosses borders or falls between cracks, it's also a way to describe works that bridge the intuitive and the intentional.

Amelia Beamer

After Verona

William Alexander

The news is getting everything wrong. Her name was Verona, and not Veronica. She was not a teenager, and would not have been flattered to be mistaken for one. She was not an edgy performance artist. She painted. She also sculpted.

The news is implying that her boyfriend is sketchy. They always imply that the boyfriend, or husband, is sketchy. I'm angry on his behalf. I am also angry because this basic, default assumption usually turns out to be right. Part of the logic behind it is that someone has to care about you very deeply if they are going to bother beating you to death with "multiple instruments."

The only fact which does not change between newspaper editions is the fact that she is dead. That part is accurate. I know because she isn't answering messages, and because she hasn't finished the painting that's supposed to be in a show next week. I know because I'm looking after her dog, and she would never leave her dog alone for this long if she could possibly help it.

The dog is small and bug-eyed. She loved it. I made fun of her for it. It never barks, it just whines when it needs to excrete.

The newspapers are retelling a familiar story, visible in the details they choose to print, the ones they ignore, and the ones they completely and utterly misrepresent. They are not doing this by choice. They have no choice. The pattern is hardwired.

They are telling a story about a girl who goes walking alone. She meets a wolf. The end. It is all very sad, but with clucking of tongues and with shaking of heads we must admit that, in some small way, she had it coming.

I am not at all sure that I want to know the other story, the one under the latex gloves of a medical examination, but I do know that it is not about a girl who went walking alone in dark woods and died there. She was smart, and she was careful, and she died at home. She did not have it coming.

$\sim$

"They're just trying to shrug it off," says Arnold. He prints out another strip of "50 % OFF" stickers and puts them on books. I stand by the register. There are no actual customers, so nothing more than standing is required of me. "That's what you get for being one of those bohemian artist types. It couldn't ever happen to one of *us*, the ordinary folk who qualify as persons."

"They're not shrugging it off," I say. "They're fascinated. But whatever, I still think you should talk to your mom. Talk about *editorial slant*. Talk about *fact-checking*, for chrissake. They could at least get her name right." Arnold's mother edits our largest local rag. I am not sure how much power she actually wields, given that the whole paper is owned by a company in Utah, but she *is* the editor.

Arnold shrugs and scratches his beard. His hair and beard are two different colors; one red, the other brown. "What I don't understand," he says, "is how there could be multiple causes of death. How can there ever be multiple causes? Rasputin drowned. That's it. He drowned. He had various and diverse injuries, but when it comes right down to it, there is only ever one cause of death, and his was drowning."

"There's never just one cause of anything," I say. Arnold, whose ears are purely decorative, gives a smug snort and goes on about Rasputin for awhile.

The bell on the door finally dings. A kid pushes his own stroller inside. A woman follows, taking kid-size steps to avoid stepping on the toddler.

"Can I help you find anything?" I ask. This is not a selfless question. Please let me help you find something. Please give me something to do. Ask me a question I can answer.

She smiles and shakes her head. I point in the direction of the kids' books, but the kid is already headed that way.

"What a great stroller," I say, interrupting Arnold. "Looks like an escape pod with bicycle tires. Why didn't we get strollers like that? Mine had tiny plastic wheels."

"I have no idea what my stroller was like," Arnold said. "But listen—thirteen inches. Seriously. Rasputin took it out for the palace guard when they demanded identification."

"You don't remember your stroller?"

"No. I don't. Kids creep me out. They creep me out under normal circumstances, and last night I got attacked by several little bastards on my ride home."

"Really?"

"Yeah," he says. "Really. Kids threw bottles at me from the overpass bridges. Happened at Ninth Street, and then again at Fifteenth." Arnold and I both commute to the bookstore by bicycle, but from opposite directions. He takes the bike path that used to be a railroad track: a long east-west ravine cutting through the city and underneath the north-south roads.

"Did you get hit?" I ask.

"No," he says, "but the broken glass blew out one of my tubes. I had to replace it this morning."

"Shit," I say.

"Yeah," he says. "That whole trail is set up just like a mountain pass in a Western. You know, the one you're guaranteed to be ambushed in. I always get that feeling. It's like when you walk into a bar and you know exactly how the kung fu fight would go down, if it ever went down. You can see it happen. So I wasn't surprised when the bottles started dropping on my head."

"Shit," I say again.

"Yeah," he says.

I ask how kung fu fighting would likely go down in the bookstore, and Arnold launches into a fully choreographed description. He has clearly thought about this before.

I wonder if Verona fought back. She probably did. I try not to imagine this happening.

The stages of grief are not linear. They cycle rapidly and at random. My own version of Bargaining has more to do with time travel than making deals with some kind of deity; I think about the one thing in the past that, if changed, would fix the present and make the whole story work out the way it should. It would be helpful if I could repeat the day in question in an endless loop, broken only by my discovery of the right thing to do. This does not seem to be happening.

Instead I keep dreaming that I am a detective. Every night I figure it out. I go to her apartment, look around, and understand what happened, Sherlock style. He could always read a place, and all the little things that make a place, as though the dining rooms and street corners of London were built out of language to be read.

In the morning I can't remember, or else I *do* remember my imaginary understanding and it no longer makes sense.

The next day I check up on Verona's boyfriend, just to check up on him. He's glad I called, but neither one of us has much to say. He asks about the dog. I tell him about the dog, leaving out the most annoying and smelly details. He would be the one looking after the dog if he wasn't allergic. He tells me that his allergies are the primary reason why he and Verona never moved in together.

There is a pause. One of us is going to ask. It turns out to be him.

"Heard anything?"

"No," I say. "You?"

"No. The police just remind me that forensic tests take longer than a commercial break."

"Yeah," I say.

He sounds broken. He sounds like he is not actually there. This might just be a bad cell phone connection.

The dog skitters across the kitchen tiles, pauses to lick my toe, and moves on. Its name is Parsifal, but I still think of it as "the dog."

"Hey," says Albert when I get to the store. "I found the *best* book cover in Alternative Health. It's a photograph close-up of someone sticking a long, purple gemstone in their ear. I kid you not. The ear takes up most of the cover, and it's like the rock is a magic Q-tip from the seventies. I put it on display. Go take a look."

I go take a look. *Crystal Healing* is propped up on an eye-level shelf beside Herbert RavenMonkey's *Athenian Vampires*. Next to that is *Confessions of a Pet Psychic*.

I pick up *Confessions of a Pet Psychic* and page through it. There is a chapter on communicating with dearly departed pets, and

189

chapters about understanding the past lives of pets (all domestic cats remember Egypt, apparently), but there is nothing about communication with pets who witness a murder in a small apartment. I put the book back on the shelf.

"It happened again last night," Arnold tells me when I get back to the register.

I stand perfectly still and wait for him to tell me who else has been murdered.

"What happened?" I finally ask.

"Hooligans ambushed me on the bike trail," he says, and I start breathing again.

"Did they throw bottles?" I try to sound concerned rather than relieved.

"No," he says. "They were hiding under one of the bridges, behind the big concrete columns. As I got closer they all came out, six or seven of them. They stretched across the trail and held hands like paper dolls, just to block my way."

"What did you do?"

He grins, impressed with himself. "First I shouted. Then I took the chain and padlock off my shoulder and started swinging it around like a lasso."

"Really."

"Oh, yes. They wouldn't budge, and I wouldn't slow down. So I swung the chain out in front of me and hit a pair of clasped hands. They let go, and I rode through the gap. No cries of pain. Nothing. Not a word. I'm pretty sure I broke some fingers back there, and I didn't even get a reaction."

"You could have killed one of them," I say.

He shrugs. His casual attitude toward violence makes me want to kill him.

"No," he says. "I don't think I could have."

"A heavy padlock to the head wouldn't have done it?"

He looks at the ceiling. "I got a pretty good look at them, and I really don't think I could have done much harm. Do you know how many places overlap with the land of the dead?"

"No," I say.

"Me neither," he says, "but I am pretty sure that the bike trail between ninth and fifteenth is one of them."

Other places of overlap include reflective surfaces, shadows, and dreams. This is because these are the three traditional methods of seeing someone without actually looking at their physical body. Be careful around people who don't have shadows. Don't trust anyone who doesn't show up on film. They have obviously misplaced their souls, or else never had them to begin with.

I know this because of a thick blue book in the folktale section, second shelf down from the top.

I am also fairly sure that the freight elevator in the back of the bookstore overlaps with the land of the dead—not because of shadows and reflections, though it is fairly dark in there, but because of the noises that the cables make.

Today the cables make a noise that sounds very much like Parsifal the dog. I'm bringing a huge pallet of books down to the basement, which is where we unpack pallets of books. I don't know what the dog-cables are saying. I don't know if there is any such thing as an elevator psychic.

This particular elevator does not stop automatically. You have to hold down the button, watch the wall of the shaft go by through the rusty fence-door, and let go of the button at precisely the right time to line up floor and elevator. You have to take inertia into account. It's tricky. I'm usually good at it, but today I'm listening to dogs in the cables and trying to understand them. Today I hold down the button until the elevator clangs against the bottom of the shaft and gets stuck.

I let go of the button, which does nothing because I am already as far down as the elevator goes. I push *up*, and this also does nothing. I do some shouting. Then I use my cell to call the front desk of the bookstore, and leave a message for Arnold when he doesn't pick up.

There is a manual crank upstairs, all the way upstairs on the fourth floor of the building. It should be possible to unstick the elevator with the crank. I tell this to voicemail, and hang up, and wait for it to happen. Then I start pacing. There is plenty of room for pacing. You could set up a Ping-Pong table in here. You could fit an entire car in the elevator, which used to be convenient because our storefront used to be a car dealership.

Verona loved knowing the history of a room, a building, or a broken piece of furniture. She figured that places have memories, and she tried to read the language of those memories. She painted moldy ventilation ducts and claimed that the mold was just the next stage of vent-evolution. It's lovely stuff, her art of urban decay, but it is also unsettling. It gives the papers another reason to imply that she flirted with dark and dangerous things, and therefore had it coming.

I'm still pacing, and I notice that I'm angry, and I wonder if I have any right to be, if the stages of grief are reserved for family members rather than friends and classmates and other peripheral mourners. I feel like a poser, monopolizing someone else's tragedy for an emotional thrill. Then I feel like a bastard for ever not-grieving, for letting Arnold's inane, ironic obsession with bad new-age books distract me. Then I feel nothing much. Then I'm angry again. Then I laugh because Verona would knock her knuckles against my forehead and tell me I'm a dink. I could always count on her to tell me I'm a dink. She would love this elevator, with its old wooden floor and its rusty fence-doors at either end.

I stop pacing to open one of the doors, behind which is the concrete wall of the elevator shaft. I can hear a faint cable-squeak. I can also hear the sound of countless people standing perfectly still.

"What happened?" I ask her. She doesn't say. She isn't there.

Cables whine, and the floor shudders.

"Shut the door!" Arnold shouts from very far above me. "I can't turn the crank with it open."

That night I dream that Parsifal has been mummified and left in Verona's apartment. The eyeballs, each one already larger than the dog's little brain in its little cranium, have been replaced by stones that are even larger. It blinks, dry skin scraping over stone eyes.

"He isn't allergic," says the mummy dog in a deep baritone.

I wake up.

I remember how Verona's boyfriend cried on my shoulder at

the wake. He left a small snot trail on my suit. I wonder if the police know that he isn't allergic to dogs.

Arnold misses his shift the next day. He doesn't pick up his phone. This is not necessarily cause for alarm. Arnold never picks up his phone.

His mother stops by in midafternoon. She wears a commanding pinstripe suit and looks at me as though she wishes that she didn't have to.

"My son will not be coming in today," she says. "He is getting stitches."

"What happened?" I ask.

"Someone threw a bottle at his head," she says.

"I'm sorry," I say.

"So am I," she says. She looks around to make sure that there are no customers nearby. "I'm also sorry about your friend." She does sound genuinely sorry. I reluctantly abandon the speech I've prepared about fact-checking.

"Thank you."

"Are they making any progress?" she asks.

I shrug. "You would know before I do."

"Not necessarily. Do you have any theories of your own?"

I am very much aware that this might be on the record. "Beats me. She knew some pretty strange and intense people."

Arnold's mom shakes her head and waves one hand in the air. "Don't worry about strange and intense," she says. "Worry about the ones who aren't really there, the ones who give shitty hugs."

She gives me a hug, and it's a pretty good hug. I can't remember the quality of Verona's boyfriend's hugs. I try to remember if I've ever seen his shadow.

That night I close the store, count the cash, and turn the key. I ride to the bike path. I take the opposite direction from home.

No one throws bottles or shoots arrows down from the sides of the ravine. I pause underneath every bridge, waiting. Sometimes I can see hands and faces in the bridge support pillars, revealed by crumbling cement.

Verona would have loved these pillars. She would have mixed pigment with the pulverized cement dust and made wonders with it. She would have known what the cement remembered, and she would have encouraged a stretched piece of canvas to know it, too.

I pause underneath the Ninth Street bridge and wait.

They come out from behind the pillars, and from within the pillars. They are all children. They are all male. This bothers me. They are not holding hands. They don't touch each other, and they do not touch me, but they have me surrounded. Two sodium lights are whining above us. None of the children have shadows.

This bridge overlaps with the land of the dead, but dead is a very big place. It is probably absurd to assume that they all know each other. When I meet someone from Australia, I always ask whether they know the only other person I've met from Australia. They never do. I still have to ask.

The dead who live under bridges and throw bottles might know what happened to her. They might be able to tell me what story she is actually in.

Maybe Verona's boyfriend will be arrested by a Violent Criminal Apprehension Unit when forensic tests are finally concluded. Maybe he will confess to every brutal detail and give a tearful and truthful confession that explains absolutely everything.

It won't happen. I'm sure of that. They may track down *who*, but never a satisfactory *why*. He won't say, whoever he turns out to be, because he doesn't have a shadow. The dog won't say, not even in dreams, because the dog doesn't know.

This is a story about not-knowing. It is frustrating, and I am sorry about that, but I don't get to know why this happened to her, and neither do you. Just please remember that she is not Red Riding Hood. She is not in that story, not unless you can accept *woods* and *wolf* as extremely large variables. She did not have it coming.

I am surrounded by children without shadows. I should ask why she died, because it is possible that they know.

"Is she okay?" I ask instead, even though I know better, even though there were multiple instruments, even though the casket was closed at the wake.

They turn around, almost in unison but not quite. Each one of them leaves, walking back between concrete pillars and across overlapping borders. This might be my answer, but I don't understand it. I can't read it. Verona might have known. She might have found this place legible, with its crumbling pillars and sodium light, but she is not here. No one is under this bridge but me, and I'm leaving.

I ride back the way I came.

It has occurred to me a couple of times, at a couple of different funerals, that eulogies are interstitial sorts of stories. They contradict, acknowledging loss while trying to put it off awhile longer. They take memories and make them more memorable for having been shaped and shared, and therefore just a tiny bit more permanent. They are stories told at thresholds, in the borderland places where the rules change, and a ghost story is a eulogy with a flashlight held under the chin.

William Alexander

Valentines

Shira Lipkin

1.

The waiter's name is Valentine. He has long, slim fingers, and he writes down my order instead of pretending to commit it to memory. I like that, his pen on the paper bringing forth one simple thing about me. My lunch. Just a tiny fragment of information. I honor him by doing the same. "The waiter's name is Valentine," I write in my battered notebook, "and he has long, slim fingers."

Information is sacred. I don't remember why, or who told me. But I know that information is sacred, so I write it down, scraps of knowledge and observations. I used to write in leather-bound journals with elegant, heavy pens, but my fetish for elegance has fallen by the wayside in my rush to commit everything to paper. Now I use cheap marbled composition books, purchased by the dozen. The pen is still important, though. It must write in smooth lines of black, not catch on the page. There is too much to capture.

I order chai and butternut squash soup. I write that down as well, just after Valentine does. I watch him walk to the kitchen, slender and graceful, and I wonder what Valentine does when he is not refilling coffee mugs. I wonder if he dances. I write that down: "Perhaps Valentine dances." I watch him flirt with the barista, their movements around each other a careful ballet of hot espresso and soup and witty banter, and I curl up in my armchair and wrap my hands around the mug of tea when Valentine brings it to me with his usual smile and nod. I observe. I record.

I write on the bus, on my way home. I write about the bus driver, and about the woman sitting across from me, wearing a too-heavy jacket ("perhaps she is sick"). I write about the barista and the patterns of her movement around the large copper espresso machine, the way she admires her reflection. When I get home, I carefully tear the pages from my notebook, and I tear fact from fact, isolating each bit of information, and I file them in the rows of small boxes nailed to my walls. Miniature pigeon coops filled with paper instead of birds. Facts. Ways to build the world. I copy things over when necessary, when I must file "perhaps Valentine dances" under both "Valentine" and "Speculation." I must separate speculation, after all. My shreds and fragments of information comprise my image of Valentine (for example). I cannot allow speculation to color that. I can allow his grace, but not the possibility of his dancing.

With enough data, maybe I can figure out the world.

2.

The waiter's name is Val. His hands are stained a burnished yellow from nicotine, and guitar-callused. He is bored and impatient, waiting for his shift to end. He does not write down my order—which is fair because it's just coffee and blackberry pie, and the pie is right at hand. He slices it and slaps it on the plate; it falls over just a bit, slides, and blackberry oozes out onto the plain white plate, the color almost shocking. I write that down, and the way the steam dances over the coffee mug. The mug is smooth and unadorned, the same bone white, and the coffee is rich and dark and bitter. The diner is a diner, no more and no less, retro-1950s tube with aproned waitresses and meat loaf and pie and Val, leaning forward by the register, staring at the door. Waiting for something else.

He talks to me, I think out of sheer boredom—I'm the only customer at the bar, the only person here alone. His dark hair is frosted blond at the ends, and his eyes are seaglass blue. He is in a band, but he worries that now that the guys have day jobs, they'll stop playing music. He doesn't think he's good enough to go solo. He shrugs a lot—he has developed his own fake-casual rolling shrug, a silent "whatever." He asks why I care, and I tell him that these are the things that make him *him*. That we are collections of information. We are what we are because our dog died or our dad left or we won the lottery or whatever. And I like to figure out what people are by examining what they're made of.

When I close my eyes, I imagine Val made of paper, all the little strips of paper I'll file later under "Music" and "Loss" and

"Resentment," cross-reference him with others, see if I can figure out "loss."

See if I can figure out data loss.

When I open my eyes, Val has gone on to the next customer. I eat my pie and write.

3.

The waiter's name is V. It's a new restaurant, sci-fi–themed; all of the waiters have names like Klaatu or Ripley. I point out that *V* is a series, not a character, and he laughs. "No one remembers character names from *V*. But everyone remembers the show. Everyone remembers the lizards."

He writes down my order, and I write down that everyone remembers *V*. I will file it under "Television" and "Things everyone remembers." "Things everyone remembers" is one of my bigger boxes; it is not nearly full. Not nearly as full as it needs to be.

Data loss. I do not remember the things everyone remembers. And I need to. In order to build a self, I need a foundation. So I write everything down, and I am always hoping that someone will let slip one of the things "everyone knows" or "everyone remembers." *V* and the Challenger explosion and 9/11 and the Smurfs. Sometimes when I get home, after I file the day's newly gathered information, I take the slips out of that box and spread them out on the floor, subcategorize them. Everybody knows this about politics. Everyone remembers that song.

My food arrives, a faux-Klingon dish I've already forgotten the name of. I must look it up later and record it. The drink V brings is not what I ordered—it's a neon-blue thing in a Klein bottle with dry ice fuming out of it. V grins and drapes himself over the chair beside me. "You looked like you could use it."

"What is it?"

"Dunno. Try some."

"I have . . . trouble. With things I don't know."

V looks around; seeing no manager, he takes a quick sip from my glass. "Perfectly safe."

I sip. It's sweet. V grins as I lower the glass. His hair is frosted silver, and I wonder if he's dyed it, or if he sprays it on every night.

His hands seem to have a mind of their own; he gestures incessantly when he talks. Italian, he says, with a shrug very unlike Val's. I write that down: "Italians talk with their hands," and also, "V is Italian."

He has to get up, eventually, as the restaurant gets busy. He brings me a spoon for dessert, with a wink like Valentine's.

1.

Valentine writes my order down with a flourish and gives me a wink like V's. I study him—none of his other mannerisms remind me of V. He does not talk with his hands. He is not flashy or flamboyant. His hands, unlike Val's, do not have guitar calluses; if Valentine plays anything it's a wind instrument, or maybe a violin.

This is speculation. I cannot allow speculation.

I study my own hands. They shake slightly, and I wonder if I ever played anything; if so, that data is lost. I should search my apartment. It has been too long since I've done anything there but file and sleep.

Valentine presents my chai with a smile. "Valentine," I ask, halting him in his graceful spin kitchenward, "do I always order the same thing?"

"In the fall, yeah." He sits down beside me in a way not entirely unlike V's draping or Val's slouch. "Other soups, the rest of the year. But always chai and soup."

"Then why do you write it down?"

"Because you like it." I must look as puzzled as I feel, because he shrugs (unlike Val, like V) and continues. "You told me once that you don't see how anyone can hold that in their heads, not really. Things fade. I might forget what kind of tea, what kind of soup."

I stretch my hand, aching from holding the pen. "I think I forget."

2.

Val pours the coffee, thick plume of steam from the stream of dark liquid, the battered pot. "Do I always get the same thing?"

Val gives his rolling shrug. "Coffee, keep it comin'. Pie. Yeah, you do."

I write that down: "I always order the same thing."

I don't know how to file that. "My brain." That box is over-flowing. I need to find a way to subcategorize it. I can't figure it out.

I ask Val if he's Italian. He's not. Mostly Norwegian, he says. I study him all shift for things that correlate with Valentine and with V. He notices, but ignores it.

I write. Everything. The clumping of the salt in its shaker. The reflection of sunlight on the silver edge of the clock. Val and the waitress, Thalia—she looks like the barista.

Everyone looks like everyone else these days. It feels like my world is compressing. I have to write more, write faster. I have to make sense of things.

3.

I don't remember entering the restaurant, but V is already sprawled across from me. He asks if I'm okay, and I tell him honestly that I don't know. I ask if he's in love with a waitress, and he laughs, says no, gestures at a waiter in Jedi robes. I tell him what I'm slowly, falteringly, worrying about: that all of them are the same person. He tells me all the ways he's different, but I find some things the same.

(A)

They all have a younger brother. They all had a dog, growing up. They are all waiters.

1.

I am so tired. Valentine brings me a chai without my asking, and he asks if I'm okay, and I tell him honestly that I don't know. He asks me when I last saw my doctor.

I say, "Doctor?"

He takes my hand and notices its tremor. He asks if he can walk me home.

4.

I am shy. I have never let anyone in.

Valentine enters, and his eyes widen at the sight of all of the little boxes lining the walls, perched on shelves, the bits of things everybody knows spread over the floor. "What is this?"

"Information," I whisper. "I—have chunks missing. Parts of the world I can't figure out. And I think—I think that bits of other worlds are melting in to cover the gaps. I think that maybe all Valentines are the same Valentine. I think the universe or the multiverse or whatever has this stopgap for data loss, and I think the human brain does pattern patching on a subconscious level—finding the things that match you and filling holes with them. Do you think that's what happens?" And I pray for an "Everybody knows," but he gives me something else.

He had been on duty when I had the seizure. He watched my body arc back; he called 911. Probably saved my life. The doctor told him I might lose some memory.

I lost more than that.

I lost swaths of long-term memory, the things everybody knew, the things I knew. I stopped being able to get all of my short-term memory into long-term. I started having trouble conceptualizing things.

I started writing. Data retrieval. Trying to make sense of the world.

I don't remember. I don't remember any of it. But Valentine so clearly does. And he is right there, holding my gaze and holding my hand, and the earth begins to tremble—

He tries to pull me to the doorway, but I refuse—I stand in the middle of the room and the whole building starts to shake, and I watch a year of carefully gathered and filed slips of information explode from the walls and shower around me like a snow globe, all of the fact and the speculation, all of the ways to learn people and make things make sense, all falling around me like ash, and I have a sort of hitching sob in my chest as I drop to my knees as the room settles, and he is there. V. Val. Valentine. His hair flashes silver, flashes blond, settles to dark, and his hands resolve from callused to slim, and he is folded back into himself; all Valentines are one Valentine. And I look up at him helplessly, all of my data scattered, and I ask: "Do you dance?"

Epileptics live in a very interstitial state, slipping from world to world with little or no warning. Some seizures induce a sort of religious euphoria. Some are stark, terrifying disconnection. In some, one hears music no one else can hear, or one experiences the scent of lilacs as a physical object.

Temporal lobe epilepsy means, at its best, walking between worlds.

In 2003, I became interstitial, and I've been trying to make sense of it ever since—of the electrical cascades in my brain that can send me elsewhere, of the battery of medications that often make things worse, and of the pervasive sense of data loss and the odd things the brain does to patch those holes.

"Valentines" could be an extended seizure state. It could be many-worlds quantum physics. It could be magical realism. It is me, like my protagonist, trying my best to make sense of this in-between world.

Shira Lipkin

(*_*?) ~~~ (-_-):
The Warp and the Woof

Alan DeNiro

Roger found the notebook in his attic, tucked in the side pocket of a kevlar jacket. The notebook contained his first novel, the one he wrote when he was twenty-two and never had the heart to revise or learn any more about. He had forgotten about it, but the smell of his old cologne on the pages awakened his memory. The world that he had written about was long dead, but he wanted someone else to sift through the notebook, to extract something marketable from it. Roger couldn't read his own handwriting anymore. He stared and stared at it—the squiggles—but did anyone know cursive anymore? No one had penmanship. For a few delusional seconds he wondered whether someone else had written it.

He went downstairs. Having no luck figuring out what to do with the notebook, and too afraid to place it with his current material, next to his laptop (which still needed to be hand-cranked for the night), he called his agent, voice only.

"I'm going to ship the notebook to you, I mean manually." Above Roger was a framed picture of Roger with the president. Roger's hair was darker then—no, not the radiation, that had no effect on the color.

"What time is it?" his agent asked.

"It's noon," Roger said. "What are you doing? Why are you still sleeping?"

The agent said nothing. The agent knew Roger didn't want to hear about Lord Manhattan, the sweeps and declarations. The agent would have moved out of Queens if she could, but she didn't have the right IDs. The agent had to conduct meetings at night, and daytime security was expensive.

"Well," Roger said, after the pause, "okay, could you look at it, then? Maybe there's something there that could be extracted from it?"

"Sure, sure," the agent said, turning over, squinting at the blinds.

It took five business days for the notebook to reach the agent. FedEx lost a few planes in a flurry of SAMs the week before. Flight schedules were blown up and reconstructed. The courier who handed the package to the agent came at 3 AM.

"Hang on, let me find my wand," the agent said, fumbling in her pockets. "Shit, do you have yours?"

The courier shook her head. "Sorry, mine got stolen."

"Just give me the package, then. I can scan it later."

The courier shook her head and eyed the corridor of the agent's building, the cameras like rifle scopes in the crown molding. "You know the rules. I could get in trouble from the Lord's Army, like that."

"Bitch, give me the package!" the agent spat. The courier took a step back and cradled the package to her chest.

"OK, OK," the agent sighed. "I think I might have a spare wand in my kitchen. Hang on." Storming back into her apartment and slamming the door behind her, she thought about her options. She hadn't been able to find her wand for week. Roger, as much as she found him a saddening figure, was her primary source of income. And he hadn't had a new book in a year. The side projects, yes—but the ghost writers and translators made their cuts larger and larger, the custom freight to Roger's market strongholds—White Vegas, Nebraskan Rhodesia, the Dobsonpods on the Yellow Sea, Pentecosta—were getting more restrictive. And they were strongholds, not strangleholds. Newer, semiliterate thriller authors were rising. Thugs, Roger called them, even some reeducated Asians and Arabs, but they gave people what they wanted. Words garnished with blood. Roger was about ideas, his ideas about the state. With each passing year after Operation Mexico Moon, the agent cared about those ideas less and less. The agent had to eat and pay for the apartment, not to mention the retainer fee for the building's security detail. She thought about what she had to do, walking to her bedroom, and what she had to do made her sad.

She would not tell Roger.

She came back and opened the door, was rather amazed that

the courier was still standing there. The agent raised her arm and Tasered the courier's face. Wasn't a clean shot; the stinger punctured her cheek, straight through. The courier fell back, and the agent kicked the package through her apartment door, rubbing the arm brace where her Taser was attached. She then unhooked the wire, which would dissolve in about an hour. Kneeling down to the courier she said, "I warned you. It's my risk. It's my package. Why should you give a fuck if I get blown up by it? I have no family left to sue you. And you can fuck your Lord, you fucking hear me?" She stood up and rolled the courier into the freight elevator, and pressed Down.

She decided she needed wine before opening the package. After half a bottle, Quebecois Concord vintage, she cut open the package with a butcher knife. Black duct tape all along the perimeter, thicker than the packaging itself. Then she extracted the notebook. Thick gray cover, gray wire spirals. The pages were soft, cheap paper, almost decomposing, unlined. Roger's cursive alternated between blue ink and pencil. The agent couldn't make heads or tails of it.

"Fuck," she said to herself, taking the wine from the bottle. "Was he thirteen when he wrote this?" Then she slept, dreaming of elephants in rivers electrocuted by lightning. They were trying to cross to tell the agent something, but she kept saying, turn back, turn back! When she woke, she took the tube out of her ear and shook it.

"Ah," she said, then stared at the notebook. Then Roger called.

"Well?" he said.

"I don't know what to tell you, Roger," she said. "It's really… dense." She rubbed her arm where she had attached the Taser. "I'm going to have to bring in a consultant."

"Who?" On the other end, she heard his apprentice scrubbing a floor and running a hose. Roger had good grandchildren, who went to good schools. He boarded writers-in-residence each year from his pool of readerly constituents. This year it was only one writer. He would not trust his apprentice with his notebook; she did his chores. The other Minnesotans in his complex, which used to be the Minnesota Zoo, tolerated him because he was famous.

"I'm . . . not sure yet," she said, although she was sure. "Don't worry about it. Listen, what is the novel about? Why don't you pitch it to me?" She laughed, uneasy. It had been a long time since Roger had had to pitch anything.

"I..." Roger stopped, and the agent could hear him fumbling for a drink. "That novel was really, really early. I was still working as a bartender, you know? I was still trying to figure out what I needed to do, find my own voice . . . It's like I put everything I didn't want to become in that novel . . ."

"Wait, so it's not a thriller? It's not a Mick Solon book?" Mick Solon was Roger's prime character. Roger wrote series after series of Mick Solon books: Mick assassinating socialist governors, Mick putting newspaper editors on the rack, Mick breaking up Mexican farmers' unions that threatened the state. Above all else, Mick was money.

"Well, not really . . . I mean, it has a character named Mick Solon, but he's not the same . . ."

"Not the same?"

"He's a bit . . . mellower."

"Christ, Roger. What am I supposed to do with this? Will you please tell me what the fuck it's about?"

"It's about relationships," he said. He sounded embarrassed, and a bit surly. "There's a failing marriage. I'm pretty sure there aren't any terrorists in it? But, who the fuck cares. You're my agent. I want you to fucking assess it and sell it. Maybe I could go over it again, add a political subplot, a liberal suicide bomber? Maybe one of the characters has an affair with a sultan's daughter, who's actually been programmed to kill the Republican senator to make sure tax cuts don't go through, because the taxes are going to fund restoration of the caliphate?"

"I don't know, Roger. It sounds kind of retro. Stuck in the past?" The Republicans shattered with the constitution, like all else, like every other party, every other public interest.

"Well, it is set in the past. I'm just thinking out loud here. Look, you're my employee."

"Contractor."

"Whatever. Just transcribe the manuscript and figure out what to do with it."

"Fine." She hung up on him. Then she called the front desk. She was going to work harder for this 25 percent cut than she ever had in her life.

"Security detail, please. I need to go to Kinko's."

She met the concierge in the front lobby. He was in urban camo and had a silver bag slung over his shoulder like a purse. She didn't want to know what he had in there. He was pretty much a kid. He must have thought she was ancient, and she knew he was trying not to stare at the cloverleaf radiation burn on her cheek.

"All right, ma'am," he said, unholstering his sword and turning its crank to power it up. *Ma'am.* "Follow me."

They put on their masks. She crossed her arms and followed him out the door. He walked a few paces in front of her in the street. The Kinko's was only two blocks away, but she didn't want to take any chances. She clutched the notebook close to her chest. It was dusk, and the clouds cast shadows over the rowhouses of Queens, in one of the few sustainable neighborhoods left in the old boroughs. Glittering dust swirled around her feet. She almost slipped on the gangplank, and a few bicycles nearly ran her over, but the concierge barked at one of the cyclists as he passed, and the other that followed got the message. From the Starbucks on the corner of Vine and Polk, a teenage girl watched them pass. The Starbucks window was about a foot thick. She must have been a viceroy's daughter, or a sphere-of-influence envoy, right off the dirigible from China. The agent felt sorry for her, for having to live in this shithole. Lord Manhattan and his revolutionary army could only survive because of the influx of humanitarian aid from Africa and Asia, most of which he kept. And the tourism—plenty of brisk trade to the vaporized sites.

"We're here," the concierge said, moving toward the storefront, looking up at the sky for any security breaches. The gangplank was short by about two feet, so the agent did her best to pick through the mud, coal, and fish bones in front of the Kinko's. Her shoes weren't the best. The concierge gave her a hand. His arm was like a steel beam that she gripped tightly.

"Thank you," she said. He opened the door. She was paying for that courtesy, too.

When she went in the door, she saw that the couriers were waiting for her there, next to the scanners. There was no point in running.

They let her scan the documents and send them to Amar, though. She was surprised about that. But they also said that an equal measure deserved equal measure. The courier she had Tasered was not there. The concierge thought about protecting the agent, but he was outnumbered five to one, and the couriers had these wiry, muscular bodies. And besides, they were under contract with Lord Manhattan, and he wanted no quarrel with him. He sheathed his sword.

"Stupid," one of the couriers said as he held the agent down next to the paper cutter.

"You can hold her hand if you want," another courier said to the concierge. The agent turned her head toward him, and her feet nearly slipped on the wet straw. She could see that he was contemplating leaving her there, and she started screaming and crying.

"What's got into you?" a courier said. "Hold still."

The concierge then took her hand, and she clenched it, dug her nails into him, to the point of almost striking blood. After that, she closed her eyes and could only hear their voices, and she wondered what Roger would think of her.

"Heat it up."

"We can't heat it up. Nothing to do that here . . . none of these machines will do that."

"The bindery? There's a glue-heater on the top—"

"Fuck that. We don't have any pamphlets to bind. I'm not going to pay-n-pedal simply to sterilize an awl."

"Fine. Fine. I don't know if Marigold would really want to cause this one too much harm, though."

"She's not the best judge of that now, is she? She was stupid enough to get wounded."

Then they started arguing in Telugu.

Thirty seconds later the awl went through the agent's cheek, through the cloverleaf lesion, to the other side, scraping against her molars. Then she passed out, and the concierge let go of her hand.

Amar didn't know any of this. He was at the beach when he received the compressed files. His family was in the water, along with hundreds of other fathers' families. Roger's novel tried to download to Amar's wristwatch, but the memory constrictions were too tight. He had worked with the agent before in the past, regarding Roger's increasingly erratic hand at writing. The agent always thought of Roger's hands shaking when he typed or dictated his novels, but Amar never got that sense. He only saw the information at hand.

He squinted at the file name report on his watch—the sun was bright—looking for clues. The scanners captured words in their filing nomenclature before downloading the scans in full at Amar's home: BARBARIAN 20-35.ppgr, DEVIL-ROCK.ppgr, LUCY-IS-AT-A-BAR 450?-.ppgr. More unusual gems: Knives . . . a kiss . . . more devils . . . a hill with a cathedra . . .

"Early draft," the agent had punched into the scanner, with fingers she could barely control, her face bandaged like a mummy's. "Please."

Amar's youngest son, Prius, came running up the beach toward him, from the bay, waving his arms like wings.

"Watch out for the glass!" Amar shouted, covering his watch with his other hand so that his son wouldn't splash any salt water on its face, large as a saucer.

"I saw an eel," his son said as he got closer, panting heavily. "But I escaped it."

"I don't think there are any eels in these waters," Amar said, looking out at the bay. "And the lifeguards would kill them on sight."

"Oh, but there are!" his son said, plopping down on the edge of the towel and pushing his feet into the gravelly sand. Amar winced and turned his body so the watch wouldn't face his son.

"If you say so," he mumbled, giving a smile. Looking at his watch again at a slant, with the file names cascading on the screen, he wondered whether there was a glitch in the transfer. Nothing of the Eighth Client's files had ever looked like this before. The enjoyable voices on the beach kept murmuring over him. Surely there were others like him here?

"You're not working, are you?" his wife said, putting a hand on his shoulder from behind. He flinched.

"You surprised me," he said, looking down.

"You are working. Amar... you need to take that stupid thing off." She stood over him, blocking the sun, crossing her arms. He had met his wife at the Technical Freelance Armory, a few years after Mexico Moon, which in their vendor conglomerate's handbook was called the Strategic Reorganization of the Americas. She was in marketing services for a Bengali pharmaceutical company. She was shy but was finding her career voice over the last few years, after birthing the two children, traveling all over India and Africa to meet her production teams. She was a team leader in a way that Amar could never be. People thought he sounded like a woman on the phone!

"I really need to . . . sorry," he said. "Sorry." He looked toward the bay, the spires of old Visakhapatnam out in the water. "Where's Puneet?"

"I thought he was getting rasgulla?" His wife looked back at the beach house, the snack bar, the Ferris wheel.

"No, no—he was with you in the water?"

"I wasn't in the water."

"He's swimming!" his younger son said. "Way out, near the towers."

"Puneet!" his wife shouted, running out to the water. Amar struggled to get his watch off, but the strap was caught on a hook. As he was fumbling, his mind drifted backward, into an undertow of time, and kept thinking: Why am I panicking? Is it because of her? Why is she panicking?

Back in the van—Amar was actually relieved that the trip to the beach was cut short by an imaginary emergency—Puneet was reluctantly explaining how he had been swimming out to the tower crowns to impress a girl. Who wasn't even Buddhist—his wife assumed, thinking out loud, working through the implications, because if this girl was Buddhist, he wouldn't have had need to impress her, on the breakwalls and ruins of the old port, because of their mutual understanding of their dual non being.

Puneet said nothing as they drove farther up into the hills, trees ripe with mango hybrids overhanging the road. Amar didn't dare venture into this emotional territory—he really couldn't care—of course, he was glad his son was safe, but he had no real doubts on this score in the first place. His wife also drifted into silence. But she had larger issues, which soon became clear after Amar glanced at his watch while driving. "I wish you wouldn't work with devils!" she said, looking straight ahead.

"Father works with devils?" his youngest said. "What are they like?"

"They're not devils."

"According to Nichiren they are," his wife said.

Amar sighed and clenched the wheel of the van tighter. They had met at sangha within the technical college, chanting together. The sanghas were subsidized by the companies; after the Japanese diaspora, Nichiren Buddhism had found a home within the corporations of India. He found it as a way to get ahead, but she fell into Nichiren's teachings, more and more every year.

"We're not going to talk about that now," Amar said.

"America is a poisoned land!"

"I've never met them, my beautiful wife," he said between clenched teeth. "They're only contracts I have with them. Now let me drive."

That night, after his children and wife were asleep, he locked himself in his office with the novel. He had managed to survive the sullen hours after they returned from the beach—helping with dinner, chanting together for world peace, doing laundry while his wife helped Prius with his Mandarin homework. Sand was everywhere. Children on motorcycles sped by on their street, which his wife tut-tutted as she was getting ready for bed. Didn't their parents know this was a good Buddhist neighborhood?

"I can't sleep," he said, sitting up after ten minutes.

"Amar, I love you."

"I know." He kissed her forehead. The night sky was still. She was asleep when she said this. She would only say these words with such fierceness and warmth when she was dreaming.

He poured a Scotch—bottle kept in a secret drawer—and started downloading the scans from his watch. He had to enter the writer's world, and this usually wasn't an enjoyable process. It was never clear what an American writer was ever trying to say. Sometimes it made it easier to move the text along, toward a vision or instinct that Amar felt within the words, but sometimes this ambiguity was a dull wall, too thick to break. Tunneling underneath the text to the other side was the only option, but it was long and painstaking. This novel was, as Amar had feared, one of the latter cases.

If it could be called a novel. The beginning picked up in the middle of the action, in the middle of a dinner party. In a castle? Amar wondered if, perhaps, the agent had forgotten to send pages, but no—the author had clearly numbered each page of the manuscript with tiny, fastidious figures and dates, as if he had been trying to assert a timestamp control that was not there in the text itself:

. . . meeting Mick inside the cathedral was not Mary's cup of tea. She was afraid of it, how it loomed on the hill, the votive candles in the vestibule. She had been there before as a child. But Mick said it was the only safe place, where his wife wouldn't discover the true feelings for Mary that he had to keep secret.

"I have to see you," he said. "That, or else I'll leave the city and backpack through Asia. You know, see the world. You may hear back from me or you may not."

"Fine. It's a deal, then," she said.

Mick's wife had learned to read lips when she was in the foreign service. At the kitchen table, she read her husband's conversation as if it were a book. As Marigold walked up the hill to the cathedral—it was a pleasant path, lit with daffodils—she had no idea that Mick's wife was following twenty paces behind. Mick Solon was already there, lighting a candle and stuffing a dollar in the donation box, supposedly for his dead grandmother.

CHAPTER SIX: Please Don't Kill Me!

This was written more than twenty years ago. This was depressing, all the more depressing after the second Scotch. The handwriting was frantic. The pages had stains—from alcohol, no doubt. Writers like this one always drank. Amar converted the cursive to type, page by page, once he entered his handwriting algorithms. It would take a few hours.

He worked until morning. Decipherment and understanding were two different things, and he was nowhere near understanding when the morning bell rang six times. He could hear his wife wake and shuffle into the kitchen and then the shrine room. He thought about joining her but would not. One of his project managers from South Africa who always sent him work gave a head's up that a two-volume commentary on the Lotus Sutra, by some Zulu pop transhumanist he'd never heard of, was going to be coming his way in a few days; just a head's up.

He was almost falling asleep at his desk, the pages churning with due industry, when his scanner choked and stopped:

Larissa paused. "Do you really expect me to discuss politics, my lord?" she said, looking downward. And then her favorite Don Henley song started playing.

White paper on the facing page. The scanner was adjusting to the typography differential. A note was caught in the agent's original scan, pressed in the pages of the notebook. Clean, dark printing, could have been from a typewriter. Creased once in the middle. A logo in the upper center—a seal, to be exact. He recognized that seal. He wished he could have smelled the page.

He blew up the page and read the note, and then read it again more quickly, as if blurring his comprehension would somehow change the placement of the words into something far more innocuous. Then he grabbed the wastebasket underneath his desk and vomited into it. He could hear his wife keep chanting, and the crossing guard's whistle for school's first shift. His children were second shift but had half-internships that started at nine. They would be waking soon, and his wife would ready them, and Amar started crying.

Then he paused the scanner and called the agent. He wasn't even sure what time it was there, but he didn't care. He waited about a minute for someone to pick up, but it wasn't the agent. The room on the other side was dark, and he could barely see the shapes: a lamp, a head, a gun. Then the head moved closer to the camera.

"Yes, hi?" the woman said. She was young, thin, had a bandaged face. Was chewing something. Kind of evil-looking, Amar thought. She dipped out of view again until she was just a shadow.

"Where's . . . where's the resident of this property?" he said.

"Who are you?" she said.

"I'm a business associate of the woman who lives here. I need to speak to her."

"Oh," she said. "Um . . ." She scratched her hair with both hands. "That's . . . that's really not going to be possible. She's been taken to the Lord."

Marigold wasn't sure what to do with the man on the other side. The agent's apartment had been given to her as part of the punishment. They kept adding conditions onto the agent's punishment; Marigold wasn't sure how she felt about that. First the lancing—Marigold was squeamish about it, but fine, it had to be done. People wanted it done. Then the agent had been told she was free to go, but then Marigold's superior had put his mask back on and said, wait, Marigold needs some place to stay to recover, to convalesce, and Marigold wasn't going to make a big deal of it, but the rest of the couriers had thought it was only proper. Marigold had never really had a place of her own, just a couch in the couriers' warehouse, on Staten Cape. The concierge—who had been quite cooperative during the entire justice operation in the Kinko's, all things considered—was beginning to balk at this, Marigold could tell. After all, the building was under his charge, and the couriers—even though they had the official backing of Lord Manhattan, with all the opportunities in the boroughs opened up to them—were beginning to press their luck a little, Marigold thought. But they insisted, and Marigold did need to sleep off all the excitement and the dull pain that was everywhere on her face, so she relented, and arrangements to move to the fifth floor were made. The concierge bit his tongue and gave the security card to Marigold. He also said to let him know if she "needed anything," but she knew what he meant to say was: "I'll have my eyes on you."

But where was the agent to go? That really hadn't been thought through by the couriers. The agent was sitting in a corner, staring at the hot glue dripping and mixing in the funnel of the binding apparatus, and the dragon moths buzzing around the ceiling bulbs, as if it all were happening to someone else. In a way, it was; she didn't seem the type, after what she had been through, to stir up trouble anymore. She wouldn't have been a recurrent threat, Marigold knew that. But the others didn't see it this way.

"She just can't be wandering Queens," one of the couriers said, as if concerned.

"No, no…" Marigold's assistant supervisor said. "She'll be safest in the Lord's custody, wouldn't she? For her own protection. Marigold, don't worry. She's going to be all right."

Her assistant supervisor might have noticed a look of concern on Marigold's face as she watched the agent trying to stand up, say something. The agent couldn't get her footing, though.

"I think she's going into shock," Marigold said, forcing herself to look at her assistant supervisor, who had plucked her from the street, literally, when she was ten, in a neutral-car derby on the old Brooklyn Slags. Marigold was ten, and steered the Acura chassis down the five-hundred-foot incline. The car came in third, even though it crashed into the breakwalls. In the wreckage, her future assistant supervisor had snatched her out and splinted her broken leg. She wasn't really hurt; he didn't know that her brother had been the brake operator in the compressed trunk and had died on impact. Marigold had never told him that. She didn't remember much about that day. But the need to protect him from her own awful truths was slipping away from her.

"I know, I know," he said. "She'll have doctors in the detention facility." He snorted. "She'll have better medical benefits than we do." That was the Lord's line. "All right, get her out of here. Hook that gurney up to my cycle. And Marigold, go to her building now and rest."

Marigold nodded. She looked for the concierge, but he was gone. When she got the key from him later, in his little lobby booth, she was going to tell him about the agent's being taken to Lord Manhattan (who wasn't even in Manhattan; White Plains, rather), but he gave her a look that said, I already know, and I'm not taking this lightly.

She had thought that the phone call might have been the

concierge buzzing her—to play a trick on her, maybe?—so it was a genuine surprise to find Amar on the other end. She didn't know that the agent was an agent. Did something with books, of course, but books weren't really up Marigold's alley. There was a five-second delay in the transmissions, so after a few minutes of meaningless back-and-forth, during which the agent's predicament was not established to Amar's satisfaction, Marigold asked him:

"Are you from Albany?"

"What?"

Albany was one of the few freestanding cities around the area that she could think of, and also the farthest away she'd ever been. To deliver heart medicine. She biked all the way up there and took the river back and lived to tell about both trips.

"You have a nice office," Marigold said. "And you sound far away. So I was thinking you were maybe from Albany."

Amar licked his lips and closed his eyes. He was sweating. He said, with his eyes still closed: "Could you tell me when she's coming back?" When he opened them, he wanted the agent to be there, to have willed the agent into existence in that room, speaking to him.

Marigold was still there. "Well, that's kind of hard to say," she said. "It depends on how long they treat her."

Amar took a lot longer to speak than the normal delay.

"Please tell me she's not hurt."

"Well, a little. But she'll really be all right." She wasn't sure if she sounded convincing.

"Okay..." He took a deep breath. "What about the notebook? You have to have the notebook there, right?"

"I . . . Wait, well, was that . . ." She didn't know why she was trying to be so helpful. Maybe she wanted to see his office a little longer—the mahogany desk, the office supply dispenser, the window overlooking what she thought was Albany. But of course it wasn't Albany—the trees and grass, even in Albany, would not have been that green, and the wind shaking those trees would not have been so clear (without specks), and the children's bicycles on the curb would not have been so unstolen.

"You have to tell me!" he said.

"Well, she was going to the Kinko's to scan something—"

Amar leaned back in his chair and sighed, relieved. "Yes, that is the document." For the first time he gave the impression that they were speaking the same language. "Yes, thank you. So where is it?"

"I'm not sure." Marigold knew, however, that her supervisor had discarded it. Maybe that was part of the agent's punishment as well.

A woman entered the office. She was in a dark suit and wore sunglasses with whirling blue lights on the sides.

"Amar, is everything all right?"

He turned around and waved both of his hands. "Not now—get out!"

"I heard you screaming, the children—"

"Out!" He stood up from his chair. "Out!"

She saw the wastebasket, the vomit. "Are you sick, Amar?"

"Please... please..." He opened the door wider and pushed her backwards. It took her a few seconds to realize what was happening—Amar never did things like that—but by that time he had shut and locked the door.

"You have a really beautiful wife, Amar."

He squinted. "How do you know my name?"

"She said it. Plus it's on the bottom of the screen.

Listen, do you mind if I pee?"

He leaned forward. "Fine. But believe me, I'm not going anywhere. The notebook is—"

She ran to the bathroom, locked the door (not sure why) and sat down on the toilet, and tried to think of what to do next. Amar was too far away to hurt her—she was pretty sure of that—but all the same she didn't want to get other couriers in trouble. If he knew the agent, maybe he knew others in Queens? She had been stupid to think that he came from Albany—her mouth couldn't be trusted.

Think, she said to herself, looking at herself in the mirror. Think before you say anything. Think.

When she sat down again, she saw that Amar was staring straight at her. Wouldn't break his eyes away.

"They threw the notebook away," she said.

He didn't get angry; not in a way that was immediately visible to her. He was resigned. "Can I tell you what is in the notebook?"

"Sure," she said.

He laughed. "No, no. You know, I thought about telling you, but..."

"Fuck off!" she said, nearly shoving the screen off the desk, kicking it. "You need to leave."

"No, wait. Wait! Listen, the author might call—"

Marigold turned off the feed. Then she left the apartment to do her routes, pushed herself to, even though she wasn't feeling well or like herself. She ran through checkpoints in silence. All the other couriers had put their funds together and bought her kicks with a passport transmitter. They were red. She tried to keep herself from crying when she delivered her packages. They were so hand-held: toys, spices, books. She could mule them all, borrow a bicycle through straightaways when cleared for it, sprint otherwise, jump over barricades, slide feet first under glass-enclosed garden overhangs arching over the streets—"fuck you gardens" the other couriers called them, on account of the old money that made such projects possible on a thoroughfare—the armed gardeners shaking pruning fists once the trespass was discovered. Too late, always too late. She was the rabbit who could slip through any fence. The exhaustion didn't slam her until she bounded up the steps to the agent's apartment, as the day was ending. The agent had nothing but wine to drink, not even safe water.

"Whew," Marigold said, catapulting onto the bed with a non-alcoholic bottle. She checked the messages; one from a V someone. Had to have been the author. She turned on the screen and flinched at the first sight of him. White hair like ash. A face that could have a training surgeon's palette—too much flesh in one cheek and not enough in the other (both were rosy), a thick nose broken and reset, though not perfectly, a jaw that had molar outlines under the skin like the baby corn cobs she liked to eat from the Chinese charity meal packets. His face was too much for Marigold. She did, upon seeing him, want to know what was in the notebook, but she wanted to hear it from Amar, not this man.

"Hi," the author said. He coughed. Marigold crossed her legs and drank half the bottle while the author gathered his thoughts in the darkness around him. "Hey. Um, listen—I hope you're doing well, by the way—I needed to check in, about your... your appraisal of the manuscript. I know, I know, these things take time. You're always telling me to be patient. But I'm ... I'm really under the gun here." He laughed and took a sip from a red straw. "Grandkids need to eat, to go to school, you know ... you know?" It was storming in Minnesota. Purple lightning. The gutter purifiers were gathering water off the roof, distilling it through pipes and into basement barrels. He lived in the savannah in the old zoo. Foundations of most of the old buildings existed, but only those. "See, here's the thing. They're raising my levies and fees here. I think it's a plot to get rid of me. I want to write for people in Nebraska, but I don't want to live there, you know?" He sucked the last liquid through the straw. "So I need your assessment... soon. Or I'll find another agent." He thought that this last threat would get her attention. "Oh! There is another small issue. There's a piece of memorabilia that happened to be in that notebook. Nothing of too much consequence... but, if you could... if you could return it to me, it would be much appreciated. You can take the postage out of the future earnings of the book." He rattled his head, to draw him back to the most important matter at hand. "I want a fast sell!" He then hung up and folded up his empty drink box.

A giant sloth brayed outside his window. Only gentle animals lived in the complex anymore, but he still didn't trust them. Then he heard the monorail approaching, creaking through the rain. He sighed and went out to his front porch and watched the monorail come in.

Inside the front car was that sloth, large as a horse, pawing at the windows. The monorail was automated. Someone from another part of the complex must have lured the sloth onto the monorail and sent it his way. The monorail halted. Could it have been the super? (The super liked to call himself the zookeeper. But he was really just an asshole.)

"Lion savannah," the monorail's calming voice said. "Please

exit carefully." The doors to the car, which should have been welded shut with rust years ago, creaked open, and the sloth exited onto the platform in front of Roger's house. The platform was narrow, but the sloth had sure feet and, bobbing its head, moved closer to Roger's front door. Its eyes were yellow and shot.

Below him, the waves of rain rustled the sedge. Swampy runoff. He didn't like venturing down there in the best of conditions, or traveling far on foot. Green Path to the theater, Red Path to the general store, Purple Path to the megafauna barn. No. He took the monorail for Friday night cinema. The other tenants liked what they showed on the giant screen more than he did. They were the type of people who enjoyed movies from Bangladesh that didn't make sense—lots of violence, but in the wrong ways and places (Mughal romantic comedies that somehow ended in bloodbaths; a series of six galling musicals following the Ural mujahideen). Roger allowed his writers-in-residence to visit the cinema only once a month. He didn't want their minds poisoned any more than necessary. Other years he had four, five writers from his readerly province learn from him. Numbers dwindled, though. He wasn't sure the sole young woman given to him was up for the job. The monorail closed its doors and creaked forward to the primate house. Roger took a step back and clanged the bell next to his front door. He didn't stop until his apprentice arrived. The sloth was taking its time. The apprentice was taller than him, and the tan uniform was too short in the sleeves for her. She was out of breath, and she smelled like woodsmoke. The walkway from the monorail platform to Roger's raised porch was about twenty feet and had flimsy railings on each side. The house itself was on concrete pillars above the veldt. There was nowhere for the sloth to go except forward, and it did. But it was groggy. The sloth had to have been tranquilized.

As it moved closer, Roger could see that something glowing was attached to the fur on its side.

"Apprentice, see what's on its fur."

"What? No."

"Do not disobey a direct order!"

She sighed.

"Did you bring your sidearm?" he said.

She shook her head. "I . . . I was fixing the furnace, like you told me to."

"It's moments like these that provide you the writing material that will change your life forever!" he barked. "And to fully seize the moment, you need to be properly armed. That's the bedrock of this household, do you understand?"

She slowly nodded.

He put a hand on her shoulder and tried to look her in the eye, though she would not meet his gaze. "Fetch your sidearm, and also the rocket launcher from my study."

"Which one?" she asked.

He paused, not wanting to seem too greedy for carnage in front of her. "The small one."

While she was in the house, the sloth did an ambling circle toward him and then shuffled sideways. He darted forward, thinking to himself how brave and stupid he was. But he also wanted to prove to his apprentice that he would not make her do what he would not do himself.

The sloth reeked like shit, and underneath the fur Roger could see sores. Reconstituted, it was not made for these times. He could also see that some bastard had tagged the sloth's hide with iridescent paint. It was a message:

BIG MURDERER

FUCK OFF N DIE

LEAVE

"I've got the weapons," the apprentice said, the pistol in her holster and the rocket launcher slung over her shoulder. "I also brought a notebook and pen..." She managed to smile. "In case the inspiration—"

"Give me that," he said, taking the rocket launcher from her, turning off the safety settings. His first thought, which immediately shamed him, was to kill her, to point the rocket launcher ten feet from her chest and to blow a hole through her and send the rest of her into the old lion sanctuary below. His hands shook; he had trouble keeping the rocket launcher level as he arced it past her body—a clear safety violation, how could he be teaching her anything—and toward the sloth. The storm was tapering, though the wind pushed the rain back and forth through the air.

"This is just another example of how the world hates us and our ideas," he said. "You have to keep being strong... persisting..."

"What's on the fur?" she said. His outbursts and directives were not reaching her. She was getting numb; too numb for his training to have proper effects. She was broken down, but he honestly didn't know whether he had the strength to build her up again. "Do you want me to—"

"It's nothing," he said. "It's one of those Shiite gang symbols."

"That's not nothing," she said.

The sloth raised its head, took a few dizzy steps, and lumbered toward them.

"Kill it!" she shouted at Roger.

He tried to steady himself, lowered his center of gravity. The sloth's tongue sloshed gray. It was a herbivore, but didn't they mix in leopard DNA? Did the zookeeper tell him that once? His feet slipped, and as he fell forward his finger pushed forward on the trigger. The shot screamed, a wall of fire and metal vapor rushed toward him.

He woke up in the middle of the night, on his bed, with the fireplace blazing. The apprentice stood over him.

"You broke your arm," she said. "I splinted it."

"The sloth . . ." he said.

"The rocket smashed into the walkway," she said. Her voice was flat. "The walkway collapsed and the sloth went down. Don't worry. I set up a rope bridge across."

"That can't be safe..."

"It's safe enough. I worked the whole day on it."

He tried to sit up. "I need to call the complex security . . . whoever did this . . ."

She gently pushed him down on his good shoulder. "Don't worry. I've already taken care of it. You shouldn't have to tolerate that kind of attack." She took out her notebook, flipping through the corners, and handed it to him. "I've written all about it. I freewrote all night."

He took it from her. He wanted to say he was proud of her.

"But you shouldn't read it until you're feeling better," she said. "I don't know what's going to happen to us, Roger."

"What…" He didn't have the strength. He smelled napalm and ash, still. He had assumed it was from her earlier chores.

"I learned explosives pretty well from my father. He used to take down Omaha rail lines in the wars. Did you know that you have bags and bags of potash in the basement?"

When she left the bedroom to set up a defensive perimeter, he read her exercise book.

THIRD-PERSON EXERCISE: MOMENT OF PLOT RESOLUTION

Charity McClune knew who had come to kill them: Dumbocrats, in league with homosexual imams and ecoterrorist Jews, with Mexican foot soldiers brought in from their misguided revolutions, financed by turban-wearing geothermal vice lords from India. They would stop at nothing. She had to stop them. How fitting that the seeds of their own destruction would be carried on a monorail—the transportation of choice for Communists and their broken dreams. She smirked as she assessed her handiwork. She had blond hair and blue eyes, blue like the glacier waters of her hometown in Free Alaska. She knew the price of freedom and was willing to pay any price for it. Those other people, they were full of hate for her and her teacher, a great American—

He flipped forward, hands barely under control.

Only one right path lies before her. In the pure fire of justice her world would be cleansed. Looking up, she almost saw in a cloudface her father's face, smiling down on her. She missed him so much, and the wind pressed up a gentle breeze on her face as her chief colonel nodded.

"'Bring down the noise, Charity!" he exclaimed, his jaw set.

As she clenched the trigger—

Roger closed the notebook. "Total shit," he said, falling asleep, drifting backward to the air force bases of his prime, when he had been a prime mover, an adviser, a prophet of policy. No one would ever understand, not even the apprentice. The only ones who understood were long dead, at one time laid to rest in desecrated Arlington graves: the rear admirals who had requested signed copies of *Fierce Power* by the boxload for mandatory frigate book clubs;

the Secretary of Information and Coercion who sent his daughter to shadow him for a week for a school project; and, of course, the president, the commander in chief, his commander in chief. Roger imagined that others in the inner circle of Washington, Lincoln, and Reagan must have felt the same thrill—not only to be living at the same time as an architect of history, but to advise great men and great decisions, by sheer accident more than anything else. He was, after all, a writer of stories, an entertainer, and he never let himself forget that. And yet . . . he was there when the world changed. He was there. He was there in the bunker, a mile underneath Minot. El Paso burning, Dallas burning, the District of Columbia cordoned, Chinese peacekeepers amassing on the Canadian border, and the choice resting on heavy shoulders.

"Tell me what to do," the president said to him in the bunker's lounge, velvet upholstery muffling any sound, any klaxons and shouts. The words and the president's face echoed in the chambers of his sleep. "Tell me what to do, Roger."

"Your advisers, sir..." Roger said, swirling his bourbon and looking down into it.

"I don't trust them. Don't trust any of them. You know that, Roger." The president could get petulant without enough sleep, but who wouldn't?

"I do know that, sir. I would..." Roger set his bourbon down on a stack of his own paperbacks on the coffee table. A poster of Roger on the door stared back at Roger—arms crossed, wearing sunglasses, an ammo belt draped over his shoulders like a scarf, a baseball cap that had embroidered on it: DON'T TREAD ON ME, and underneath that: KILL ZONE. Roger tried to think of what that Roger would do, what Mick Solon would do.

"You have to root out the problem at its source, sir." The commander-in-chief stared at Roger. "Do you understand what I mean, sir?"

The president thought about this, licking his lips. "Do you mean to bomb Mexico City? Nuclearly?"

Roger shrugged and tried to keep his eyes on the president. When the president didn't say anything, Roger said, "Have you seen the war games for that, sir? With the bunker busters?" Roger had no idea whether war games for that even existed, or what his real advisors would say.

"No... no. But maybe that's for the better." The president stood up, and Roger followed suit. The president reached out to shake hands, and Roger moved right away to salute, leaving the president's hand dangling there. But then the president returned the salute.

"Stay here as long as you want," the president said before leaving, and in two hours the bombers were in the air, reaching their cruising altitude. And Roger did stay in the bunker, for five months, as winter set in, and then—instead of spring—winter set in again throughout the Americas. Then, after that, another winter of fog and ash, and the president's hanging at Mount Vernon. Then the third winter skipped right to fall, winds of acid and ice, the fall of two or three provisional governments, and then no governments at all, at least in the old sense of the word. Roger took a Humvee from Minot to Minneapolis, and he had to pay for the trip with his collection of Liberty dollar coins. The soldiers never talked with him, joshed with him, as they had before. The zoo was the safest place he could find.

Of course, the world stabilized, after a fashion, and he was able to write again. People were still hungry for his stories. They were the same people as before, for the most part, the same survivors. And their children, who had little in the way of television, grew up with Mick Solon instead. Roger found an agent who understood this—his old agent having disappeared in the Manhattan reorganizations. Enclaves still believed in the rightness of Mick's causes, that Mexico Moon was necessary and cleansing, only one salvo in the war for civilization.

Roger obliged them.

When he woke from his long sleep, he was put under house arrest. Not in so many words; no one announced this to him. But there was always an armed groundskeeper within sight of his house. The apprentice had disappeared and was found a few days later on the outskirts of the old zoo, where she had set up a makeshift bomb-making factory and blown herself up by accident. The apprentice's family demanded that Roger pay for her funeral. He used the request for a fire-starter. There was no body, he wanted to tell them. How can you bury a person without a body? Do you want to bury her jaw? Her femur? Her dental records? The investigation into the destruction of the sloth and the walkway found him neither guilty nor innocent, but rather complicit in a long-standing pattern of harboring and brainwashing terrorists. No charges came, though. On the other hand, they did arrest the fucker who had drugged the giant sloth—tampering with megafauna was a serious crime. She was one of the medical assistants who administered chemo at the free clinic and hated everything Roger stood for. He tried to follow her trial on the daily bulletins, but the painkillers he took for his legs would not let him focus on anything for too long, except for sleep. He tried to call his agent but couldn't remember the right access codes, and the screen would always stay blank, no matter what he did. Then in the middle of the night he heard the apprentice calling for him, pausing with her blowtorch and asking, Isn't this what you would want me to do? And he would have said, No, not exactly—see, action has to be clean like writing is clean; there have to be clear consequences and no loose ends. Self-defense has to be guided by the conscience of liberty. The fight has to be a true one. People just want to forget about their problems. Also, you're really fucking scaring me.

And she might have paused, after listening to that impromptu lesson, letting it sink in.

But she always went back to her welding.

After a few weeks of this toss-and-turn, he received a package. The sky was clear and inviting when the courier knocked on his door and asked him to sign. The courier was young, barely out of UPS U. It was the first time Roger had gone outside, even a few steps, since the apprentice died.

"What if this is a bomb?" Roger asked.

"I've scanned it," the courier said, waving his black wand. A little too casual for Roger's taste. "It's fine."

Roger pulled the package to him and closed the door. The box was taped over and over again. He set it on the kitchen table and then saw it had a passport from India.

"Shit!" Roger said, swiping at the package and pushing it to the floor. Maybe there was a contact poison. Those stupid wands couldn't account for everything. He let the package sit there for a few more days, until he summed up the courage to face his own death. Placing the package back on the table, he closed his eyes as he cut it open with scissors and reached inside. It was a manuscript. His manuscript, a copy of it, scribbled upon in red ink. In his haze he had forgotten about it. There was a handwritten letter attached to it.

Dear Sir:

You may be surprised to find this returned to you, as you have not had any dealings with me in the past. However, your agent—who I now fear to be dead—has often utilized my services to doctor your recent synopses and novels, though I am rarely able to make sense of them. It took me great trouble to track you down. I assume you are in hiding.

I have enclosed my transcription and my edits, in order to complete my contract and rid myself of you. I have to say that I found the ideas devoid of meaning, the characters cold, the prose poorly written—like everything else of yours. And yet, in a manner utterly alien to your later projects, there is a vulnerability, too. The people who inhabit these pages are shallow, but they are not inhuman. You started with something at least honest—in your own fashion—and cast that aside.

You had a letter stuck in the pages of your notebook. Do you remember this letter? You must. It's a letter of commendation from the last president of the United States, "personally, and with great warmth, thanking you for defending the Constitution and the integrity of the nation during a time of great trial." The letter goes onto list the names of the bomber pilots who "would vouch for the great effect your writing had on their thoughts as they dropped the collateral payload on the enemies of America and freedom." These words made me—

Amar felt his wife's hands on his shoulders in the middle of his composition. He flinched, though he didn't want to.

"Let it go for now," she said. "The children are asleep." She curled closer into him, arms around his neck. He felt that she was naked. A torrent had come into her when he had told her everything, about every distant monster he had to face, the innocent blood embedded in every file. The planes taking off and landing lighter six hours later.

She told him that even monsters needed to be forgiven—not right away, of course. But even Devadatta, the Buddha's worst enemy, the traitor of his inner circle, was able to be a great enlightened teacher after many successive lives, after many hells and trials. She had told him that calamity was the loom and that all sentient beings were the cords of silk on the loom, interwoven in the warp and the woof, bound tightly together. She struggled to find the spirit of these words, but even this attempt comforted him. It gave him the courage to write the letter to the American—which his wife needed to interrupt. She told him she needed him. He turned around his chair and kissed her neck and then licked each nipple as she pushed herself onto him. She unclasped his pants and slid his cock out, rubbing its head and pressing it against the tangle of her pubic hair. He put his hands on her ass and guided himself into her.

She came first. After he came, she lifted herself off and knelt in front of him. She sucked his softening cock and ran her tongue on the foreskin until it was clean, and then placed her head against his thigh. He stroked her hair and told her he was ready to finish the letter. He wanted to finish strong, vicious, to devastate the author so that he would never be able to write another word again. And then Amar could go on with his life.

After she left, he sat there for a long while. No words came to him. He had no idea what to say next. That girl who thought he lived in Albany—what would she have told him? She would have told Amar (or so he imagined) that he didn't have the right to say anything, really, even to a war criminal, that he was trying to dredge up memories he didn't possess of a time he didn't live through. And that it was better to quit while he was ahead and pretend none of those false memories ever existed.

Really, she would be all right.

The wound on her cheek—he closed his eyes and saw her lean forward—look, Amar, it's healing.

❖

I had a prescription for myself that I followed for many, many years: "Don't write stories about writers." It seemed like a great rule of thumb to avoid self-reflexivity for its own sake and therefore tedium. However, no rule is hard and fast, and sometimes it can provide a temptation: "How can I get away with it?" So there was a basic challenge in writing the story in a way that was creatively fruitful.

A few more impetuses came together with this story, and combining them was part of the interstitial act. I wanted to put a thriller writer in a world that he has helped bring into being. What happens when writing's power (and pedagogy) gets out of control? I think a lot of right-wing-leaning thriller writers play fast and loose with their content, but what does that mean in terms of a country's political discourse?

Another motif I wanted to play with was that of a "cursed manuscript." However, I wanted to ground that "curse" in a future political reality that would reflect back on our own. Finally, I wanted to explore the idea of middle-class comfort and how it's shaped, and how the middle class perceives the world through a narrow view.

The obvious reversal, of course, is that America and the "developing world" change places in this story. If a cursed manuscript comes to us from halfway around the world, how do we handle it? Do we even have the tools at our disposal to adequately assess it? Finally, the story's form (no section breaks) gave me an opportunity to thread all of the characters together on one spool, so to speak. Whether all of these elements together make the story "interstitial," I can't say—but definitely having these thematic elements bumping up against each other was part of the thrill of writing this story—I wasn't ever sure how they would collide.

Alan DeNiro

The Marriage

Nin Andrews

This is a story about a man who ties a woman to his bed. *No, it's not what you think*, he says. *Please understand*. But how can he explain? All those nights his wife turns into other things. Would anyone believe him?

He should have known the first time he saw her, he thinks: her waves of dark hair spilling down her back, her torn jeans, her look of *fuck you, too,* her scent of wet leaves, sweat, and dirt. It made him horny. What else can he say?

She's wild, his friends smirked. As if they knew. But he'd always wanted a woman like this. Not one of those local girls who knit and pray and stare at the ceiling all night. But these days he's not so sure.

Each night when he comes home, he suspects something is amiss. And it is. She's not there. She returns so late at night. *Where have you been?* he asks. She doesn't answer him at first. So he asks her again, and that's when her soft skin grows fur, her head sprouts horns, the buttons on her blouse burst off and fly across the room like seeds. She charges after him, lunging again and again, letting loose such bellows and curses. *What do the neighbors think? What if someone knocks or calls the police?* he asks.

After a while, he has no choice. (Or so he says.) He takes out the harness, the ropes, the bucket of oats and corn. He talks to her softly, crooning her name. And she lets him get close. She lets him do with her whatever he wants.

But the mornings after, the house is in shambles. The tables and dressers are cracked and splintered. Clothes are torn and tossed over chairs and lamps. Even the framed wedding pictures are shattered into glass splinters that shimmer on the bed sheets and floors.

Sometimes he tells her, *I can't live like this anymore.* Her eyes fill with tears. Her voice, a whisper, she begs him, *please, please.*

Then she showers and washes the night from her skin. She slips into one of her silky underthings and stands there, hosing her hair with a hot wind. *How can I resist?* he thinks. *What man is as lucky as this?*

He bends to kiss her again and again. *My wife, my love, my forever after,* he says. *Don't leave me again. Please.* And she promises she'll stay. She won't go anywhere. She'll just be happy in their home. She will cook dinner and wait for him to come home. There is nothing she would rather do than wait for him to come home. And he almost believes her. He almost believes she's his.

I suppose this is a bit of a fairy tale, or maybe an anti–fairy tale, an anti-happily-ever-after tale. I've always loved fairy tales and ghost stories and the like. I think in some ways they often tell the ugly truths in a magical way, or an indirect way, which is oddly more believable. I particularly love tales of shape-shifters. I think we all do that—turn into other things, I mean. But by the time we grow up, marry, have a home, etc., we have learned to pretend we are one thing. After a while, pretenses are all we are. But that, of course, is another story.

As to the questions of interstitial versus regular fiction, I've never been one thing or another. Fiction writer or poet or, occasionally, a memoirist. I recently received a letter from an editor saying, *We like this, but what is it?* I'm happy to take on any labels and no labels. And I never have a clue what *it* is. I'll go anywhere they will let me in.

Nin Andrews

Child-Empress of Mars

Theodora Goss

In the month of Ind, when the flowers of the Jindal trees were in
blossom and just beginning to scatter their petals on the ground like
crimson rain, a messenger came to the court of the Child-Empress.
He announced that a Hero had awakened in the valley of Jar.

The messenger was young and obviously nervous, at court for
the first time, but when the Child-Empress said, "A Hero? What is
his name?" he replied with a steady voice. "Highest blossom of the
Jindal tree, his name is not yet known. He has not spoken it, for he
has as yet seen no one to whom he could speak."

The Ladies in Waiting fluttered their fans, to hear him speak
with such courtesy, and I said to Lady Ahira, "I think I recognize
him. That is Captain Namoor, the youngest son of General Gar,
who has inherited his crimson tongue," by which I meant his eloquence, for an eloquent man is said to have a tongue as sweet as
the crimson nectar of the Jindal flowers.

Lady Ahira blushed blue, from her cheeks down to her knees,
for she had a passion for captains, and this was surely the captain
of all captains, who had already won the hearts and livers of the
court.

"Let the Hero's name be Jack or Buck or Dan, one of those names
that fall so strangely on our tongues, and let him be tall and pale
and silent, except when he sings the songs of his people to the
moons, and let him be a slayer of beasts, a master of the glain and
of the double adjar." The Child-Empress clapped her hands, first
two and then four, rapidly until they sounded like pebbles falling from the cliffs of the valley of Jar, or the river Noth tumbling
between its banks where they narrow at Ard Ulan. And we remembered that although she was an Empress and older than our
memories, she was still only a child, hatched not long after the lost
island of Irdum sank beneath the sea.

"Light upon the snows of Ard Ulan, he is indeed a slayer of beasts," said the captain. The Ladies in Waiting fluttered their fans, and one sank senseless to the floor, overcome by his courtesy and eloquence. "He wounded two Garwolves who approached him, wishing to know the source of his singular odor. He wounded them with a projectile device. They are in the care of the Warden of the reed marshes of Zurdum."

"This cannot be," said the Child-Empress. "The Hero must go on his Quest, for that is the nature of Heroes, but he must not harm my creatures, neither the Garwolves singing in the morning mist, nor the Ilpin bounding over the rocky cliffs of Jar, nor the Mirimi birds that nest in the sands of Gar Kahan, nor even the Sloefrogs, whose yellow eyes blink along the banks of the river Noth. He must not bend a single wing of an Itz. Let us give him a creature to speak with, who can learn his name and where he has come from. Let us send him a Jain, and with her a Translator, so that he will perceive her as resembling his own species. Is there one of my Translators who would travel with the Jain to meet the Hero?"

All three of the court Translators stepped forward. From among them the Child-Empress chose Irman Adze, who was the oldest and most honored, and who signaled her willingness to make such an important journey by chirruping softly and nodding her head until her wattles flapped back and forth.

The Child-Empress said to Irman Adze, "Your first task is to remove his projectile device and replace it with the glain and the double adjar, so that he is suitably equipped but can cause no great harm to my creatures and the citizens of my realm." Then she turned to the court. "And let us also send an Observer, so that we may see and learn what the Hero is saying and doing." The Observers whirred and flew forward. She selected one among them and entered its instructions.

"And you, Captain," said the Child-Empress, turning to Captain Namoor, "because of the pleasure you have brought us in announcing the arrival of a Hero, you shall be permitted to wear the green feather of a Mirimi bird in your cap, and to proceed after the Chancellor on state occasions."

His training prevented Captain Namoor from blushing with the intensity of his emotions, but he must have blushed inside, for not one in a thousand receives the honor that the Child-Empress had bestowed upon him. Lady Ahira squeezed my upper left hand until it went purple and I winced from the pressure.

"What beast shall he slay, great—green feather of the Mirimi bird?" asked the Chancellor, in his ponderous way. He fancied himself a poet. The Ladies in Waiting hid their ears with their fans, and even the Pages giggled. His words were so trite, and not at all original.

"What beast, indeed?" asked the Child-Empress. "Since I have said that none of our creatures must be harmed, let us send our own Poufli." Hearing his name, Poufli rose from where he had been lying at the Child-Empress's feet and licked two of her hands, while the other two stroked his filaments.

"Go, Poufli," said the Child-Empress. "Lead the Hero on his Quest, but allow him eventually to slay you, and when you have been slain, return to me, and I will think of a way to reward him that is appropriate for Heroes."

The next day, the Jain, with the Translator strutting beside her and the Observer whirring and darting around them, left for the slopes and caverns of Ard Ulan, where the Hero had awakened. Poufli bounded off in the opposite direction, to where the Child-Empress intended that the Hero should encounter his final Obstacle.

We watched, day after day, as the Hero traveled across the valley of Jar. The images transmitted by the Observer were captured in the idhar at the center of the Chamber of Audience. I preferred to watch in the mornings, when the mist still hung about the bottoms of the pillars but the dome high above was already illuminated by the rising sun, and the Mirimi birds were stirring in the branches of the Gondal trees. I would splash water on my face from one of the sublimating fountains, eat a light breakfast of Pika bread spread with Ipi berries, drink a libation made from the secretions of the Ilpin that were kept at court, and then sit on one of the cushions that the Child-Empress had provided, watching, with the other early risers, as the Hero performed his ablutions and offered his otherworldly songs to the gods of his clan.

As the Observer transmitted, the Translator interpreted for the Hero and simultaneously showed us what he saw, so we were confronted with our own landscape made strange, like the landscape of another world. The Ipi bushes, the yellow Kifli flowers that grew at the edges of the reed marshes of Zurdum, the waters of the marshes, all were flatter, as though they had lost one of their dimensions and were lacking many colors of the spectrum. The Jain had become tall and pale, although the Translator did not disguise her undulations. The Observer had become organic. It bounded rather than flew and was covered with a fine brown fur.

"Dog! Come here, dog!" we heard the Hero say, and, "Would you like something to eat?" to the Jain, whose articulations he listened to with care, as though she were speaking a language he did not understand.

I preferred these quieter, intimate moments, although each day, in the late morning or early afternoon, the Child-Empress sent the Hero an Obstacle: once, a swarm of Itz to sting him, so that he swelled up and the Jain had to cover his arms and legs with the leaves of an Ipi bush soaked in marsh water; once, two Habira that he fought off with the glain and clever use of a flaming reed; once, a group of warriors from the town of Ard, so that he would know he was approaching the towns and cities where the citizens lived. Once, the citizens came out of a town to offer him welcome, placing a garland of pink Gondal flowers around his neck and giving him cups of the intoxicating liquor that westerners make from an iridescent fungus they call Ghram, which grows on the roots of the Gondal tree. Once, he was placed in a cage at the center of the town, and the citizens came to see him, until he said a word that was the name, they told him, of an ancient god who was still secretly reverenced.

As court Poet, it was primarily my responsibility to create the events and Obstacles of the Quest, although the Child-Empress was an enthusiastic collaborator. After my morning viewing, I would go to her chamber. However early I went, she was always lying upon her couch, absorbed with matters of state, attending to the well-being of the citizens. But she would put aside her work, waving away the Chancellor and the Courtiers who were gathered around her, and say to me, "Good morning, Elah Gal. What have you thought of for my Hero today?"

The morning that the Hero reached the court of the Child-Empress, the Translators occupied themselves with interpreting us to the Hero. We looked at ourselves in the idhar, translated. We were still ourselves, yet we were no longer ourselves—Lady Ahira still blushed blue, although her knees were stiffer, and an entirely different shape. The Courtiers were stiffer, as well, more angular—and silent. I must admit that I did not miss their chirring. Many of us were only partly visible, and the Translators themselves appeared only as a shiver in the air. The Pages still ran back and forth behind the cushions where we sat, but on two slender legs, like Ilpin. I had to remind myself that they would not fall—they were only translated.

The Child-Empress was still herself, still a child, still an Empress, and yet how different she was. Substantial parts of her could no longer been seen, and when she clapped, it was with only two hands.

"That must be what a child of his species looks like," whispered Lady Ahira, and she would have whispered more had not the Hero walked in, with the Jain at his side and the Observer, grown positively shaggy, by his feet.

"Welcome, visitor from another land," said the Child-Empress. "Do you come from far Iranuk, or fabled Thull? Tell us what land you come from, and your name."

"No, ma'am," said the Hero. "My name is Jake Stackhouse, and as far as I can make out, unless the stars are lying to me, I'm from another planet altogether. What planet is this I've landed on?"

"Planet?" said the Child-Empress. "This is Ord, the crimson planet. Have you truly learned to travel across the darkness of space? You must be a great wizard, as well as a great warrior."

"No, ma'am," said Jake Stackhouse. "I've got no idea how I ended up on your planet, though I sure would like to find out, so I can go home again. And I'm not a warrior or a wizard, as you call them. I'm just a ranch hand, although I've had a few knocks in my life and learned how to take care of myself."

"You do not know your way home?" said the Child-Empress. "I am sad that you are not able to return to your clan, but what is a misfortune for you may be fortunate for us. I have heard that you fought the Garwolves and defeated the warriors of the western marshes. Surely you are the most courageous man on Ord. I ask for your aid. We are threatened by a fearsome beast, called a—" I suddenly realized that when we had created this encounter, the Child-Empress and I, we had not given our beast a name "—a Poufli. This beast is ravaging our eastern cities and towns, eating and frightening our citizens. If you will defeat this beast, I will give you ten hecats of land, and one of my Ladies in Waiting to be your mate."

Captain Namoor, who stood next to the Chancellor, turned orange down to the tops of his boots. Let him, I thought. A little jealousy would do him good.

"I don't want a mate, ma'am. Just this girl here, who's traveled for the last three days, the strangest days of my life, at my side. She's saved my life a couple of times, I reckon. I don't know her name, so I call her Friday."

"You would have that female for your mate?" said the Child-Empress. "Then know, Jake Stackhouse, that she is a priestess of her people, the Jain of Ajain, from the far north, where the river Noth springs from the mountains of Ard Ulan. To mate with her, you must win her in battle with the glain and the double adjar. Are you willing to fight for her, Jake Stackhouse?"

I could not help blushing pink with surprise and appreciation. What an improvisation this was, not the words we had created together and so carefully rehearsed, but the Child-Empress's own, created at that moment. Around me I heard a scattering of applause as the court realized what had just happened. I applauded as well, pleased with her spontaneity. How honored I was that my Empress, too, was a poet.

"All right," said Jake Stackhouse, "I'll fight this Poufli for you, and then fight for the girl I love best in all the world. I never thought I'd marry a green bride, but underneath that skin of hers, she's as sweet and loyal as any woman of Earth."

"It is well," said the Child-Empress. "Defeat the Poufli for me and I will give you ten hecats of land by the upper reaches of the river Noth, where the soil is most fertile, and I will ensure that the Jain becomes your mate. Now, take some refreshment with us, Jake Stackhouse."

The Pages brought platters of the roasted fruit of the Pandam tree, and a sauce made from the sap of the Pandam, and stuffed roots, and the sweet lichen that grow on the roofs of the houses of Irum, in the south, and Ghram that had been brought from Ard for the Hero's Feast. The Hero sat on a cushion, with the Jain beside him and the Observer at his feet, and told us stories of his planet and the place he had spent his childhood, the Land of a Single Star. He spoke of towns in which warriors battled each other with projectile devices, thieves who stole from transport vehicles, and herds of creatures that stretched over the plains so you could see no end to them. He spoke of females so beautiful they were given the names of flowers. The Ladies in Waiting were so eager to hear his stories that they listened without respiring, and some of the more delicate Pages swooned or emitted the scent of marsh water. I myself, Elah Gal, the court Poet, listened and recorded, so that these stories of another planet could be placed among the Tales of the Heroes, which my ancestress Elim Dar had begun when the Child-Empress herself was only a dream of her parent's physical manifestation.

Grief and consternation spread throughout the court on the day the Observer transmitted the tragic news: the Hero was dead. His body was brought back to the palace, and three Healers examined him to determine the cause of his death. They reported their findings to the Child-Empress. Poufli was not to blame. He had played his part both enthusiastically and with care. The Hero's wounds were minor. But his dermal layer, when they examined it, had been covered with red spots. He must have had a reaction to Poufli's emissions, or perhaps to the touch of his filaments.

But Poufli was not to be consoled. He lay submerged in one of the palace fountains, beneath the translucent fish from Irum, refusing to eat; refusing to sleep, as had been his custom, at the foot of the Child-Empress's couch.

The court grieved. The Courtiers put on their white robes of death, and I myself put on the death robes that my mother had worn when her spouse of the second degree had chosen to de-manifest. The Ladies in Waiting would not blush. Lady Ahira postponed the celebration of her union of the fourth degree with Captain Namoor, for which luminous mosses had already been grown on the walls of the Chamber of Audience. The Pages stood silent, neither giggling nor emitting scent. By orders of the Child-Empress, the murals on the walls of the palace were muted, un-til only faint outlines reminded us of their presence. The palace Guards wore mourning veils and drifted around the halls of the palace like gibhans of the dead. The Jain was inconsolable and filled the halls with the mourning wail of her kind. A cold wind seemed to blow through everything.

I sat beneath the Jindal tree in the palace garden and tried to create a poem about the Hero, but how can one commemorate defeat? The Child-Empress herself would not leave her chamber. I went in once a day to try to consult with her, but she simply sat by the aperture, looking out at the garden. I did not wish to inter-rupt her contemplations. Even the Chancellor stood by her couch without stirring, waiting for her to emerge from her grief.

On the seventh day, she came into the Chamber of Audience. She wore robes as red as the Jindal flowers, and she had adorned her arms with bracelets of small silver bells, which jingled as she moved. Poufli was at her side, pushing his noses into her robes.

"Citizens and creatures," she said, "you are sad because the Hero has died. We cannot now celebrate his victory, nor follow with fascination the story of his life here on Ord. Is this not so?"

The Ladies in Waiting, the Courtiers, the Guards, the Pages, all nodded or waved or emitted to signal their assent.

"But we should not be sad," she said. "To watch the triumph of the Hero would have been like listening to a poem by Elah Gal, or watching the blossoming of the Jindal flowers, or attending the union of Lady Ahira and Captain Namoor. It would have been most satisfying. But there is another sort of satisfaction, when Elah Gal pauses and there is silence, or the blossoms fall from the Jindal tree, or lovers part in sorrow after their time together has ended. Do we not take satisfaction also in the passing of things, which we can no more control than we can control the way of the Mirimi bird in the air, or the way of two loves once they are mated? The death of the Hero reminds us of our own demanifestations. This, too, is a poem, perhaps a greater poem than the Hero's triumph would have been, because it is more difficult, and to understand it we must become more than ourselves.

"Let the Hero, whose physical manifestation our Healers have so artistically preserved, be placed on a pedestal of stone from the quarries of Gar Kahan, beneath the branches of the Jindal tree in the garden, where their blossoms will fall upon him. And let us celebrate the death of the Hero! Let us celebrate our own demanifestations, which are to come. Let the Jain be returned to her clan so that she can differentiate and deposit her eggs, and let her offspring be raised at court, in recognition of the service that she has performed for us. Let Elah Gal create a poem about the Hero, a new kind of poem for a new time, and let it be included in the Tales of the Heroes. And let us all celebrate! Come, my friends. Let song and laughter and blushes return to the palace! But I shall withdraw, for I have important work to do. Tonight, as the moons rise over Ord, I shall begin to dream, so that, in your children's children's lifetimes, another Child-Empress will be born."

For a moment, there was silence around the Chamber of Audience. Then, the murals on the walls began to glow. The Ladies in Waiting began to clap and laugh and blush. The Pages leaped into the air and landed again on their toes, emitting the scent of Kifli flowers. The Guards cast off their veils and clashed their disintegrators on their shields, so that they rang through the halls. Everywhere, there was the sound of joy and of wonder. I myself could not keep my orifices from misting. To live at a time of the dreaming! The Hero had indeed brought us something greater than we could have imagined.

I wondered, for a moment, if I would become one of those poets who are celebrated for having created what no other poet could have—if I would create the poem of the Child-Empress's dreaming, of her becoming no longer a child but the full essence of herself, until eventually she emerged in the perfection of her nonphysical manifestation. But then my humility returned. Such poems were still to be created. The first of them would be about the Hero, of how he had died and yet fulfilled his Quest.

But today was a day of celebration. We sang and danced in the Chamber of Audience, celebrating the union of Lady Ahira and Captain Namoor. At the height of the festivities, the Child-Empress withdrew. But we knew now that it was not to contemplate her grief but to begin an important new event in her life. And we leaped higher and turned faster with joy, while the Musicians played their kurams and their dharms, until night fell and the mosses illuminated the ancient murals, and the moons rose, and the Jindal flowers spread their fragrance over the palace.

Is this an interstitial story? I don't know. Maybe it's just the way I write science fiction . . .

It refers to, but is not about, the Edgar Rice Burroughs series of adventure stories, which I have not read. (I've only, like a bad student, read the Wikipedia entry describing them.) It's about a literary genre that I began to call, in my own mind, Blank of Mars, turning Burroughs's series into a symbol for the genre, which might more accurately be called the swashbuckling interplanetary romance. Somehow, in the middle of a particularly complicated week, I started thinking about the Blank of Mars stories and Ray Bradbury's *Martian Chronicles* at the same time, and started wondering what those stories would sound like from the perspective of the Martians.

I have a hunch that if you look at things from the "other" perspective—the perspective of the alien, the monster—they become interstitial, because aliens and monster are themselves in-betweeny, liminal, interstitial sorts of creatures. As an alien (of the sort we more politely refer to as an immigrant), I seem to see things from that perspective myself. Perhaps that's why I so often write not the story, but the underside of the story, which can be another story altogether . . .

Theodora Goss

L'Ile Close

Lionel Davoust

To Eldritch, walking the many ways ...

Guinevere

Dear Diary,

I wonder why I still write you. After all, tomorrow you will disappear, yesterday you disappeared. Nothing changes, and everything is in flux on this island that shrinks, that swells . . . Do you know how hard it is to lead an infinity of lives all at once? I say an infinity, when, really, it's just a great many lives in which I remain essentially the same. I have unendingly committed these words to paper and I have never done so. I am young and old, the wife who loves and deceives, the hieratic figure.

But above all, I am weary.

Oh, I'm not complaining. Of us all, Arthur bears the heaviest burden—but also the most glorious. The heaviest because he dies endlessly, struck down by Oedipus, by Mordred, the son he loves and hates, without ever really dying—since, in leaving for Avalon, he always returns here, and it all begins again. He acquires the sword, and then his troubles begin—for when all is said and done, his story doesn't really start until the moment he becomes the incarnation of supreme authority. The rest is just a prologue, conceived only to satisfy the mind's appetite for beginnings.

I no longer dare consider what I am. What I truly am. I've lived so many variations of the Geste, and always the same story, the same betrayal, without power to change or to escape. I know there are boundaries I cannot cross; I don't know where they are, and yet I sense them, invisible, around me, shaping my acts, defining what I am throughout all my incarnations. And I will never be anything else. I will forever be remembered as the queen who betrays her husband, plunges him into uncertainty and grief, and hurls the realm into night.

But I can't stop myself.

All things considered, I'd rather have been Morgana la Fay, Merlin's mysterious student, the enchantress from another world: dangerous, unpredictable. Her reputation is no better than mine, but her aura of mystery veils her acts in romance. She is feared. Me, I'm not even hated; I am despised. I would have liked to be wicked, but no: I am merely weak.

There had to be someone like me in the story, I suppose.

Lancelot

Beneath a leaden sky, where the brown earth slid under the seas' calm waves—or of a lake so vast that fog hid the far shore—the inhabitants of the isle were gathered round the knight.

Clothed in shining armor, perched proudly on an immense caparisoned palfrey, square-chinned and hair blowing freely in the wind, Lancelot cast his unsullied gaze one last time over the company. He smelled of iron and ginger, of candles and sex. All Camelot held its breath, respectfully silent at the approach of an event which, through its regularity and heroic character, had taken on the formality of a ritual.

The knight finished the golden apple he'd picked from the royal orchard—he'd eaten it down the core—and took the lance offered by his squire. He brandished the weapon, crying out in a ringing voice: "For the king!"

The faceless crowd raised their fists vaguely in response and let out a few dubious cheers.

Before lowering the visor on his helm, Lancelot turned toward castle, toward his lover, agent of a tragic force. Guinevere had not come down to the shore, but he knew that their gazes would meet no matter the window they chose. They were bound to each other. Camelot never took the same shape twice; but on the island, only the meaning mattered.

The king's favorite turned back to the bank, leveled his lance, and spurred his steed.

The charger galloped joyously into the water without the slightest hesitation. The crowd took a few steps back to avoid the great sprays of mud.

The animal soon sank beneath the weight of armor and rider, disappeared, and quite likely drowned. Lancelot tried his best to swim but, dragged down by the iron in his turn, sank like a stone under the gray waters.

For a little while longer, Camelot followed the knight's progress by the trail of bubbles that traced his stolid, imperturbable march toward the open sea.

Then, when the bubbles grew so infrequent they were almost completely gone, the onlookers turned on their heels and hiked slowly back to the castle.

It was starting to rain.

Shadow

That very night, Lancelot returned—or perhaps it was the early hours of morning; the flow of time seemed to elude consciousness. When everyone's back was turned, a kelp-covered mound rose noiselessly at one end of the island, climbing to the low-hanging clouds.

The knight descended from the heavens' vault, still resolute, but with a glimmer of despair in his eyes. He was dripping wet, rust and seaweed splotched his armor, sand clung to his beautiful hair, and little fish wriggled from his chausses.

No trace of the horse. But another had doubtless already replaced it in the stables.

At the foot of the slope waited a large figure dressed in a voluminous night-black cloak, its face concealed by an unfathomable hood. Lancelot did not spare him the slightest glance, the smallest word. He even brushed it as he went by, but he kept walking, refusing to see it, to acknowledge its existence.

The shadow being, which seemed to float, immaterial, on the barren moor, turned toward the knight with infinite slowness.

He then raised his arm in a timid "Hi" before letting it fall again and shaking his head sadly.

Arthur

Mordred won. The Grail didn't save me. This son of incest, this hatred I myself sowed, rose up against me, gathered the forces of darkness, and crushed us. Mordred! You are an insult to my eyes, the essence of your mother's treason—my own half-sister! Your steps poison the barren moor! You are the High King's Nemesis.

There had to be one.

And yet I seem to remember another time, when we fought side by side.

I lie wounded, Excalibur at my side. The king passes, leaves this heathen land, unable to save it, unable to atone for his sins . . . I die, struck down by a lance piercing my side, crucified on the pommel of my sword to save mankind . . . My sword, Caledfwlch . . . No, its name is Balmung. No, I slew the dragon with Balmung when I went by the name of Siegfried. That's another story, and the same one.

Ah, a red veil is falling over my eyes . . . I can't see . . . I'm rambling . . . I am human, all too human.

I call Girflet to me. I have but one thing left to do.

I feel the loyal knight kneel beside his fallen master. I know I cannot trust him. And yet I must go through the stages of the Geste, again and again.

"Here I am, sire," a solemn voice says.

"Good." I sigh. Pain stabs my ribs. I feel the world draining away with my blood, which spreads over the earth without nourishing it. A light breeze scatters the chill mist and smoke, bringing the fresh smell of the lake, or the sea. Like everything else, the island changes shape, but it is always contracting—I'm sure of it.

"Take Caladbolg," I tell him, pointing to the sword, "and throw it in the water."

He barely has time to open his mouth before I cut him off: "Yes—in the water. And do it the first time around. For you will disobey me: you'll hide it and come back and lie to me. I'll ask you what you've seen, and you won't be able to tell me that an arm clothed in shimmering brocade seized Durandal and drew it beneath the waves. You'll make three trips before following my orders. Must we really go through all this *again*? I'm tired, Girflet— or Bedivere, what does it matter, today you are the same—I'm tired."

I sense my knight is taken aback. Through the scarlet veil, I can just see him leaning toward me like a conspirator.

"But everything has to go in threes, sire," he whispers. "It must be so."

What idiocies we have decreed. I dare not answer that everything has to go in pairs, by fours, fives, sevens, or twelves: each number has its own symbology, but it's pointless to argue with him. He cannot transcend himself. Today, he is the archetype of my second-in-command.

"Well, hurry up, at least."

Guinevere

Dear Diary,

Something new, at last! Of course, whenever a new pattern is added to the Geste, it becomes immortal and fits in as though it has always been there. We ourselves forget this change; we become the new development. That's why I must set what happened down on paper.

The enchanter came to see us with many rolls of parchment under his arm. He conferred with Arthur for a long time, and when they left the council chamber, my husband had a gleam in his eye that I hadn't seen in a long time. He gave the lumberjacks, the weavers, the faceless servants orders; soon they brought the materials the bard-wizard had asked for to the court—long wooden staves, squares of cloth, a few metal mechanisms—and put them together according to the old man's instructions.

What a strange creature stood before us! A spidery web, a delicate bird, holding at its heart a cradle where Merlin settled.

. . . I can feel the memory fading! As if my mind can't retain this story. I must finish quickly.

Slowly, the machine's wings began to beat and its tail to swivel. The mentor flew away in his machine, headed west; we lost sight of him in the fog around the isle. He returned from the east, of course.

Or . . . did he rise from the waters?

Did he fall from the sky?

I don't know anymore! What does it matter—the Geste has refused this new development, I can feel it. And so I'll forget even the existence of this object, even this strange vision . . . After all, Merlin is a sage, a guardian of arcana and mystery. His magic lives in the rustle of the trees and the murmur of the waves, not in a sterile construct. None of this fits his role. I'll lose this tale like all the others, or perhaps, in a random reordering, I have found it once more.

One thing, however, is certain: the isle seems even narrower than before. This morning, the seas were almost lapping at Avalon/ Camelot's west wall.

The Round Table

"Repent," roared the Grail, "repent!"

Lancelot leaped to his feet, pounded a silver-gloved fist on the table, and exploded: "I won't let some golden gravy boat tell me what to do!"

Arthur cast upon his knights a gaze in which emptiness jousted with disenchantment. On the walls hung the same tapestries that had hung there since the dawn of time, and yet the symbols embellishing them changed, coexisting in a single spot, melting one into the other—the Celtic tree of life, the Christian cross, the medieval coat of arms: blue, with six golden lion cubs.

The space seemed to stretch itself around the Round Table so that it might accommodate twelve or a hundred men, depending on the version. But their number didn't matter; the table stayed the same shape even if sections of it sometimes seemed parts of a giant cosmic wheel of fortune. At the current table, only a few faces could be clearly identified. The stony charm of Lancelot. The angelic perfection of Galahad the Pure, seen by some as the incarnation of Christ. The youthful wonder of Perceval, who began the Quest in all innocence, in all ignorance, and failed before succeeding.

And yet, Arthur reflected, his face was partly hidden by the Grail, which he'd put on his head. No one knew how to take this; Perceval, who symbolized youth and naïveté, never stopped surprising, never stopped following a path whose internal logic defied all reason. This was a nice way of saying that he behaved, perpetually, like a simpleton. Arthur couldn't help thinking there was something rotten in the kingdom of Britain.

The Grail took the form of the lance that pierced the Savior's side and fell to the ground with a metallic clang, splattering the company with blood. Involuntarily, Galahad hugged his sides. The king, too.

"I am not a gravy boat," clucked the Grail. "I perform my role, as do you all."

Exclamations rang out in the great hall.

"Silence!" Arthur broke in.

The king had spoken. All fell silent except the Grail, which became the Lia Fáil that sings at the coming of the true king, which, quite logically, began to sing "We're Knights of the Round Table."

"Let the Grail take another shape," Galahad murmured, "and the Quest be over. I shall ask the Question, I shall come again, and I shall heal the king and the kingdom."

"All in good time," Arthur assured him. "Your hour of glory will come again. Right now, it's Perceval's turn."

Having come to the second chorus of "We eat ham and spam and jam a lot," the Grail suddenly broke off.

"It's gone again," Perceval announced, a bit sad.

Probably one floor down, Arthur thought. *There, where I play the Fisher King waiting for a knight to come ask me the Question that will deliver me from the evil spell, thus ending the Quest. Everything is simultaneous.*

"We should declare war on the renegade Mordred," declared Lancelot, stiff as a broomstick.

Arthur's expression clouded. His gaze hardened, his jaw froze, but after a precarious moment, he sighed and raised his hands peaceably. "Your enthusiasm is getting the better of you. I already died yesterday, and I'll die tomorrow; let me at least reign over a prosperous kingdom tonight. My fall is only as great as my grandeur. The more noble I am, the more cruel a blow to my soul will be the treason of those I love. The purer my love, the deeper my wound, the graver the fall of the kingdom, and the more important the Quest. Be great, Lancelot, and betray me well. It is necessary."

A bit embarrassed, the knight dropped his gaze to the table and mumbled, "Sometimes I stay virtuous, too."

Arthur left the man in peace and gazed on the infinitely variable company—especially the recognizable faces. The others were condemned to remain anonymous, to have no worth beyond their presence, to impress by sheer numbers and nothing more.

At the far end, a small voice piped up: "We're not numbers, we're free men!" But no one paid attention except the shadow, the figure dressed in blackness that stood propped against the wall. People seemed to look right through it. It glanced furtively at the protester, but the crowd had already swallowed and censored him.

The shadow turned its attention to Arthur and his knights.

"I did not summon you for reasons of the Geste," the king went on. "I think it's time we had a talk as *ourselves*. We perform the Quest, our rise to power and afterwards, our fall . . . Oh, what's the use. As the ideal king, I come into power and die betrayed a thousand different ways; heroes, characters, even mythological figures, we embody an infinite set of variations on the same idea, the same archetype, at once figures of the mind and independent concepts."

All the knights were turned toward their king, petrified, staring at him uncomprehendingly, as though they'd heard his words but didn't understand them.

Arthur—the Bear, Ambrosius Aurelianus, the god Lir, or even Beowulf—felt dizzy.

"We are . . . archetypes," he repeated, nodding, hoping to lend weight to his words. "And yet we all seek to flee the isle . . ."

"I nevere!" roared Lancelot, rising to his feet. "Lord, it is blaspheme! Myn armes ben thyne, and I nyl nat straye."

Arthur was dumbfounded.

"But, Lancelot . . . you leave the isle every three days, and you drown every time. Don't you remember?" He could almost hear Girflet/Bedivere scolding him, as though he'd proposed something obscene: *But everything has to go in threes.*

Outraged, the knight dumped his wine on the floor and stormed from the great hall.

"He'll be back," Galahad whispered. "None of us could desert you, Sire."

Except Mordred, Arthur thought bitterly.

"I'm hungry. Can we eat yet?" asked young Perceval, an idiot's smile on his lips.

Mordred

"What a bunch of losers," the renegade grumbled, contemplating his army of hairy peasants.

"Countryfolk, my son, countryfolk," Morgana said placatingly.

"Still," Mordred sniffed disdainfully. "They stink, and they're filthy. In *Excalibur*, John Boorman gave me a real army."

"Boorman? What knight is this?"

Mordred glanced at his mother, who wasn't always Morgana la Fay. Tall, powerful, of indeterminate age, she gazed back, her eyes full of love and ferocity.

"Never mind," he said. "I don't understand how I always manage to win with such a band of underfed savages."

Morgana let her hand fall on her son's armored shoulder and whispered in his ear, "Because you have the vigor of youth, my son. A new wind blows across the isle. A storm that will overthrow Arthur's reign."

"Yeah, I know. I'm the archetype of change, the unconscious force that always pushes men to outdo themselves, to overcome what came before them."

Morgana gazed at him proudly, one brow raised in surprise. "Exactly. How well you speak! I couldn't have said it better myself."

Mordred sighed. *So, even a goddess can forget. How many among us have let ourselves be gulled by the illusion that we are self-aware, human, and have forgotten our symbolic natures?*

He bit into one of the golden apples that a spy regularly brought him from the gardens of Avalon, and then he held it out to Morgana.

He readied himself to play his role to the hilt, to drown in it with all the energy of despair.

"We'd better start training these savages," he said with disgust.

~

Déjeuner sur l'herbe

The knights, clad in their eternal silver armor, and the ladies, richly bedecked in diaphanous veils, strolled in the orchard, chatting gaily of the news of the realm, lunching in high spirits on golden fruit they plucked from the trees. To one side, Arthur watched, disillusioned and not without worry.

Can't they see this kingdom and our very existence are only fictions?

"Mm. Wars not make one great," said a deep voice behind him.

The king started and turned, irate. "I hate it when you do that, Merlin."

The enchanter, dressed in a long habit—his face sometimes bare and sometimes covered with an imposing white beard—approached him, a long rod in his hand.

"It's part of my nature. I am mystery. I do try, but it's impossible for me to approach someone from the front."

Merlin reached the king and gazed out on the people of Camelot.

"They've forgotten," Arthur said. "Or rather, they refuse to remember. The isle dwindles when we're not looking, Merlin. They all want to leave, but they all deny it. Lancelot even pretended that he's never tried to leave Avalon. And yet it's uncontrollable. We're burying ourselves. We're becoming fossils. We need to transcend our symbolism, but we're so frozen in our forms I fear it's too late. It's a real . . . neurosis."

"What is the sound of one hand clapping?"

"I'm in no mood for riddles."

"Forgive me." Merlin picked a golden apple from a low-hanging branch. "When man was emerging from barbarism and awakening to civilization, he thirsted for an ideal. This thirst was so great that the burgeoning collective unconscious named, fashioned, and codified the heroic archetypes it lacked. Neither being, nor idea, but something intangible halfway between. Unfortunately, the Geste is so powerful that nothing can replace it."

The mage smiled.

"We are, rather, so human that we refuse to get out of the way,"

Arthur argued. "We'd rather anchor ourselves to this miserable speck of dust than go have a look elsewhere."

"But no one can see elsewhere, Arthur. Even you, when you die, when you leave the realm on the funeral barge sailing for Avalon—you return here, because you never really leave."

"So, help me."

"I don't know what you're talking about, little grasshopper. Good morning!" Hastily, Merlin stalked away from the king, without a backward glance.

We are all constrained by our madness.

Not far away, wearing a straw hat, perched on a ladder, the shadow trimmed the golden apple trees.

Three little turns and then . . .

Since we are constrained by our roles, perhaps I could try something completely random, thought Arthur, desperate, walking aimlessly, his hands behind his back.

He reached the edge of the sea-lake and picked up a yellowish, half-rotten apple. One end of a worm poked through the bruised flesh.

To be or not to be. On the isle of archetypes, how many inchworms to a metric foot? He eyed the beast. *And if I dubbed thee a heroic couplet?*

I, too, could leave thought behind and hurl myself headlong into endless rehearsal of the Geste.

Elsewhere, somewhere, Arthur was dying, receiving the sword from the Lady of the Lake or pulling it from a stone, meeting Guinevere for the first time: blonde, brunette, or redhead.

The problem is, I've had it up to here, quite frankly, and everyone around me is nuts.

Suddenly irritated, Arthur threw the apple with all his strength against the bank of fog that drew inexorably nearer to Avalon/Camelot. The grayness swallowed it greedily.

Of course the fruit came back from behind and hit him in the head. Disappointed, the king mumbled a vague "Eureka, yeah right" and paid it no more attention.

He began to shuffle along the shore.

Do something completely random. Why not, since I'm at the end of my rope. He started to skip like a child, tried a cartwheel and crumpled under the weight of his armor, picked a flower and picked off its petals—she loves me, she loves me not—while thinking of Guinevere, etched insults in the dust with Excalibur's point to shock the skies.

Nothing happened. Dripping with sweat, staring at the bank, Arthur walked on, discouraged.

Deviance isn't the answer. The others deviate all the time, and nothing changes. All I've done is act contrary to my usual vision, which is not really random. It's just the exact opposite of my fundamental nature. Which reveals it as much as anything else.

Arthur passed by the orchard where his court picnicked, bewildered and careless. The shadow climbed down his ladder, took off his straw hat, and went to walk beside Arthur. The king didn't notice a thing.

He finished his lap round the isle, returning to his starting point, where the same moldy apple lay on the ground. Elsewhere, at the same time, he was marrying Guinevere, discovering Lancelot's betrayal, recruiting Perceval or Galahad.

I am a code, the incarnation of a concept. Tragically, I am only myself. How can I understand what I lack, if my wings are clipped? The Grail Quest is, above all, a journey of enlightenment. But even the Quest can't give us answers; it, like everything else, is part of the Geste. It belongs to the system.

The shadow matched Arthur's progress, hands—or sleeves—joined, head tilted forward like a monk in his cloister. They passed the trees again. The knights were finishing their feast and returning to the castle.

The Grail, too, is a symbol. The human mind gave it the form of something to be sought in a wilderness because that was easy to understand, but in the end, the Grail is just an illusion. Only what it signifies matters here.

Arthur picked the rotten apple off the ground and, without thinking much about it, bit down. He began methodically to chew its flesh, sickly sweet and still crunchy in places. Swallowed the syrupy juice squeezed out by his teeth. Felt the sugary aroma of rot rising into his nasal cavities, choking his throat, burning the sides of his tongue. Ignored the wild wriggling of worms going down his royal gullet.

He finished the putrefied fruit and turned on the shadow.

Which nodded in return. Far off, emerging from the fog, rose the evanescent pillars of a misty and immaculate bridge, woven from light, appearing bit by bit, reaching the shore of l'ile close.

Somewhere, the first few measures of "O Fortuna" from *Carmina Burana* rang out.

Staggered by fear of what was to come, the king fell to his knees and vomited forth the awful seeds of reality.

The Third Way

Anonymous corpses littered the plain of Camlann all the way to the horizon—a very close horizon: the sea was lapping at the castle on all three sides now, and before the battle, the two armies had faced off only a few yards apart. And yet the epic charge of the final battle of Arthur's reign had seemed to last an eternity, and the faceless dead were heaped up in their thousands.

Arthur, his handsome armor scarlet-stained, his hair and beard sticky with mud, sweat, and blood, advanced unsteadily through the groans of the dying, Excalibur in his fist. The sticky sword was heavy, still heavier to bear than the crown: his royalty resided in the weapon, in divine glory, and not in the human symbol of kingship.

A single idea, one sole desire drove the king to the end of his era: to find Mordred, his treason, the heir he'd never have.

"Mooordred!" he shouted over the plain.

A young man with a face too perfect to be beautiful emerged from the smoke, bloody lance in hand, and advanced with a faltering step, a grimace of hatred on his lips.

"Here I am, father," he growled.

The true king and the usurper met in the center of the plain of Camlann among the remnants of past grandeur, amid fire and death, beside Stygian waters.

The Geste neared its end. Again.

Mordred let out an animal roar that grew in intensity. With a final effort, burning with hatred, he brandished his lance, ready to commit parricide.

Arthur opened his arms. And flung Excalibur aside like a fence picket.

"I abdicate," he announced.

There was a moment of uncertainty. Mordred remained frozen, as though he'd been hit in the stomach, and then gathered himself. "It's a trick—you're trying to win by cheating, you want to keep things as they are!" he hissed through his clenched teeth.

"No, I promise," Arthur replied. "I'm fed up with this story, with these patterns whose infinite repetition has pretended to immortalize us. The human unconscious needs—*we* need to evolve. But I'm too old, too attached to the old order to give it a new ending. I embody wisdom and you change. It's your turn to take the throne. Do you want it?"

He picked up Balmung and gave Mordred an ambiguous look. "Here, take my phallus and give the earth back its fruitfulness."

Dumbfounded, Mordred contemplated the sword without touching it. He stuck his lance in the earth and leaned on it, and then frowned.

"I . . . " he stammered. He looked around him at the dying men, who would breathe their last only at the battle's end, when the scene was over. Then he turned back to his father—frowned, all hatred extinguished.

"Don't want it," he said sulkily.

Arthur felt a wave of dizziness. He stared at his son.

"But . . . you wanted it so much! You have to lead the kingdom to a new age. What'll become of the world? Of the island?"

Mordred shrugged.

"Dunno. Not my problem." The words flowed naturally now, as if they'd just been waiting to ripen, to blossom, and give his ideas new meaning. "I was only making war on you because Mom hated you. And because you represented everything I didn't have and would never have. But if you just give it all to me, well, that's another story. It doesn't interest me anymore. I don't want to become you."

Embarrassed, father and son studied their armored feet for a moment.

"Just like that?" Arthur asked, panic creeping into his voice.

"Yeah, well—I like the idea of kissing it all off on a whim," Mordred replied with a cynical laugh. He sat down on a soldier, who protested faintly.

More respectful, Arthur remained standing, pensive.

"I know how to leave," he confessed at last. "But I can't. I have responsibilities to this world." A pause. He took a deep breath. "No, that's not true. I'm just scared."

Mordred half-smiled. "This world, it's us. And I've had it up to here. "C'mon," he said, getting up. "Let's blow this joint. Hey, do you know that guy in black who's waving at us?"

The Depths

In the bowels of the isle, far beneath the castle, in the heart of the earth, of the dragon, the shadow made its way among stony sculptures, columns joining floor and ceiling. In the sub-basement of the collective unconscious, the odor of sulfur reigned.

The figure came to an underground lake, an unfathomable mirror whose still waters no wind had ever stirred.

The Lady rose from the waves without a ripple, without a splash. The lake seemed to sculpt her shape from water, its impossible curves draped in a veil woven of space, time, and stars. In her right hand, she held the king's sword.

Facing the shadow, she set foot on the black stone where scarlet veins pulsed, tracing incomprehensible patterns.

In silent answer, the shadow's cape collapsed, as though the forces sustaining it had suddenly tired. With barely a rustle, the fabric fell empty to the floor.

A snake slid from the folds of the cloak and curled itself around the Lady's calves. By touches on her veil and the slip of scales across her skin, the animal asked, "You got it back?"

The Lady of the Lake traced a complex alphabet on the serpent's skin with her fingertips. "Yes. Despite his king's absence,

Girflet still remained blindly loyal to the Geste. After three trips, he threw Excalibur into the water."

"But now there's no one left to reclaim it," the snake replied with a few flicks of its tongue at the insides of her thighs. "Arthur and Mordred have left the isle. The enemies have called a truce and, without denying their natures, have taken their first steps on the path of evolution."

"Yes, but toward what?" the Lady asked, petting the serpent's scales most insistently.

"I know no more than they. I am only the gardener. They've taken the bridge, but its far end is still shrouded in fog."

The serpent climbed languorously toward her groin, insinuating itself under the cloth. Cool scales sent a shiver up the length of the Lady's spine.

"They say the true king will return one day. But even then, I don't think he'll need this prop any more." She glanced at the royal sword and then chuckled, breaking the age-old silence of the cave. "You know, Lucifer, one day the human mind will no longer need the mystery we embody, and the death of myth will open these caverns to the light of day and reveal all their secrets."

The serpent stopped. "That day is not yet come. I concede we're only tools, but there are still so many archetypes on the isle who haven't yet discovered the secret of the apples of immortality."

Before surrendering to the cold sensuality of the Bringer of Light, the Lady answered him with a final caress, smiling under her veil: "Yes. But something's going on in the human mind all the same."

Translated from the French by Edward Gauvin

When the French anthologist Lucie Chenu first asked me to write a story about the Arthurian myth, I enthusiastically accepted—only to curse myself later. How does one rewrite such an archetypal story, manage to find something new to say in a framework within which, I felt, everyone—especially much celebrated writers—had already tackled all the important aspects? Well, I thought, let's tackle all the aspects at once, then.

That is, for me, one of the greatest joys of being a writer: to look for resonances, echoes, relations between ideas, concepts, feelings, things in the world around us and inside us. To build some kind of synthesis (or synaesthesia?) from them, to imbue them with meaning in order to form a story. For me, there are no boundaries of any sort in the world—only those people build for themselves, consciously or not: limitations we should strive to tear down, in art as well as in everyday life. I do write in the SF&F fields, but I am really a child of surrealism and magical realism. I am convinced that all creations, all thoughts, do exist somewhere, elsewhere. Their physical impact on our world is proof enough of that—reality is not all material. The world is shaped by what we think; thought and action are two sides of the same coin. The world is a decision.

That is why I like to think that I build my life in the image of my writing—and not the other way round. Is this madness? Well, that's fine by me. Being crazy sure beats the hell out of consensual reality.

Lionel Davoust

Afterbirth

Stephanie Shaw

My obstetrician has four heads.

She stands in front of me, arms crossed, tapping one foot.

She only has the two feet.

We are in Evanston, a socially-politically-ecologically aware suburb of Chicago, and she wears sensible shoes, expensive clogs, and natural fibers to draw the eye away from the four heads.

I sit on the edge of the exam table, in a nest of feathers, twine, and bits of bone. The stirrups are up, flanking me, each giving me the great big hairy eyeball, just like my obstetrician. Only she has eight eyes.

My obstetrician holds out her hands.

She only has the two hands.

In them, she holds a small, opaque lump.

Fleshy and purple-veined, it is about the size, color and texture of a large plum tomato, recently blanched and peeled. She holds it out in front of her, cupped in her hands, like a priest about to bless the host. Almost imperceptibly, the lump shifts and sighs, whether on its own or under some subtle manipulation from her gloved fingers is impossible to tell, and I realize that (oops!) this is my amniotic sac, one of them. Containing (oops!) the fetus, one of them. I had somehow managed to misplace it, scatterbrained me, and my obstetrician is not angry with me, she is just very, very disappointed.

"Just because there are two of them," she tells me, "does not mean we can afford to be careless."

I cup my palms, and my obstetrician dumps the thing cautiously into them. It is warm and sticky.

My obstetrician has four mouths, of course, lipstick faded after a hard day of blood and afterbirth. She has four noses, all of them very thin bridged and possessed of expressive nostrils, like the noses of young female movie stars. Her eyes number eight and they are so sincere that they have no choice but to be pale blue. She is varying shades of sandy, no-nonsense blond. One of the heads tells me that she needs to punch a needle through my abdominal wall and into my melon belly, so she can extract secret baby juice and read its code. Another deciphers my blood results and tells me that one or both of my babies stands an increased risk of arriving in this world with Down syndrome. One tells me to get into bed and stay there. The other says nothing, just snaps on a glove, reaches inside me, and punches me in the cervix to make sure it's still closed.

It is difficult to argue with a four-headed obstetrician—she has three more mouths than I, and many more degrees of higher education, and anyway, I have been taught not to argue with doctors. They are high priestesses, and best avoided altogether, if possible.

I cannot avoid them. I am manacled with a blood pressure cuff.

I breathe, as I have been instructed.

I examine the living tomato in my hands. I squint at it, trying to see the child inside, looking for claws or webbed feet, pearly horns or wisps of smoke from tiny, dilated nostrils. But the sac I have built is tough, and it resists my scrutiny. I see nothing but the throb of it. It doesn't believe in long-range predictions any more than I do.

Before anyone can stop me, I put it in my mouth and am reminded of my grandmother's spaghetti sauce before I swallow it whole.

Now, bear with me, because here is where it starts getting a little weird. A little of the fairy tale comes into play here.

And why not?

A fairy tale often starts with a childless woman, doesn't it, one who would give anything to anyone—her soul, for instance, to the devil or the witch or the toad in her bathwater—for the gift of a child? And let me tell you something about this woman. It's not so much that she has love in her heart to spare or that she's known all her life that mothering was her destiny or that she woke one morning with all her nurturing powers suddenly revved up and ready to be unleashed on an unsuspecting infant.

It's that she thought it might be kind of cool to have a baby.

After all, she has the reliable life partner; and she has the life insurance; and let's face it, she's never going to finish writing that postmodern sword-and-sorcery novel she started ten years ago, and suddenly, for inexplicable reasons, the majority of her art is about poultry.

But the main thing—the main reason she wants to have a baby—is that after an extended period of fucking in various efficacious positions, and even consulting a wizard or two, nature seems to be telling her she can't.

She cannot seem to get pregnant.

This woman, who, whatever else can be said about her, is almost certainly descended from a long line of mothers, cannot be one herself.

And so comes the mystical line of pharmaceuticals, the Clomid and the Pergonal and the subcutaneous injections administered daily, and the praying and the paying and the sacrificing of the nanny goat and the blood in the stone basin offered up to the goddess on the mountaintop and the witch in the woods and the occasional urologist.

And this woman perseveres. She is awarded a child. Or two. Or more.

And a four-headed obstetrician.

I open my mouth, unnaturally wide, place the sac on the back of my tongue, and swallow. There is heat; there is oregano and basil and bay leaf, red wine, a touch of cinnamon, just a pinch of sugar to cut the acidity. I am reminded of my grandmother's kitchen. I never liked my grandmother very much, but she made a kick-ass spaghetti sauce.

The nest of feathers on the examination table begins to unravel, and the feathers float separately upwards, as if there has been a shift in the density of the air around us. Slowly, I follow them. Scattering bits of ivory and agate from my nest, I rise from the table in full lotus position, my navel eclipsing my crossed ankles, serene as a long-haired Buddha, but only for a split second.

Then, I fluoresce.

I emerge from my thin, cotton gown tied only at the back of my neck, eyes lighting, gloriously naked, my blood-heavy belly swinging in slow-motion majesty, nipples magenta with maternal rage, my hair lifting in a sudden ripple of internal heat. My rib cage cracks open with the terrible popping sound of tendons under duress, a taste like lighter fluid on my tongue, a high-pitched keening at the center of me.

My obstetrician steps backwards, confused, attempting to shield all her eyes with two inadequate hands. Civilization, inhibition, thought, fall away as my limbs stretch forth into talons, wings evolving like time-lapse photography Darwin, dark purple, filling the examination room with Giant Bat Majesty.

I open my mouth and my tongue unfurls, sparking like flint; a jet of flame shoots out, triumphant, along with the words, "Fuck your amniocentesis, ladies!"

I eat them, and their speculums, none of them virgins. Then I notice something twitching out of the corner of my eye and turn to pursue it. I spend a pleasant hour in the wrecked examination room, just chasing my own tail.

That night, I wake to the sound of my ribs creaking under my own weight. The ratio of baby to bladder is not in my favor. The pillow I had so carefully positioned under my abdomen and between my legs when I went to sleep is flattened under all this potential. I hear my daughter sigh and shift in her crib, down the hall. I have been pregnant, or recovering from pregnancy, most of the last two years. I am a stunned dutch oven. The man beside me snores and sweats, but both of them lightly, and his knee against my back offers a comforting counter-pressure to the babies pressing from within. He will not be going with me, tomorrow, to see the specialist. We have already been told the birth is "high risk." Before sleep, my husband shakes the information off like drops of water from his shower and shifts in between the sheets.

"A specialist is just going to throw some numbers at us and repeat what the OB said," he tells me. "We can't know anything until they're born."

I am going anyway.

"I am going anyway," I tell him, but he is asleep.

My belly is a hollowed-out boulder filled with soft bone and heavy syrup, and during the course of my sleep it has slung itself hard right of center, dragging my resisting hips with it, skewing my spine.

Everything is heavy and dark, as if Pompeii has fallen on me. I wait in the dark, for some speck of light, for some rugged archeologist to brush the dust from my twisted form and lift my bones from my wrecked bed.

I will probably never sleep again, and so to amuse myself, I go over my list of anxieties. There are currently thirty articles, and I tell them like rosary beads, roll them like olives in my mouth, rearrange them like twigs in a nest.

1. The babies haven't moved in two hours.
2. Money.
3. The sound of wind chimes when there isn't any wind.
4. Symptoms of senile dementia in my cat.
5. God is definitely this Guy, and he never wanted me to be a mother to begin with, and I have subverted nature, much like Dr. Frankenstein, and remember what happened to Mary Shelley, her husband ran screaming from her that time they were vacationing in Geneva because he swore he saw eyes where her nipples were supposed to be.
6. I need more folic acid in my diet.
7. My eighteen-month-old is on to me.
8. Someday she will meet someone who wants to fuck her.
9. I'm turning into Erma Bombeck.
10. Erma Bombeck is dead.
11. Satan.
12. Jesus.
13. Incontinence.
14. Now I'll never be a movie star.
15. That beer I shouldn't have had last weekend.
16. The public school system.
17. I'll never be sexy again.

18. I was never sexy to begin with.
19. I place too much importance on being sexy.
20. What is sexy, anyway?
21. My bathwater was too hot; I have inadvertently boiled my babies' brains.
22. Lead paint.
23. What is that? Is that a goiter?
24. I'm a fraud.
25. Soon everyone will realize I'm a fraud.
26. Down syndrome.
27. Global warming.
28. The pros and cons of circumcision.
29. My life is like the first twenty minutes of a disaster movie.
30. The babies haven't moved in two hours.

So when the dragon comes barreling down on me like a whistling, murderous Chinese New Year, I am not surprised. It arrives in a blast of red-black heat, rolling eyes, and charcoal-tinged farts. At the foot of my bed it pauses to sneeze, a stringy line of flaming snot escaping its nostrils and narrowly missing the cat, which sleeps on, like my husband, unperturbed.

It is red.

Not fire-engine red, but heart's blood. Aortal.

It sort of hangs there like an unexpected metaphor, filling the room with its lizard funk, its wings spread and riding an impossible updraft, or maybe just floating on its own heat. The air beneath it bends and ripples. The streetlight from outside our bedroom window filters in through the bamboo shade and picks out the black edging that scallops the scales of its wings.

It looks like my grandmother's spaghetti sauce tastes—pepper-tempered, oily, irresistible, with just a whiff of anchovy on its breath.

It is staring at me stupidly.

Stupid, stupid animal.

I know I should leap to my feet, grab a sword from somewhere, defend my family; I should go for its belly, as it would go for mine. But I haven't been able to leap to my feet for some time now, and the closest thing we have to a sword is a meat cleaver, and I would have to get out of the bed, past the dragon, and all the way to the kitchen to get it. Besides, it would disturb both husband and cat if I were to engage in battle with a creature from my girlhood at this absurd hour.

So I wait. I wait and see. I wait for the dragon to speak, to make dire predictions about the fate of my children, my husband, my cat. But it doesn't say a word. It just swivels its lizard head around and gazes momentarily at my husband.

At the bookshelves from Crate & Barrel.

At the desk from the Container Store.

At the Little Tikes plastic kitchen set that my daughter got for Christmas.

At the Pampers, the cell phones, the iPods, the printer/scanner/fax machine. Its gaze travels out to the red minivan in our detached garage, and then back inside where it sneers briefly at the cable TV. It causes the edges of last year's tax return to curl slightly with heat, and it notices the Christmas card we got from our mortgage associate, Dan Kozar (which, if you're looking for someone, he has been nothing but helpful to us).

I see the pale underside of the dragon's throat as it raises its head to observe the ceiling fan; with its eyes it tries to follow the fan's circling blades for one confused moment, and then it abandons it. The dragon glares at me, shuddering, wings arching inquisitively.

I shrivel, not with its heat, but with its disapproval.

"I have to pee," I tell it, finally.

It flees out the back way, through the kitchen door, knocking over a pile of fastidiously stacked recyclables. I hear paper and plastic scatter and bounce off the kitchen floor.

In the silence that follows, the cat yawns, in that sudden way cats do.

Once I am certain that the dragon is gone, I pry myself from sweat-soaked sheets. The floorboards creak under my weight.

In the bathroom, after I pee, I check for blood in the bowl and on the toilet paper. The toilet paper is white, and the bowl is blameless—I am peeing so often, my urine is nearly colorless.

No blood floats in the water there. But I'll keep checking as I have done, nearly compulsively, for the last four months.

I pause in the kitchen and clumsily squat to gather the bundles of newspaper scattered around in the dragon's wake. The tile in this kitchen is a delightful Italian slate, cold as hell, even in August, and receptive to stains. My daughter has come to grief on it more than once, I've broken a number of wine glasses on it, and now the dragon has tracked what looks like smoke damage across it. I will try to scrub it out in the morning. I close the kitchen door, wondering why we left it open in the first place.

In the dark hallway, I pause at my daughter's door listening to the wet, uneven breathing typical of toddler sleep.

She is some kind of sea creature, a baby squid, hard where you expect her to be soft and vice versa. Not a sweet, cooing, ornamental baby, but an inquisitive force of nature, and a humorous one. She will need all of her humor in the weeks to come.

Back in my own bed, arranging my pillows just so under my big, white belly, I consider weeping, but I can't spare the salt.

My husband snores like an oblivious summer storm.

In the morning, over orange juice and a prenatal vitamin, I will tell him about the dragon. I will show him the smoke damage on the cold slate tile. I will tell him that, while house hunting, we cannot consider anything red. No red barn board, no red kitchens, no red trim around colonial blue shingles.

I'll never see the color red again without my heart breaking for that vision of it that flew in on smoke-streaked wings and paused to sneeze all over our lifestyle.

The babies stir. I sleep.

This is not at all like the first time.

The first time goes like this.

It is a very warm day, but in the time it takes us to walk from the car to the emergency room (I insist on walking, because I'm a Trooper), the wind has changed and it is downright chilly in my flowing summer maternity dress.

(I wonder what portents lie behind this sudden ominous change in weather.)

Pretty Evanston hospital.

Pert RN.

Pretty labor and delivery room complete with glider rocker and medical equipment hidden behind flowered panels in the walls. I speak to my mother on the phone while a no-nonsense intern decides to insert what looks like a long crochet hook up me to break my water. The sound is like a rubbery balloon resisting attack. The fluid leaves me and hits the tile floor with a resounding splat, and I say "No, Ma, look, I've got to go now, things are happening here," while the contractions come and go with great regularity; but I do not twist and moan like in the movies or even on TV, I just feel the need to inform everyone when the contractions are coming and when they are peaking and when they are going away, and I think this isn't so hard, it's not like taking a math test, for instance, I can't fail it, for instance, people stupider than I have given birth, lord knows, and, yes, I'll take the drugs, any drugs, all drugs, and that's much better except I feel sick so I throw up into a bedpan and I push and the drugs wear off and I push and there's conversation about how hospitals used to give the placenta to cosmetic companies to put in shampoos and things but that was before AIDS, now they just throw it away, and it's bright and cheerful in the room like a sporting event and I don't even get to yell at my husband like they do on TV, I don't feel the need, just once he's talking a little too rapidly and I say "shhhh" (and he does!) and I feel sick again, I've been pushing two hours, so I throw up into the bedpan again, and that does it.

That is how my daughter arrives. With a rush of vomit and me too busy clearing my mouth to notice.

Later, she and I stared at each other from our respective beds. I was afraid to pick her up. I didn't know if it was allowed.

I'm not afraid of giving birth. That's the least of my worries. I'm afraid of what comes after.

Some things they don't tell you about.

Hemorrhoids: Wherein the tortured veins around your anus rise to the surface in swollen masses of tissue and cry revolt. Not every woman gets them, but many do. They come from straining during the birth, and they will cause your fully dressed husband to wince when he is standing there like a great big hairy cheerleader between your shaking legs. If you're lucky, he will later remark that they put him in mind of that time he was at the zoo and was mooned by a female baboon in estrus. Your mother will warn you, with typical grim glee, to forever after be wary of sitting on hot concrete, or a radiator, as the heat will "bring them out again." This may prove to be untrue. But something does bring them out again. From time to time. For the rest of your life.

Episiotomies: Wherein the doctor makes a small incision to the perineum (that's the area between the anus and the vagina, for you amateurs) in order to facilitate the birth. Midwives hate them and swear they're not needed. Doctors swear by them and say it keeps the woman from getting torn up. The woman in labor doesn't give a shit. The trauma surrounding her cunt is, by that point, so transcendentally mind-blowing that a quick snip with some silver surgical scissors is more or less an unremarkable event. Though the stitches may itch, later.

The Fluid: Wherein you empty out. There's a lot of it, and it pours out of you, and it gets all over. It is amniotic fluid and blood and in some cases shit, but don't worry, the orderlies mop it up. Don't worry about the orderlies. Don't wonder what would've happened to you if you'd grown up in the sort of dire circumstances that makes orderlies out of people. You are not an orderly. You do not have to mop up the juice bucketing out of a helpless privileged white woman with her legs up and her eyes up and her belly heaving like that of an albino mare. You are not an orderly. You are not responsible for someone else's goo. Yet.

The Dragons: Wherein they perch on your very chest, like in a painting by Hieronymus Bosch. They may just be metaphors. Ignore them as best you can.

This is not like the first time.

For one thing, the last time had been in a different hospital, a nicer hospital. In this hospital there is no gliding rocker and the equipment is not hidden like wolves in the walls, it's right out there in the open.

Last time, there had been no dragons.

This is no tasteful birthing suite, but a small, hard room with monitors and no windows and the ubiquitous TV screwed high on one wall, because we know what's important. I can understand why the dragon crouches there. It's a good roosting spot, the highest spot in the room.

As the student nurse stands next to my bed and attempts to find a likely spot on the inside of my elbow, she brushes aside leathery wings, irritated, mostly, by the color of them. "The color of these things," she complains, the dragon wings flapping lazily around her. She is a tiny woman, herself caramel colored, with an accent I think might be Philippine. The lilt of her voice is tropical, but she is trying for a brisk bedside manner and her hands are not confident. Her needle drags across my nerves before finding its way into my vein. I hiss, which is what I do when I'm in pain. I breathe in. I have been told, in birthing classes, that you're supposed to breathe out. But a person can't breathe out all the time.

I hiss, and the dragons answer; they hiss and flutter, drawing the student nurse's eye.

"I can't get over the color of them," she marvels, but not over their actual presence. "The color of what is it now? That trendy poison all the French artists drank?"

I am surprised out of my middle-class, liberal-arts complacency. What does a Philippine student nurse know about symbolist poets?

"Absinthe?" I venture.

It's true. My student nurse has got it right. The dragons glow like something distilled from nature but mixed by mankind, potentially lethal, a gleaming riot of green under dull fluorescent light.

"That's right!" The student nurse unsnaps the rubber tourniquet from around my arm with a flourish. "You teach art or something?" she asks.

I am not so far gone yet that I will admit to being a poet, even under torture. But I am disturbed by the assumption that I am a "teacher" and not a "doer." It takes my mind off the Pitocin drip that is about to be directed into my bloodstream, and the stink of hot linoleum.

"Hey, can we do something about the animals in here?" my husband asks, sparing me the difficulty of answering the poet question. He has come up from the cafeteria with a milkshake for me.

"She can't have that," the nurse says and promptly confiscates it. "Empty stomach, remember?"

"Shitfire," I say, morose in the bed, with a fetal monitor strapped to my belly and an armful of Pitocin guaranteed to start my labor.

"Hello?" says my man, as the little Philippine nurse walks past him, out the door. "About the dragons?"

She has an eye for color, but her work here is done, and she doesn't spare my husband a glance.

"I'll see what we can do," she says, in passing.

My husband finds the dragons distasteful, but he's not alarmed. There have been hints of them around before. Most notably at our wedding, when the cake burst into flame as we cut it, and at my father's funeral, where many of them showed up dressed as professional Sicilian mourners. They may have been at our daughter's birth, come to think of it, but he was too busy looking at her to notice, and I was too busy watching him look at her. The dragons may have been hiding, that time.

Now there are two dragons, we think, but it's difficult to tell them apart. They're both the same poisonous green, and they're off in a corner, coiled into one another like snakes. It's difficult to tell where one starts and the other begins. They are smallish.

It is not lost on me that I am now beginning to think of certain dragons as "smallish."

These are not quite the size of certain prehistoric alligators I'd read about in the second grade. It is their wings that take up so much room. Like the elbows of adolescents, they shoot out at odd moments and knock magazines out of our hands. One of them knocks my husband's coffee cup over onto one of the monitors; the machine whines and hisses, and a nurse trots in to frown and adjust it. She is not my little student nurse, but stern and large-bosomed and dark brown, and I am afraid of her. My dragons have made a mess, and I'm afraid I will be scolded.

Instead, she picks up the chart by the bed, sponges coffee off with a tissue, and squints at it severely.

"How are the contractions?" she asks.

Pitocin is an evil chemical made from the piss of pregnant horses, or so I've been told. It is designed to jump-start labor, and all the midwives and the other mothers have warned me about it. "Worst contractions you'll ever experience," they all predicted with funereal cheer.

So far, it hasn't been so bad. Deep within, the contractions announce that they are still a long way off, like the distant rumblings of a train that hasn't reached my station yet.

"I'm fine," I tell her, which is my stock answer to any person I catch in a lab coat, or working anywhere near a doctor's office or a hospital. "I'm fine." Please don't work your voodoo on me.

"We'll just crank up the drip, then," says the nurse, and adjusts my IV.

A train whistles ominously. One of the dragons lifts its head.

"Did anyone else hear that?" I ask.

"I can't hear anything," my husband says, gesturing toward the dragons, "with these things, here, wheezing like this. Nurse, can we either get them out of here or get another room?"

"There's been a bit of an infestation, I'm afraid," says the stern nurse.

"You mean they're all over the hospital?" I ask.

"No. Just in here."

"Can we get another room?"

"I'm afraid not."

Having wiped the coffee off the monitors with common paper towels, she leaves us.

My husband has gone to get more magazines.

There is nothing left to do.

We have observed the habits of the dragons (one of them has defecated, sizzlingly, against the far white wall), but we don't talk about the number of neonatal specialists who have checked in with us, or what we think we might have seen on the last ultrasound screen. We don't talk about the number of chromosomes we are hoping for.

Down syndrome babies are awarded an extra chromosome.

As open-minded as we try to be, my husband and myself find it a dubious award.

We are hoping, and trying not to be crass about it, for forty-six chromosomes per cell.

There are forty-six chromosomes in a normal cell.

But what's normal?

I am huge with two infant boys, pregnant mare piss is pumping through my veins in an effort to startle me into labor, and I have no idea how many chromosomes the average dragon needs to rack up, in order to appear ordinary. Their wings are folded on their backs, and they nap, one on top of the TV, one in the corner, on the floor behind my husband's chair.

My husband sighs and shifts and finds the chair too hot, eventually. He pulls back the hospital blanket and rubs my feet. He puzzles out the monitors, absorbs himself in the green blip of my heartbeat on the screen, and tries to follow the quicker heartbeats of Baby A and Baby B on the screen below.

I send him for magazines.

I tell him I want something thick and glossy, smooth-haired and full-lipped and the kind of shoes I would never wear because (although I am proud of my legs) I feel hobbled and helpless in high heels. I want a scented page full of nothing but a single Prada sling-back. I want to meditate on it, on its knife edges, designed to keep a woman off-balance, spread-legged, unable to dig in or to flee, tilted forward, ass out, constantly on the verge of being tipped over and fucked. I am a mother, and currently my feet are bare, but I took care to shave my legs for the birth, and I find myself craving that sort of frivolous, self-imposed imbalance.

They have given me a wee drop of morphine.

So when I thumb the remote for the TV, and hear the sounds of kids screaming over cell phones, and see helicopters circling a nondescript high school in a nondescript suburb, it takes me a long time to sort it out. There is gunfire, and students, their shirts riding up to expose their backs as they drop one another from broken windows. The dragon sitting on top of the TV is awake now. It has brought its hind leg up to its mouth and is gnawing industriously on its talons.

"What is this?" I ask it. "Where is this? A bombing? Israel?"

The dragon is so pretty, and green, and lethal as a Prada sling-back. Like the shoe, it has no answers but spits heat.

When my husband returns with copies of the *New Yorker* and *Harper's*, I am sweating.

"There's something going on in Colorado," I tell him. "Something biblical. Two boys. Ow."

The morphine has worn off. The contractions feel like fists. I am being pounded from the inside. My husband drops the magazines and does this beautiful thing where he runs to my side and picks up my hand and starts rubbing it, and my arm. Unfortunately, it's the arm with the IV in it.

"Ow!" I yelp. "Goddamit, ow, there's a needle in there, man!"

"Sorry," says my husband. "Two boys," he says.

"Colorado," I say.

"No, here," he says. "Soon."

"Two boys are killing their classmates in Colorado," I say.

I push the green power button on the remote control and we watch emergency vehicles circle, hear the kitschy pop of automatic weapons, listen to panicked high-school kids on cell phones conferring with media vultures.

My husband's face is like a soufflé, at first; soft in the middle, collapsing, and then hard around the edges. I feel I have spoiled his party by turning on the TV. He doesn't like TV, and this is his day, the day he will stand back and watch sons emerge like some sort of magic trick, like rabbits out of a hat. For him, it is as though he cut the deck thirty-eight weeks ago and is only now being presented with his card, the two of hearts.

Maybe he is not counting chromosomes; maybe I'm the only one doing that.

He despises standing by.

He cannot watch what is happening in Colorado, he is powerless when it comes to Columbine, but when it comes time, he will take his children in his hands and study them thoroughly. He will catalogue their parts, and he will not flinch.

He puts his hand on my forehead now and keeps it there, walking alongside my bed as the orderlies roll me into the OR.

There are two boys in Colorado who have had it. They will not live out the day.

They will kill themselves while I am having my legs taped to the stirrups. I do not realize I'm having my legs taped to the stirrups. There is a dragon on my belly. The two boys who are killing themselves do not realize that somewhere in the Midwest, a woman is lying on her back, spread open among strangers in a hard white room, wondering about those same two boys, wondering why no one will do anything about the goddamned dragon. It's unhygienic, to say the least, and it is drooling napalm, which runs in hot lines down either side of me. It hurts.

"I thought you left," I tell it. "I thought you were so done with me. I thought you were all red and black and sneering at my tax returns and my varicose veins."

But it is here, as undeniably green as a new fig leaf. It inches forward, puts its head down on my breasts, and nudges the underside of my chin with the top of its horny jaw. I realize I do not want it to leave. It flinches slightly at the sound of the duct tape being ripped from the roll. A nurse heaves one of my legs onto the stirrup and tapes my ankle to it.

My four-headed obstetrician is draped in OR green, which clashes with the dragons, but I can tell by the way her surgical masks crease that all four mouths are smiling reassuringly at me. Four neonatal specialists stand guard next to two empty incubators, quietly discussing their weekend. One of them mentions a sailboat, the other his prize-winning rose bushes. The orderlies hold their mops at the ready, and an anesthesiologist with an unpronounceable name and deft fingers quickly slips a needle in between the vertebrae of my lower back.

They all move around the room like geese, with their green paper caps and their quick hands and feet.

I raise my head and meet the eyes of the dragon. In their many facets, I can see the hairline fractures of time and space and all the blood that fills them up, and beyond that my own bare knees, spread wide apart. The fists inside of me flex and try to knuckle their way out.

This will all end in tears, I think, and have to close my eyes to dispel the sudden, quick headache. A soft voice in the room draws attention to my blood pressure. They have taped my legs to the stirrups because I can't feel them. The fists inside me relax.

I tilt my head back on the table and stare at the anesthesiologist, who has worked his mojo on me. He smiles pleasantly, swarthy and competent, with strong-looking teeth, one of Ali Baba's thieves. Along with the pain, he has robbed me of my ability to cut and run. Plastic tubes lead to plastic bags leading to my spine, to my arm, to my monitors. The Philippine nurse keeps her lovely accent in her mouth while she rearranges metal carts on wheels and soaks rolls of gauze in a basin full of yellow-brown disinfectant.

"Should I push?" I want to know.

"No, no, no, no," says my four-headed OB.

"I don't like where your blood pressure is going," says one.

"Baby A is breech," says another.

"I'm going to try to turn him around," says the third, and puts one arm inside me, up to her elbow. Her other arm is on my belly, manipulating. Because my anesthesiologist is so Ali Baba competent, this affects me only slightly, as though I were a purse and the OB was rooting around in me for a set of lost keys. Her eyebrows draw together, and the crease between them deepens as she concentrates, the one face close to my belly, the others hovering, watching my blood pressure. She frowns in frustration and swivels her head around to communicate a silent message to her sisters.

"You need to sign this," says the fourth OB, presenting me with a clipboard and a Bic Rollerball pen. I scribble my signature on a release form as the stern black nurse introduces a catheter into my bladder. Knives are readied while the nurse who knows a thing or two about the French symbolists tents me. My pregnancy disappears from my sight by a surgical screen arranged just above my breasts. My arms are free of it, but I am cut off from the action. The dragon is still there, peering out, kittenish from beneath green draping.

"Fuck off," I tell it. "You're gonna have to move." It retreats beneath the tent.

My obstetrician steps forward, eyes as sincere as the four surgical masks that cover her mouths. She bends over me. I am her work, now, and she has taken no chances, she knows my tricks. I cannot rise up righteous this time. I feel nothing below my pumping heart.

She selects a scalpel and holds it up casually. There is nothing that catches the light like a brand new scalpel.

I breathe, as I have been instructed.

I am splayed, filleted, my spine does not know itself. I am a beached sea creature dredged up from its purple cave and tied down, gray, under white lights. Who knows what could come out of me; a cloud of ink, a hail of bullets, a sermon, some dice, a pair of dragons. My husband, in his green paper shower cap, waits nervously by my head, ready to do his duty and cut the cord. Will he still get to cut the cord? No, he is not allowed past the tent around my belly; huh, they let a dragon hang out in there, but not a tenured college professor; this is some crazy hospital.

My OB's hands disappear behind the draping, and I imagine a thin red mouth opening from east to west in the flesh of my belly, below my navel.

A tugging commences, just barely north of my groin. The OB has set her scalpel down and has slipped her gloved fingers into the incision, in order to pry me apart. The dragons shriek and fly up with a great commotion of wings and claws, as my abdominals are muscled apart. In a panic, the dragons knock the ceiling fixture askew, throwing light into the eyes of the anesthesiologist, my gentle kidnapper, who swears softly.

As they spread their wings and attempt to circle the small OR, I lift my head to follow their flight but find I cannot lift my ribcage.

I wonder, wildly, if my feet are cold.

My hands are free, and unaffected, and I raise one arm to shield my eyes from the glare of the light. The anesthesiologist, seeing that it is the arm with the IV, reaches across my face to grab me and keep me from pulling the needle out.

I can't help it; I bite him.

I bite him right on the underside of his arm, in the meaty part just shy of his armpit. He tastes like very good Volpi salami. His shriek joins that of the dragons, higher pitched, and I release him. He jerks away from me, pivoting to show one of the nurses the damage I have done. My husband has my other hand in his, and he bends to put his mouth close to my ear.

"Don't do that, honey," he says. His breath is coffee stale and the only familiar thing in the room. I can see the gray in his razor-stubbled cheeks.

My obstetrician turns one head to frown at the fracas the dragons are causing, and one of the orderlies reaches over my open belly to adjust the light, and another takes a swipe at one of the dragons with a mop head.

"Don't," I say.

Orderly and dragon face off, baring teeth at each other. The dragon clings high in one white corner, scrambling with its talons to find a claw hold. The frill around its head extends, threatening, and the orderly responds by puffing out his chest and swinging a (mercifully empty) galvanized waste bucket by the handle in widening circles, like a mace on a chain. Nurses dodge. A metal cart falls over with a clang, scattering gauze and tubes of ointment.

"Don't," I insist, loud now. "Leave him alone, cut it out." The other dragon takes refuge under an incubator and spits sparks at the neonatal specialist who takes it upon himself to chase the creature out with a surgical tool.

"You're frustrating them," I warn, familiar with the signs of incipient temper tantrum. "You're not giving them good choices," I say. The neonatal guy ignores me and jabs at the dragon with a pair of silver forceps. There will be fire soon, and blood.

I have been known to go into paroxysms of panic over the sight of a spider, or a worm-white cicada struggling out of its shell. Once a week, I get into a sweat contemplating death by automobile, a scenario in which I imagine my sternum penetrated by a steering column while the radio continues to play a Steely Dan song. The sound of a single wind chime from the neighbor's yard on an otherwise still summer night can make my mouth go dry and rob me of sleep. I know exactly who my husband's coffin bearers will be, in spite of the fact that he does not want a coffin, he wants ashes and an urn, but whoever heard of urn bearers, and anyway, I'm determined to die before he does. Since my daughter was born, my nightmares no longer end in my death. My nightmares begin with my death, and they deal in the details of my girl's miserable existence as an orphan in, for some reason, the streets of Victorian London.

Everything is just so fucking fragile, you know?

Flat on my back, skinned, unable to move, I recognize fear that, for once, is not mine, although very like.

"Call Security," says one of my OB's heads, just as the dragon under the incubator lunges and draws blood from the hand of the neonatalogist. A sweet-looking young nurse gives a little scream, and the dragon high in one corner gives off a puff of flame that sterilizes the instruments on the surgical table. The OB's fingers are singed, but she remains calm and involved in her work, peeling away layers of my belly, digging for gold. "Call Security," she repeats.

Security, I think, will have crew cuts, and guns. Security will walk in and smell blood and see my fatty tissue gleaming yellow, and they will want to *fix* everything. They will be in uniform. They will think they know what's best.

I lift my head and shoulders from the table. "NO!" I bellow, monstrous and wounded, like Grendel's mother.

Grendel's mother is never properly described, except that she is something like Grendel, only worse. I am worse.

"NO!" I roar and bawl. "*No* Security, Security makes *no* one feel secure, *no* one's calling Security, if Security comes in here, I am calling the whole thing off, so everyone just calm the *fuck* down! And that includes you two!"

The dragons close their mouths with a snap. Everyone freezes except for the nurse who is cleaning the wounded doctor's hand, and the other nurse who is bandaging the wounded anesthesiologist's arm, and my OB, who has made it to my uterus.

"*These are mine,*" I tell the room at large. There is a heart monitor pinching my finger like a clothespin, and I use it to point at the dragons. "No one touches them, or I will sue for malpractice."

All eight of my OB's eyebrows rise at this, and she concentrates on unzipping my womb.

"You two—" I address the dragons, "—need to understand

that you are a scary couple of motherfuckers and you can't fly off the handle every time you get spooked. There is *work* going on here. Stay out of the way and let people concentrate."

Before the dragons can so much as sulk, the thin wail of infants interrupts the momentary silence, and suddenly everyone is moving.

I glimpse only a flash of new pink before four doctors converge on the squirming things, carry them to the other side of the room, cover them, suction them, and rub them with what seems unnecessary vigor.

One of my dragons is still cowering up in the corner, held at bay by a distrustful orderly. My husband strides forward, St. George, snatches the janitorial bucket from the surprised man's hand, and throws it down at the foot of the operating table, just in time to catch the steaming placenta the OB has tossed away. The dragons slide out of their defensive postures and slink casually toward the bucket.

My husband stops by my monster head, puts my stretched mouth back into place by kissing it, scrapes the scales off my face with his unshaven cheek, and then goes to take a look at the infants. As he examines them, I cannot see the expression on his face.

I turn my head and close my eyes, listening to the OB hum in four-part harmony while she sews me back up. I try to rest, and concentrate on the pulling and pushing sensations somewhere in the vicinity of my navel, as I am threaded back together. I breathe, as I have been instructed.

Something warm is placed on my chest, and something else, bundled, in the curve of my neck.

I can feel their wet breath on my skin.

When I open my eyes, the first things I see are the dragons, in the corner, snouts thrust into the big galvanized steel pail, eating the smoking afterbirth. I lift my head and turn away from them.

I study my sons. They glow like miraculous larvae.

I push back blankets and categorize all their parts.

I can smell my blood on them.

I do not flinch.

❖

My first discipline is theater.

I've written and read many press releases for theatrical productions, and I know that if you want to appeal to the widest possible audience, you have to define the work in no uncertain terms, with simple, broad adjectives.

I also know that in order for theater or art of any sort to be interesting and alive, it has to tell the truth.

Or some form of it.

I know that truth is subjective: difficult to define and almost impossible to explain with simple, broad adjectives.

I know that every time I try to define myself I become tongue-tied.

I can't even explain to people what it is I do for a living.

I write in the small spaces between being a teacher, a performer, a mother, and "a middle-aged, mildly anxious white female," which is a definition I once read on my chart in a neurologist's office.

"Afterbirth" is autobiographical, of course, but one has to be careful these days, so I call it a story.

If dragons show up in an otherwise banal hospital delivery room, what can I do?

If they're honest dragons, they stay put, making the story difficult to define and therefore a tough sell to any known market. The dragons don't care. They're not there to appeal to the widest possible audience. They're there because they really mean it. I see them in color, in far clearer detail than I see my husband or my children in the story, which may be why I occasionally find myself in a neurologist's office, sneaking a peek at my chart when she leaves the room.

Stephanie Shaw

The 121

David J. Schwartz

People always get my origin story wrong. I wasn't "born in an explosion," I *am* the explosion; if I'm the chicken, the bomb was the egg. It's just that no one's ever taken responsibility for laying it. Anything else blows up, anywhere in L.A., and the gangs and factions fall all over each other to take credit, but someone takes out the craft services tent on the set of a minor erotic space opera and no one says a word.

One hundred and twenty-one people died; I know because I killed them, but also because parts of them are still with me. Their souls, maybe. They're kind of . . . suspended, I guess. Like me. It's kind of a hard thing to talk about. Most of the 121 hate me, and they withhold themselves from me—including the bomber, who-ever it was. It's exhausting, being hated. Hating yourself. On the other hand, without all that rage I'm pretty sure that whatever I am would have burned out by now.

Not knowing who the bomber was used to bother me more than it does now. It was a real problem for Marty, my agent. Be-fore he signed me, we spent an hour going around the question of whether I was Muslim. Marty doesn't like Muslims. He didn't like the fact that I spoke Arabic and Farsi, but then it turned out I spoke Hebrew, too, so he didn't know what to think. He wanted to see all the evidence files from the investigation, but they haven't even let me see those. He was like, "Do you worship Allah?" I told him I'd never thought about it. I was four days old at the time. Then he's like, "Do you *feel* Muslim?" Sometimes Marty is really stupid.

I would fire him, but Marty keeps me working, and as long as I'm working, the Trinity doesn't bring out the hoses. Besides, he was Phil's agent, too. Phil Lima is my writing partner, and my best friend.

~

I never knew L.A. before the war, with its club music, its price-tag elegance, and its plastic charm. You can still spend a few thousand for a pair of shoes, here, but that's got more to do with inflation than with any designer's name. You're better off resoling what you've got or buying off the black market. Not that I have to worry about shoes, myself.

Phil knows all about the black market. Screenwriting wasn't bringing in a lot of money, the way things are, so Phil had his hands in a lot of things. If he'd been caught, he'd have been in deep trouble; the Trinity will put you to work at the desalinization plants if they catch you smuggling. Phil says there was an agency that handled smuggling, and immigration, too, but they were Homeland Security, so they're landlocked in St. Louis with FEMA. After Justice captured L.A., the attorney general placed everything under the jurisdiction of the FBI, the DEA, and the ATF. That's the Trinity. There's still an LAPD, but they mostly handle security and take orders from whichever acronym is standing closest.

I'm fuzzy on all the history and the way the old USA worked before it splintered into a hundred-odd pieces. Everyone tells a different story. Sometimes it was the drought that led to the war, sometimes it was the strikes, sometimes it was the election protests. Phil tries to give me the facts; he says you have to know a lot about the world if you're going to write about it. But the war is one thing that the 121 all have an opinion about, and we can't have a conversation about it without every single one of them jumping in to share a theory, not to mention reminding me how much they hate me. As if I could forget.

I'm not much of a writer, on my own. I don't know much, and a lot of the things I *do* know, I don't even know that I know. The 121 have a lot of life experience, but most of them are too busy hating me to share it. Sometimes bits seep through. I know things that I shouldn't. I know how to drive a cement truck, and how to light a scene that's supposed to be in the dark, and twenty-seven different recipes using chorizo sausage. I speak fifteen languages that I know of. Most of this is passive knowledge, not active. I have no idea it's there until it comes up.

Still, I learn things from them. They're kind of like parents, I guess. Except I don't really like to think of the bomb or the people who built it as my parents, so I'm not quite comfortable thinking of the 121 as my family. A family with one really bad egg, maybe.

After I didn't burn out and dissipate into smoke and ash, I needed a name, so I called myself 121 in their honor. Marty doesn't love the name. Sometimes he'll tell the casting agents that he calls me "Hunter," which he doesn't, because I hate it. Marty thinks Hunter sounds like an old Hollywood name. Marty thinks there's still a Hollywood.

Today I'm working on a DEA film about a kid who falls in with a rebel gang and plans to smuggle his family up the coast to the Free Cities. Only he has to sell drugs to make the money for it, and a rival gang tries to steal the drugs. They get into a shootout, and a little girl gets killed. The ship he finally puts his family on is destroyed in an accidental explosion. That'll be me, in the credits: Accidental Explosion.

If the details of the plot sound sort of vague, that's because they are. They'll film about forty different versions, one for each of the major ethnic gangs in the city. But they'll use my footage in all of them.

Sometimes I like working, but this job is pretty dull. For one thing, they're filming in black and white. The director says it makes the characters easier to empathize with. That's important, because the purpose of these films is to convince people that as shitty as it is to live in a place where most of the drinking water is recycled urine—and even that's rationed—you're better off waiting to be discovered at the salt docks or with the salvage crews than trying to leave.

So I roil and billow and all that, and they film me from multiple angles to milk it for maximum dramatic effect, but it's all in monochrome. I'm better in color. The first film I was on, the director wanted a look that was "less smoky, more flame-y." He said all the white and black smoke was boring, and he asked if I could do more in the yellow-to-red spectrum. I'd never tried it before, but I discovered I could. It's something I practice now in my spare time, trying out new color patterns and progressions. Being able to feel beautiful helps a little with the self-loathing.

While I wait for my fourth take ("Let's try it a little bigger this time, Hunter"), I work with Phil on our script. Mostly it's Phil's script, but he tells me we're partners. It's about these three former caliphs—al-Qahir, al-Muttaqi, and al-Mustakfi—who lived as beggars on the streets of Baghdad back in the tenth century. They'd all been deposed and had their eyes put out in pretty quick succession, and by 946 they were all three on the streets at the same time. Phil's idea is that they hate each other but end up working together to solve a murder. It's kind of a buddy picture. He wants to set it in L.A., with the ruined buildings and the paranoia and the starvation and all, but he knows that'll never happen. The three caliphs are supposed to echo the Trinity, see? Only they're blind, which is Phil's comment about Justice, I guess.

The film where I was born, that was a lot different. It was an adaptation of one of Holly Martinez's books. Holly wrote pulpy lesbian science fiction erotica about a spaceship captain named Carolina Dakota; books that sold ridiculously well and had been made into a half-dozen softcore features. None of the 121 had read any of her books, but I've seen some of them. They have taglines like "SHE WAS A SMUGGLER OUT FOR JUSTICE—AND LOVE!" and painted covers of a woman in a skintight black bodysuit. They were a little outside the propaganda guidelines, but Justice kept making them because they made money on the outside.

Holly and I don't talk much. About the only thing we have in common is that I killed her, and I don't even remember that. All I remember of being born is confusion. I didn't know who I was or what I was, just that I was growing and knocking things down and burning people. I think I knew I was killing them, but not what they were or what that meant. My insides got to 800 degrees Fahrenheit, which means they died pretty much instantly. I think that's supposed to be a comforting thought.

My core burns about that hot, still; hotter when I shrink down, like I have to do to in order to get into Marty's office. I can get down to about the size of a volleyball; any smaller, and I'm afraid I'd collapse. Or explode again. Or both. I worry about that a lot. I worry that all the anger inside me will overwhelm me and I'll take out the entire city. I'd have to change my name, then. Two-Point-Five Million just doesn't have the same ring to it.

No, I know it's not funny.

We wrap for the day, and my own personal Three Stooges meet me at the studio gates. I guess I better explain: after I was born and didn't die, the Trinity shot at me for a couple of days. The bullets didn't do much, but I didn't like the hoses. I was preoccupied with all the angry souls inside me, but I ended up flying up out of reach, which was when someone picked up a bullhorn and started talking to me. Until then I hadn't realized I could speak English.

After I made my deal with Justice—I do film work for them, and they don't bother me with hoses—protestors started following me. They thought I was a sign of the end times, I guess. They carried signs that talked about a sixth bowl and something called the "Mountain of Megiddo." I don't know what any of it means. Anyway, after the world didn't end, a few of them changed their minds and decided I was actually sent by God. There were some fistfights then, and the Trinity locked some of them up, and I guess most of the rest of them got tired of waiting. By the time I was two months old, there were only three of them still following me around.

They don't really talk to me, and I don't know their names, but I've overheard them talking, so I know where they stand. The one I call Moe is convinced that I'm a harbinger of the Antichrist. Once he threw a bucket of holy water at me; that scared me, but it wasn't enough to put me out or anything. The Trinity warned him, and now he carries a Super Soaker and sprays the ground when he loses his temper. Larry, on the other hand, thinks I'm a messenger of the Lord, like the Burning Bush. Sometimes he tosses fast food wrappers and other flammables from a safe distance. I swear he's just getting rid of his trash. Then there's Curly, who's undecided. He thinks I'm important, and he follows me around because he thinks Something Big will happen eventually. He just hasn't decided if he thinks that something is going to be good or bad.

The three of them argue a lot, but I think they're actually

friends by now. They follow me around in an old VW Bug. Larry's skinny, so he usually sits in the back. Phil thinks they're Trinity spies, but then Phil thinks everyone is a spy.

Sometimes when it's just me and the Stooges, I can listen to them argue and pretend I'm not even there. It's like the turmoil outside matches the turmoil in, and they cancel each other out. I like that, feeling like I'm just part of the scenery, something people don't even notice. Like a ghost, or a painting. But after a day on set I have a lot of trouble getting to that place, so I head down to Grand Avenue Beach and out over the ocean, leaving the Stooges behind.

I float out past the swimmers and the patrol boats and just hang there looking at the sun, the only other sustained explosion I know. I wonder sometimes if anyone dies when a star is born.

I have another job lined up for tomorrow, an ATF training video. Training videos are kind of my bread and butter. Not that I need money, but I like working, and it's part of the deal. The Trinity propagandists like to use explosions as exclamation points, and with me around they don't actually have to spend money destroying anything.

I stay out until sunset and echo the colors back at the sky while the surf echoes us both. I stare down at the fragmented colors and wonder if I could still burn beneath the waves.

Al-Qahir was the earliest of the three blind caliphs to rule. By the time of his reign the caliphate was in decline, and he did what he could to accelerate that. He tortured the mother and sons of his predecessor (who also happened to be his brother) in order to gain their fortunes. He had his nephew and heir walled up alive, Cask-of-Amontillado style. Finally the courtiers got him drunk, put out his eyes, and threw him in prison for eleven years.

In our script—Phil's script—al-Qahir is the eldest of the caliphs, with a long gray beard and a beige suit with too-long pants and sleeves, who used to be head of Columbia Studios before Justice captured L.A. The script begins with al-Qahir speaking over shots of the city's ruins:

AL-QAHIR (V.O.)

You must know by now that the United States of America never existed. It was a fraud perpetrated by idealists and idolaters, storytellers and slogan writers. Even the dream of it would have collapsed long ago, if not for the movies. Hollywood told comforting lies about the imagined country, assuring citizens that crime didn't pay, that lust was love, that the government was doing its best. What is *Mr. Smith Goes to Washington* but a consolatory fiction? Once we gave them the dream, it was a simple matter to splinter it, to divide them by the lies they believed. We appealed to sexual depravity, naked greed, and godless humor; at the same time, we indulged fears and doubts in order to allay them with fairy tales of law and order and crime scene investigations. The America of the mind disintegrated into 300 million separate nations, and all we had to do was give the infidels what they wanted.

Sometimes when Phil and I are working, Holly starts criticizing. She wants to know why al-Qahir sounds like the attorney general, or what the idea is behind having tenth-century Muslim caliphs running Hollywood Studios. Phil and Holly met in a creative writing course in college, and as far as I can tell they've been arguing ever since.

"For twelve weeks we argued about everything we read," Holly says, "and then he asked me out. I told him I was a dyke, and he said OK. We went out anyway, just to hang out. Our politics and our sense of humor were just about identical. It was our aesthetics that differed."

I still haven't figured out why Holly doesn't hate me like the others. Phil thinks she just appreciates the dramatics of it all.

"So why did you ask him to work on your films?" I ask her.

"Because he's good."

"I think so, too," I tell her.

"You're a little sweet on him, aren't you?"

I have to think about that, so I don't answer.

⌒

Nights are long when I'm not working. Sometimes Phil wants to go to Westwood to check out Marilyn Monroe's grave or climb to the ruins of the Griffith Park Observatory. The thing is that I've been to all of those places a hundred times before, or at least my ghosts have.

A little before curfew, the Stooges take off for the night, and I head up the 101 to the Hollywood Reservoir. The guards at the checkpoint between the reservoir and what's left of the Hollywood Bowl get nervous when I hang out there. I'm supposed to inform Justice of all my movements—Marty always lets them know where I'm going to be working—but at night I don't bother. It's not like they could stop me from leaving if I wanted to, and leaving is something I've been thinking about lately. I probably won't, though. The 121 are like psychic anchors; sometimes it's like I'm just a vessel for their nostalgia.

Hanging over the depleted reservoir I fall into a meditation of things the 121 recall: a yellow prom dress, a golden retriever, the face of a child. I find myself reproducing the images of these things on my surface. I am drawn to my own reflection on the low water, and without realizing it I drop close enough to raise steam. Through the haze I stare at the buttery orchid a key grip has conjured out of me. I hover a moment, and then fly high over the hills to wait for sunrise.

Before dawn arrives, a dark sedan drives up to the reservoir, and a man in a dark suit gets out. He walks to the edge of the water, lights a cigarette, and waves. I move closer.

"Mr. 121?"

"Just 121," I say. "I'm not a Mister or a Miss."

"Right," he says. "Sorry about that. My name is Howard Callaghan. Special Agent Callaghan. Can we talk?"

"We're talking now."

"Yes." He takes a long drag off his cigarette and then picks something off his tongue. "We've learned something about the bomb," he says. "A man named Phil Lima built it. We believe it detonated accidentally—"

I guess I flare up a little, because he takes a step back and shades his eyes. Inside me the 121 are rioting. If they had bodies, Phil's would be torn to shreds.

Callaghan holds up a manila folder. "We have evidence that he intended to use it—"

I lash the folder with a tentacle of flame, setting it ablaze. Callaghan drops it and steps back, his hand going to his pistol. After a moment he must realize how foolish that is.

"I have other copies." His hands shake as he replaces the pistol in its holster.

I expand to my full size and hang over Callaghan, so close that I see my reflection in the sweat on his forehead. I know I would burn him if there was no other way to shut him up. I hang there, rotating, breathing black and orange gouts. I can't tell my rage from that of the dead inside me. I'm not sure I want to keep it under control.

He spreads his hands and takes a step back; the cigarette falls from his lips. He gets in the sedan and drives away.

Phil hasn't said a word.

I spend the night wandering the city, blazing up at the stars, wondering if they burn rage as well as helium. At some point I realize I'm moving down Highland Avenue. It's morning, although I can't see the sun. The Stooges are walking behind me, arguing.

"Here's what I don't get," says Moe. "Muslims don't allow their dead to be cremated, right? They consider it a desecration."

"I didn't know that," says Larry.

"It's true. So how do the people who train suicide bombers convince them that it's OK to vaporize themselves like that? It's the same thing, isn't it?"

"They're fanatics," says Larry. "The Quran doesn't condone religious violence, either, but it still happens."

"That isn't the reason," says Curly. "It's very simple—it's the difference between life and death. The bombers are alive when they're blown apart. No one is desecrating them; it's their final act, their choice."

An unmarked black sedan is following us, creeping along the curb about twenty feet behind the Stooges. No lights, no siren. I turn off Highland onto Santa Monica, heading west toward the mountains and the Pacific. Two more squad cars turn to join the first.

Lots parked with rusted weed-catchers, caved-in strip malls picked clean. A red-and-yellow Shakey's Pizza blazes on the right, a shredded "GRAND RE-OPENING" banner in front. There's not enough water to fight all the fires. The ATF Studio Lot is on the left; Phil told me it used to be United Artists, back in the day. Not so long ago. Sometimes I have to remind myself how young I am.

I asked Phil once if he missed the way things were before Justice won the war. He said he missed the way things never were. The way he said it, I could tell it was something he'd started saying a long time before, maybe back when he first met Holly. I'd like to ask him about it now, but I'm too angry.

Phil was right about L.A. and Baghdad, though. This is just a desert town surrounded by enemies, trying to keep up appearances.

AL-MUSTAKFI
This will be the end of the Abassids.

AL-QAHIR
Idiot. You equate your own fortunes with those of the caliphate? *L'État, ce n'est-pas toi.*

AL-MUTTAQI
Now that the Turks are gone from the city, the Shi'a will rise. I have seen it.

AL-MUSTAKFI
You see nothing. You are blind, have you forgotten?

He laughs, and al-Qahir joins in. Al-Muttaqi throws a punch in the direction of al-Mustakfi's voice, and the three of them begin scuffling. Behind them, a parade of conquerors marches: the Bayids, the Seljuks, Ayyubids, Mongols, Jalayirids, Quyunlu, Safavid, Ottomans, British, on and on and on, grinding the great city into ruins beneath their feet.

∽

West Hollywood. Sex and hamburgers. Inside me, Phil is talking to Holly, while 119 other voices shriek a backing soundtrack.

"It was an accident," says Phil. "I was going to put it in the administration offices."

"Because that would have been OK," she says.

"There are only two choices in life: you live or you fight. Not because the fighting kills you, although it often does, but because to really fight you have to give up living."

"What is art, then?" Holly asks.

"Art," says Phil, "is not making the choice."

Behind me the ululations of the mourners become sirens. I am a long way from the ocean. The vizier's men—the attorney general's, I mean—are lined up behind me for almost a mile, two and three cars abreast. Helicopters thunder above. I haven't seen the hoses yet, but I know they are coming.

They have taken the Stooges into protective custody, but I know what they are saying. This is the moment. They don't want to miss it.

I can move fast when I want to. I rise above the shopping towers and the apartment complexes, shining down brighter than the sun behind the city's gray haze. I hear Callaghan's voice through a bullhorn, but I can't distinguish the words through the polyglot of voices demanding blood.

I fly toward the ocean.

By now Justice has blacklisted me. Marty's going to flip out. I'm seven months old, and I'd never threatened one of the Trinity before last night.

It's sort of a desert palette I've been given. It seems appropriate. Not quite enough green, I suppose. But a little gray mixed in with the yellow might work. Colors of destruction and desire. Red like a fruit, or a warning, or skin flushed with need. Yellow for sunlight and cowardice and gold. Black, and white, and gray for all the choices in between.

Phil's choice killed him, but it also gave me life. The script we've created together has given me purpose, and the rage of those he killed has given me resolve. This won't make up for their deaths, but maybe it will mean something to the ones who are still alive.

The ocean is far enough below that no ships will reach me, far enough that the spray does not hiss along my underside. I could let go, dive down, see if I can be extinguished after all.

But for now I am making something, a moving image I cannot see, a story that will shift over the hours and days and—if I can sustain it for that long—the years. I invite my cast of dozens to speak through me, to let me be their medium. This can't be just Phil's script, not now. It has to come from all of us to mean anything. If that means we will contradict ourselves, then so be it.

The angry voices of the 121 carry over the water in all the languages we know. We don't know who will choose to watch or listen. We don't know what they will take from what they see and hear. We have to set aside hoping for that, and just hope they will look at us, stretched out to our fullest size, brushing light and heat across ourselves like a living canvas.

Look at us, world.

Look at us not making the choice.

If interstitial art is art about the *between*, about gaps, then I think that's where I live, and probably where all of us live at one time or another. Whether it's in small ways, like living in so-called flyover country, or in big ways, like waiting to find out what happens in an economic apocalypse.

In "The 121" things get a bit recursive; part of the foundation of the story is stolen from the film *The Third Man*, which is about life in fragmented Vienna after World War II. Except that the setting is a fragmented United States, and the protagonist is a movie star with a fragmented self. Sometimes I think that's what an artist is, someone who's always moving in all directions, seeing the world from every angle, looking in as much as out. Sometimes that's paralyzing. To keep creating it, you have to believe that art is worth something, that the gaps you expose will resonate with others, that we all know that between and what it feels like to be there. That's a shaky faith, sometimes, and in large part that's what this story is about.

David J. Schwartz

Afterwords: An Interstitial Interview by Colleen Mondor with Christopher Barzak and Delia Sherman

Colleen Mondor: *In discussions on the idea and definition of interstitial writing, writers and editors often describe it as a "crossing of literary borders" or "filling of gaps between literary conventions." I'm curious as to why we need to formally address this so-called Interstitial DMZ (to quote Heinz Fenkl) at all. Will these stories gain following without the title of "interstitial" to describe them? How does the "interstitial" label help a story gain readership?*

Christopher Barzak: I was initially skeptical of creating a term to categorize the uncategorizable, to be honest. It was only after I began to think about the term and its openness that I started to understand how apt it is. By calling attention to the wilderness that exists between conventional genres (such as the focus on the observable, material world in realism), readers can locate a kind of writing for which they are being asked to hold no expectations whatsoever. "Interstitial" is a term that informs readers of a book's content the same way that the "romance" label signals sex, adventure, women who get their dream man, etc. As a term, "interstitial" tells readers to expect the unexpected. This may seem simple, but I think telling readers straight up that what they're reading is a narrative based on a set of rules that they may never have encountered elsewhere is not only a selling point in some cases, but also an honest contract.

Delia Sherman: In a world of too much marketing and too many choices, labels give people something to latch onto, something to signal whether a work of art is worth their time and energy to pick up or not.

Interstitial art, by definition, is art that's hard to describe or pigeonhole, art that stretches definitions and asks its audience to leave its expectations at the door. Some people like that experience. Some don't. Some would enjoy it if they were warned ahead of time to expect it.

A lot of beautifully written, highly literary stories were submitted for this anthology. The question I always asked myself when I was reading something I really loved was, "who else might publish this story?" If the answer was *The Magazine of Fantasy & Science Fiction*, then I suggested the writer send it there. If it was *Weird Tales*, then I suggested that. If the answer is "beats me," then I put it in the "to be seriously considered" pile. Because the whole point of *Interfictions* is to publish stories I thought wouldn't find their audience otherwise.

Can a story (or novel's) structure mark it as interstitial regardless of content? Are there certain story elements (ghosts, hauntings, reliance upon myth or legend) that would move an otherwise literary tale into interstitial territory?

CB: I do think that a narrative's structure in and of itself may make a piece interstitial regardless of its content. For example, though there is a sort of mysticism in M. Rickert's "The Beautiful Feast," the story's interstitiality resides not in the mysticism so much as in the structure, which weaves in and out of time and space in the most effortless manner and is more a war story than it is a fantasy. Or consider Peter M. Ball's "Black Dog: A Biography." Here's another story that has a sort of strange legendary creature involved in a fairly domestic account of a man who has absolutely terrible luck in love, but it wasn't the inclusion of the black dog itself that interested me so much as the story's pull between fiction and autobiographical narrative.

Sure, I think that a blend of content—ghost stories, alien invasion, slave narrative, historical, romance, etc.) can move a story into the realm of the interstitial. The problem I have with the term "literary" is that it connotes "realism," when in fact I think it's a much more usable term for any writing in which not only the tale but how the tale is told—its structure and style—are particular features. For example, Alan DeNiro's "The Warp and the Weft" is particularly easy to categorize in terms of its content: it's science fiction. But the structure of the story and the language he invents in the telling are completely unlike the plate glass prose of conventional science fiction. In this case, it's not the content of the story that makes it interstitial, it's the language and structure that take it outside of its own genre's expectations.

DS: All serious fiction is literary fiction. Domestic realism, which is the genre that so-called mainstream literary fiction properly belongs to, is as circumscribed by genre convention and expectation as the hardest SF or the most formulaic bodice-buster romance.

That said, interstitial fiction isn't just domestic realism with ghosts or gods inserted like raisins in a pudding. Of the twenty-one stories in *Interfictions 2*, only three include ghosts, and in no case is the ghost the primary point of the story. In "The Score," Jake's ghost is almost incidental—a by-product of the media controversy surrounding his death. In "The Assimilated Cuban's Guide to Quantum Santeria," the ghost of Sal's mother is a problem to solve according to scientific principles as understood by a ten-year-old boy whose father had been a Santero in Cuba. In "After Verona," the ghosts are mysteries without answers—mysteries a lot less pressing than how and why Verona died.

Certainly, most of these stories have an unusual narrative structure. "The Long and the Short of Long-Term Memory" is structured around a series of medical diagrams illustrating the physiology of memory. "Valentines" is a series of recursive descriptions of three different men who might or might not be the same man. "L'Ile Close" cycles repetitively, like its characters, through all the variations of the Arthurian legend. But "Remembrance Is Something Like a House" is a fairly straightforward narrative of a cross-country journey undertaken by a house that has something it really, really wants to communicate—from the house's point of view.

So, I guess the real answer is: it depends.

The problem with trying to pin down interstitial fiction is that the examples are going to change from year to year. Stories that were interstitial when they were published are now the proud centers of their own subgenres: steampunk, mythic fiction, fairy-tale retellings. I wouldn't say that any of the stories we published in *Interfictions 1* looks sweetly old-fashioned after only two years. But I expect some of them will after ten years. As will the stories we have collected here.

Well, not *sweet,* maybe, or exactly old-fashioned. But no longer outposts on the edge of genre.

Chris, I thought it was interesting that your story "What We Know About the Lost Families of _____ House," a haunted house story, was published in the first Interfictions *collection while your first novel,* One for Sorrow *which relies heavily on the protagonist's interaction with more than one ghost, is categorized as literature. In your own writing, where do you think the line between interstitial fiction and general fiction lies?*

CB: For my own writing, I believe the line between interstitial fiction and general fiction exists in a couple of places. Contentwise, I tend to treat fantastical elements as realistically as I do anything that we typically consider part of the real, observable world. So when a boy falls into a hole where a murdered boy was initially buried, he comes out transformed, a bit of death caught inside him, the same way, say, Frodo Baggins begins to slowly wither toward death after being pierced by the blade of a death knight in *Lord of the Rings.*

There is a logic to all of this, and I treat it logically, rather than fantastically, even though I set my stories, for the most part, in the recognizable world, rather than in Middle Earth. In terms of structure or style, though, as in "The Lost Families of _____ House," I tend to try to write around the ordinary conventions that make up a haunted-house narrative; to erase the expected trappings and setup and follow-up; and also (at least in that story) to hold the narrative together in a collective narrator's voice ("we" of the small-town setting) while at the same time breaking the narrative with subheadings and jumps in time between past and present, and with arguments among the members of the collective narrator about how to interpret anything that occurs in the story (and sometimes argument arises within the collective narrator in regard to a belief the narrator claims for the entire community, while others disagree with that same statement of belief). So for me the interstitial is both a way of treating the fantastic as if it is real, and the real as if it's strange, and also a way for me to push against the rules of the techniques and various aspects of fiction—structure and point of view, etc.—that I've chosen to use in a given piece.

What do you think of a book like Michael Chabon's The Yiddish Policeman's Union, *which is about an alt-history Jewish settlement in Alaska, being marketed and shelved as literature rather than fantasy? Aren't these interstitial titles?*

CB: I'd definitely say that book is interstitial in several ways. It's being marketed as general fiction rather than as any one of the various genres from which it draws, but in a bookstore, sellers like to pigeonhole for the sake of convenience. In an ideal bookstore, such books would be tagged under each category that they partipate in, but apparently this is too difficult to manage, at least from what I've been told by people who work in sales and marketing. They've never clearly explained why it's difficult, only that it is. I myself think it would be worthwhile to find a way to help bring books to a much broader audience.

Perhaps "literature" is already being used as a term to hold some interstitial books. For example, Jeanette Winterson's novel *Art and Lies* ends with a musical composition and is told in prose as well as using dialogue and voice structure from a playwright's toolbox. Regardless of its content, the book blends the structures and techniques of several different forms of art. Then, looking at the content, you can see that it is a combination of the magical and the real and the historical as well as several other elements.

DS: I definitely think Chabon has written a lot of interstitial fiction. When *The Amazing Adventures of Kavalier and Clay* came out, I saw it as interstitial, existing at the confluence of historical, literary, and fantastic fiction, all in the service (and this is the kicker) of turning a pair of schlubs who imagined superheroes into superheroes themselves (for a Chabonesque value of superhero). And *The Yiddish Policeman's Union* is like Chandler transported to a different plane of reality and turned inside out, which is certainly a boundary-breaking kind of thing to do.

Consider also Angela Carter—my personal patron saint of interstitial fiction. She always wrote everything: realism; fantasy; SF; weird, uncategorizable imaginative stuff. She was published as literature, I suspect, because that's the only category her beautifully written, thematically ambitious work definitely fell into. For the same reason, the novels of our own Jeffrey Ford have been published as mainstream, even though they are clearly as rooted in speculative fiction as they are in any of four or five other literary genres. His story "The War Between Heaven and Hell Wallpaper" slides around between domestic realism (yes, really), dream narrative, satire, and possibly one or two other genres I'm not familiar enough with to identify. He might have sent it to the *New Yorker*— I've seen stories just as weird printed there under the bylines of T. Coraghessan Boyle and Ursula K. Le Guin. I'm glad he sent it to us instead.

The bigger names in fiction seem to embrace the literature label over those of genre. Cormac McCarthy's The Road *and David Brin's* The Postman *have almost everything in common in terms of setting and general plot, but one is strictly literature and the other solidly science fiction. McCarthy's fans seemed particularly resistant (along with most reviewers) to referring to his book as SF. How does the interstitial community build a bridge with publishers who seem unwilling to stray into any suggestion of genre territory?*

DS: I suspect the Internet is going to be our friend in this, because the Internet is all about crossing genres and blending communities. Sure, there's always going to be a large part of the population that is entirely unwilling to step out of its narrowly defined comfort zone. There are far more comfort food restaurants in any given country than out-there fusion experimental joints. It is also true that if you're a big-name anything, the mainstream is more willing to embrace you.

The reason we started this foundation was that there's more power in community than in isolation. Writers like Michael Chabon and Barbara Kingsolver and Alice Hoffman don't have to make common cause with anybody unless they want to. The rest of us, less established, less lucky, maybe less accessible, need something behind us, a passport out of the genre ghetto into the wider literary world.

CB: I think in many ways this is where the term "literary" begins to raise its head. Very little difference exists in terms of content between *The Road* and *The Postman*, but their use of language and structure and tone does differ. McCarthy's prose is stark whereas Brin's is full to the brim with detail, and though those seem like small differences, I do think that typical readers of science fiction will read Brin's book and feel it meets their expectations (at least in terms of language and detail) more closely than McCarthy's.

How to build bridges? The best way, I think, is to have this sort of discussion, and to create the language necessary to talk about these differences that seem like huge gulfs when they aren't, really. Take, for instance, Amelia Beamer's "Morton Goes to the Hospital," a metafiction that places the reader in a position of active participation in the imagining of its characters after the last word. It's a sort of story that, while not having much fantastical content in the actual story line, asks a question of its readers that creates a fantastical readerly experience in a story that is mostly about the ordinary lives of two elderly characters. Likewise, Elizabeth Ziemska's "Count Poniatowski and the Beautiful Chicken" feels more like a Margaret Atwood story, recounting personal and family history amid discussions on the nature of time and space and history, a fiction about science (or ways of knowing) that was a delight to encounter in our submissions.

Chris, what roadblocks do you think exist for writers who resist standard genre definitions? What should authors do when their writing takes them into that gray area in the middle? Are fantasy markets the best place to consider for interstitial stories? Or should the boundaries be pushed at straight literary markets?

CB: I think the roadblocks will be determined by what aspects of standard genre definitions writers are blurring or doing away with in their writing altogether. For example, Kelly Link's short stories were very much welcomed first within the fantasy and science fiction marketplaces. I think this was because, though Kelly presented stories with structures and voices that were often unfamiliar to standard fantasy readers, they still delivered the wonder and magical aspects of standard fantasy. A writer like Alan De-Niro, however, has had better luck with literary magazines like *One Story* and the *Santa Monica Review*, even though his stories use the iconography and content of sci-fi stories. His technique and structures, like Kelly Link's, are not those of typical sci-fi, and neither is his mix-and-match, almost pastiche, approach. He has created his own language, one a bit further removed from standard genre audiences than Kelly's more friendly and open prose. So here you have two examples of people doing the same thing, in certain ways, and not at all the same thing in other ways, and the majority of their (at least early) successes were published on different sides of the fence. (It didn't take too long for literary magazines to catch on to Kelly after her work began to make its way into the wider world, of course.)

So which markets are better for interstitial stories? I think both are fine, but it depends, again, on what exactly you're making available to your readers in your stories, and that will end up being the deciding factor. I think it's best to push at the boundaries from both sides—fantasy and literary publications—and however many other sides may exist.

In his introduction to Interfictions I, *Heinz Fenkl describes the publication of his own interstitial title,* Memories of My Ghost Brother, *which was published as a novel but is drawn from his life and is in fact the story of his childhood. This brought to mind the books of Tim O'Brien, whose highly successful Vietnam titles wind their way through all manner of nonfiction, memoir, and novel territory. Does interstitial writing dwell also between the lines of fiction and nonfiction? If so, how does it differ from creative nonfiction? If a story is truth but not factual, is that where it crosses the interstitial border?*

CB: Yes, interstitial fiction does exist between the borders of fiction and nonfiction, as well as between poetry and prose. You'll see some of those divisions broken down in several of the pieces we chose for the new anthology. Like Camilla Bruce's "Berry Moon," which employs a kind of language that hovers between prose and poetry. And Nin Andrews's "The Marriage," which carries the arc of a full story in the small space of a prose poem, with the evocative language as well as the jumps in logic and time that poems do so well. I think when a story begins to work in a variety of modes and manners, though, as in O'Brien's books, the terms "fiction" and "nonfiction" no longer even apply.

DS: This is a part of the interstitial forest I haven't spent much time in—like, any. For what it's worth, though, my gut feeling is, sure. Writing is writing, and the line between fiction and nonfiction (and mythology and legend) has always been more permeable than most people realize. Colette's memoirs, for instance, partake enthusiastically of a number of genres, although she certainly meant for them to be read as sober nonfiction. Perhaps that's where the difference lies—in the writer's intent (yes, I'm aware them's fighting words, and I already yield; I do not pretend to be a theorist). If a work of nonfiction artfully bestrides genres, making that uncertainty (Did that really happen? Is this event/character a metaphor or even a convenient lie?) part of the experience of reading the book—well, that's what Stephanie Shaw's "Afterbirth" does, and we bought that for this anthology.

As for the "truth but not factual" statement—well, I don't know. It's what I usually say about folk- and fairy tales, and we all know what genre they belong to, right?

Chris, what surprised you the most working on this anthology? Is there a subject matter or style that dominated the submissions?

CB: I did notice that there were a lot of politically oriented stories in the submissions, which doesn't actually surprise me considering the upheaval of the past decade and the now occurring change of the political landscape. We selected several of the most interesting of those stories for the anthology, too, and each comes at its subject matter very differently. Brian F. Slattery's "Interviews After the Revolution" and Alaya Dawn Johnson's "The Score" both arrange their politics through a polyphonic display of voices and media. Alan DeNiro's "The Warp and the Woof" posits an extreme vision of today's politics played out on a futuristic backdrop. Lavie Tidhar's "Shoes" takes a magical realist perspective on current political strife in the Middle East, and in "The 121" David J. Schwartz creates a voice-oriented piece about a political event that is unforgettable. Aside from that, there were also a lot of gender-oriented submissions, and stories that talked about race or ethnicity or cultural identity. One of the most remarkable of these was Theodora Goss's "Child-Empress of Mars," an exploration of the tragic effects of cultural blindness and well-meaning prejudice, set in a lushly described and exotic Mars that owes as much to non-occidental fantasy as it does to science fiction. It was amazing to see all of these stories coming from so many different parts of the world, too, which is part of what the anthology does: it creates a space for writers of varying cultures and nations to come together and mingle their perspectives on the world. So it's interstitial in that way, too, avoiding the standard anthology feature that presents mainly writers working from within one nation, culture, etc. It's an anthology series very much focused on diversity, which is what interstitial writing draws its strength from most, I think. Cross-fertilization, difference, deviation, rather than homogeneity.

Acknowledgments

Thanks to all the Interstitial Arts Foundation board members without whom this would still be just a good idea:

Deborah Atherton, Wendy Ellertson, Elizabeth Genco, Ellen Kushner, Geoffrey Long, Larissa Niec, Katherine Pendill, Victor Raymond, Stephen H. Segal, Erin Underwood

and to the Art Committee:

Geoffrey Long and Connie Toebe

and to the many great IAF volunteers who have worked so hard to fund and to publicize this anthology:

K. Tempest Bradford, Deborah Brannon, Elissa Carey, Cris Fisher, Alaya Dawn Johnson, Felice Kuan, Amy Lau, Emily Wagner

Delia wishes personally to thank Jeff Pinty, Shana Cohen, Christopher Schelling, Davey Snyder, Racheline Maltese, and Tempest Bradford for technical assistance, advice, and support above and beyond the call of anything but friendship. Also Ellen Kushner, for patience and help in every step of this project. And Christopher Barzak, for calm, responsiveness, and excellent good taste.

Chris thanks Delia Sherman for a steady hand through the process of making this book, Rick Bowes for his steady sense of humor, and Tony Romandetti for his steady heart.

About the Interstitial Arts Foundation

Just as how in nature the greatest areas of biodiversity occur in the margins of land between ecosystems, it is our belief that some of the most vital, innovative, and challenging art being created today can be found in the margins between categories, genres, and disciplines. Because such works are hard to classify, they are often misunderstood in a culture that has become overly dependent on branding and selling art by category labels. Border-crossing works of literature, for example, which consciously borrow tropes and themes from both genre and mainstream fiction, are classified as one or the other—and then critiqued according to the terms of that classification rather than on the book's own terms, often to the detriment of the work. This happens in other areas of the arts as well: in visual art forced to declare itself as either "illustration" or "fine art," for instance, when in truth it falls into the interstices between the two; in music labeled as "country," "jazz," or "roots," when it actually utilizes elements from all those genres; etc.

Though labels make for convenient marketing tools, they misrepresent the work of artists who don't fall neatly into one category or another. Rigid categorization by critics and educators is an unsatisfactory method for understanding the border-crossing works to be found in all areas of the arts today. As interstitial artists from a variety of disciplines, we are increasing our visibility, claiming a place in a wider artistic and academic community. The mission of the Interstitial Arts Foundation is to give all border-crossing artists and art scholars a forum and a focus for their efforts. Rather than creating a new genre with new borders, we support the free movement of artists across the borders of their choice. We support an ongoing conversation among artists, academics, critics, and the general public in which art can be spoken of as a continuum rather than as a series of hermetically sealed genres. We support the development of a new vocabulary with which to view and critique border-crossing works. And we celebrate the large community of interstitial artists working in North America and around the world.

www.interstitialarts.org

About the Editors

Christopher Barzak grew up in rural Ohio, went to university in a decaying postindustrial city in Ohio, and has lived in a Southern California beach town, the capital of Michigan, and the suburbs of Tokyo, Japan, where he taught English in rural junior high and elementary schools. His stories have appeared in many venues, including *Nerve*, *The Year's Best Fantasy and Horror*, *Salon Fantastique*, *Interfictions 1*, and *Lady Churchill's Rosebud Wristlet*. He is the author of the novels *One for Sorrow* and *The Love We Share Without Knowing*. Currently he lives in Youngstown, Ohio, where he teaches fiction writing at Youngstown State University.

Delia Sherman was born in Japan, raised in New York City, educated in a small town in upstate New York, overeducated in Providence, Rhode Island, and lived in Boston, Massachusetts, for many, many years before moving back to New York in 2006. She has worked in a bookstore, taught Freshman Composition, edited novels, written full-time, and taught creative writing workshops, the last two jobs being her favorites. Her stories have appeared most recently in *Realms of Fantasy*, *Coyote Road*, *Poe*, and *Troll's Eye View*. Her latest novels are *Changeling* and *The Magic Mirror of the Mermaid Queen*, both for younger readers. As an editor, she is dedicated to publishing more stories of the kind she likes to read—strange stories, unexpected stories, diverse stories, interstitial stories.

Contributors

William Alexander lives in Minneapolis with spouse (an artist) and cat (a poly-dactyl lunatic). His fiction has appeared in magazines (*Weird Tales, Zahir, Post-scripts,* and *Lady Churchill's Rosebud Wristlet*), anthologies (*Fantasy: The Best of the Year 2008, ParaSpheres 2,* and this one), and sometimes on the interwebs at willalex.net.

Nin Andrews is the author of several books including *The Book of Orgasms, Why They Grow Wings, Midlife Crisis with Dick and Jane, Dear Professor, Do You Live in a Vacuum?,* and *Sleeping with Houdini.* Her next book, *Southern Comfort,* is forthcoming from CavanKerry Press.

Peter M. Ball lives in Brisbane, Australia, writing stories and notes toward his thesis in roughly equal measure. His work has appeared in *Fantasy* and the *Dreaming Again* anthology, and he attended the Clarion South Writers Work-shop in 2007. More information about his recent work is available at his website, petermball.com.

Amelia Beamer's fiction has been published in *Red Cedar Review* (winning the 2007 Flash Fiction Contest), *Lady Churchill's Rosebud Wristlet,* and other ven-ues, and was shortlisted for the 2008 Raymond Carver Editor's Choice Award at *Carve Magazine.*

Camilla Bruce is a Norwegian writer who has published several short stories and novellas in English over the last few years. She lives in the itsy bitsy city of Trondheim, in an itsy bitsy house with an itsy bitsy cat, her itsy bitsy son, and a strange and peculiar menagerie of other people.

Cecil Castellucci is the author of three YA novels, *Boy Proof, The Queen of Cool,* and *Beige,* two YA graphic novels, *The PLAIN Janes* and *Janes in Love,* illustrated by Jim Rugg, and numerous short stories. She is currently working on a hybrid novel and the libretto for a multimedia opera. She has played in bands; produced and directed a feature film, a few one-woman shows, and a play; and does the oc-casional confessional stand-up comedy gig. She is always on the lookout for new ways to tell stories. Having lived on both coasts and both sides of the forty-ninth parallel, she appreciates a well-coordinated snow removal operation but wisely hides out where none is needed. For more information go to misscecil.com.

Lionel Davoust is one of the most promising French writers of his generation—and something of a personal patchwork. Originally a fisheries engineer studying marine mammals, he returned to his true calling at the turn of century: litera-ture. He edited the French fantasy magazine *Asphodale* before focusing solely on SF&F translation and writing. His stories have been reviewed by the French and Belgian press (*Le Monde, Le Soir*) and nominated for major French awards. Sometimes bittersweet or just plain crazy, he loves to change styles and voices, to try new story angles, to subvert genre boundaries—in short, to tell compelling stories without limitations.

Alan DeNiro is the author of a short story collection, *Skinny Dipping in the Lake of the Dead*, which was a finalist for the Crawford Award, and a novel, *Total Oblivion, More or Less*. His stories have appeared in many literary magazines, genre magazines, and anthologies. More of his work can be found on his website, goblinmercantileexchange.com.

Jeffrey Ford is the author of the novels *The Portrait of Mrs. Charbuque*, *The Girl in the Glass*, and *The Shadow Year*. His short stories have been collected into three books—*The Fantasy Writer's Assistant*, *The Empire of Ice Cream*, and *The Drowned Life*. He lives in South Jersey and teaches writing and literature at Brookdale Community College.

Theodora Goss was born in Hungary and spent her childhood in various European countries before her family moved to the United States. Although she grew up on the classics of English literature, her writing has been influenced by an Eastern European literary tradition in which the boundaries between realism and the fantastic are often ambiguous. Her publications include the short-story collection *In the Forest of Forgetting* (2006); *Interfictions* (2007), a short-story anthology coedited with Delia Sherman; and *Voices from Fairyland* (2008), a poetry anthology with critical essays and a selection of her own poems. Her short stories and poems have won the World Fantasy and Rhysling Awards. Visit her website at theodoragoss.com.

Carlos Hernandez is the coauthor of *Abecedarium* and the author of the novella "The Last Generation to Die" and many short stories. By day, he is a professor of English at the Borough of Manhattan Community College, CUNY. He lives in Queens, which is the best borough in New York.

Alaya Dawn Johnson's short fiction has appeared in *Interzone*, *Strange Horizons*, *Fantasy Magazine*, *Year's Best Fantasy 6*, and *Year's Best Science Fiction 11*. Her first novel, *Racing the Dark*, appeared in 2007 and the sequel, *The Burning City*, in fall 2009. In 2010, Thomas Dunne will publish *Moonshine*, the first in a series of 1920s vampire novels set in New York City. You can contact her via her website, alayadawnjohnson.com.

Shira Lipkin lives in Boston with her husband, daughter, and the requisite cats, most of whom also write. Her poetry and short fiction have appeared in *ChiZine*, *Electric Velocipede*, *Lone Star Stories*, *Polu Texni*, *Cabinet des Fees*, and the *Ravens in the Library* benefit anthology. You can track her movements at shiralipkin.com. Please do. She likes the company.

Will Ludwigsen didn't know he wrote interstitial fiction, though his disparate appearances in *Alfred Hitchcock's Mystery Magazine, Asimov's Science Fiction*, and *Weird Tales* should have given him a clue. When he isn't writing interstitial fiction, he writes interstitial nonfiction for the federal government, challenging genre boundaries with disquieting documentation and training materials. He lives in Jacksonville, Florida, with writer Aimee Payne and two greyhounds, also possibly writers of some sort. His website will-ludwigsen.com is even stranger than his fiction.

Colleen Mondor is a writer and reviewer who resides in Alaska and the Pacific Northwest. She has been published in *Eylsian Fields Quarterly* and *Identity Theory*, among others, and her monthly column of young adult book reviews can be found online at Bookslut.com. She also reviews for the ALA's *Booklist*. Her personal website is Chasingray.com, named for her literary hero, Ray Bradbury. It was a toss-up between Bradbury and Louis Armstong, who she maintains is one of the coolest people who ever lived. In a perfect world, *Dandelion Wine* would be on everyone's nightstand with "What a Wonderful World" as our global theme song. It's something to aspire to.

M. Rickert has won a World Fantasy Award for best short story, and the Crawford and World Fantasy awards for her short story collection, *Map of Dreams,* published by Golden Gryphon press. She lives in Cedarburg, Wisconsin.

David J. Schwartz's short fiction has appeared in numerous markets, including the anthologies *Paper Cities, The Best of Lady Churchill's Rosebud Wristlet*, and *Twenty Epics*. His first novel, *Superpowers*, was nominated for the Nebula Award. He lives in St. Paul, Minnesota.

Stephanie Shaw has been an actress, a theater critic, a Neo-Futurist, and a solo performer around Chicago for the last twenty years. She has recently completed her MFA in Creative Writing at Columbia College Chicago, where she is a senior lecturer in the Theater Department, teaching acting, solo performance, and (strangely) musical theater. She has been published in the *Chicago Reader*, the *New City, Analemma Magazine, Neo-Solo: 131 Neo-Futurist Solo Plays From Too Much Light Makes the Baby Go Blind*, and *200 More Neo-Futurist Plays From Too Much Light Makes the Baby Go Blind.* Her novella "Mademoiselle Guignol: A Theatrical Romance with Blood" will be published by Doorways Publications this summer. She lives in a barely functioning household in Oak Park, Illinois, with her husband and three children.

Brian Francis Slattery is an editor, writer, and musician. He has written two novels, *Spaceman Blues* (2007) and *Liberation* (2008), both for Tor Books. This is his fourth published short story.

Lavie Tidhar is the author of linked-story collection *HebrewPunk* (2007);

novellas *An Occupation of Angels* (2005), *Cloud Permutations* (2009), and *Gorel & The Pot-Bellied God* (2010); and, with Nir Yaniv, the short novel *The Tel Aviv Dossier* (2009). He's lived on three continents and one island-nation and was last seen in Southeast Asia.

Ray Vukcevich's fiction has appeared in a wide variety of magazines. Some of the stories have been collected in *Meet Me in the Moon Room*. Read more about the fiction at sff.net/people/RayV.

Elizabeth Ziemska received an MFA in Creative Writing from Bennington College. She lives in Los Angeles with her husband, stepson, three dogs, and one rabbit. She has previously been published in *Tin House* and nominated for a Shirley Jackson Award, and she is currently at work on a novel titled *Muse of Vengeance and Sorrow*.

If you enjoyed the stories in this book, be sure to check out the Interfictions Annex online for these additional stories:

Kelly Barnhill, "Four Very True Tales"
Kelly Cogswell, "For the Love of Carrots"
F. Brett Cox, "Nylon Seam"
Chris Kammerud, "Some Things About Love, Magic, and Hair"
Eilis O'Neal, "Quiz"
Ronald Pasquariello, "The Chipper Dialogues"
Mark Rich, "Stonefield"
Genevieve Valentine, "To Set Before the King"

at
www.interstitialarts.org/annex

The Interstitial Arts Foundation thanks the many, many
supporters whose donations made this volume possible.

Sponsors
Anonymous
Doris Egan
Neil Gaiman
Peter Straub
Catherynne M. Valente, S.J. Tucker,
and the artists of the Orphan's Tales Tour

Cover Art Sponsors
Irving & Enid Kushner
in honor of Ellen Kushner & Delia Sherman

Booklovers
Samantha Casanova
Chris Claremont & Beth Fleisher
Eleanor & Leigh Hoagland
in honor of Ellen Kushner & Delia Sherman
Robert K.J. Kilheffer
in memory of Jenna Felice & Robert Legault
Ellen Klages
Kushner & Hamed Co., LPA
Geoffrey Long
Allison Stieger
Steve Weiner & Don Cornuet
in honor of Ellen Kushner & Delia Sherman

Online Annex Sponsor
Ellen Kushner
*in honor of Terri Windling's editorial and visionary
contributions to interstitial fiction*

For a full list of all the Friends of *Interfictions 2*,
please visit our website at interstitialarts.org.

If you wish to make your own tax-deductible donation to
support interstitial art and the publication of further
volumes of *Interfictions*, please visit our website
or contact us at info@interstitialarts.org.